AN UNFORTUNATE
WAR

JOE EAST

AN UNFORTUNATE WAR

This is a work of fiction. All of the characters, names, incidents, organizations, and dialogue in this novel are either the products of the author's imagination or are used fictitiously.

iUniverse books may be ordered through booksellers or by contacting:

iUniverse
1663 Liberty Drive
Bloomington, IN 47403
www.iuniverse.com
1-800-Authors (1-800-288-4677)

ISBN: 978-1-4917-7628-5 (sc)
ISBN: 978-1-4917-7630-8 (hc)
ISBN: 978-1-4917-7629-2 (e)

Print information available on the last page.

iUniverse rev. date: 11/10/2015

PROLOGUE

Following the discovery of hyperdrive technology, manned exploration of our galaxy was undertaken. America's interstellar explorers discovered, claimed and colonized Haven; a planet 367 parsecs from Earth.

Haven is almost identical to Earth in size, climate and natural resources. Two hundred fifty years after the first settlers arrived; Haven's residents are now completely loyal to their world and no longer feel any attachment to Earth.

In the meantime, Earth is no longer able to feed all of its population. Desperate for food, America has turned to Haven and demanded that Haven grow and produce more agricultural products for export. Haven's government has refused America's latest demands because it means allowing millions of farmers to immigrate to their planet. Haven's peaceful residents now face an invasion by Earth which will force them to give up their sovereignty and way of life.

John Collins, a skilled and highly-paid construction worker, has been drafted to serve in Haven's expanding militia as a vehicle mechanic. On reporting for duty, he meets Helen Ramses, his commanding officer. Helen has both a tough reputation and a fiery temper and she treats John like her personal servant. Sparks fly as their personalities clash. Other members of Helen's fire team wonder if John or Helen will survive their tense relationship as Haven prepares for war.

CHAPTER 1

NEGOTIATIONS (EARTH)

President Phillip Reginald Williams studied his visitor; Ambassador Jonathan Allen, Haven's representative on Earth. Ambassador Allen patiently waited for President Williams to speak.

Phillip Williams was acknowledged as Earth's most powerful leader because he governed fifty-five percent of Earth's remaining arable land.

The dwindling supply of arable land occurred when poorer nations failed to promote sound agricultural practices; resulting in less land available for farming. Recently, millions of hectares of East European farmland were temporarily lost due to a terrorist group infecting winter crops with a genetically modified variant of wheat rust.

Today, most nations are forced to import food from America to feed their citizens. Interestingly, the increasing demand for American agriculture products triggered a reversal of earlier land use practices. Arable land is now being reclaimed from urban sprawl and converted back into farmland. Suburbanites are moving into compact cities and living in skyscrapers or below ground.

Two hundred fifty years ago, an American space exploration team discovered and claimed Haven; a planet similar to Earth in age, size, climate and land mass. Shortly afterward, American pioneers began arriving on Haven; thus cementing America's claim to that

1

planet as its territory. During the past seventy-five years, Haven has become an important source of food controlled by America.

Focusing on his visitor, President Williams said, "Ambassador Allen, the Taxation Commission has given its final ruling. Haven is required to lower its export tax to 1.25% of the wholesale value of all goods being shipped to America. Further, the Commerce Commission has ruled that Haven cannot limit the quantity of goods being shipped. There is really nothing more you can say to change our position in these matters."

"President Williams, surely you understand that Haven must be permitted to protect its environment and conserve our way of life. Allowing unlimited immigration to Haven will forever change our unique culture and our deeply held religious beliefs."

"Ambassador, as a religious person, you must look at the greater good for mankind. We estimate over ten million people on Earth will starve each year if we don't increase Haven's farming capacity."

"Mr. President, your exploration teams have recently discovered another planet which can grow food for earth's populations."

"Unfortunately, this planet is not readily available for this purpose. As you undoubtedly know, terraforming a planet takes years and costs trillions of credits. No, we require Haven's immediate assistance."

"President Williams, while I sympathize with the plight of Earth's population, it is not Haven's problem. Social policies encouraging population growth, weak environmental regulations, wars, and rampant consumption by the wealthy has decimated Earth's ability to continue supporting its population. Your predecessors have utterly failed to provide leadership which might have circumvented your current dilemma."

"Ambassador, while I respect those who have critical opinions of Earth's past and present leadership, there is another detail I hoped we could have avoided mentioning. But the fact is, Haven is a territory of America and our laws and policies take precedence over Haven's wishes. If you cannot persuade your government to accept our final position on immigration, our Agriculture Commission is prepared to send enough growers and equipment to Haven to substantially increase agriculture production."

"Mr. President, my government gave me explicit instructions regarding Haven's position on trade and immigration. These new policies proposed by your government compel me to return home for further instructions."

"Ambassador Allen, please convey my respects to Governor General Johnson. Have him contact me if there are additional questions. I look forward to our next meeting and wish you a pleasant trip home."

After the door closed behind Ambassador Allen, President Williams grinned, turned to his Chief of Staff and said, "Harry, if Haven's leadership is anything like that little wimp, I'll crush them like a bug. These conversations held under the guise of diplomatic negotiations have been a total waste of my time. I want large numbers of Americans to immigrate to Haven. We'll show them what Earth-style farming is all about. I want you to make it happen. As you well know, we've got to do something fast. Sporadic rioting has been reported on three continents. You and I know widespread insurrection is just around the corner."

* * *

Ambassador Jonathan Allen left the President's office and hurried to his official residence to start preparations for the long trip home to Haven. As he entered his residence, he summoned an aide to his office.

After switching on 'white noise' equipment designed to ensure privacy, he said, "Sergio, please contact Jim Anderson. Tell him I am going to visit Haven for a few weeks. Ask him to bring me any notes and gifts he may have for his family. Also, please schedule an embassy staff meeting to convene at 3:00 PM today. We must begin preparations for a trip to Haven."

* * *

Sergio met Jim Anderson at the Lafayette Restaurant for lunch. "Jim, it's good to see you today. How is your family?"

"Oh the family is fine. Jenny is growing so fast. She started kindergarten this year."

"Wow, it seems only yesterday when I saw you and Victoria at the Tupelo hospital. That was the day you were taking Jenny home."

"Sergio, your memory is phenomenal. But I'm sure you called this meeting for another purpose. What can I do for you?"

"Jim, the Ambassador is leaving Earth and returning to Haven for consultations with the Governor General. He is volunteering to take any letters or gifts you may have for Victoria and Jenny."

"That's very kind of the Ambassador. Shipping items home is expensive and this will save me lots of money. Please tell the Ambassador I'll bring some personal gifts for my family this afternoon."

After returning to his apartment, Jim opened his safe and selected four chips containing data purchased or stolen during the past few months by his team of agents.

Jim left a fifth chip in his safe. It contained a large collection of personal data giving the chip owner access to a number of America's computers. These computers were connected to power stations, banks, water treatment plants, air traffic control, shipping, communication satellites and selected automated production facilities.

Agent Anderson put the four chips in his suit pocket and drove to the Ambassador's Residence. After entering the Ambassador's office, he handed the chips to the Ambassador for inclusion in the diplomatic case.

"Mr. Ambassador, these chips contain specifications and drawings for the latest hyperpulse engines used on Earth's interstellar

4

transport ships; specifications for a new armored vehicle; and specifications for a revolutionary fighter design. The fourth chip contains the most recent intelligence on America's invasion plans. That specific information was furnished by a Haven agent serving on America's military planning staff. Until today, we considered this merely contingency planning and nothing to be concerned about. However, after hearing President Williams' conversation with this Chief of Staff following your meeting this morning, there can be no doubt about America's real intentions toward Haven."

"Jim, how the devil did you manage to install a listening device in the President's Office?"

"Sir, I must decline to answer that question and it is imperative you keep this most secret. When America invades Haven, this information source could be our key to victory."

"Jim, I'm impressed and deeply appreciative of what you and your team have accomplished. Regretfully, you must stay behind and prepare for the worst possible scenario. The sad state of Earth and America's planned actions toward Haven is placing our world in a precarious position. We need you and your team to remain behind and available to continue helping Haven."

"I fully understand, Mr. Ambassador. My team will await your signal. We have finalized our plan; code named Dragon's Spoon, which inflicts destruction, delay, and confusion to America's manufacturing and sustainment capability." Jim paused; then continued, "Sir, I wish you a safe trip home and please let our families know we are doing well and not to worry about us."

"After the invasion begins, America will block all transmissions from Haven. Jim, if America sends an invasion force, I want you to implement Dragon's Spoon. Here is a chip containing Governor General Johnson's written authorization. Commence your operations one day after the first Earth soldier lands on Haven."

"Mr. Ambassador, my best wishes to you on your upcoming trip. May Haven prosper; forever."

Ambassador Allen replied, "And may you prosper, too."

CHAPTER 2

GRADUATING FROM WEST POINT (AMERICAN FORCES)

Cadet Bill Anders was taller and more muscular than most of his classmates at West Point. He also possessed a fiery temper and an overwhelming desire to get ahead - no matter what it cost. Bill was a member of the West Point ice hockey team and was noted for his rough play and frequent penalties. His nickname was The Sandman because of his many knockouts.

"Bill, why don't you leave it alone? Cadet Smith didn't mean to bump into you this morning. Speaking as your friend and roommate, you're 'making a mountain out of a mole hill.'"

"Jerry, I won't have that smug asshole going around telling people that he hit an upperclassman and got away with it. I've even heard there is a betting pool among freshmen cadets on how many upperclassmen they can accidentally hit."

"Buddy, you're imagining things. I don't know about you but I want to graduate next month, get my commission and get outta here."

Looking down at his clenched fist, Bill added, "Maybe I should catch that little punk alone and have a frank conversation with him. It would be easy to get the truth out of him."

"Bill, if you mess with that kid, you risk getting kicked out of the Academy. And just to teach the little punk a lesson? That doesn't make sense."

"Yeah, maybe; we'll see what happens."

* * *

A month later, Bill's class received their commissions and was given assignments in a wide range of Army units. The 1,000 graduating cadets hurriedly exchanged their school uniforms for regular Army attire and headed out en masse.

Lieutenant William Anders was assigned to the 415th Armored Battalion stationed at Fort Boende in the Democratic Republic of the Congo. This remote location was the secondary launch site for the big American interstellar ships. A small military force was stationed there to protect the launch facility. Located near the equator, Fort Boende was not considered a choice assignment. At West Point, assignments are awarded based on a cadet's academic standing. Fort Boende was ranked near the bottom which mirrored Lieutenant Anders' grade point average.

Newly commissioned officers customarily take a month of leave prior to reporting for duty. Accordingly, Lieutenant Anders requested thirty days of leave to be with his family in Connecticut prior to reporting to his unit.

Instead of immediately going home, Bill put his plan to kidnap Cadet Jonathan Smith into action. Wearing civilian clothes, he purchased a ticket to New Haven and gave it to a shabbily-dressed man who was panhandling outside the ground transportation terminal.

Using a false identity, Bill rented a nondescript personal hauler and checked into a hotel about seven kilometers from West Point. He scouted the area, made a few purchases and found the perfect place in which to meet privately with Smith. Bill then began his reconnaissance by quietly watching places frequented by cadets.

A couple of days later, Bill spotted Cadet Smith walking near a pizza restaurant. Bill identified himself as Lieutenant Anders and invited Smith to go for a drink. The cadet was flattered that an officer would invite him for a beer and readily accepted. A couple of beers later while Smith visited the toilet, Bill put a Rohypnol derivative into Smith's drink and waited for the expected effect. It didn't take long for the drug to begin working. He helped Smith out of the bar and into his rental vehicle and drove to the secluded site.

Bill fastened Cadet Smith's arms and legs to a chair in an old wooden structure located near an abandoned farmhouse. The building appeared to have been a workshop.

"Cadet, can you hear me?"

Bill slapped Cadet Smith's face a couple of times and repeated his question, "Wake up! Can you hear me?"

Slowly, Cadet Smith's eyes opened slightly. His head was bobbing and he seemed to be trying to focus on Bill's voice.

"Let's wake up, Cadet!"

Smith slowly focused his eyes on Bill and softly responded, "Where am I?"

"Cadet Smith, you're in my 'truth chamber.' I'm going to ask you some questions and I expect you to answer each question truthfully and without reservation. Is that clear?"

Smith's head bobbed again as he said, "What questions?"

Bill slapped Smith again and said, "Cadet, you'd better stay focused; I'm not playing with you."

Bill slapped him again even harder and said, "Are you getting my drift?"

"Y-y-yes, sir"

Bill grinned and continued, "Okay, now that I have your full attention, I want you to tell me about your little game of 'accidentally' hitting upperclassmen."

Smith looked at Bill and didn't say anything at first – then slowly answered, "Sir, seven of us have a pool going to see how many upperclassmen we can accidentally bump without being caught. I know what I did was wrong and I apologize for my inappropriate action."

Bill smiled. He was pleased about getting the confession and validating his suspicions. He thought, *'Okay, now that I have his confession, what punishment is appropriate?'* A few moments later, Bill made his decision and hit Smith's jaw with his right fist using a quick uppercut. Almost in slow motion, Cadet Smith and his chair toppled backwards to the floor.

Bill heard a dull crack as the back of Smith's head smacked a loose brick lying on the floor. Smith's body went limp and Bill noticed a trickle of blood spreading into a small pool.

After vainly feeling for a pulse in Smith's neck he thought, *'Oh crap, he's dead. I didn't hit him that hard. His head bounced off the brick and his skull must be cracked! It was an accident. Holy crap; why did this have to happen to me? Well that doesn't really matter, does it? He's dead and I have to get rid of the body unless I want to lose my commission and spend a long time in prison for manslaughter.'*

After pacing the floor for a few minutes, Bill came up with a plan to get rid of the body. Outside the workshop was an old well. Bill heard a reassuring splash as Smith's body hit the water. That evening, Cadet Smith's absence would be noted and reported to authorities.

Bill thoroughly cleaned his 'truth chamber' before leaving for Connecticut. The remainder of his family leave was uneventful. Bill contacted some friends who graduated with him from high school and even had a few dates. He enjoyed the fact that women were attracted to an officer; especially when wearing a uniform. He made sure everyone knew that he had spent a few days in New Haven before coming home to Stamford. His initial regret about accidentally killing Cadet Smith faded completely from Bill's conscious. A month later, it was as if it had never happened.

CHAPTER 3

FORT BOENDE (AMERICAN FORCES)

Bill's flight from New York arrived just outside the city of Boende at 9:00 AM local time. The rocket powered plane crossed six time zones in only two hours. As he exited the plane and began walking toward baggage claim, he immediately noticed the many different aromas which seemed to permeate the terminal. Bill was met at baggage claim by a sergeant.

"Lieutenant, welcome to Boende. My name is Sergeant Jerry Rogers. Let me take your bag. My hauler is parked just outside and to the right."

"Thank you, Sergeant."

Exiting the terminal, Bill was struck by a wave of hot air. The heat outside the terminal felt like you were standing in front of a blast furnace. Regretfully, the hauler was not air conditioned, either.

As the hauler departed the airport, the sergeant looked over at Bill and said, "Sir, it takes several weeks to get used to this stinking heat. I've found the best thing to do is drink lots of water and limit your physical activity outdoors until your body adjusts. Luckily, we have air conditioned offices and barracks. Even our gym is air conditioned."

"Thank you, Sergeant for the health tip. This is my first time to be so near the equator. I suppose it is like this year round?"

"Yes sir, pretty much so."

"What do you do for entertainment out here?"

"Sir, some soldiers date contractor personnel and others have found local girlfriends. The Fort sponsors tours to various places during our time off and we have lots of vids in our day room. We have a well-equipped gym complete with a bowling alley and swimming pool. There are a few good restaurants in town and several bars where they serve local beer. The beer is pretty good, too. Boende also has a casino filled with a variety of games invented to separate you from your money. That's just about all there is to do around here. The most exciting thing to see is a rocket launch. The Colonel insists that everyone not on guard duty be permitted to see the launch. Lieutenant, a rocket launch is well worth seeing. It beats fireworks any day."

He continued, "Sir, when we get to Fort Boende, I'll drop you off at battalion headquarters and stow your gear in your quarters."

"That's very kind of you, Sergeant. How far is it to the fort?"

"Sir, it's about sixteen klicks from town to Fort Boende.

* * *

"Welcome to Fort Boende, Lieutenant Anders."

"Thank you Sergeant Major. Is the Colonel expecting me?"

"Yes sir. I'll take you in."

Sergeant Major Tinsdale knocked on Lieutenant Colonel Miles Harper's door and entered with Lieutenant Anders in tow.

"Colonel Harper, Lieutenant William Anders reporting for duty."

Returning Bill's salute, Colonel Harper said, "Lieutenant Anders, welcome aboard. Please have a seat. I'll brief you about our battalion and will give you my expectations. Afterwards, I'll introduce you to your company commander."

"Thank you, sir. I'm really excited about joining this battalion. I've heard a lot of good things about your unit."

"Lieutenant, I'm proud of the 415th. Our primary mission is to protect the launch facility. Since our battalion assumed responsibility for security, there have been no unauthorized entries."

He continued, "Boende is scheduled for four launches this year. Seeing, feeling and hearing a rocket launch itself into space is an unforgettable experience. Everything stops and everybody gets to see each launch. It's really the highlight of your tour of duty."

"Yes sir, I'm looking forward to seeing a launch."

After meeting with Colonel Harper, Bill walked over to the B Company area with Colonel Harper and was introduced to his company commander, Captain Melissa Steiner.

Captain Steiner walked up to Bill, extended her hand and said, "Welcome to Company B, Lieutenant Anders."

As Bill shook her hand, he quickly noted her appearance. Captain Steiner stood just above one and a half meters, weighted roughly fifty kilograms, with short blonde hair and blue eyes. Her only noticeable physical flaw was a wide scar running from the corner of her mouth to her ear; possibly caused by a vehicle accident or bullet wound. She didn't try to hide the scar with makeup nor did she appear to be self-conscious about its presence. Bill concluded she was a career-oriented armor officer and the Army was all that really mattered to her.

After the battalion commander departed, Captain Steiner asked Bill to be seated. She sat behind her desk and quietly announced, "Lieutenant Anders, I've received a message from the New York State Police notifying me that you are to be formally deposed as part of an ongoing investigation. Do you know anything about this?"

Bill replied, "No Ma'am. I have no idea why they want my testimony. But I'll be happy to cooperate."

"That's good to hear. Please be in my office when they call at 7:00 PM this evening and let me know if you want an attorney present during the deposition."

"Ma'am, I'm sure I won't need an attorney."

She continued, "Fine. Now let's talk about your platoon. I am assigning you the 1st Platoon. You are replacing an officer who was selected to command an armored company in Florida. Lieutenant Don Marks was one of the highest rated officers serving in the 415th Battalion and the soldiers assigned to 1st Platoon adored him. I'm afraid you'll have your work cut out for you in filling his shoes."

Bill was thinking, *'It sounds like Lieutenant Marks was more to his company commander than just a platoon leader. At the very least, Captain Steiner must have been president of his fan club.'*

After an awkward silence, Melissa continued, "Lieutenant Anders, our battalion's training budget was cut again this year. Although we have a full complement of cheetahs, we can only afford to operate them during our annual two-week battalion level maneuvers. The remainder of our time is spent on simulators, physical fitness programs and in patrolling our assigned area outside the launch facility. In spite of funding limitations, morale is high and my company is ready to fight.

"Your job is to ensure your platoon maintains its high readiness level. If you have questions or need my help, don't hesitate to see me. As you know, my job is to prepare you for company command. But before you can become a company commander, you'll have to prove yourself as a platoon leader. Have you any questions?"

"No Ma'am. Everything is perfectly clear."

"Take it easy for a few days until you become acclimated to the weather and adjust to the six hour time difference between here and New York. If you feel up to it, you're invited to have dinner with myself and your fellow officers of B Company tomorrow evening."

"That sounds like a lot of fun. I'll be there, Ma'am."

After the briefing by Captain Steiner, Bill walked out of her office thinking, *'Not only I am stuck in the middle of nowhere, I'm saddled with a giddy-headed commanding officer who has "loser" written all over her. She does have a cute figure though. If I get desperate for sex; maybe I'll favor her with my attentions.'*

Bill took a quick tour of his quarters where he noted that his gear had arrived. He next walked over to his platoon area and met with Sergeant Roland Miller; the platoon sergeant.

Sergeant Miller said, "Lieutenant Anders, may I suggest we go to the dining hall and have lunch?"

During lunch, Bill asked, "Sergeant Miller, where and at what time is formation?"

"Sir, company formation is held at 0600 each morning in the company headquarters' parking lot."

"What is the uniform of the day and do you have an extra set of unit patches?"

"Lieutenant, based on the clothing sizes listed in your personnel file, six sets of tropical combat uniforms have been put in your closet. Regarding the unit patch; a couple of patches have been placed on your desk in your quarters."

"Fine; now what is on our training schedule?"

"Sir, tomorrow 1st Platoon is having an open locker inspection followed by a tour of the motor pool. Time has been set aside for you to meet with the squad leaders, address the platoon, and observe our physical fitness training."

Thank you, Sergeant Miller. I'll see you in the morning." Bill returned to his quarters and put away his gear and took a long shower.

At 6:45 PM, Bill returned to Captain Steiner's office and waited for the call from the New York State Police. While waiting, he and Captain Steiner talked about his plans for 1st Platoon.

Bill asked, "Captain Steiner, what can you tell me about our Boende launch facility security mission?"

"Bill, platoons in the battalion are assigned guard duty on a rotating basis. Each platoon works an eight hour shift. This means a platoon has guard duty about ten times each twenty-eight day period. Your platoon is scheduled ..."

They were interrupted by the call from New York.

The call was displayed on a vid unit. "Lieutenant Anders, my name is State Trooper Reynolds from the Special Investigations Division. With me is Mr. Paul Archer; a New York Assistant District Attorney. This interview is being recorded."

Bill responded, "Trooper Reynolds, present with me is Captain Melissa Steiner, my company commander."

"Lieutenant Anders, we're conducting an investigation into the disappearance of Cadet Jonathan Smith who is assigned to West Point. Please describe your relationship with this cadet."

Bill responded, "I met Cadet Smith during my senior year at West Point. We talked on several occasions. I concluded that Cadet Smith had a lot of potential as a future Army officer. He was not my friend because upperclassmen are not permitted to fraternize with plebes. In summary, our conversations were brief and always related to military subjects. I don't recall ever discussing any personal subject with Cadet Smith."

"Have you seen or have you been in contact with Cadet Smith since you graduated from West Point?"

"No. After graduation, I was on leave for thirty days and then departed for my current posting."

"Have you heard anyone discuss Cadet Smith in any capacity since your graduation?"

"No. I have not spoken with anyone from West Point since graduation."

"Lieutenant Anders, thank you for your cooperation in our investigation. Please contact us immediately should you remember or hear anything about Cadet Smith. This interview is over."

Bill said, "Trooper Reynolds, I'll call you should I hear anything pertaining to Cadet Smith."

After the interview ended, Captain Steiner paused a few moments then said, "Bill, how much experience do you have operating cheetahs?"

"I spent three months between my junior and senior year in a cheetah unit. That summer convinced me to become an armor officer."

"Okay, let's assume you may be a bit rusty. I want you to spend time in the simulator refreshing your skills. Our battalion is scheduled for its annual training exercise in October. Following this event, a one-on-one competition is held among the platoon leaders. Last year, Don Marks, your predecessor, eventually lost to Lance Stallings of A Company in the finals. As you might imagine, a lot of unit prestige is at stake."

She added, "I've also been informed the local casino operates a betting pool on the annual competition and even posts odds on each lieutenant. And in spite of regulations against gambling, some of our soldiers will bet several months' salary on the outcome."

"Ma'am, thank you for the challenge; the cheetah simulator and I will become best friends during the next eight weeks."

"Bill, you've had a busy day. Why don't you turn in? We'll have time for further discussions tomorrow."

"Good night, Ma'am."

CHAPTER 4

THE TRIP HOME (HAVEN)

Key members of the Embassy staff accompanied Ambassador Allen to the Cape Canaveral Spaceport where they boarded a transport ship bound for the month-long voyage to Haven. A majority of the staff remained behind to maintain the appearance of 'business as usual' at the embassy.

Jonathan Allen smiled as he boarded the ship. He was looking forward to seeing his family and returning to his home world. His momentary elation was quickly replaced by a feeling of dread lurking in the back of his mind. The meeting with President Williams had gone badly. He had failed to persuade President Williams to moderate his demand for unlimited immigration and he knew that few options remained; none of which were acceptable to Haven's government. Jim Anderson's bombshell about America's planned invasion made his trip home all the more critical.

The ship's captain personally greeted Ambassador Allen and escorted him to the bridge as his special guest. The Steward showed other members of the embassy staff to their quarters.

"As you will note, Mr. Ambassador, we are fully prepared for takeoff. I am delighted to have you join us on this trip to Haven."

"Thank you, Captain. I feel safe knowing you have taken this trip many times. Your enviable safety record and reputation for meeting schedules are well known throughout the diplomatic community."

"That is very kind of you to say so, Mr. Ambassador. We have calculated this trip to Haven will take only thirty days."

After a slight pause, Jim continued, "Captain, do you mind my asking what cargo you are taking to Haven?"

"Mr. Ambassador, in addition to you and your staff, we have on board almost 7,500 settlers with farming equipment who volunteered to immigrate to Haven and start a new life. My crewmembers are telling me these settlers are excited about the prospects of breathing Haven's fresh air and a new start. Due to our large number of passengers, we've modified our holds and installed temporary shelters for our additional passengers. After arriving on Haven, these temporary shelters will be taken off my ship and reassembled as the settler's homes."

Jonathan inwardly cringed at this news but showed no emotion as he stated, "Captain, after the ship's launch, may I be shown my cabin? It's been a long day and my aging body requires rest."

Jonathan was thinking, *'President Williams, it's apparent you're not waiting for Haven's official response. Instead, you're taking preemptive action. This unilateral declaration will not go well with Haven's leadership; especially Governor General Johnson. I fear there will be no further negotiations.'*

"Certainly, Mr. Ambassador, my Chief Steward will show you to you cabin immediately after launch. And now, if you will kindly strap yourself into the seat to your left, we'll get underway."

A klaxon sounded throughout the ship followed by; "All stations, prepare for takeoff."

The Captain turned to his crew on the flight deck said, "Gentlemen, cast off all lines and initiate maximum thrust."

CHAPTER 5

SIMULATOR INCIDENT (EARTH FORCES)

Cheetah simulators were housed in a large air-conditioned building near the gym. The building contained four simulators; one for each armored company with one available for additional training and which was used as a spare if a company's simulator was down for maintenance. People signed up for usage on a 24/7 basis but individual usage was limited to 30 minutes per soldier.

Suspecting Lieutenant Anders needed extra training on cheetahs, Sergeant Miller suggested, "Lieutenant, because you may want to spend some additional time in the simulator, all of the platoon members have voluntarily signed up for simulator training. You are welcome to take the slots of those who don't actually need the simulator time. Sir, we want you to be on top of your game for the one-on-one competition this year."

Bill wryly replied, "Sergeant Miller, how very thoughtful of you and the platoon members. I know your desire to see me become more proficient on a cheetah has nothing to do with the large betting among the soldiers on the outcome of these contests." After pausing, Bill grinned and continued, "However, I also want to win the competition this year. Let me know which soldier doesn't need the refresher and I'll gladly use his or her time allocation."

That brought a big smile to Sergeant Miller. "Yes sir and don't worry sir, I'll keep close tabs on the soldiers and not let them get out of shape while you're in training."

Bill devoted himself to the simulators. He got to know the sim room technicians and maintained good relations with them. He became a fixture in the sim room due to his numerous training sessions. It was a good thing he took Captain Steiner's advice; he had become rusty since his previous cheetah experience and would have failed miserably during the upcoming competition.

One evening Bill was about to enter a simulator when someone behind him said, "Sorry bub, that simulator is taken. You'll have to find another."

Bill turned around and saw another Lieutenant impatiently waiting to get into the simulator. Bill said, "Take a look at the sign-up sheet '*bub*' and you'll see that I own this time slot for Simulator #4."

"I don't give a rip what the sign-up sheet says, this simulator is assigned to Company A and you are standing in *my* way."

Smiling at the angry Lieutenant, Bill replied, "Why don't you go outside and play with yourself, sonny. I'll be done in 30 minutes."

As Bill turned to climb into the simulator, he was grabbed by the arm and pulled around to face the irate Lieutenant. Bill dropped his helmet and slammed his fist into the gut of the Lieutenant. The startled Lieutenant's eyes became big and his mouth formed a big oh as he began leaning forward. When the Lieutenant's head was approximately waist high, Bill kneed the Lieutenant in his face which sent him reeling backward. The Lieutenant fell and his head smacked the concrete floor with a dull thud. He lay sprawled on the floor without moving. A couple of simulator technicians came running over and Bill ordered one to call a medic. After ascertaining the lieutenant was still alive, Bill turned around, picked up his helmet and entered the simulator. Once inside, he began grinning as he set the scenario for an offensive operation.

CHAPTER 6

COURT MARTIAL (EARTH FORCES)

"Lieutenant Anders, you have been accused of attempted manslaughter and conduct unbecoming an officer. You have the right to an attorney. Do you wish to make a plea at this time?"

Bill looked at each officer sitting behind the table in front of him. The impromptu courtroom was set-up in the battalion dining hall and there was not one familiar face in the group of officers. He turned his attention to the senior officer and replied, "Sir, I am innocent of all charges."

"Lieutenant Anders based on the evidence collected, you are hereby notified that a court martial is being convened and you are formally charged under the following articles of military justice:

- Article 133 – Conduct unbecoming an officer
- Article 134 – Assault with intent to commit voluntary manslaughter

"You have the right to an attorney of your choosing. If you prefer, your battalion commander may appoint an officer to represent you. Do you have any questions?"

"I have no questions at this time."

Lieutenant Anders, you are hereby relieved of duty and confined to your quarters until further notice. Your court martial will commence on September 15th."

Bill walked out of the dining hall and to his quarters. He called battalion headquarters and requested to speak with Colonel Harper.

"Colonel Harper speaking, may I help you?"

"Sir, this is Lieutenant Anders. I am requesting Captain Melissa Steiner be assigned as my attorney."

"I can do that. However, you do know she's not a trained attorney."

"Yes sir but she is my choice."

"Very well, I'll have her appointed as your attorney. I'm very sorry this incident occurred. It gives me no pleasure to know that one of my brightest officers is being court martialed and the other is receiving intensive care in the hospital. Good luck, Lieutenant."

"Thank you, sir."

* * *

A loud voice announced, "All rise."

"Lieutenant Anders, this court martial finds you not guilty of assault with intent to commit voluntary manslaughter. You have been found guilty of conduct unbecoming an officer. As punishment, you will forfeit 30 days' pay and will be confined to your quarters for 15 days. Additionally, you will receive anger management counseling."

The gavel struck the table and the chief judge said, "This court martial is adjourned."

* * *

After hearing a knock, Bill opened his door and saw Captain Steiner standing in the hall.

"Lieutenant Anders, forgive me for barging into your quarters, but we need to talk."

"Please come in." As Melissa walked into his room, Bill continued, "Ma'am, thank you for representing me at the court martial; I doubt anyone else could have rescued me from that predicament."

Melissa said, "Lieutenant, I'm not here to celebrate. You were damn lucky this time. Don't let it happen again. *Am I clear?* Your uncontrollable temper almost killed that officer."

She continued, "Bill, you have been assigned to my company for less than two months and during that brief time; you have damaged your personal reputation and your penchant for violence has reflected poorly on *my* leadership skills. One more screw-up like this and I can practically guarantee you'll be discharged from the Army and sent packing! And there is nothing I'll do to save you next time. Do you understand?"

"Ma'am, I read you loud and clear."

In a quieter voice Melissa continued, "As you recall, I was present during the deposition you gave to the New York State Police. After hearing about you beating Lieutenant Stallings, I began thinking about Cadet Smith. I pray you didn't harm him. In addition to having a violent temper, you may be a very clever man. For example, by requesting me as your attorney, you knew I couldn't mention the deposition during the court martial. In my book, this coincidence places you on shaky ground."

After pausing for several moments, she continued, "Bill, as long as you're a member of B Company, I have an obligation to mentor and help you. In that spirit, between anger management counseling sessions, I want you to study these vids of prior cheetah one-on-one competitions. Also, I've asked one of the technicians from the simulation lab to stop by and debrief you on your simulation sessions. You need to absorb these lessons because we don't have much time remaining before battalion maneuvers. Winning the one-on-one competition this year will go a long way toward repairing your reputation in this battalion."

"Thank you, Ma'am. I won't let you down."

"Lieutenant, you've already let me down; just make sure you don't disappoint me again."

After Melissa left his quarters, Bill began thinking, *'Bill, it's time to begin planning how you can permanently silence Captain Melissa Steiner. That little bitch suspects too much and has become a direct threat. She must be neutralized.'*

CHAPTER 7

PLANNING FOR
THE INEVITABLE
(HAVEN FORCES)

Ambassador Jonathan Allen arrived at the Governor's Residence on Haven and was immediately escorted to the private office of Governor General Peter Johnson.

"Come in, Ambassador Allen. Welcome home. Won't you please be seated?"

"Thank you, Governor Johnson. It's a pleasure seeing you again but I'm afraid I bring bad news from Earth."

"Jonathan, I suspected as much. In fact, I've convened my Cabinet in anticipation of your report."

"Governor, my information is vital to the continuing survival of Haven. I wish I could've sent this over the Hyperpulse Communication Network but America's military intelligence is able to decipher any coded message transmitted over that communications system."

"I understand perfectly, old friend. Now what is this news you dread telling me?"

"Sir, America intends to invade Haven within the next four months. According to my sources, they are planning an invasion made up of three waves. The first wave will consist of eight armored and four infantry battalions supported by two aviation units. The second and third waves will consist of additional combat units plus logistics, military police, intelligence and medical teams. This chip contains the details of the American force to include biographies of the command staff."

Jonathan continued, "I also have specifications of a hyperpulse drive engine, a new armored vehicle and America's latest fighter design. Perhaps Haven can use this data?"

Governor Johnson grimly reflected on this news. *'Haven is ill-prepared to repel an invasion of this magnitude. The size of their invasion force coupled with their having newer technology does not bode well for Haven's defenders.'*

Focusing on his ambassador he replied, "Jonathan, this is sad news, indeed. Let's adjourn to the conference room and share this information with my cabinet. It appears we have no time to waste."

The conference room door was opened and the Master of Arms announced, "All stand for the Governor."

"Good morning, ladies and gentlemen. Please be seated. I have with me Ambassador Jonathan Allen from Earth who is the bearer of sad news. Following the Ambassador's briefing, we will discuss our path ahead. Jonathan, please proceed and spare no details."

After Jonathan's presentation, Governor Johnson looked at the shocked faces of his cabinet and asked General Turner for comment.

General Albert Turner, Commander of Haven's Militia, cleared his throat and said, "Governor Johnson, the first wave of the planned American invasion force is bigger than our entire militia. They could annihilate us in one pitched battle.

"We must not face the invaders head on until the size of our militia is substantially increased. We must also modernize our militia with weapons comparable to those America is surely bringing. Until we get these modern weapons and a larger force, we must limit our militia to fighting the enemy using 'hit and run' tactics. This means the invaders will be able to occupy Haven's cities and military installations. Our militia will be restricted to the countryside until we amass sufficient forces."

Governor Johnson then turned to Dr. Harold Winters, an industrial specialist, and asked, "Even before you and your team thoroughly review the plans for the new armored vehicle and fighter aircraft, how long would it take Haven to produce quantities of these new items?"

Dr. Winters cleared his throat and said, "Governor, I hesitate to give an estimate because of the many variables contained in producing complex systems. For example, will American forces leave our existing production facilities intact and permit us to produce weapons which will be used to defeat them? If not, we have to relocate our production facilities to remote regions of Haven and start anew. Regarding the production of new weapons; even if we have complete specifications, an optimistic estimate to begin production is four years. A likely estimate is five to eight years."

Governor Johnson replied, "Dr. Winters, because Haven will be invaded within four months, what must we do in order to shorten your optimistic estimate?"

"Sir, I believe I have given you the best estimate. To produce new weapons, we must first build the manufacturing tools. However, in order to build manufacturing tools, we need a research and development facility, raw materials, access to power, skilled workers, food, water and housing for our workers, exemption from existing rules and regulations governing production, and physical security. While a hidden facility is being prepared, our engineers could commence designing and developing the production tools. Given these requirements, we could build the machinery and tools needed to produce the weapons at the hidden facility. Following this critical step, we could transport the completed production tooling and begin building the weapons at any production facility. This proposed course of action could save valuable time."

Governor Johnson asked, "Does anyone have an idea where such a facility could be located?"

Linda Harris, an environmental expert said, "Governor Johnson, what about the Isaac Schmidt Caverns? They're extensive, located far from any city, and the Centennial Hydro Electric Power Facility is less than forty kilometers away."

"How large are these caverns?"

"Nobody has completed a full survey but the caverns explored thus far average five meters in height and fifteen meters wide. I've heard estimates that the main cavern and its branches extend hundreds of meters into the mountain."

"Excellent. General Turner, could you defend that area?"

"Yes Governor, we could defend the facility. The caverns are in a wilderness area accessible only by air and one hard surfaced road."

General Turner added, "Ladies and gentlemen, let's not forget our existing weapon systems. Until we have the newer weapons, we need many more of our current weapons; especially the cheetah armored vehicles and anti-aircraft missiles. The current production facilities must be relocated and we need to add factory workers for a three-shift operation."

Governor Johnson stated, "My Chief of Staff will coordinate with each of you on your requirements. Now let us address manpower. How can we rapidly expand the militia?"

Dr. James Patterson, representing the public health sector, suggested, "Governor, why not institute a draft? We should draft all men and women between the ages of eighteen and thirty-four."

Dr. Winters objected saying, "Drafting that age group will cut into the manpower available for production."

General Turner said, "Governor Johnson, we've got to dramatically increase the size of our military and that age group is ideal for soldiers. Further, we need more land on which to train draftees. Our existing training facilities are inadequate for a rapid expansion."

"General Turner, while you're expanding your training facilities, I assume you cannot train all the young people who are available for the draft this year. Governor Johnson, may I be given some of these young people? They will be needed for construction and factory relocation."

Governor Johnson announced, "The age group encompassing eighteen through thirty-four will be subject to the draft. General Turner, you have first choice from this pool to meet your requirements. Dr. Winters, those not inducted into the militia are yours. Men and women thirty-five and above will also be available for farming, construction and production jobs."

"Governor, this means only the disabled, young and very old will remain in our cities. How will they be cared for?"

"First of all, I believe our children should be sent to farms throughout Haven for their safety. Children are the future of our planet and they must be protected. Secondly, others not being drafted into the militia or in defense-related work should be encouraged to move into the countryside and stay with relatives or friends. Further, it's safe to assume not every person thirty-five and above will be drafted to serve in our industries. Our hospitals and many retail stores will remain open. When the Earth forces arrive, we will ask that our cities be given neutral status and we be allowed to provide food and health care for residents living within each city. Since these citizens are the most vulnerable and least threatening, the invaders may grant our request. However, we must not permit the invading army to hold these citizens hostage and force our cooperation. I know this sounds harsh, even draconian, but I see little option. We cannot defend every city and every person. We must carefully choose what and who we will defend; otherwise we'll be forced to surrender everything."

After much more discussion, Haven's leaders unanimously voted to fight rather than surrender. A citizen's draft would be implemented immediately, work would commence on constructing a development facility in the Isaac Schmidt Caverns for war production machinery, current manufacturing plants would be relocated, surplus food and raw materials would be gathered and hidden, new immigrants would be put under local police surveillance and the Government would be transferred away from the capital. Prior to the invasion, commercial broadcasting equipment would be moved and reserved for Government use.

General Turner was given the mission to plan and defend Haven using all available resources. He was also allocated a wide frequency spectrum for military use and full access to Haven's satellites and land-based communications. Based on the information contained in the stolen invasion plans, the invaders would not be able to block or intercept all militia communications. Only the planned third wave of invaders would bring equipment capable of jamming and intercepting the full range of militia communication signals.

Civil rights of Haven's citizens were to be temporarily suspended and all utilities placed under immediate control of the Government. A formal declaration of war would be issued to America immediately after Haven was invaded.

CHAPTER 8

DRAFT NOTICE (HAVEN FORCES)

My name is John Collins and I live in Tupelo. Tupelo is Haven's capital city of eight million residents. After a hard day's work, I got off the city transit unit and began walking to my apartment. Haven's weather is beautiful this time of year. Early September through October is my favorite; we are blessed with a long stretch of warm days and cool evenings.

Near my apartment, I stopped at the incoming box and retrieved some advertisements and a couple of personal notes. As I scanned each, I noticed one of the notes looked official.

I quickly opened the note, read it, and started laughing. The note stated I was being drafted into the Haven Militia.

I immediately activated my comm unit and called my brother. "Hello, Jerry? Yeah, it's John. Are you trying to play one of your stupid jokes on me?"

Jerry replied, "John, what are you talking about?"

"What am I talking about? I just got a personal note which says I'm being drafted into the militia. Did you send this as a prank?"

"No John, I got a draft notice, too."

"Wait a minute, you got one, too? What's going on? I'm twenty-seven years old and you're thirty-four! Haven doesn't draft its citizens; especially not people your age."

"John, where have you been? It's all over the news. Haven't you been watching the vid?"

"No, I just got in from work and haven't seen the news. Hold on a second while I turn it on. Which station?"

"Any station, this news is on every station."

"It's on all of them? Okay, I'll call you back."

I disconnected the comm unit and began watching the vid. The commentator was saying, "All men and women between the ages of 18 and 34 are being drafted into Haven's militia. Individual exemptions from the draft will be awarded based on a number of factors. Poor physical and mental health and employment in critical jobs are examples."

Between these special announcements, a world in shock heard its politicians and military leaders discussing Earth's decision to send an army to occupy Haven. During the interviews, a repeat of the draft notice scrolled along the bottom of the vid screen.

I carefully read my note. It said I was to report to the Tupelo Shopping Mall #2 on Thursday, September 13 at 9:00 AM for induction into the militia. I thought, *'Oh that's just great, I've got at least five days of work to do before the ferrocrete can be poured. Smitty won't like that one bit. He hates construction delays with a passion.'*

I activated my comm unit again and called Smitty. "Hey Smitty, did you hear the news?"

Smitty replied, "Are you talking about the draft?"

"Yeah, I got a draft notice and it says I have to report on Thursday. You're lucky they're not drafting old farts like yourself."

"John I'm sorry you're being drafted. However, I need you to complete the excavation before you leave. Are you willing to work overtime during the next two days?" He hesitated and then continued, "I'll pay you double the overtime rate."

"Smitty, you must be desperate to offer me that kind of money. Yeah, well I'll do it on one condition; you get somebody else to maintain and service the excavator and let me concentrate on digging. Is that a deal?"

"Okay, you work your magic with the excavator and I'll get Frankie to keep it serviced and make any repairs."

"Thanks, Smitty. I'll see you bright and early tomorrow morning."

I next called my latest girlfriend. "Hello Sarah, have you heard the news?"

"Hi John, I've been trying to contact you for the past 30 minutes. Your comm unit has been continuously busy. You won't believe this, darling; I got a draft notice!"

"Sarah, I don't understand. You have a college degree, a great job with a law firm and you're still married to that high priced lawyer."

"John, I wish you wouldn't mention Leonard. But yes, I got my draft notice today."

"When do you report for the draft?"

"The notice says I have to report on Thursday."

"What a coincidence, so do I. Wouldn't it be a hoot if we get assigned to the same unit! What's-his-name would have a heart attack! Sarah, can you come over to my place tonight?"

"I'll try. I love you, John."

"Love you, too, Babe."

I had met Sarah through a mutual acquaintance. We felt an immediate physical attraction toward one another. I'm 180 centimeters tall and weigh about 81 kilograms with blonde hair and blue eyes. Sarah is 167 centimeters tall, weighs about 56 kilograms and has blonde hair and hazel eyes.

She had recently separated from her husband and was lonely for a man's attention. Being single, I felt it was my duty to help her in any way possible.

My mother was not happy with me dating a married woman even though I told her repeatedly that Sarah was separated from her husband and was in the process of getting a divorce. Because of my family's feelings, I didn't take Sarah to my parent's home.

I contacted my brother again after ending the conversation with Sarah. "Jerry, I heard the announcement. How is Allison taking the news about you being drafted?"

"John, Allison received a draft notice, too. She's been crying all afternoon."

"Holy crap, Allison's being drafted, too! Who is going to take care of Danny?"

"Allison's mother has volunteered to keep Danny."

"Wow, I'll bet that idea will excite our mom and dad! I can see the boxing gloves coming out already."

"John, Allison's mother is able to provide exceptional care for Danny and she loves him a lot."

"Hey, I know that. Allison's mother is wealthy and she really loves Danny, but you and I know that don't mean squat to Mom and Dad."

"I know. Hopefully, they'll work out a sharing arrangement for Danny."

"Okay, bro; I know you have lots to do. Tell Allison I love her and I'll talk to you later. Good luck, huh?"

Sarah came over late that evening. She was still in a state of shock about getting her draft notice. All she could talk about was how unfair the draft was and what she would be leaving behind. I was getting the impression that she cared more about losing her possessions, job and social life than our budding relationship. It was interesting to see how a little stress can bring out the 'real person.' Deep down, I was glad to discover this side of her before investing too many thoughts about our future together. After Sarah left my apartment, I thought, *'Sarah, I'll always remember you as a beautiful but spoiled woman who loved sex.'*

* * *

I completed the foundation excavation late Wednesday evening. I moved a lot of dirt in two days and was proud of getting the job done in record time. Smitty deposited a fat paycheck in my bank account, thanked me several times for the work and wished me luck in the militia. He also told me I would always have a job with him after the war.

Immediately after the digging was completed, workers began tying reinforcement rods, setting forms and roughing in plumbing in preparation for ferrocrete deliveries on Friday. Once built, Haven's capital city would have a new hospital for its rapidly growing population; regardless of who was in charge.

On Thursday morning, I reported to the shopping mall. Hundreds of men and women were lined up in front of a battery of clerks seated behind temporary counters. When I stepped up to the counter, I was asked a bunch of questions including name, date of birth, home address, comm unit number, next of kin, education and work history. They also took my photo, recorded my fingerprints and issued some papers. The process was smooth and quick. It took less than five minutes per person. There were also a lot of police on hand to keep things under control.

After stepping away from the counter, I looked at the papers the clerk handed me. One page gave instructions on emptying my refrigerated food storage unit, where to take pets for their safekeeping and notifying my landlord and the personal note delivery office. The other paper listed things to pack and where and when to meet for transportation on Friday morning. I thought, *'Friday morning – that's tomorrow! I was hoping for at least a week to party with Sarah. This Draft Board is acting like there's a war on.'* The second paper also contained some legal jargon to the effect that showing up was not optional and that anyone not reporting would be arrested.

That afternoon, I stopped by my parents' house. "Dad, may I come in?"

"Of course you may. Jerry and Allison are here. They're in the kitchen with your mother."

I followed Dad into the kitchen and noted everybody sitting around the table. They looked my way as I said, "Hello folks; you're staring at the newest member of Haven's militia."

Mom said, "Oh dear. I'm so sorry all three of my children are getting involved in this terrible situation. I've been listening to the news but I can't understand why America is sending soldiers to Haven. We're a peaceful world and have never had any problems with Earth."

Dad said, "Martha, that may be true, but the news media is blaming widespread starvation on Earth as the reason their soldiers are invading our planet."

Jerry added, "It seems America is not satisfied with trading with Haven; they want to rule our planet and our people."

"Sending soldiers to Haven is not going to make our crops grow faster. Maybe they intend to force all of us to work on farms in order to grow more food for Earth?"

A teary –eyed Allison answered, "John, maybe Earth will also send millions of settlers to Haven? My sixth grade geography students recently read that over fifty percent of our planet is available for farming with the balance consisting of forests and fresh water lakes. With more farmers, Haven could easily quadruple its crop production and Earth could reduce its population through a massive migration."

"Allison, that may be true, but adding millions of new settlers will generate more pollution and deplete our own natural resources; not to mention the increased crime and a host of other social problems."

"Dammit, it's not right that Haven must be destroyed to solve Earth's problems. In fact, ruining our world will only drag us down into the same plight as Earth is experiencing. What kind of solution is this?"

"Evidently, our Government has decided that we're not going to be sacrificed to give Earth a reprieve from its own self-destruction."

"John, what are your plans for this evening?"

"Sarah and I are going to dinner and celebrate our last evening together. I've been given orders to report for duty tomorrow."

"Wow, that's fast! Allison and I have a week to report. Guess we were given more time because of Danny."

After saying goodbye to the family, I got reservations at Sarah's favorite restaurant and met her at the bus stop near her home.

"John, you should let me drive my personal carrier this evening. I have to turn it over next week to the Government for their use. The person who interviewed me for my militia assignment said I wouldn't need it while serving in the militia and if I did need a vehicle, they would issue me one."

"Sure. We can take your carrier. The restaurant isn't far from here but I know how much you enjoy driving. On another subject, do you know what assignment you're getting?"

"Not really. Since I'm a lawyer they're assigning me to Militia Headquarters. I was informed I would be given specific duties upon arrival. The interviewer did say that I'll be awarded a commission in the militia as a lieutenant. When I asked about the pay, he quoted me a number. John, the pay is laughable; my clothing expense is more than I'm going to earn!"

"Sarah, the good news is you won't have to wear expensive designer clothing while you're in the militia. I'm sure they'll issue you a uniform."

"Funny you should mention that. Here is another piece of bad news. Because I'll be an officer, they're giving me a 'uniform allowance' which means I have to buy my own uniforms. Again, the amount they are giving me won't even pay for my bras!" She grinned and continued, "Fortunately, I'm allowed to take my underwear and cosmetics with me."

The remainder of the evening continued in the same vein, Sarah constantly complaining about how inconvenienced she was going to be for the foreseeable future. I was actually relieved when she offered to drive me to my apartment. Sarah declined my invitation to come in because she had to finish some legal drafts associated with her law firm. We said our goodbyes on the street and I promised to think of her often.

As I got ready for bed, I reflected on the fact that Sarah had not asked me anything about my upcoming assignment. She is a walking definition of self-centered.

CHAPTER 9

DRIVER TESTING (MILITIA FORCES)

On Friday at 8:00 AM, I arrived at the intersection of Fourteenth Street and B Avenue as instructed. Several people were already there. A Tupelo city transit unit and a green military hauler were parked along the curb. Between 8:00 and 8:30, more men and women joined our group. At 8:30, a soldier ordered everyone to either board the transit unit or get on the hauler. Since most began crowding the transit unit door, I walked over to the hauler, threw my duffel bag into the back and climbed the tailgate. I turned around and helped a tiny woman who was struggling to reach the elevated cargo bed.

After helping her up, we sat on a wooden bench and introduced ourselves.

"Thanks for the lift. My name is Brittany Fellows. You are?"

"John Collins and you're welcome for the hand up. These cargo beds aren't made for easy access."

"You're right about that, but I'll have to learn how to climb up on these things since I'm being drafted into the militia."

"Brittany, what did you do before becoming a militia recruit?"

"I operated a fork lift at Castle Brewery here in Tupelo. What about you?"

"I ran an excavator for Ajax Construction. In fact, I finished a project yesterday."

Our conversation was interrupted as others began climbing on board. Some were complaining that the bus had filled up too quickly and they shouldn't be forced to ride in the back of a hauler like livestock. I looked over at Brittany. We both smiled but said nothing.

Before the vehicles departed, the soldier stood at the back of the hauler and conducted a roll call. He said, "When I call your name, answer up."

One guy asked, "Where are we headed, General?"

After calling everyone's names the soldier replied, "I'm a corporal; not a general. And you're being assigned to Johnson Springs Reservation. It's about 300 kilometers away. Good luck, recruits."

Afterwards, the hauler started and we rode about four hours before arriving at our destination. Once there, the tail gate was lowered and a soldier ordered everyone off the hauler.

Looking around, I noticed that we were inside a large fenced area and several tracked vehicles were lined up across the street. On the opposite side of the street was a set of bleachers. Using a voice amplifier, a soldier with three stripes on his sleeve announced, "You recruits have thirty minutes to use the portable latrines located a block down the street to my right. Afterwards, I want to see everyone sitting on these bleachers."

Thirty minutes later, "Ladies and gentlemen, welcome to Johnson Springs Reservation. My name is Sergeant Andrew Thigpen and I'm in charge of warrior and mechanics training. You fifty recruits are here because you either have experience operating heavy equipment or performing vehicle maintenance. Today we'll test your driving skills. Those passing the test will be designated as warriors. Those not passing the driving test will be mechanics."

He continued, "Our armored vehicles are named cheetahs. As you look behind me, you will note that a cheetah is a small one-man vehicle mounting a medium caliber rail gun and an anti-personnel weapon. Their light-weight armor provides protection against anti-personnel fire but the vehicle's low silhouette and high speed is its best protection against the heavy stuff. Notice that large numbers have been stenciled on each cheetah we're using today. Does anybody have any questions? Okay, when your name is called, run to your assigned cheetah and await further instructions."

My name was the first called. I trotted over to the parked cheetahs and stood beside the one assigned to me."

A soldier with two stripes on his sleeve walked up to me and said, "Recruit, my name is Corporal Charles. Have you ever operated a tracked vehicle?" I replied, "Corporal, I operate a tracked excavator every day at work."

He said, "Okay recruit, crank it up, back it up slowly and give me a 180 degree turn."

I scrambled up the cheetah's hull and dropped down into the driver's compartment. The controls were familiar so I pressed a button and activated the engine. Powered by a Lithium Thorium Hydroxide (LTH) battery, the cheetah's engine was almost completely silent. The engine readout displayed 250 RPM at idle and showed a red line of 20,000. Wow! This vehicle was built for speed! No wonder it was named after the legendary Earth animal. By comparison, my excavator's engine was limited to 1,500 RPM. I remembered the ancient tortoise and hare fable and smiled at the comparison.

Looking out the windscreen, I noticed everyone in the bleachers was staring at me. Using the corporal as a guide, I backed the cheetah about 10 meters; clearing the other parked cheetahs. Feeling cocky, I decided to execute a 180 degree spin by applying full throttle to the engine, locking the right track and allowing the left track to run at top speed in reverse. Unfortunately, my showing off was my undoing. I made a rookie mistake and threw the left track! The cheetah was never meant to be spun about with the engine running anywhere near its maximum RPM.

The corporal came running up to the front of the vehicle and made a chopping motion with his hand signaling me to cut the power. He was red in the face and I could tell he was really pissed.

Sergeant Thigpen hurried over and ordered me back to the bleachers. As I sat down, he addressed everyone saying, "Ladies and gentlemen, this recruit has demonstrated what *not* to do while operating a tracked vehicle. His showing off has cost us valuable time and deadlined one of my training assets. With only five cheetahs at my disposal, he has singlehandedly reduced my training capacity by twenty percent."

Looking directly at me he said, "Recruit, stand up and tell me your name."

I stood up and said, "My name is John Collins."

Sergeant Thigpen said, "Well Private John Collins, I want everyone sitting in the bleachers to meet the militia's newest vehicle mechanic. And since you're our newest mechanic, you can help Corporal Sanders put the track back on his cheetah. Go to the motor pool, find the corporal and tell him you're volunteering to help him."

It's hard for me to express the level of humiliation I was suffering; especially when other recruits started laughing. I was glad to get away from everyone.

Eventually, I found Corporal Sanders in the motor pool. "Corporal, Sergeant Thigpen told me to report to you because I threw a track on a cheetah and I've been told to help you get it back on."

Corporal Sanders said, "What's your name, recruit?"

"My name is John Collins."

"Private Collins, your dumb stunt has caused extra work for us; especially you."

Back near the bleachers, Corporal Sanders supervised while I sweated for forty-five minutes jacking and prying the stubborn track back onto the cheetah's bogies. Other recruits had to walk around me as they tested their driving skills on the four remaining cheetahs. It didn't help my feelings when I heard several of them laugh as they walked by. I wanted to get up and beat the crap out of them.

Afterwards, with my duffle bag in hand, Corporal Sanders escorted me to the barracks.

"Okay, Private Collins here is the mechanics' barracks. This is where you'll be staying. Next door is the warrior's barracks. The dining hall is a block down the street. Across the street from the mess hall is the motor pool. I know you're already familiar with that facility. After stowing your gear, you should get something to eat because the mess hall closes in less than an hour."

Dinner consisted of a green salad, macaroni and cheese with sliced ham and shortcake for dessert. I noticed warrior trainees were sitting in groups and seemed to be having a good time. I sat by myself and quickly finished my first meal as a militia recruit. At least the food was good. Later, I claimed an empty bunk in the mechanics' barracks. A sleeping bag was furnished with each bunk. Although several recruits were engaged in conversation, I didn't feel like joining in. After a quick shower, I crawled into my sleeping bag and fell asleep.

Corporal Sanders woke us early the following morning. As we got dressed, I counted ten recruits assigned to mechanics training; four women and six men.

Corporal Sanders interrupted my thoughts by announcing, "Good morning, ladies and gentlemen. In case you forgot, my name is Corporal Sanders and I'll be one of your instructors. During breakfast, everybody needs to sit at the same table so you can watch and hear the Militia Orientation vid. Afterwards, I'll escort you to the infirmary for your shots; then to the supply room where you'll be issued your uniforms. After lunch, we'll meet in the motor pool where you'll be partnered with a fellow recruit, issued tools and assigned a shop bay. Counting myself, there are five senior mechanics on staff who also serve as your maintenance instructors. Does anyone have questions? If not, I suggest you go to the dining hall."

As we settled around a table, one of the recruits stuck out his hand and said, "My name is Jesse Clark. I remember you from yesterday. You're John Collins."

"Hi Jesse; it's good to meet you. Where are you from?"

"I'm from New Albany. What about you?"

"Tupelo. Jesse, what did you do before being drafted?"

"I worked as a transit vehicle mechanic. What about you?"

"I operated and maintained a tracked excavator for Ajax Construction."

Another recruit suddenly joined our conversation. "John, my name is Alexis Holden. Pardon my intrusion, but I have a question. If you're a tracked excavator operator, why did you attempt a one-eighty yesterday? I would have given my eye teeth to become a warrior but got stuck as a mechanic. I just don't understand why you threw away a golden opportunity."

Looking around the table, I noticed other recruits had stopped eating and were listening to our conversation.

Grinning, I replied, "Alexis, my tracked excavator weighs seventy-two thousand kilograms and is not built for speed. The cheetah is a lightweight vehicle with a powerful engine. I guess I wanted to see what it would do." After pausing for a moment I continued, "There is a bright side to becoming a mechanic."

"And what would that be?"

"Mechanics are less likely to be shot at and most of our work will be done inside."

"John, aren't you concerned about Earth planning to invade Haven?"

"Alexis, I love Haven and will defend our world against any invader. But I've no ambition to be a hero and I didn't volunteer for the militia. Incidentally, did you volunteer to serve in the militia or were you drafted?"

"Point taken; I was drafted, too."

I noticed several recruits nodding their heads in agreement. I was thinking, *'I'm glad Alexis broached this subject in front of everybody. Maybe I won't have to relive my moment of stupidity again.'*

Another recruit joined in the conversation. "John, my name is Jo Anne Davis. I agree with Alexis and believe you should try to succeed at whatever task is assigned. By giving your best effort, our leaders will have better information to make decisions."

I glared at Jo Anne but refused to take the bait and said nothing. I was thinking, '*Here we have a miss goody two shoes. I pity the person who gets stuck with you as a maintenance partner. Your meddling in my business makes me want to slap the snot out of you.*'

Following an awkward silence, the breakfast conversation shifted to another subject.

After watching the vid explaining the militia and its role, we walked to the Infirmary for our vaccinations.

At the Supply Room, we were issued our military clothing consisting of two sets of coveralls, a pair of boots, six pairs of socks, six sets of underwear, two caps, a duffel bag and a poncho. We were each given a copy of militia regulations and told to read the book on our own time. Everyone had been instructed to bring their own toiletries.

Corporal Sanders gave us time to put on a uniform and store the remainder of our stuff in our lockers before lunch. Our barracks was equipped with self-service laundry machines and free soap which meant we washed our own clothes. Everybody slept in a large open area and used a communal bathroom. I already missed my apartment because the barracks was not equipped with a vid screen or kitchen.

There were five shop bays in the motor pool and each pair of maintenance recruits was assigned a bay for their use. Lucky me; I was assigned to work with Jo Anne Davis and Jesse Clark was teamed with Alexis Holden. Jesse and I had hoped to be partners but Corporal Sanders dictated otherwise. Jo Anne and I inventoried our tools and cleaned the shop bay.

While cleaning the shop bay I asked, "Jo Anne, what maintenance experience do you have?"

She replied, "Not much, I'm afraid. I worked on an assembly line before being drafted."

"What did your company make?"

"We manufactured motorized wheelchairs." She continued, "Guess I'm lucky to be working with a highly skilled tracked vehicle operator."

I stopped sweeping, looked at her and said, "Jo Anne, you're pretty damn quick with the sarcastic comments. I hope you learn your maintenance skills just as fast." I was determined not to let her snide comments go unchallenged.

"Oh I don't think you have to worry about me, big fella. Unlike some people around here, I'm a fast learner."

I resumed sweeping the floor while thinking, '*Okay, another smart-ass comment coming from somebody who probably doesn't know how to open a can of oil. Keep mouthing off, smart-ass. I can see you and I are destined for a little one-on-one session.*'

Around 4:00 PM, forty-four cheetahs entered the motor pool. Each maintenance team was given eight or nine to service before turning in that evening. A maintenance instructor told us what had to be done to each vehicle but he didn't help do the work; he just stood around and supervised.

During the next four weeks, a typical day consisted of sitting through vehicle maintenance classes each morning and repairing equipment in the late afternoons and evenings. During the first week, our work was supervised by senior mechanics. After that first week, they let us figure out what was wrong and how to make the repair. We didn't stop until all vehicles were ready for use the next day. Because of my previous hands-on experience with tracked vehicles, other recruits often asked for my help. I enjoyed helping them solve mechanical problems because it helped take the sting out of failing to be designated as a warrior. It was also nice when other recruits visited our maintenance bay with their questions because it reminded Jo Anne that others valued my expertise.

During the second week, we were given small arms training. I had never fired a rifle and this was a unique experience. Our rifles were made of a carbon fiber material and fired small rocket-assisted projectiles. The instructor informed us that scopes could be added for engaging targets beyond 100 meters. Our targets were set at 25, 50 and 75 meters.

It was a lot of fun shooting at silhouette targets shaped like people. After a few lessons from the instructor, I began hitting the target more times than I missed. I figured that with practice, I could get even better.

My chance for additional small arms practice came when Sergeant Thigpen ordered me to help him on the firing range one Saturday morning. He said, "Private Collins, the instructors have to qualify with small arms and I need someone to pick up expended launcher cases after their practice session. Meet me at the firing range at 7:00 in the morning."

Recruits had Saturday and Sundays off so this amounted to additional work with no additional pay. According to my copy of the militia regulations, superiors were permitted to assign soldiers additional work as they chose.

After the cadre had completed their firing, Sergeant Thigpen stayed back and let me fire his weapon. He was an exceptional shot and a good teacher. After a half hour of practice, he said, "Private Collins, you're a natural shooter. Every unit needs an expert marksman. With a little more practice, you can qualify as a sharpshooter. I suggest you continue practicing at every opportunity."

"Thanks Sarge. I enjoy shooting and being designated as a sharpshooter sounds cool."

"Okay Collins, that's it for today. Police up the spent cases before you leave the firing range."

* * *

During training, we occasionally heard the cheetahs' main guns firing. The rail gun made a cracking sound similar to a bolt of lightning. The cheetah's main gun consisted of a barrel containing a series of electrical coils which rapidly accelerated a projectile and launched it toward its target. The speed of the projectile leaving the gun barrel approached Mach 7 and had an effective range of three kilometers. The cheetah's battery was used to power the main gun. Each time the main gun fired, the outer coating of the projectile remained inside the barrel. Lucky me; scrubbing the residue from inside the barrel was a mechanic's responsibility.

After hearing a mass salvo one afternoon, Jo Anne said, "Oh crap, it sounds like we'll be up past ten o'clock tonight repairing vehicles and cleaning guns."

I replied, "Yeah, I just hope they're hitting their targets."

The hardest job was going to the field and retrieving a damaged cheetah. We used a special hauler equipped with a flatbed and large winch. It was a two-man operation. Not only did it take two mechanics away from the normal workload; it meant having to make substantial repairs to the cheetah after returning to the motor pool.

* * *

One day Corporal Sanders walked into our shop bay and said, "Collins, you and Davis get a hauler and go to this grid coordinate. One of the cheetahs threw a track this afternoon and it has to be retrieved."

"Corporal, that's not fair. If you recall, John had to replace a track on our first day here. Why can't the warrior replace his own track? After all, he caused the problem."

"Davis, I don't have the time or inclination to argue with you about this. When Collins threw the track on the first day, he was showing off. Based on his employment record, Collins can operate and maintain a tracked excavator. The militia needs skilled mechanics as much as they need warriors. Remember, a warrior can't accomplish his mission unless his cheetah is operating. Now if you're finished defending Collins, get your ass out there and bring that cheetah back to the motor pool."

As I drove the hauler to retrieve the cheetah I looked over at Jo Ann and asked, "Jo Anne, what were you trying to prove by arguing with Corporal Sanders?"

"Well excuse me for standing up for you! I thought you would be grateful that I tried to get Corporal Sanders to make the warrior fix his own track."

"Jo Anne, Corporal Sanders doesn't have the authority to change the maintenance manual."

"What does a maintenance manual have to do with anything?"

"Well, if you took the time to read it, you'd discover the mechanic is required to perform all maintenance on a cheetah. That's probably why the militia assigns a mechanic to each warrior."

"Okay, Mister Smarty-pants, you got me. I haven't read the cheetah maintenance manual cover-to-cover."

"Had you bothered reading it, you would have known better than to argue with Corporal Sanders."

"Well I guess this incident will teach me not to come to your defense in the future."

"Jo Anne, I didn't ask you to defend me in the first place. I think you're pissed because you have to do extra work."

"John, why don't you stick it up your butt!"

* * *

Warrior trainees were hard on their cheetahs so there was plenty of maintenance work for us mechanics. I began to understand why mechanics don't like to see their vehicles abused. Our small group of mechanic trainees began to believe that the forty cheetah warriors were being treated like prima donnas; leaving us to clean up after them. Also, living in segregated barracks and eating separately at the dining hall reinforced a feeling of 'us versus them.'

In order to get out of the motor pool and back to our barracks, mechanic trainees voluntarily worked together to complete their work. This practice built teamwork among the mechanics and increased individual competency.

One exception to this was Hugo Forrest. Prior to being drafted, Hugo repaired heavy equipment owned by the Tupelo Public Works. According to Hugo, he had a cushy job back home and only worked when it suited him. Evidently, his former boss set and maintained low performance standards.

Hugo was unwilling to do his share of the work in our motor pool and that quickly became a problem. He was a big man and a bully. Even his maintenance partner was afraid to say anything to Hugo's face. Eventually, some trainees began grumbling to Corporal Sanders about Hugo's low productivity. Corporal Sanders quietly suggested I have an informal talk with Hugo behind the maintenance building.

After lunch, the trainees walked back to the maintenance building to await the cheetahs. I said to Hugo, "Hugo, one of the cooks gave me a container of ice cream as payment for a favor but I can't eat it nor do I have any way of keeping it frozen. Are you interested?"

Hugo actually grinned and said, "You bet! Lead me to it."

"Okay, I put it behind the maintenance building. Let's go."

Hugo and I walked around the building and I picked up the container and handed it to Hugo. He pried the lid off and brought the container to his lips. As soon as the container blocked his view, I shoved the container into his face and pushed him backwards. A surprised Hugo lost his balance and fell backwards onto the ground.

After catching his breath, he let out a yell and began scrambling to his feet with ice cream dripping off his face. As soon as Hugo began rising to his full height, I kicked his shin and drove my fist into his fat nose.

He went down again and began cursing as blood gushed from his nose. While still on his hands and knees, I kicked him in the side; causing Hugo to fall again. He lay there trying to catch his breath.

I leaned close to his bloody face and said, "Hugo, we're sick and tired of you not doing your share around here. You may have avoided work back in Tupelo, but your days of loafing on this team are over. Starting today, you're going to work hard and make us all proud. And Hugo, if I hear that you've taken this out on somebody or if I find out you aren't doing your share, I'm going to give you another beating. Only next time, I'm going to break something."

Having delivered my motivational speech, I left Hugo lying in the dirt. His productivity increased dramatically and I never heard a peep from him.

A couple of days later, Corporal Sanders grinned in passing and quietly said, "Good job."

* * *

On Friday afternoon of our final day of training, I said, "Jo Anne, you're a fast learner and willing to do your share of the work. I'm glad Corporal Sanders assigned you to train with me. I predict you're going to make some warrior very happy!"

Jo Anne looked up from the part she was repairing. She was obviously surprised to hear my compliment. Finally, she replied, "Uh thanks, John. I've been meaning to confess that you've been a good teacher and very patient with me. Four weeks ago, I may have misjudged you."

"That's okay Jo Anne; a lot of things can happen in four weeks. Changing the subject, have you been given your assignment?"

"Yes, Corporal Collins stopped by a few minutes ago. He informed me I'm being assigned to the Fifth Armored Battalion. Did he contact you?"

"No, I must have missed him. Wait a minute, since you think I'm such a good teacher, maybe they'll keep me here as an instructor?"

"You wish! No, I have a feeling Private John Collins is destined for greater things."

I was thinking, *'I may be destined to get my ass shot off, too!'*

CHAPTER 10

FIRE TEAM SIX
(MILITIA FORCES)

Helen Ramses was newly-promoted to warrant officer and given command of Fire Team Six. Colonel John Maxon reorganized his battalion into twelve fire teams after Militia Headquarters transferred his officers to form additional armored battalions. His lieutenants and captains became the nucleus of three new battalions bolstering Haven's defenses.

Helen's positive attitude and expertise in handling a cheetah earned her the position of commanding one of the fire teams in the battalion. Outwardly, she didn't appear to have any limitations. Helen was a stunningly beautiful twenty-five year old career soldier. She was an exceptional cheetah warrior who displayed a reckless abandon during battalion maneuvers. Helen was unafraid of any opponent; regardless of the odds. After assuming command, she would unhesitatingly commit her fire team to attack any size force. Her own casualties during these mock battles were high but because she led from the front, her team members continued following her without reserve.

As her mentor, Colonel Maxon discussed tactics with Helen and frequently talked about risk versus reward options. These talks seemed fruitless because Helen was unwilling or unable to exercise caution during subsequent exercises.

Headlong assaults against superior forces are the grist for adventure novels and vids. Unfortunately, during war this tactic is a recipe for defeat and excessive loss of life. The old Earth poem entitled, "The Charge of the Light Brigade" comes to mind. It was her 'attack at all cost' mentality which caused Colonel Maxon to reject her application to attend Officers Training School.

Being a perfectionist, Helen insisted on her cheetah being maintained at the highest level. She was especially tough on her maintenance chief, Roger Hale.

"Private Hale, Colonel Maxon has announced a new series of battalion-level exercises starting tomorrow. Let the other mechanics know that every cheetah in my fire team has to be ready by 6:30 in the morning."

Roger raised his voice and replied, *"Ma'am, your mechanics have been working overtime for the past two weeks to keep your cheetahs running. These upcoming exercises are pushing us past our limit."* In a quieter voice he continued, "We need down time to get some rest and perform important maintenance tasks which have been deferred. For example, your cheetah's engine is due for an overhaul. That's something which cannot be done overnight."

"Private Hale, you need to stop complaining so much. This isn't a union or a social club. We're preparing for war. Everyone is under stress; but that's part of the job. As my chief mechanic, you need to figure out how to get the job done."

Raising his voice once again he retorted, *"Ma'am, I've been in the militia for four years. We're not at war and it seems to me you're more interested in making a reputation for yourself at the expense of the welfare of your soldiers."*

Helen became angry and shouted back, *"Private Hale, I'm placing you on report for insubordination and dereliction of duty. My warriors need the additional training and I'm not going to permit some whining mechanic to keep me from meeting our readiness goals!"*

After hearing these words, Roger's face turned a bright red and he began grabbing his chest. As Roger slowly sank to the ground, Helen quickly activated her portable comm unit and called for a medic.

A few minutes later, a med team arrived and transported Private Hale to the infirmary. Helen reported the incident to Colonel Maxon and requested a replacement for Roger Hale.

CHAPTER 11

ONE-ON-ONE COMPETITION (EARTH FORCES)

With the battalion seated in bleachers, Colonel Harper stood behind the podium and said, "Ladies and gentlemen, twelve lieutenants will represent their platoons and companies in this year's one-on-one competition." Looking at his lieutenants sitting on the first row, he gave a big grin and continued, "I have never seen a group of officers more eager to show their skills piloting a cheetah. I wish each of you good luck as we pair individuals for these contests over the next two days. Your best scores in the simulators have determined the brackets. As they said in ancient times, 'let the games begin!'"

The battalion operations officer walked to the podium and announced, "The one-on-one competition among platoon leaders will consist of two cheetahs engaging one another in mock combat. The arena for this year's competition is a ten square kilometer area surrounded by electronic fencing designed to disable a vehicle if it ventures outside the arena's boundary. The terrain inside the arena is a mixture of dense vegetation, ravines, and open fields. We have installed a large vid screen and placed numerous cameras throughout the arena so everybody sitting in the bleachers can watch each contest as it occurs.

He continued, "For those of you who are new to our competition, you should know each cheetah is fitted with sensors which register hits. These sensors have different values assigned; depending on where the sensor is located on the cheetah. For example, a hit on the track will disable the engine but the cheetah can still shoot. A hit between the turret and the hull will count as a kill and the entire vehicle will be disabled.

"The cheetah's main gun is fitted with a low-powered laser set to the maximum range of a live round. The number of laser shots available is limited to the number of rounds carried when the cheetah is 'combat loaded.' If two vehicles fire at one another at practically the same time, only the first round to register a hit is scored."

Although sensors had been around for hundreds of years, the reliability and accuracy of new sensor technology was amazing.

The operations officer continued, "In our first contest today, Lieutenant Tracey Lynn from Charlie Company has drawn a newcomer, Lieutenant Bill Anders from Baker Company. I've been informed that this is Bill's first time competing in a cheetah. Tracey, don't mess him up too bad. [Laughter] Ladies and gentlemen, the arena is hot. Officers; when you hear the signal, go to your vehicles and good hunting!"

A loud whistle signaled the start of the event. Bill and Tracey ran to their cheetahs which were parked about 200 yards apart. Bill jumped in the driver's compartment, started the engine, and raced away. Laser sensors were activated after the vehicle traveled a minimum of one hundred meters. He thought to himself, *'Okay Tracey, as I recall from your simulation room records, you favor a frontal assault in a one-on-one situation. Let's see what I can do to make you uncomfortable and keep you unbalanced.'*

Bill ran his cheetah at full throttle until he arrived at his pre-selected route. He headed into a large ravine, raced along a twisting and narrow bottom, and found an ideal spot for an ambush. He backed his cheetah into a tight space and killed the engine. He got out and quickly draped some foliage over his vehicle to break up its outline against the ravine wall. After scrambling back into the driver's compartment, he began a waiting game. He didn't have long to wait.

He heard Tracey's cheetah a few seconds before it appeared. Apparently, Tracey was following his cheetah in hopes of finding him and attacking from behind. Bill patiently waited until he had the perfect shot.

As her vehicle rolled by his position, Bill slowly squeezed the main gun's trigger and, *wham!* Tracey's cheetah stopped dead in its tracks. Smoke poured out of the turret and her laser device began signaling a kill shot.

Bill started his cheetah and slowly drove past Tracey's disabled vehicle. Tracey was holding her helmet at her side and standing in the driver's seat looking at Bill in disbelief. Bill grinned and gave her a mock salute; knowing this scene was being displayed on the large vid screen at the bleachers. Score one kill for Baker Company and Lieutenant Bill Anders.

* * *

After dinner, Colonel Harper said, "Ladies and gentlemen, please raise your glasses and join me in congratulating the winners of today's competition. And those winners are: Lieutenants Lance Stallings of A Company, Heather Chong of A Company, Gail Webber of A Company, James Homer of B Company, Bill Anders of B Company, and Ralph Gordon of C Company."

"In our next round of competition, Lieutenants Stallings and Gordon will receive a bye because they were the top two seeds. I recommend everyone get some rest; especially our contestants. Tomorrow will be a busy day. We'll have round two in the morning, round three in the afternoon, and the final contest tomorrow evening."

Bill returned to his quarters shortly after the speech and watched a vid showing Gail Webber's strategy in several scenarios. He thought, *'Gail; I know how you fight. Fortunately for me, you never change tactics. Beating you tomorrow should be easy.'*

* * *

Gail's favorite strategy was a standoff attack firing her main gun at maximum range. She missed some shots using this tactic but only needed to score one hit in order to win the contest.

After the whistle blew, Bill raced to his cheetah, started the vehicle, and drove directly toward Gail. Bill had covered forty meters before Gail realized Bill's cheetah was bearing down on her. She frantically tried to back away but this was a big mistake. Before Gail's cheetah had rolled to its minimum arming distance, Bill fired and hit her vehicle at point blank range. Gail's cheetah immediately stopped moving and smoke began billowing out of the turret. Game over; it was the quickest one-on-one victory ever recorded. Bill slowly circled Gail's stalled cheetah in a victory lap before driving to the assembly area.

Bill's platoon members were loudly cheering for their champion as Bill walked to the bleachers. Melissa congratulated him on an exceptional victory. After the cheering subsided, spectators turned their attention to Lieutenant Lance Stallings doing battle with Lieutenant Heather Chong. The contest did not take very long. Lance Stallings might not be a physical brawler, but he was an artist with his cheetah; a fact that Bill noted for future reference.

* * *

Following lunch, Bill and Lieutenant Ralph Gordon fought in the semi-finals. Sergeant Miller informed Bill, "Sir, the betting line has Lieutenant Gordon a two to one favorite due to his higher ranking. But I believe you can take him. He's a cautious warrior who seldom makes mistakes. His favorite strategy is springing an ambush on his opponent. He favors the same strategy you used on Lieutenant Webber during your first fight."

Bill said, "Thanks for the intel report. I have a plan for Lieutenant Gordon."

After the whistle blew, Bill ran to his vehicle and raced away. He hid his cheetah and waited until Ralph began his move. Sure enough, Ralph chose an ambush as his strategy.

Knowledge is power. Bill began tracking Ralph's movement by maintaining a track parallel with Ralph's vehicle. Bill found Ralph's ambush site and stopped his cheetah nearby. Creeping up on Ralph, Bill physically caught Ralph in the process of camouflaging his vehicle. The man-to-man contest was quickly over and Bill was credited with single-handedly capturing a cheetah without firing a shot. This was another victory for the record books. Nobody had ever achieved this feat. The cheering was deafening as Bill returned to the bleachers bringing a humiliated Lieutenant Gordon draped over his main weapon.

* * *

That evening, Bill and Lance were scheduled to battle for the championship. Because Bill's court martial over beating Lieutenant Stallings was known throughout the battalion, this was the match everyone wanted to see. It was no secret that Bill had knocked Lance unconscious in the simulation room. Everybody was wondering, 'who is best in a cheetah?'

Sergeant Miller took Bill aside and said, "Lieutenant, the platoon has bet everything on you to win the final match. Because of Lieutenant Stallings' previous wins, he's a huge favorite to win tonight. Sir, I've seen you handle each opponent by using his or her strength against them. Tonight is no exception. However, Lieutenant Stallings is a complete cheetah warrior. We don't know of any weaknesses on his part."

"Don't worry; I've studied Stallings' moves and I have a plan for him. Did you place a bet with my money?"

"Yes sir. I bet all of it on you to win."

"Okay thanks. As a reminder, keep that information to yourself; officers are not supposed to bet."

Sergeant Miller grinned and said, "You got it, sir!"

Standing in front of the noisy bleachers waiting for the signal to begin, Lance looked over at Bill and said, "Anders, you got lucky three times. Now I'm going to bring you back to reality when we get in our cheetahs. I'm going to toy with you for a while then embarrass you in front of everybody."

Keeping a grin on his face Bill replied, "Sonny, you shouldn't boast about a victory over me. Do you remember the beating I gave you a few weeks ago? Tonight, I'm going to make that look like a love pat."

The whistle blew. Bill ran to his cheetah, started the engine and raced directly toward Lieutenant Stallings. Lance tried to avoid Bill's cheetah but Bill's rapidly advancing vehicle rammed into Lance's cheetah with a bone-grinding crash. Both vehicles were immobilized and smoke blanketed the crash scene.

Lance felt himself being pulled from the driver's compartment and thrown to the ground; landing on his stomach. His arms were jerked behind his back and he felt a flexible cord binding his hands together. Before he could scramble to his feet, his legs were pinned and Bill was binding them with the same type cord. Lance struggled but to no avail; he was hog-tied.

Bill pulled Lance to his feet and literally threw him over his shoulder. He stepped out of the billowing smoke and walked toward the bleachers carrying his struggling prize. Although both vehicles had been disabled, the judges had no choice but to award Bill the victory since he had captured Lance before the contest officially ended.

At the bleachers, Bill carefully lowered Lance to the ground then raised both arms in victory as he walked toward his platoon. Widespread cheering and applause erupted and drowned any words being spoken over the public address system. The great cheetah warrior Lieutenant Lance Stallings had been decisively beaten by the rookie, Lieutenant Bill Anders. By demonstrating his careful treatment of Lance, nobody could accuse Bill of brutality. He won converts that evening and gained respect from many.

A lot of people lost huge amounts of money betting on the finals. Lance had been a four-to-one favorite at the casino. Those betting on Bill winning the match were overjoyed at the outcome. Soldiers would discuss this unique one-on-one contest for months to come. Bill's winnings greatly exceeded the fine placed on him by the court martial.

Because Lieutenant Anders had won two victories using his superior physical strength, the Rules Committee called a hasty meeting and outlawed future one-on-one contests which relied on physical force.

CHAPTER 12

OFFICER'S CALL (EARTH FORCES)

Following highly successful battalion maneuvers, Colonel Harper sent invitations to all officers and senior non-commissioned officers to join him for a formal dinner at the battalion mess hall. This was one of those 'attendance is mandatory' events which all are required to attend.

Bill sent his dress uniform to the cleaners and mentally rehearsed the names of officers assigned to the battalion. As the winner of this year's one-on-one competition, Bill was invited to join Colonel Harper at his table. His biggest decision was whether to invite one of his fellow platoon leaders as his guest or invite Captain Steiner; his company commander. He thought, *'If I invite Captain Steiner to be my guest, it may appear as though I couldn't get a date with one of the lieutenants. If I invite Lieutenant Montgomery or Richards, it may irritate Captain Steiner and make her feel I don't appreciate all she has done for me. Aw hell, this is complicated. Nancy Montgomery is a blonde beauty. She can't handle her cheetah worth squat but she's been friendly with me. I'll ask her. This will show Captain Steiner that women are interested in being with me.'*

"Hello Nancy? This is Bill Anders. Will you accompany me to the formal dinner?"

"Bill, that is very sweet of you to ask. Yes, I'll be happy to be your guest at the dinner. What time and where should we meet?"

"I'll come by your quarters at 6:30 PM."

"That's great. See you then."

Bill thought, *'Well that was easier than I thought. I guess my recent success earned me some points with the women. The old saying is probably true; most girls are attracted to bad boys.'*

The week went by quickly, Bill's platoon adapted to his leadership style and morale was high; no doubt helped by their platoon leader winning the one-on-one competition. For a couple of weeks, members of Bill's platoon had lots of money to spend in Boende.

Captain Steiner called a staff meeting on Wednesday morning to discuss parts availability and servicing the cheetahs after the battalion exercises.

"Lieutenants, what is the maintenance status of your cheetahs?"

LT Montgomery said, "Ma'am, I have fourteen fully operational cheetahs and one requiring a left track replacement. This morning, we sent a hauler to the battalion parts store for the track. I expect to have the fifteenth cheetah back to fully operational status by this afternoon."

LT James Homer stated, "Captain Steiner, I have fifteen fully operational cheetahs."

LT Anne Richards reported, "Ma'am, I have thirteen fully operational cheetahs. One is waiting for a servo motor replacement and the other needs an engine overhaul. I expect to have fourteen operational by this afternoon and the fifteenth will be operational Thursday afternoon.

Bill said, "Captain Steiner, I have fourteen fully operational cheetahs. The fifteenth is requiring extensive repair due to a recent collision. I plan to have it fully operational by the end of this week."

Nancy added, "Yes, Lieutenant Anders, everybody witnessed you abusing your cheetah last week!" [Laughter]

Bill retorted, "That's correct. However, I should have been given Ralph Gordon's cheetah since I captured it intact. Captain Santiago, Commander of C Company, wouldn't even entertain my request!" [Laughter]

Captain Steiner sternly interjected, "Lieutenant Anders, stop razzing those officers; especially Gordon and Stallings. You've humiliated them in front of the entire battalion. It'll take a while for them to get over being captured and manhandled like a sack of potatoes. I recommend you lay low for a few weeks at least."

"Wilco, Ma'am; I don't want to create bad feelings between B Company and the others."

"Okay, if no one has anything else, I'll let you get back to your platoons. I must attend a battalion staff meeting this afternoon. See you at the dinner on Saturday evening."

The platoon leaders stood as Captain Steiner walked out the door.

CHAPTER 13

THE FORMAL DINNER
(EARTH FORCES)

Bill knocked on Nancy's door precisely at 6:30 PM on Saturday. Nancy opened the door and asked, "Bill, won't you come in?"

"Thanks. You look great, Nancy."

"Well aren't you the charmer! I'm sure you know it is tough looking feminine in a dress uniform. Thank you for the compliment. Bill, would you care to take off your jacket and join me for a drink before we leave?"

"Sure. We've got time. Have you attended one of Colonel Harper's dinners before?"

As Nancy poured two drinks, she replied, "Yes. I attended his dinner last year. It was a lot of fun but I had to constantly remind myself to go slow and not drink too much. Apparently, some people in the battalion keep a running tab on who drinks and how much they consume. Being labeled as someone who drinks too much can hurt your career. And that, dear sir, is wise advice from our Captain Steiner."

"Cheers. What other advice do you have?"

Nancy walked over to Bill and looking him in the eye said, "Well, since you asked; don't brag about your recent exploits at the one-on-one competition. Everybody knows you beat the best in our battalion and you are physically stronger than most men. It's not necessary to remind them at dinner. Just put on the charm and we'll get through this ordeal."

"Nancy, with you by my side, I feel confident we'll get through this evening unscathed. And to show my appreciation for your words of wisdom, I want you to wear this small token. Please turn around."

As Nancy stood in front of Bill, he placed a small gold necklace around her slender neck. It was something which could be worn underneath her formal attire and Bill knew women loved jewelry. He had recently purchased the necklace from a goldsmith in downtown Boende. His winnings more than covered the cost of the necklace.

Nancy walked over to her wall mirror to see the necklace. She said, "Bill, I love it!"

Walking over to Bill, she tiptoed and gave him a peck on his cheek. "Thank you, Bill. You are so sweet and thoughtful." Looking at her watch, she added, "We need to leave; don't want to be late to the Colonel's shindig!"

As they left Nancy's quarters, Bill was thinking, '*Nancy, you're so cute! I want your body. This formal dinner means my intentions toward you are only delayed. I saved the honor of B Company and it's time somebody showed some gratitude around here. And I'm ready to start with you.*'

The Colonel's formal dinner was held in the battalion mess hall. Bill noticed how much it had changed from the time he spent here during his court martial. Tonight, decorations festooned the walls, ceilings and tables.

Colonel Harper had established a reception line and was flanked by his senior officers. As Bill shook hands with Colonel Harper, he noticed Captain Steiner standing immediately to the Colonel's right side. Evidently, the Colonel also had a date to his formal dinner. Bill was happy he followed his instinct and asked Nancy to be his date instead of asking Captain Steiner.

Bill found Colonel Harper's table and introduced Nancy to those already seated. They were joined shortly afterward by Colonel Harper and Captain Steiner.

As the Colonel stood behind his seat, he said, "Ladies and gentlemen, please join me in a toast to the gallant men and women of the 415th Armored Battalion!"

Everyone stood up and replied: "Hear, hear" which was heard throughout the dining hall.

As everyone sat and began eating, Captain Santiago looked across the table at Bill and said, "Lieutenant Anders, you owe me an apology for suggesting I give you a cheetah because of the manner in which you humiliated Lieutenant Gordon."

A silence fell over the table as everyone began staring at Bill.

Bill felt Nancy squeezing his hand as he glanced over to Captain Steiner and noted the pained expression on her face. Bill shifted his gaze back to Captain Santiago and replied, "Sir, what humiliation are you referring to?"

Santiago said, "You know damn well what I'm talking about. You captured my officer then humiliated him by bringing him back to the assembly area hogtied and draped over the barrel of your gun."

Bill paused a moment before responding, "Captain Santiago, I don't owe you an apology. It's true I did humiliate Lieutenant Gordon. But through my actions, he probably learned a valuable lesson about how dangerous it is to leave his armored vehicle in the middle of a war zone. In actual combat, he could have been captured or killed for his carelessness. His carelessness was compounded by giving the enemy an operational armored vehicle. Sir, in my opinion, you owe me thanks for giving you an opportunity to teach your lieutenant a valuable lesson in combat survival."

Captain Santiago's face became visibly red as he retorted, "Lieutenant, I'd like to take you outside and teach you some manners. I don't know what they're teaching cadets at West Point these days but if you're an example, I shudder to think about the future Army."

Bill countered, "Sir, I'm here at the invitation of Colonel Harper. I'm escorting a beautiful woman and hope to have an opportunity to dance with her later this evening. I didn't come here to engage in a schoolboy brawl with a superior officer."

Colonel Harper spoke up for the first time. "Gentlemen, that's enough. Captain Santiago, please show some restraint. Lieutenant Anders acquitted himself in the one-on-one contest with honor. I suggest you take his advice and ensure Lieutenant Gordon benefits from his experience."

Captain Steiner came to Bill's rescue by raising her glass and saying, "Ladies and gentlemen, let's change the subject to a more pleasant topic, shall we?"

Bill felt his hand being squeezed again by Nancy. As he looked her way, he was rewarded with a subtle wink and smile. Unless he miscalculated, he would be spending the night with her.

The remainder of the evening was fine. Nancy and Bill danced and spent time talking with other officers.

As they arrived at Nancy's room, she said, "Bill, won't you come inside for a nightcap?"

"Sure. That would be great, Nancy."

"Bill, I'm so proud of the way you handled Captain Santiago tonight. You came across looking like the adult. While I was in the latrine, Captain Steiner informed me Colonel Harper was also impressed with you."

Nancy took some coaxing, but eventually Bill was able to persuade her to allow him to spend the night in her quarters. After some uninspired sex, they began talking.

"Bill, I don't want you to think of me as a 'one night stand.' I want our relationship to be more than dinner and sex."

Bill thought, *you stupid little bitch, what makes you think I want anything more from you?* But he said instead, "Nancy, I believe we have a lot in common and I really enjoyed our first date. If it's okay with you, I'd like to see more of you."

Those were the right words. Nancy answered by snuggling close to him and whispering, "Oh darling, you've made me so happy." After he gave her a tender kiss, they began making out more passionately than before. The sex which followed was much better, too.

Before going to sleep, Bill's last thoughts were, *'Now that I have a steady girl, I won't have to waste my time going to Boende and spending money on a prostitute.'*

CHAPTER 14

FIRST ASSIGNMENT (MILITIA FORCES)

After a month of training, warriors and mechanics were given their unit assignments. Corporal Sanders saw me at dinner on Friday evening and said, "Collins, you're being assigned to the Militia's Fifth Armored Battalion. You and three other mechanics will be leaving first thing tomorrow morning for Camp Shelby."

I asked, "Corporal Sanders, where is Camp Shelby?"

"It's adjacent to the Haven Wildlife Refuge. It's our most remotely located armored battalion." Grinning, he added, "The good news is there are no cities nearby to distract you from your work."

After Corporal Sanders departed, I spotted Brittany sitting alone in the mess hall and walked over to her. "Hi, Brittany, I don't know if you remember me but we met during the ride down here from Tupelo."

She gave me a big grin and said, "Hi, John. Of course I remember you. In fact, everyone remembers 'John Collins' since Sergeant Thigpen made such an issue about your reckless driving. Your name was often used by our instructors throughout warrior training. Please sit down."

I felt my face turning several shades of red but I sat down anyway and said, "Have you been given your assignment?"

Brittany replied, "Yes, I'm being assigned to the Third Armored Battalion which is based at Fort Mantachie; a few kilometers east of Tupelo. This assignment is what I really wanted because I'll get to see my parents every weekend. What about you, John?"

"I'm going to the Fifth Armored Battalion. They're stationed in the middle of nowhere just outside the Haven Wildlife Refuge." I continued, "Brittany, rumor has it that the Third is getting new armored vehicles."

"Yes, I've heard one of the fire units in the Third will be converting from cheetahs to a new armored vehicle named the leopard. I'm hoping to earn the right to drive one of those babies."

"I have yet to see anyone here who is a better driver than you. I've watched you several times during this past month. You have great driving skills; second to none."

"Thank you, John. That is a nice thing for you to say. I'm sorry you didn't get designated as a warrior. I'm sure you're very talented and know more than most people about handling tracked vehicles - in spite of what happened on our first day."

Shortly afterwards, we wished one another luck and went our separate ways.

After returning to the barracks, Jo Anne asked, "John, where are you being assigned? I saw you speaking with Corporal Sanders in the mess hall but I didn't get a chance to talk with you."

Unable to resist, I replied in a somber voice, "Jo Anne, Corporal Sanders informed me that you needed a bit more maintenance training so they're sending me to the Fifth Battalion with you to complete the job."

She laughed and quipped, "I don't think so, big boy. I learned everything you know after our second week of training. For the past two weeks, I continued acting impressed in order to stroke your enormous ego."

I thought, '*damn, that woman has the fastest mouth in the militia! She would make a great lawyer.*'

* * *

At 7:00 AM on Saturday morning, four of us mechanics and three warriors assigned to the Fifth Battalion were ordered to load up on a hauler headed for our new unit. Before getting on the hauler, Sergeant Thigpen called me aside and said, "Private Collins, Corporal Sanders has given me his instructor's evaluation report citing your outstanding work and extensive mechanical knowledge. Based on his comments and my own observations, I've sent my personal recommendation for you to the Sergeant Major in the Fifth. He's a close friend of mine. Stay out of trouble and continue working hard. I predict you'll accomplish a lot."

"Thank you, Sergeant Thigpen. I'll try."

The 450 kilometer hauler ride to Haven's National Wildlife Refuge took six hours. We stopped at a roadside diner and had lunch. At 2:30 PM, we arrived at the main gate. There was a sign which said, "Welcome to Camp Shelby." The guard checked our identity discs before allowing the hauler to proceed to the Fifth Battalion's Motor Pool. After getting off the hauler, we got into a single rank and were introduced to our battalion leaders.

"Good afternoon ladies and gentlemen. My name is Sergeant Major Randle Peters. I want to introduce you to Colonel John Maxon; our battalion commander."

"Ladies and gentlemen, welcome to the Fifth Armored Battalion. We're very proud of our unit and I know your presence will make it even better. Normally, an armored battalion will have commissioned officers serving as platoon leaders and company commanders. Five weeks ago, our officers were reassigned to build new armored units for our militia force. Subsequently, I've reorganized my battalion into fire teams which are led by experienced warrant officers. Fire team leaders report directly to me."

"Should you need to talk with me, please remember that my 'door is always open.' Sergeant Major Peters, please take over and resume the orientation." With that brief introduction, Colonel Maxon left the area.

After Colonel Maxon departed, Sergeant Major Peters said, "Colonel Maxon has a tremendous responsibility leading this battalion. He typically works sixteen to eighteen hours every day. A word to the wise, make sure you talk to me before going to see the Colonel."

He continued, "After reorganizing our battalion, Colonel Maxon allocated five cheetahs to each fire team. We have a total of twelve fire teams in this battalion. Warriors, when I call your name, your assigned leader will raise his or her hand. Join them and they'll complete your orientation."

After the three warriors departed with their fire team leaders, he continued, "Mechanics, you'll be assigned to a specific cheetah warrior as his or her maintenance chief. Senior fire team mechanics have been reassigned to help our junior warriors. Because you mechanics are new, you'll be working with experienced warriors. Listen to your warrior and do what he or she says. From now on, they're your boss."

He continued, "It's important that you remember, 'Cheetahs are the tip of this battalion's spear and our mechanics are responsible for keeping the point sharp.' If you encounter a real problem and cannot get it resolved with your fire team leader, come and see me."

Eventually, I was introduced to Warrant Officer Helen Ramses, the commander of Fire Team Six. She motioned for me to walk over to where she was standing. As I walked over, I noticed Helen was a stunningly beautiful brunette who appeared to be in her mid-twenties. She was about one hundred and sixty centimeters tall and was wearing black highly polished boots and a fitted two-piece uniform which accentuated her athletic figure. I began thinking, *John, you are one lucky devil. Stuck in the middle of nowhere; you've been assigned to work with one of the most beautiful women on Haven.'*

My mental appraisal of Helen's outstanding physique was interrupted when she began talking.

"Private Collins, you may address me as WO Ramses or Ma'am. I'm ranked among the best warriors in this battalion and my goal is to become number one. As my mechanic, your job is to ensure my cheetah is one hundred percent operational and ready to go at any time. I will not tolerate insubordination, incompetence, laziness or lame excuses. Are we clear?"

I immediately sensed that Helen and I would never be friends. I looked directly into her beautiful eyes and said, "Perfectly clear Ma'am. Will you show me our cheetah?"

"Let's go. And in case you are wondering; when you're accompanying me, always walk one step behind and to my left."

I slung my duffel bag over my shoulder and dutifully followed Miss 'High and Mighty' to her cheetah. I couldn't help noticing she looked great from the rear, too. I would enjoy doing some 'maintenance' on her.

After a thorough inspection, it became apparent Helen was driving a well-maintained machine. Everything was spic and span. None of the usual oil leaks, external rust, scratched windscreen or even dust accumulation appeared on her cheetah. Whoever did her maintenance before my arrival spent a lot of time servicing this cheetah. I examined the meticulously-kept log book and noticed the engine was due for its 5,000 hour maintenance service. "Ma'am, the log book indicates the engine is due for some extensive preventative maintenance. It will take a couple of days to perform this service. When should this be scheduled?"

Helen got into my face and with eyes blazing said, "This is *exactly* what I mean about laziness and lame excuses. We're scheduled for live firing tomorrow and I want my vehicle ready. If the engine needs maintenance, then you had *better* get your ass in gear. Your job is to have my cheetah ready to roll by tomorrow at 7:00 AM. My fire team is assigned Shop Number 6; it's the long building behind me. Shop Bay 1 is assigned to you. *Now get to work!*"

After her little speech, she wheeled around and left me standing there.

Without missing a beat, I raised my voice and shouted, *"Just a minute, Lady!"*

Helen froze in mid-stride. She slowly turned around as I walked up to her. In a normal voice I continued, "Ma'am, this is a two day job regardless of your training schedule. However, two people working all night can overhaul the engine if you're willing to get your hands dirty helping me. You have to decide if you want to participate in tomorrow's exercise."

Her nostrils were flaring as she stared intently at me. Finally she said, "Get started on the job. I'll change into coveralls and will be back in twenty minutes."

True to her word, Helen was back in less than twenty minutes and we worked through the night; stopping briefly for dinner and only speaking when necessary. I found myself admiring her willingness to pitch in and help.

Near midnight, Sergeant Major Peters wandered into the shop and watched Helen and me working on the engine. He left a few minutes later without saying a word.

By 5:30 AM the engine was reassembled and ready to go. "Ma'am, if you like, I'll test the engine while you change uniform and eat breakfast." She thought a moment and just nodded and walked toward her barracks.

At 6:30 mechanics and their drivers began arriving at the motor pool. Vehicles were started and the familiar low hum of electric engines filled the air. I was hungry and dead tired but stayed with my vehicle.

Helen arrived with a group of warriors. I could hear them laughing and talking. She looked as though she had slept through the night. Walking over to me, she asked about her cheetah. I reported, "Ma'am, she's running very smoothly. No maintenance issues to report."

She looked at me for a few moments then said, "Private Collins, after we leave the motor pool get something to eat and find a place to sleep. You look like shit."

Ignoring her jab I grinned and replied in a low conspiratorial voice, "Thanks for your help last night. I couldn't have completed the job without you. I think we'll make a great team, don't you?" This was followed by my giving her a wink.

At that moment, a recharging station mounted on a hauler rolled by and before Helen could respond to my cheeky comment, I signaled him to stop so I could fully charge the cheetah's battery.

After the cheetahs left the motor pool, I entered Fire Team Six's barracks and noticed Helen's name on the door of a private room in the barracks. Everybody else slept in a large open bay. I found my assigned bunk and dropped off after a quick shower. I figured I would eat after sleeping.

* * *

Around twelve thirty, I awoke and went to the mess hall for lunch. Only a few people were there. I got a tray and joined a couple of mechanics who were drinking coffee.

One of them looked at me and said, "Hey, aren't you the new mechanic assigned to Warrant Officer Ramses?"

Between mouthfuls I answered, "Yeah, that's me. My name is John Collins."

"I'm Fred Rendon and this is Chuck Diehner. We're also mechanics in Fire Team Six. Chuck and I were wondering who would be assigned to work for Queen Bitch. Man, you have everybody's sympathy."

"Uh, thanks - I guess. Warrant Officer Ramses is pretty exacting in her demands. But I don't mind as long as she's not too rough on my vehicle. By the way, who was her previous mechanic?"

Chuck replied, "His name is Roger Hale. Roger was here about a year and he was a good mechanic. A few days ago, Roger and 'the

Bitch' got into a shouting match. After a couple of minutes of them yelling at one another, poor old Roger began grabbing his chest and had to be taken to the infirmary. We heard he's being transferred to a cushy job at the New Albany armor assembly plant. Lucky for her you showed up. No mechanic here would have willingly taken Roger's place; even if she is our fire team leader and one of the most beautiful women we've ever seen. In this battalion, the word on her is out; stay away from Ramses at all costs."

A picture of a beautiful but deadly creature came into my mind as Chuck finished his last sentence. I was determined to avoid Roger's fate and quietly decided the best defense against Helen would be a strong offence.

After lunch, I ambled over to the motor pool and straightened up my area, inventoried my tools, and swept the floor. I had just finished cleaning up when cheetahs began pouring through the gate.

Helen pulled into my shop bay, switched off the engine and got out of her cheetah. She walked up to me and said, "Collins, I think something's stuck underneath and the engine is running hot. I need it ready by 6:30 AM." With that said, she left the shop bay.

It took me almost two hours to extract part of a metal fence post and some barbed wire wrapped around the vehicle's torsion bars and bogies. The engine seemed okay but I cleaned the air intake duct and changed the filter. Afterward, I took the cheetah to the wash rack and thoroughly washed the entire vehicle. It was after 7:00 PM before I had fully serviced the cheetah to include adding lubricants and recharging the battery. I parked it in line with other Fire Team Six cheetahs. After a quick shower, I immediately fell asleep.

It seemed that I had just fallen asleep when I felt someone shaking my bunk. I awoke to find Helen standing at the foot of my bunk shining a portable light in my face. She said, "Private Collins, get up and meet me in the motor pool."

I got up and looked at my watch. Crap! It was 5:30 AM and raining hard. After hurriedly dressing and pulling on my poncho, I ran to the motor pool. Helen was standing beside her cheetah and not looking very happy.

"What's the matter, Ma'am?"

"There's water standing on the floorboard of the driver's compartment."

I got up on the cheetah's deck and looked down. Sure enough, about a centimeter of water covered the floorboard. I dropped down into the compartment and pressed the spring-loaded floor drain valve with my foot and the water dumped onto the ferrocrete. I got out of the driver's compartment and sarcastically asked, "Is that all you need, Ma'am?"

She got into my face and shouted, *"Private Collins, your work on my cheetah is sub-standard. Do you expect me to drive this vehicle with a wet floorboard? Get some towels and dry the floor. And do something about your breath; it stinks."*

After thoroughly drying the cheetah's floorboard, I began grinning as I depressed the drain valve cover and locked it in the full open position before heading back to my barracks.

The cheetahs departed at 7:00 AM for an all-day training exercise. It rained really heavy at times throughout the morning and I knew the vehicles would be covered in mud when they returned from the field.

* * *

Late that afternoon, I was in the shop bay inventorying parts when Helen returned driving her mud-streaked cheetah. Her vehicle raced into the shop bay and stopped so quickly the tracks locked and the cheetah skidded about a meter. As she exited the driver's compartment, I noticed her boots and trouser legs were caked with dried red mud.

Her face was a bright red as she stomped up to me and yelled, *"Collins, if I could prove you deliberately left that drain valve locked in the full open position, I'd have you court martialed for insubordination!"*

It was all I could do to keep from laughing but I bit my tongue and let her finish her rant.

Finally she said, "Private Collins, do you have anything to say for yourself?"

I replied, "Ma'am, the operator manual clearly states drivers should always check the compartment's drain valve before operating the vehicle."

She exploded and started screaming. *"How dare you stand there and quote an operator's manual to me! Maybe I should make you clean my muddy boots for your impudence?"*

I glanced over Helen's shoulder and noticed other mechanics had gathered around the shop bay entrance and were listening to her chew my ass.

Struggling to keep from laughing, I grinningly replied, "Ma'am, when I take our vehicle to the wash rack, I'll be happy to hose your boots, too. Will you leave them with me or should I come to the barracks for them?"

Helen stared at me for a few moments. Her eyes were blazing and she was physically shaking with emotion. Finally she said, "No, Private Collins. On second thought, I don't want you cleaning my boots. You've demonstrated you have difficulty maintaining my cheetah properly. Adding to your workload would overtax your limited ability." Having hurled the final barb, she quickly walked out of the shop bay.

After Helen was out of earshot, the mechanics gathered around me howling with laughter, slapping my back and giving me a 'thumbs up' signal. I didn't say anything but I was still grinning from ear to ear as I drove Helen's cheetah to the wash rack. It took extra time to clean the muddy driver's compartment but it was worth every minute.

At dinner that evening the mechanics assigned to Fire Team Six joined me at my table. I had met Fred and Chuck previously but everybody wanted to introduce themselves to me. I guess the conflict between Helen and me had made me the 'hero of the hour.'

Fred started, "John, as you recall, I'm Fred Rendon from Crystal Springs; a small town about 500 kilometers from Tupelo. I've been in the militia for 13 months and my warrior is Ralph Taylor; a newbie."

"John, I also met you yesterday. I'm Chuck Diehner from Rosedale. I've been in the militia for nine months and my warrior is Sergeant Frank Delucca. Sergeant Delucca has been in the militia for over six years."

"John, we haven't been formally introduced. I'm Misty Ransom and my warrior is Crystal Rogers. We're both from Calhoun City. I've been in the militia for six months but Crystal has been a warrior for almost two years."

"Hello John. I'm Wendy Norton from New Albany. I've been in the militia for 8 months and my warrior is Sean Ellis. Sean has been in the militia for 12 months. Now tell us about yourself."

I replied, "Folks, I was drafted and I've been in the militia about five weeks. Prior to that, I was a tracked excavator operator in Tupelo for several years and maintained my own equipment."

Chuck said, "John, with your tracked vehicle experience, why didn't they make you a warrior?"

"Well, that's a long story."

Wendy interrupted me and said, "Wait a minute; are you *The John Collins* I've been hearing about?" She started laughing then looked at me and said, "Oh I'm sorry, John. I overheard one of the new warriors telling a group of people about a recruit at Johnson Springs Reservation who jumped in a cheetah and threw a track showing off before a large group of fellow recruits. I didn't realize until just now that *you* are the infamous John Collins!" I turned several shades of red as Fred, Chuck and Misty joined Wendy in laughing. I noticed people sitting at other tables were staring at us.

When their laughter subsided, I said, "Okay. Okay, I was hoping I would be remembered for doing something important in this war but it appears my reputation has been made by doing something stupid. After you grease monkeys finish laughing, I'd like to talk about anything else."

* * *

Over the next six weeks, Helen put in long hours training her fire team. I serviced her cheetah each evening. She never spoke to me unless it pertained to maintaining her vehicle. She never complimented my work, either. Fortunately, becoming friends with my fellow mechanics made up for Helen's lack of civility.

Because of her snotty attitude toward me, I made it my mission to play practical jokes on her whenever possible.

The other mechanics gleefully observed the ongoing conflict between Helen and me. One day Wendy privately informed me, "John, bets are being made about how long you'll survive as her chief mechanic. With that latest practical joke you played on her, the betting odds are even."

Wendy paused then continued, "Installing a hair dryer in the driver's compartment of her cheetah! Misty, Chrystal and I laughed until our sides hurt. Where do you come up with these ideas? But John, why don't you consider slowing down a bit? If this comes to physical contact between you two, the Colonel will transfer you to another unit."

"Wendy, I didn't start this. WO Ramses earned her reputation as a bitch before my arrival. And I'll be damned if I'm going to let that little snob treat me like her personal slave and get away with it. If we were in civilian life, I'd take her behind a building and slap some sense into her."

"Well, just so you know, our warriors have instructed us not to get involved in this contest between you and WO Ramses. I think everybody in the fire team likes you; I know all the mechanics do. We don't want to lose you to another fire team." She grinned and continued, "This is the best entertainment we've had in months."

"Thank you, Wendy. That means a lot to me." I added, "You know, living here way out in the boonies; we have to find our own source of amusement. And I confess I thoroughly enjoy pissing off that little stuck-up bitch."

As Wendy left, I began thinking, '*The entire fire team is aware of the friction between us? I hope this doesn't get back to Sergeant Major Peters. He's my best chance of getting a better assignment in this battalion.*'

* * *

While off-duty, I spent time in the gym. Working out with weights and running kept me in top physical shape. I noticed that Helen was a regular in the gym, too. That helped explain why she had such a perfect body. We never spoke while in the gym because of our mutual dislike of one another. However, I enjoyed sneaking peeks while she worked out. To me, there's nothing more attractive than a woman exercising. I rationalized my looking at her by comparing that to visiting a zoo and watching the exotic animals.

* * *

My final practical joke played on Helen was probably my favorite. Since meeting Helen, I had observed her taking a great deal of pride in her appearance. Her hair, uniform, and boots were always perfect. She could have been featured on a recruiting poster. No question about it, in spite of her aloofness, Helen was one of the most beautiful women I had ever seen.

During the latter part of November, early mornings at the National Wildlife Refuge were cold but it got warm during the day. It was customary for cheetah warriors to run their heaters for a few minutes then turn them off after the driver's compartment became comfortable.

One afternoon in late November Helen pulled into the shop bay after a long day of training. As she slowly climbed out of her cheetah and removed her helmet, I noticed her hair was plastered to her head and her uniform was soaking wet. She looked like she had been swimming with her clothes on. I couldn't help chuckling at her disheveled appearance.

She walked up to me and said in a hoarse voice, "Private Collins, the damned heater has been running all day and I couldn't turn it off. It has been like an oven in the driver's compartment. And because you think this is so funny, I'm having another mechanic look at the heating unit and its controls. If evidence of tampering is found, I'm bringing you up on charges. Sabotaging a military vehicle is a court martial offense and I can't wait to see if you think a court martial is funny."

Dropping my grin, I angrily replied, *"Ma'am, you've been treating me like dirt since my arrival. You go right ahead with your investigation and when you're informed that there is no evidence of sabotage, I hope you're 'man enough' to apologize for being stuck-up, overbearing, ill-considerate and just plain rude. You may consider yourself 'god's gift' to the militia but you'd go nowhere without mechanics like me."*

Helen glared at me for a long moment before leaving the shop bay.

As expected, the inspection done by another mechanic did not reveal sabotage; just a stuck thermostat. Although she couldn't prove it, Helen probably believed I was responsible. I didn't get an apology from her nor was I surprised.

After that incident, I didn't get a chance to play another prank on Helen. What happened next put all thoughts of practical jokes aside.

CHAPTER 15

ALERTING THE 415TH BATTALION (EARTH FORCES)

All officers in the 415th Battalion assembled in the battalion dining hall. Everyone was wondering what was happening. It became clear after Colonel Harper made his announcement.

"Ladies and gentlemen, the 415th Armored Battalion has been notified to commence preparations for war. This is no drill. Earth is invading Haven and our battalion has been chosen to be part of the initial invasion force. Our scheduled departure is two days from today. This mission is classified TOP SECRET and all leaves and passes are cancelled. Soldiers on leave are being recalled and nobody is permitted to leave the fort. My Executive Officer will coordinate with each company commander about the details. That is all."

Bill thought, *'Everybody is confined to the fort? No problem; I have my own little whore living a few doors from my quarters. With the excitement of going to war, Nancy will be even more enthusiastic in the sack. In the meantime, I'd better contact Sergeant Miller and give him the news. He and I will be very busy during the next two days.'*

* * *

During a B Company staff meeting that afternoon, Lieutenant Homer asked, "Captain Steiner, do you know why the 415ᵗʰ Armored Battalion was chosen to join the first invasion wave?"

She replied, "James, Colonel Harper didn't say but I contacted a friend of mine assigned to Army Headquarters. She said we were chosen because we had recently completed our annual battalion training and were already pre-positioned at a launch point. My friend also said Fort Boende would be abandoned after our launch. She hinted that the Army doesn't have enough manpower to keep peace throughout the world while sending a large invasion force to Haven. Fortunately, that's not our problem. Our immediate goal is to get all of our equipment to one hundred percent operational readiness and gather as much ammunition, supplies and rations as we can carry."

Bill asked, "Captain, why do we have to worry about rations? Why not just take what we need from the people of Haven?"

"Bill, we want to maintain good relations with the locals. It's important to remember that we have no argument with the residents of Haven. The purpose of our invasion is to force the government on Haven to send more food to Earth. Implicit in this is the mandate we avoid property destruction."

"How do we accomplish this, Ma'am?"

"We're planning a surgical strike which will incapacitate Haven's militia and force their government to cooperate."

Lieutenant Montgomery asked, "Ma'am, what do you mean by a surgical strike?"

"Nancy, the first wave of this invasion will be commanded by General Paul Dietrich; an armor officer who has a reputation as a tactician and is highly regarded for his political astuteness. He has issued his first directive stating, 'We will minimize collateral damage and avoid harming citizens. Earth soldiers guilty of violating this and other directives will be subject to court martial.'"

Looking directly at Bill she continued, "I want every platoon leader to download all directives and ensure each of your platoon members follow these instructions to the letter."

Bill maintained a blank look on his face as he thought, *'Steiner, you can't just leave things alone, can you? You'll never trust me and will always suspect the worst. Lady, you've already sealed your own fate. All I have to do now is to figure out when and how you'll have a fatal accident. If I do this right, maybe I'll be given command of your company.'*

*   *   *

The mighty ship began to shake and noise from its motors made Bill grateful for the earplugs he was wearing. He thought, *'I'm not sure this is what Colonel Harper intended when he encouraged me to witness rocket launches from Boende. Cooped up in this windowless cabin, you can't tell what's happening outside the hull of this ship. It's a good thing I don't have claustrophobia.'*

Looking across the seventy centimeter space between bunks, he caught Nancy's eyes and smiled. Nancy's tightened face visibly relaxed when she saw Bill's smile. He thought, *'you stupid cow. You take comfort in my smile but ignore the many thousands of hours of research and development that was put into the design of this ship. Creating an airtight ship designed to overcome gravity and other forces of nature is the fact which should give you comfort; not my smiling face.'*

The trip to Haven became quiet and smooth after the ship achieved hypervelocity. People were free to move around within the confines of the ship and its cargo.

Spending thirty days in cramped quarters was long and boring. Bill spent most of the time engaging in battle simulations, reading and working out using specially designed fitness equipment. Captain Steiner regularly met with her platoon leaders and discussed battle tactics. She revealed the master invasion plan during one of these sessions.

"Ladies and gentlemen, Colonel Harper has been briefed by General Paul Dietrich, the invasion commander." She pointed to a map of Haven and continued. "We're landing at Tupelo, the capital city of Haven. General Dietrich will remain in Tupelo. His headquarters will be defended by a battalion of infantry augmented by a couple of special military units from other nations. The bulk of his invasion force has been divided into four separate commands. Each command is being led by a task force commander. Colonel Harper has been appointed to command the task force at Columbus. His task force will consist of the 415th and 420th armored battalions and the 320th infantry battalion. We'll be bivouacked in Columbus; a fairly large city located about 250 kilometers to the east of Tupelo. Our area of operations will fan out in an easterly direction from Columbus."

"What will be our assignment, Ma'am?"

"Our job will be to neutralize militia forces and perform other tasks as ordered by General Dietrich."

"How big is Haven's militia?"

"We don't have a precise count but we believe their militia consists of three armored and five infantry battalions supported by an outdated aviation unit."

"What's the size of our invasion force?"

"Our first wave consists of two aviation units supporting eight armored and four infantry battalions. Four of our armored battalions each have a squad of leopards augmenting their cheetahs."

Lieutenant Homer said, "Ma'am, I've heard about the leopards. How did the Army decide which battalion would get leopards and which battalions would have to wait?"

"That's a good question, James. The Army issues its newest equipment to its highest priority units. Unfortunately, the 415th is not among the Army's highest priority units."

Bill interjected, "Ma'am, the Army could regret that priority allocation since the 415th is in the first invasion wave."

"Bill, that's true, but maybe the Army heard about you being able to defeat a cheetah with your bare hands and decided the 415th didn't need leopards."

Laugher erupted following her comment.

Lieutenant Richards stated, "Ma'am, it sounds like our invasion force will greatly outnumber the militia units. This war could be over in a matter of hours or days at most."

Captain Steiner replied, "That's correct, Anne. Unfortunately, military offenses almost never go as planned. The enemy may choose to hide and use guerilla tactics rather than meet our invasion force head on. It could take months to locate and defeat the militia units. This is why General Dietrich is dividing his force into four commands and giving each task force responsibility for a specific part of Haven."

During the long journey to Haven, Bill even spent some time with Lieutenant Lance Stallings; picking his brain about advanced cheetah strategies. Since they were headed to war, Lance was amenable to helping Bill. Naturally, Bill had ulterior motives in seeking Lance's help. Bill was presenting himself as someone who didn't carry grudges.

Although Bill didn't have a high opinion of Nancy's military skills, outwardly he treated her with the utmost respect. Bill viewed this as another opportunity to show everyone he was a caring and sensitive person.

One evening Nancy whispered in Bill's ear, "Bill, I've been over this entire ship and there's not even a broom closet we can use for privacy!"

Bill grinned and softly replied, "That's okay Babe. I appreciate you searching for a love nest. I can wait until we get to Haven. Once we've landed and found some housing, I'm looking forward to getting you alone and wearing you out."

A blushing Nancy replied, "Oh Bill, sometimes you are so crude. You embarrass me talking like that; even when no one else can hear."

CHAPTER 16

INVADING HAVEN
(EARTH FORCES)

Eight ships carrying the first wave of Earth's invasion force landed at the Tupelo Launch Facility on the third of December at 2:00 AM. There was no opposing force present at the launch facility. A committee of Tupelo residents headed by the mayor presented General Dietrich an official document signed by the Governor General requesting neutral status for Tupelo and other major cities on Haven.

General Dietrich didn't have to issue any orders. Every Earth soldier knew his or her mission. Equipment was quickly unloaded and defensive perimeters established. After each battalion was fully assembled on the tarmac, it began rapidly moving toward its objectives. The invasion was proceeding according to plan.

The 415th and 420th armored battalions and the 320th infantry battalion were assigned to occupy Columbus, a large city to the east of Tupelo. From this location, Task Force Columbus would carry the fight to the countryside of Haven.

Colonel Harper was given orders to attack the Third Militia Battalion garrisoned at Fort Mantachie a few kilometers outside Tupelo. This military post was on the road to Columbus and needed to be neutralized. An air strike was launched before Colonel Harper's task force reached the post. When the 415th armored battalion arrived, they quickly overran the facility and captured the few surviving militia.

Colonel Harper called his company commanders together and said, "Captain Steiner, leave one of your platoons to guard the prisoners and equipment until they can arrange a transfer. Afterwards, they will rejoin the battalion. Everyone else, let's go to Columbus!"

Captain Steiner contacted Lieutenant Anders and said, "Bill, I want you and your platoon to stay and guard the prisoners and their equipment; especially the cheetahs. Call headquarters and arrange a pickup of prisoners and equipment. Join us in Columbus when the transfers are complete."

"WILCO, Ma'am"

After the task force departed, Bill contacted General Dietrich's Headquarters and requested haulers to transport the captured equipment. He also requested a military police unit to collect prisoners. Bill was informed it might take several hours to make the arrangements.

Bill said, "Sergeant Miller, it appears we have several hours to wait before headquarters sends help. While we're waiting, make the prisoners dig a large pit down beside the wash rack. The dirt is loose there and it should be easy to dig a hole 2 meters wide by 2 meters deep by six meters long. I want the prisoners to bury their dead comrades. Also, collect all militia dog tags and give them to me."

The equipment haulers finally arrived. Bill assembled the drivers and said, "We've captured 30 salvageable cheetahs and 22 haulers. I want you to take these vehicles to our headquarters in Tupelo.

As the grave was being dug, the militia's cheetahs and haulers were taken away. No military police showed up to take the prisoners.

At 5:00 PM, it became apparent that someone at headquarters forgot to send a military police unit to collect the prisoners.

An idea came to Bill. "Sergeant Miller, have the prisoners kneel on the ground in front of the grave."

Bill took his pistol and walked behind each prisoner. A single shot to the back of the prisoner's head was all it took and a dead soldier collapsed on top of his fallen comrades. Bill then ordered his platoon members to cover the grave while he took the dog tags and hung them over a hydrant at the wash rack.

After Bill's platoon completed their work, he gathered everybody and said, "Those thirteen militia prisoners were scum. By wiping out their entire battalion, our action today will put fear in the hearts of others. The remaining militia forces may even lose the will to fight. None of you were involved in executing these prisoners. I did the job so your conscience is clear. What I ask in return is that you keep your mouths shut when we rejoin our battalion. If asked, just say 'the equipment and prisoners were transferred.' Does everybody understand?"

"*Yes sir!*"

"Okay, let's get moving. I want to reach Columbus before 9:00 PM tonight. Sergeant Miller, contact Sergeant Major Tinsdale and find out where we're staying. Also, I'm in the mood for restaurant food. We've been living on rations for over a month and we need a change. See if he can recommend a good restaurant for us. Your meal tonight will be my treat."

CHAPTER 17

GOING ON ALERT (MILITIA FORCES)

On December 3rd, at 3:28 AM, members of Fifth Battalion awakened to sirens blasting. Everybody hurriedly dressed and raced to the motor pool. I was standing beside Helen's cheetah rubbing sleep out of my eyes when Helen arrived. After a couple of minutes, the sirens stopped and Colonel Maxon got on a voice amplifier and spoke to a hushed audience assembled in the motor pool.

"Ladies and gentlemen, Earth has invaded Haven. All militia units have been placed on alert and we must be ready to take military action. We don't know the size of the invasion force but I've been told a lot of equipment and enemy soldiers are arriving at the Tupelo Launch Facility. I have to assume the enemy will achieve air superiority so we must load everything we can carry and disperse. This compound is no longer safe because its location is probably known to the invading forces."

"Warriors, take your cheetahs to the armory and pick up a full combat load of ammunition. Get small arms and ammunition for yourself and your mechanic. After you load up, move outside the compound and disperse your vehicles."

"Mechanics, load your haulers with supplies, spare parts, tools, battery charging generator, ammunition reloads, food and your personal items. Take everything not nailed down and join up with your fire team. We're leaving Camp Shelby and will not return for the immediate future."

"Fire team leaders, take your team and set up in your assigned area. I'll visit each fire team during the next four to five days. Stay off the main roads and commo silence is in effect. Let's move out in one hour or less. Battalion, *dismissed!*"

There was a mad scramble as we raced to get our equipment and supplies. I drove my hauler into the shop bay and began loading tools, parts and a recharging generator. I fully charged the hauler's battery; drove to the mess hall and loaded several cases of food rations, then drove to the armory for ammunition reloads. As you might imagine, there was a lot of confusion and jostling as haulers competed for space in food and ammo lines. Before leaving the compound, I stopped at the barracks and hurriedly stuffed my clothing and personal items into my duffel and grabbed my sleeping bag. I hesitated a moment before breaking into Helen's room and gathering her clothes and toiletries and cramming them into her duffle bag. Although I didn't think she deserved this service, I made sure I packed all of her belongings. I tossed her stuff into the hauler's cargo bed and drove outside the gate looking for her. When I finally spotted her, Helen was pacing in front of her cheetah impatiently waiting for the fire team mechanics. After the last hauler arrived; she lost no time in getting us on the move.

Helen commanded five cheetahs and five haulers. We quickly moved through the forest along dirt roads and fire breaks. After driving about thirty kilometers, we arrived at our assigned location just as daylight was breaking. We stopped in an opening and dispersed our vehicles underneath overhanging foliage.

Helen got out of her cheetah and walked over to my hauler. She said, "Private Collins, what do you have in your hauler?"

I leaned out the window and said, "Ma'am, I have my tools, spare parts for vehicles, charging generator, and fifteen cases of food rations. I also have ammo reloads for your cheetah and our personal items."

She said, "What do you mean, 'our' personal items?"

"I broke into your room and picked up your sleeping bag, clothes and toiletries on the way out of the compound."

"You took a big risk in stopping for my things. You could have been attacked and lost all of our support items."

I dryly replied, "It was a calculated risk, Ma'am."

She turned and walked away; but not before I caught sight of her smile. "*Well, that's a first,*" I thought.

After a brief staff meeting with the cheetah warriors, Helen called everyone together. She said, "Ladies and gentlemen, I don't know how long we're going to be separated from our battalion. We may be here for an extended period. With that in mind, I'm making the following assignments.

"Sergeant Frank Delucca, my senior warrior, will be second in command and responsible for perimeter security. Sergeant Delucca, you and the other warriors will serve as our primary security team. However, if we're attacked, warriors and mechanics will man the perimeter and fight."

She then looked at me and said, "Private John Collins will serve as our lead mechanic." She paused then continued, "I know Private Collins is our newest mechanic. However, in the short time he has been assigned to our fire team, he has demonstrated outstanding technical knowledge and shown lots of initiative." At the mention of the word, initiative, everybody started laughing. After the laughter subsided, a red-faced Helen continued, "Private Collins, as lead mechanic, you'll organize and supervise maintenance operations and will be responsible for all vehicles and supplies."

I was dumbfounded at hearing her praise my mechanical skills. I finally managed to say, "Yes, Ma'am."

Helen continued, "Sergeant Delucca, after breakfast, break out the rifles and ammo and issue a weapon to each person. Also, please make up a guard roster to cover dusk to dawn hours. Okay, if there are no questions, let's eat some of the food our mechanics scrounged for us."

Following a quick breakfast, I called the mechanics together. "WO Ramses said that she didn't know how long we would be here. Whatever time we have, let's get organized. Unless anyone has a better idea, I suggest we work on our haulers and cheetahs for the remainder of today. Make sure they're one hundred percent and ready to roll. If you run short of parts or need help, sound off. We're in this together and we have to rely on each other."

I added, "Before turning in tonight, please give me a list of parts and quantity of rations and ammo you have on hand and I'll consolidate the list. By doing this, we'll know if there's a potential problem."

Later that morning, we heard explosions going off in the distance. They weren't cheetah rounds; but whatever they were, they sounded really loud. Everyone stopped working and gathered around the center of our unit.

Fred asked, "What the heck is that?"

Sergeant Delucca replied, "It sounds like somebody is bombing Camp Shelby. It's not likely any ground soldiers are involved because we're over seven hundred kilometers from Tupelo and they haven't had time to get here. That's why I suspect it's probably bombs being dropped on Camp Shelby. You can bet I'm glad we left before those aircraft arrived!"

That was a sobering thought; we got out of Camp Shelby just in time to escape becoming a casualty from an air strike.

One by one the four mechanics handed me their list before turning in that evening. I thanked each one for his or her efforts and climbed into my hauler cab to consolidate the list. I suspected Helen would ask for the list.

Thirty minutes later, Helen surprised me when she opened the passenger side door and climbed inside the cab. She said, "What are you doing, Private Collins?"

I said, "Getting this list for you, Ma'am." I handed her my noteputer.

She scanned the list and said, "Good job, Collins. I'm glad I followed my instinct and put you in charge of the mechanics."

"Ma'am, I know the real reason you appointed me as the fire team's maintenance chief."

She stared intently at me and quietly asked, "And what do you think is my real reason for giving you this assignment?"

"You want to punish me by giving me extra work."

"Private Collins, you've misjudged me completely. Aside from our numerous disagreements, I've found you to be an exceptionally competent mechanic and based on my observation, you have natural leadership abilities."

Ignoring her compliment, I changed the subject and asked, "Do we have water?"

"Yes, a few minutes ago Sergeant Delucca got us some potable water. It is in a lyster bag located near the dining area."

"Ma'am, it looks like you've thought of everything. If it's okay with you, I'd like to turn in. We may have a busy day tomorrow."

"No, I have nothing else. Where are you sleeping tonight?"

"I'll be sleeping in the cargo bed of the hauler."

"Got room for me? I think it may rain later."

"I'll make room for both of us, Ma'am."

I climbed into the cargo bed, turned on a battery-powered lantern and shifted boxes and cans to one side; leaving enough space for two sleeping bags placed side-by-side.

A few minutes later, Helen climbed into the cargo bed. She looked at the space I had made and nonchalantly unrolled her sleeping bag beside mine without comment.

After turning off the lantern, she crawled into her sleeping bag and said, "Goodnight, Private Collins. You did excellent work today."

"Goodnight, Ma'am. You did well, too." I lay awake for a few moments thinking, *Today marks the first time she's ever given me a compliment. I wonder how long will there be a truce between Helen and me. Maybe Helen is beginning to realize she can't win this war alone. Maybe the spoiled princess is trying to change.'* I fell asleep hoping that Helen's attitude was changing.

CHAPTER 18

OPERATION SABOTAGE (EARTH)

Jim Anderson was watching his favorite program on the vid when an announcer interrupted with breaking news. "Ladies and gentlemen, we've just been informed American and some international forces have invaded the planet Haven. We also know Haven has declared war on America. In thirty minutes, President Williams will address this important issue."

"Oh crap! Why did President Williams have to do something so stupid? I warned Ambassador Allen this was going to happen. I hope Haven is prepared for invasion and that my wife and child are okay."

Jim turned off the vid and started contacting his team. Jim was the controller of a network of seven highly-placed spies who would be given the additional task of sabotaging Earth's economy.

Jim's spy network consisted of men and women who had been thoroughly vetted by Earth's security system and who worked in sensitive areas including the military, communications network, banks and shipping. These individuals were recruited by Jim and given special training in espionage. As leaders, they recruited individuals who furnished them information. These seven teams collected high quality information which was divided into two categories; long range or strategic information and operational data which had immediate value.

Strategic information is intelligence which may not have immediate use but is extremely valuable in predicting upcoming events or capabilities. Examples are technical data describing a new weapon system design, two year crop yield forecasts and military planning scenarios. Alternatively, operational data is something which could be used immediately. A new computer password is a good example.

An avid chess player, Jim maintained contact with team leaders by playing chess games. Each team leader was assigned the role of a famous chess player. A listing of their most notable games complete with play-by-play moves had been prepared and distributed with one copy given to the spy and the other kept by Jim. Each day, Jim would make one move and his team member would respond by making a corresponding move; exactly following the sequence played by the champion chess players a long time ago. A different move by either Jim or his team member was a signal to meet at a predetermined location and time.

Jim alerted his network by sending out incorrect chess moves. At the appointed times and places, Jim gave each team leader explicit instructions along with a timetable for executing the instructions. From this point forward, Jim's teams would assume the role of saboteurs.

The sabotage plan had taken months to prepare. In addition to carefully selected targets, there was a specific sequence to each action being undertaken. For example, after an unusually heavy rain, sluice gates on a dam inexplicably opened and trillions of gallons of water was turned loose on towns and farms located below the dam. Computers controlling grain storage units would suddenly cause the grain to be exposed to the elements. Ships containing life-saving grain being transported to hungry people living on one continent were suddenly diverted to another seaport where the grain was used to manufacture bio fuels. The most damaging action taken by Jim's network was taking control over communication and navigation satellites and sending them off into space or crashing them back to earth. Entire regions lost communications resulting in economic chaos. For example, shippers couldn't locate their products, trains slowed to a crawl, financial transactions ceased and thousands of aircraft flights were cancelled.

Earth's government was forced to assign many of its personnel into stopping the sabotage activities. During the ensuing months, most of Jim's espionage network were caught and summarily executed. In the meantime, hungry people demanded relief. Rioting and looting became commonplace when acute shortages appeared.

Jim's team was hugely successful in their mission. Their efforts ensured Earth could only send the first wave of the planned invasion force to Haven. All remaining soldiers originally designated for the invasion had their orders changed because they were needed on Earth to help quell worldwide rioting caused by a crippled food production and distribution network.

CHAPTER 19

TO CATCH A RABBIT
(EARTH FORCES)

Bill and his platoon arrived at Columbus at 9:00 PM. Nancy met his convoy and quietly invited him to share her quarters. She had not eaten so they dined with Bill's platoon members.

Since Bill's platoon had arrived late, they were permitted to sleep in the following morning. An early riser, Bill walked to headquarters and said, "Sergeant Major Tinsdale, I need a few minutes with the commander."

"May I ask what this is about?"

"Yes, I wish to suggest a mission for the Colonel's consideration."

"Please wait and I'll see if he has time for you."

* * *

"Colonel Harper, Lieutenant Anders reporting."

Colonel Harper looked up from his paperwork and replied, "Yes Anders, what's on your mind?"

"Sir, I'd like to take this opportunity to congratulate you on being appointed Commander of the Columbus Task Force. Giving you command of two armored battalions and an infantry battalion must keep you very busy.

Bill quickly added, "The second reason for my seeing you is to present an idea for a surveillance mission. Sir, the enemy must be curious about what happened to their Third Battalion. I propose we ask headquarters to post a lookout to report any attempt by the militia to visit their Third Battalion's post. In fact, their lookout might be able to plant a tracking device on an enemy scout vehicle which could eventually give us the location of their home base."

Colonel Harper studied Bill's proposal for a few moments then said, "Bill, I like your idea. Why shouldn't I send an infantry unit to do this surveillance and not bother headquarters?"

"Sir, headquarters is in Tupelo which is only a few kilometers from the former militia unit whereas we are over 250 kilometers away."

"I see your logic. A militia scout could investigate the battle scene and leave before we could get a lookout posted in the area. Bill, if the lookout spotted a militia scout, who would give chase?"

Bill smiled and answered, "Sir, I propose taking my platoon of cheetahs and a platoon of infantry and concealing them a few kilometers from Fort Mantachie. After our lookout gives us the signal, we will track the enemy to his lair. We can catch them by surprise and defeat another militia unit."

"That's very ambitious of you, Bill. However, if you find a battalion of enemy armor at the end of your quest, you would be overwhelmed and captured – or killed. No, I applaud your initiative and will act on your suggestion for a lookout. However, we will not attack the enemy until we know their strength."

Bill left his meeting with Colonel Harper in a foul mood. *'I give him my idea and he'll take credit for it. I don't know how such a timid little man got promoted to colonel and placed in charge of a task force.'*

After Bill left the Colonel's office, Colonel Harper placed a call to General Paul Dietrich. "General, this is Miles Harper calling. Lieutenant Bill Anders suggested that a lookout be posted near the militia's Third Battalion post and see if we can plant a tracking device on any scout vehicle sent to reconnoiter the Third Battalion's area. Sir, I endorse his proposal."

"Yes, I fully agree Colonel. I'm only a few kilometers from the site so I'll send someone to be a lookout. Give the Lieutenant my thanks for his idea."

* * *

"Corporal Timmons, I need to see you right away."

"Yes sir. What may I do for you?"

"General Dietrich wants someone to go to Fort Mantachie and stay there as a lookout. We suspect the militia may send a reconnaissance team to investigate the status of their people. Also, I want you to take a homing device with you and hide the locator on their vehicle without being seen."

"Captain Ramos, how long is this mission?"

"Take two soldiers with you and prepare to stay three weeks. Check in daily with a status report. Remember, we don't want to stop the militia's reconnaissance team; we want to locate their headquarters."

* * *

On arrival at his destination, Corporal Timmons settled into a wooded grove three hundred meters from Fort Mantachie's main gate. He was able to see both entrances to Fort Mantachie from his vantage point. He reminded his two soldiers this was a great assignment; they could sit around for the next three weeks while their fellow soldiers back at Tupelo would be on foot patrol duty.

CHAPTER 20

AMBUSH (MILITIA FORCES)

The sound of a hauler engine woke me from a deep sleep. I looked over at Helen's sleeping bag and noticed Helen was gone. Hurriedly dressing, I jumped from the cargo bed and saw several others straggling from their vehicles.

Colonel Maxon had arrived and was talking to Helen. He pulled out a map and they huddled for several minutes. After shaking hands with Helen, he got back into his personal carrier and left our area.

Helen called us together and briefed us on the situation. "Ladies and gentlemen, Colonel Maxon has informed me that Earth forces are rapidly dispersing across Haven and are taking up positions in cities, villages, airports and at former militia bases. They've established broadcasting stations and are using them to make public announcements and send out propaganda. They're checking identities and arresting both Haven police and suspected militia members. While they've grabbed a lot of places, holding them will be another matter because one; their forces are spread pretty thin and two; we've already heard stories about people getting knocked about and their personal possessions and homes being confiscated. If they alienate the population, we should have no problem getting our citizens to support us. Also, we need to be on the lookout for settlers who recently emigrated from earth. It's possible they're loyal to Earth and will turn us in if they get a chance. Fortunately, people living in each community are also watching new migrants and Colonel Maxon doubts anyone will get a chance to inform on the militia.

"Initially, we're going to use hit and run tactics. We'll ambush convoys and take everything for our own use. Militia Headquarters has issued one rule about upcoming engagements. If an enemy unit doesn't fight; we spare their lives. We'll disarm them, confiscate their identity cards and send them back to their bases. But if they fight, we take no prisoners. Our militia doesn't currently have prisoner of war facilities and we can't afford to capture enemy soldiers.

"The enemy has air superiority for now. They're using both manned aircraft and drones. Militia air defense units will use anti-aircraft missiles to take them down. Because our missiles are in short supply, don't expect us to win the air war anytime soon. With that in mind, always be on the alert for air attack. Are there any questions? If not, I need to see Sergeant Delucca and Private Collins on a related matter. Everyone else is dismissed."

After the group dispersed, Sergeant Delucca and I remained behind. Helen said, "I plan to move three cheetahs early this morning. We'll travel about 100 kilometers north of Camp Shelby and set up an ambush site along Highway 47. Which cheetahs should we leave behind to protect our camp?"

Sergeant Delucca said, "We should leave Sean Ellis and Crystal Rogers behind."

Helen looked at me and asked, "Private Collins, how many haulers do you recommend we take with us?"

I thought for a moment then replied, "Ma'am, I recommend two haulers and four mechanics. After an ambush, we may need additional drivers for captured vehicles. We should leave three haulers here and use them for our consolidated supplies." I added, "I also recommend we take a first aid kit, extra ammo, charging generator, food rations, sleeping bags and water with us in case we need to be away for several days."

Helen thought over my suggestion for a few moments then nodded and said, "Excellent. Gentlemen, let me know when you're ready to move out."

I met with the mechanics and briefed them on our mission specifics. "Wendy will drive her hauler and Fred and Chuck will come with us. Since we may be gone a few days, we should bring our sleeping bags, food, some water and extra ammo. Misty, you're staying behind with Sean and Crystal. I'm asking that you consolidate and sort the parts and store them in the remaining haulers."

I loaded my hauler with supplies and helped Misty unload my spare parts and some extra rations.

* * *

We arrived at our ambush site at 5:00 PM and prepared our positions. The cheetahs required a good field of fire with overhead cover to hide from aerial observation. We parked our haulers about 100 meters behind the cheetahs and planned emergency escape routes in case we 'bit off more than we could chew.'

Three days later, I was talking with Fred about not seeing any targets when someone spotted an enemy convoy of 10 haulers being escorted by two armored vehicles.

Helen designated specific targets for Sergeant Delucca and Ralph. She gave instructions for the haulers to intercept the convoy after the two primary targets were removed. We waited for her command.

"FIRE"

The armored vehicles protecting the convoy were hit simultaneously and burst into flames. The remainder of the enemy convoy halted and didn't move. Helen held her own fire in case of additional resistance. Sergeant Delucca and Ralph immediately sped down the hill and took up positions at the front and rear of the convoy. Seeing no additional movement, Helen signaled for Wendy and me to drive our haulers down to the convoy.

As we arrived at the convoy, Fred, Chuck, Wendy and I began searching the enemy haulers. I took the first hauler and peeked inside the rear. Instead of being loaded with supplies, I found Haven police and some militiamen chained to the cargo bed. They were guarded by a frightened Earth soldier. I pointed my rifle at the Earth soldier and said, "Sonny, release these prisoners and be quick about it." Once this was done, I told a militiaman to get the soldier's weapon and help free the other prisoners.

Each enemy hauler contained about twenty prisoners. In all, we freed almost two hundred and captured ten enemy haulers. Not bad for a day's work.

We gathered the surviving twenty Earth soldiers and confiscated their identity cards. Helen addressed the soldiers while Sergeant Delucca captured the event on vid. "Gentlemen, I'm letting you walk back to your base. Get off our planet. Your names and pictures will be distributed throughout the militia and if you're captured again, you'll be executed. Now get out of my sight."

We gathered around the rear of the vehicles and watched the unarmed Earth soldiers hurriedly walk away from the convoy.

"Sergeant Delucca, please clear the wreckage from the highway and set up for another target. I'll return as soon as I transfer these men to battalion headquarters."

She led the convoy of freed prisoners riding in captured haulers to a rendezvous point where she met Colonel Maxon. After Helen reported her actions to him she returned to our ambush site; leaving the freed prisoners and the ten enemy haulers with Colonel Maxon.

After Helen returned, she and I sat down and discussed the fire team's equipment and maintenance status. Our conversation suddenly turned personal when she asked, "Private Collins, what did you do before being drafted into the militia?"

"I worked for Ajax Construction Company in Tupelo. I started working a couple of days after graduating from school. My first six months as a common laborer and the past eight years operating a tracked excavator."

Frowning, she said, "With eight years' experience as a tracked vehicle operator, I don't understand why they didn't designate you as a warrior at Johnson Springs Reservation."

I grinned at her and said, "I would probably be a warrior today if I hadn't thrown a track showing off on day one." I then gave her the details of the incident.

After hearing my story, Helen got to her feet and looking down at me said, "Idiot!" and then walked away.

That stung! It was now apparent that my childish action on that fateful day would likely haunt me forever.

With seven of us at the ambush site, Helen and I shared our cargo bed with Fred. Sergeant Delucca, Wendy, Chuck, and Ralph slept in the other hauler. Warriors and mechanics took turns on guard duty; watching for two hours before waking the next couple on the duty roster.

Taking our turn on guard duty that evening, Helen and I sat under the stars watching the road. Our conversation was limited to whispering because sound travels a long distance at night.

"Ma'am, what did you do before joining the militia?"

Helen replied, "My parents emigrated from Earth when I was ten. I completed school on Haven and helped my father on the family farm until I was twenty. I joined the militia and have been a warrior for the past five years. I love being in the militia and don't believe I could ever return to farming."

"You were raised on a farm? Well, that explains a lot."

Helen asked, "What do you mean?"

"You helping me overhaul the cheetah's engine, for one thing. I've known women who would literally cringe at the thought of getting grease on their hands; much less risk a broken nail turning a wrench. You really impressed me that evening."

"Collins, you're such a flatterer. Does your flattery actually work on any real women you've known?"

"Yes Ma'am. And you'd be surprised how many."

"Oh my god; Collins, I don't believe the crap you're spreading. You sound like some little schoolboy bragging about imaginary conquests."

"Ma'am, is it bragging if I'm just being truthful?"

"Collins, if we ever meet an enemy who desperately needs flattering, I'll send you over. I'm certain victory would be ours."

Not to be outdone, I continued, "And Ma'am; seeing you leave the motor pool in dirty coveralls and reappearing one hour later looking like you were ready for a photo shoot was also impressive."

"Private Collins, will you stop already? We're supposed to be on guard duty and maintaining silence. If you tell me one more tale, I'm going to start laughing so loud the enemy will be able to get a fix on our position!"

After being relieved by another pair, Helen and I climbed into the hauler's cargo bed for much-needed sleep. I was rewarded with a brief smile before she turned off the lantern.

* * *

Following breakfast, Helen called me over to her cheetah. She said, "Private Collins, since you obviously know how to operate a tracked vehicle, you should learn how to use one in combat."

That got my attention!

She continued, "I've loaded some scenarios on the fire control computer. The system is set on training mode. All vehicle and weapon responses to each scenario will appear real to you. I borrowed this helmet from Private Taylor; it should fit. Plug the jack into the panel and I'll activate the blackout lens. You should see the scenario shortly; it'll be projected on the rear of the blackout lens. Listen to the voice on the scenario and follow the instructions. This first exercise is a freebie; all future scenarios will be scored. Incidentally, if we spot a real target while you're playing, I'll hit the top of your helmet. That will be your signal to vacate my cheetah and return the helmet to Taylor."

'Damn! This is fun.' I missed the first two targets but was able to diagnose and correct my mistakes. The follow-on scenarios were scored and a running total was displayed. I practiced for three hours until the screen went blank. After removing my helmet, I saw Helen motioning me to get out of the cheetah. After exiting, she reached into the driver's compartment and removed the monitor. We climbed into the hauler cab where she thoroughly debriefed me on each scenario. She patiently pointed out tactical errors I had made and praised me for making correct decisions in other scenarios.

She concluded by saying, "Private Collins, based on your scores in these scenarios, you appear to be qualified to serve as a warrior. While your shooting skill needs improvement, your mastery of operating the cheetah in simulated combat conditions can only be matched by someone with years of experience."

"Thank you, Ma'am. I learned a lot today. You're a good teacher."

"Are you being serious or is this a continuation of your bullshit from last night?"

"I'm serious. And you were right about me; I was an idiot back at Johnson Springs Reservation."

Helen smiled and said, "Since you're confessing, does this mean you're also sorry for playing those awful practical jokes on me back at Camp Shelby?"

I grinned at her and replied, "Nice try but I'm not admitting to playing any practical joke. However, if I had played a practical joke, I'd never apologize for it."

As Helen prepared to get out of the hauler she looked back at me and said, "Despite your denials, I know you were responsible for pulling those vile pranks on me. I predict that someday you may want to apologize."

I thought to myself, *'Like hell I will!'*

CHAPTER 21

RECONNAISSANCE MISSION (MILITIA FORCES)

After spending six days at the ambush site, we received a new assignment. Colonel Maxon contacted Helen and ordered her to conduct a reconnaissance mission near Tupelo. Militia Headquarters was unable to contact the Third Battalion and Helen was ordered to find out what happened at Fort Mantachie.

"Collins, I'll take you and your hauler on this mission. According to the map, we'll be required to drive over 2,000 kilometers round trip. I'm planning a route which will minimize our chance of being detected. It's not the shortest route to Fort Mantachie, but we can't afford to use major highways."

When I got a chance to speak privately with Helen I said, "Ma'am, are you sure you should be coming on this mission? This fire team needs your leadership."

"Private Collins, while your concern about my safety is touching, let me worry about my team and my actions. When you and I get back to the base camp, get your hauler loaded and ready to move out."

"Yes Ma'am."

* * *

Helen drove the hauler that morning. I felt a little weird sitting in the passenger seat while my commander drove. I thought, *'I've got to hand it to you, Helen; you do more than your part.'* We stopped for lunch after finding an area shaded with large trees. Although we had not seen any aircraft, we could never be sure that a satellite had not spotted us and relayed our position to the enemy. My hauler made a small target on Haven. Hopefully, the enemy would not hear or see us. Throughout the morning, Helen and I talked about a wide variety of things. Talking made the time go by faster.

With lunch over, I took the wheel of the hauler. After driving for a couple of hours I finally asked, "Ma'am, since we're alone on this mission, why don't you call me John and I call you Helen?"

Helen looked over at me and hesitated a few moments before answering. She said, "I'm not sure that would be a good idea. I don't know you that well and I must maintain a command presence."

"That's bullshit. You know me pretty well by now. The only question I have is why you think it's necessary to maintain a barrier between us when we're alone. We both know you're in charge and that I've never disobeyed one of your orders."

"That's fine for you to say but what would Colonel Maxon or members of the fire team think if they knew I was fraternizing with an enlisted soldier?"

I decided to take a chance using her first name and replied, "Helen, what we say and do alone out here doesn't mean we drop the commander-subordinate role in front of others."

"I'll think about it. In the meantime, why don't you pull off the road for a short break?"

I drove two additional hours before stopping for the night. Dusk was approaching when I parked the hauler underneath a large tree. I connected the battery to the generator to ensure we had an ample charge for the next day. Helen helped me camouflage the vehicle using some brush we found nearby. After washing up and eating a cold dinner, we climbed into the cargo bed and unrolled our sleeping bags.

After I lay down, Helen quietly said, "Goodnight, John."

I found myself smiling in the darkness as I replied, "Goodnight, Helen. We had a good day today. I hope tomorrow will be uneventful, too."

The best thing about this mission was getting to know Helen on a personal basis. During the long hours spent in the cab of the hauler during the three day drive, we shared a lot of information about one another and I found myself becoming more than just physically attracted to her. She helped make me like her after she dropped the snotty stuck-up attitude.

* * *

"Helen, are you awake?"

Helen stretched and murmured; "Now I am. I was having a dream. And before you get too excited, I was dreaming about home." Yawning, she added, "What time is it?"

"It's four forty-five. You said last night you wanted to get an early start today."

"You're right. Let's get ready. I'm anxious to complete this mission and get back to our unit."

Helen and I arrived at Fort Mantachie at 7:00 AM. We left the hauler parked outside the main entrance gate. Using available cover and concealment, we entered the base armed only with our rifles. The fort was in ruins. Buildings had been burned. There were vehicle carcasses scattered throughout. We counted 15 cheetahs and 23 haulers utterly destroyed. According to Helen, that was over a third of the battalion's vehicles. Hopefully, the remainder had escaped. I couldn't tell if the base had been attacked from the air or assaulted by a ground force. I didn't see any enemy equipment. Helen captured the entire scene using her vid recorder.

At the motor pool's wash rack, Helen called me over. "John, look at this; there must be dozens of identity discs hanging on this fire hydrant. I don't understand. If the Third Battalion militia members were captured, Earth soldiers would have taken their identity discs."

Shifting my gaze, I said, "Helen, look over here; this freshly turned dirt indicates something large could have been recently buried."

"John, you need to dig in that area. Find out what was buried. I'm going to photograph these discs using my vid recorder. I'll spread them on the ferrocrete pad."

I found a shovel underneath a smashed tool shed and started digging. Not far down, my shovel hit something. I scooped the dirt away and discovered a body. "Helen, come over here! I've found someone. This could be the remains of a militia soldier." Rigor mortis had set in so it was difficult for me to roll him over and the smell was awful.

After brushing the dirt from his back Helen said, "Look at the back of his head. Doesn't that look like a bullet hole? This militia member was executed! I'm taking a picture of this." She added, "I wonder if he the only one who was murdered?"

I resumed digging and quickly found another body. "Here's another body."

After inspecting the second body and finding an identical bullet hole, she said, "Okay, after I get pictures, put the bodies back in the grave and replace the dirt. We've uncovered evidence of a massacre. This will not go well with the people of Haven."

After filling the hole, I put the shovel back underneath the shed and Helen replaced the identity discs on the hydrant.

Helen walked around and took more pictures of the mass grave before we returned to our hauler and left the area.

"John, we need to hurry back and report. I can't risk transmitting a message this close to the enemy's headquarters but Colonel Maxon needs to know what happened to this unit. It is 9:00 AM. We'll stop for lunch in four hours. By driving more hours each day, I estimate we'll be back at our unit in maybe two and a half days."

After getting the hauler moving I said, "Helen, I met a girl from Tupelo during basic training who became a warrior and was assigned to the Third Battalion. She is a really nice person. I hope she escaped that carnage."

"Maybe she was lucky, John. I also know several warriors assigned to the Third. In fact, my first platoon leader was promoted to command Company C a few months ago. Honestly, it's possible some survived but it's not likely. Recall we couldn't account for all the cheetahs and haulers. If some members of the Third had escaped, they would have contacted Militia Headquarters by now. I'm guessing the Earth soldiers captured the equipment unaccounted for and left the unsalvageable stuff behind."

"Helen, it's also likely militia members killed in the fighting were buried first and the survivors were shot and added to the grave."

"John, those Earth soldiers have made a huge mistake. With the evidence we've gathered, the entire Haven Militia will become enraged and will fight harder. I hope we capture the soldiers who did this. Hanging is too good for them but it will have to do."

"Helen, I don't understand why they didn't do a better job covering up the massacre. Everybody knows it's a criminal act. Why would someone leave evidence such as the identity discs out in plain sight near recently disturbed dirt? It's almost like they were proud of their actions and wanted to show us what happened."

"I suspect whoever ordered this didn't see the long range implications of murdering our soldiers. Maybe they thought doing this would scare us. If so, they thought wrong! Based on historical books I've read, most armies engaging in mass murder end up losing the war."

Having to stay on dirt roads cost us a lot of time. On the other hand, had we chosen to ride on a paved highway, it's likely we could have been spotted and killed. For the first three hours, we only talked about what we had discovered in the Third Battalion's compound.

"Helen, how many identity discs were there?"

"There were ninety five discs on the hydrant. Some discs could have been destroyed during the attack. John, if any militia prisoners were taken, it's only logical that all identity discs would have been taken as well. Based on the evidence we uncovered, I can only conclude the Third Battalion has been annihilated."

I stated, "You know, when Earth invaded Haven, the Third Battalion's close proximity to Tupelo gave them less time to prepare. For the first time, I'm grateful we were posted far away from the capital. We probably left Camp Shelby just ahead of those killers."

* * *

After driving another hour in silence, Helen asked me to pull over and stop underneath some large trees. I was really glad we stopped because I was in desperate need of a latrine break. After washing, we had lunch and took a short rest before moving again.

Helen was sitting nearby with her eyes closed and her back against a tree when I said, "Helen, what do you think will happen to us?"

"What do you mean?"

"Well, aside from discovering the fate of the Third Battalion, I've really enjoyed being with you during this mission. Three weeks ago, I could never have imagined how much my feelings for you have changed during these past few days."

Without moving, she opened her eyes and said, "John, getting to know you personally has been very special to me, too. In fact, I was sitting here thinking how hard it's going to be once we get back to the unit. I won't be able to call you by your first name or openly discuss my feelings with you." Helen narrowed her eyes and glared at me when she added, "This is totally your fault; using your boyish charm to get me to lower my guard."

I grinned at her and said, "Yeah, I take full responsibility for putting a smile in your heart and I plead guilty to making you happy. Are these court martial offences? I remember you wanting to court martial me once."

Helen crawled over to me and pushed me onto my back. After straddling me she said, "John, you're incorrigible! You constantly say and do the most outrageous things. One moment I want to choke you and the next I want to smother you with kisses. No man has ever affected me like this. Oh crap, I was afraid this would happen."

Catching her wrists and looking up at her I replied, "Helen, when we return to camp, you'll call me Private Collins and I'll address you as, Ma'am. We can do this."

She stared at me and finally said, "John, we may be able to fool people for a while, but our new feelings for one another will eventually betray us. On the other hand, I know one day or one month from now we could meet the same fate as the militia in the Third Battalion. The possibility of us dying makes me want to be with you every possible minute."

I released her wrists and replied, "Helen, we'll figure something out. In the meantime, I'm dreading the next four or five hours of driving. We've been pretty lucky so far but I'm beginning to worry about how much luck we have remaining."

Helen got up and extending her hand to me said, "Okay Mr. Pessimist, let's saddle up and go."

That evening, I suggested we fasten our sleeping bags together to make a double. Helen agreed and after a quick kiss goodnight, we fell asleep in a spooning position. After spending two hours examining the remnants of the Third Battalion, we both needed to be held.

CHAPTER 22

TRACKING THE ENEMY TO HIS LAIR (EARTH FORCES)

Corporal Timmons looked over at Privates Neighbors and Barrett who were sleeping. He was about to call his company headquarters and give another negative report when he heard a hauler arrive. Leaning over, he nudged Neighbors and whispered, "Neighbors, wake up Barrett and be quiet about it. Someone's coming."

The two soldiers rubbed sleep from their eyes and joined Corporal Timmons on lookout. Barrett whispered, "What do you see, Corporal?"

Without removing his field glasses, Corporal Timmons softly answered, "I see a hauler and two soldiers; looks like a man and a woman getting out. They're taking their rifles and are entering the fort. Okay Neighbors, I want you to sneak down to the hauler and put the locator on the rear axle. Make sure it's armed before you leave. And be quiet about it. I don't want them to hear or see you."

After Private Neighbors departed, Corporal Timmons said, "Barrett, follow Neighbors and give him covering fire if necessary. The main thing is, don't get caught. Now go."

Corporal Timmons breathed a sigh of relief when Privates Neighbors and Barrett returned. After receiving confirmation that the homing device was operating, Corporal Timmons reported their success to Captain Rogers and asked for further instructions."

"Good job, Corporal Timmons. The signal is coming in very strong. Wait until the militia scouts leave; then you and your team return to headquarters."

* * *

"Colonel Morrissey, General Dietrich is calling."

"Sir, what may I do for you?"

"Bill, I'm sending you the final location of a tracking device we planted on a small militia reconnaissance team scouting the Fort Mantachie area. You may want to act quickly on this information because I suspect the militia unit may have discovered the tracker."

"Thank you, sir. We'll get right on it. Haven's militia units have been good at eluding our troops. We may finally get to hammer those slippery bastards."

* * *

"Sergeant Reynolds, I need to see Captain Hernandez right away."

* * *

"Captain Hernandez, here is a map reference showing the location of a militia reconnaissance team. Take some men and crush those traitors. Hit them quickly before they can escape."

"Wilco, sir."

Captain Hernandez immediately left Colonel Morrissey's office and contacted his first sergeant. "Sergeant Higginbotham, I want a platoon of infantry and two cheetahs loaded on haulers for an immediate mission. Get Lieutenant Glenn's infantry platoon and ask Lieutenant Langley for two of his cheetahs. I want to move out in thirty minutes. Oh, and tell Glenn to bring four mortars."

"Captain, may I tag along?"

"Absolutely; you're driving my hauler."

* * *

The hastily assembled Earth combat team raced along Highway 47 toward the final reported coordinates of the homing beacon. Captain Hernandez briefed his team members via comm link along the way. "Ladies and gentlemen, listen up. We're chasing a militia reconnaissance team which has returned to their unit. They've been on the road for a few days and don't know we're closing in on them. According to my map, we should arrive near their base at 10:00 this evening. I am sending you the coordinates. I want the mortars to drop off 700 meters before our line of departure and give us covering fire. The mortar barrage will commence at 10:27 and end at 10:29 plus 30 seconds. Our main attack will begin at 10:30. We'll attack in a line formation with direct fire support from the two cheetahs.

"Our line of departure will be 200 meters from the enemy's location. We don't have time to reconnoiter the enemy's position before launching our attack and nobody had better make any noise.

"I suspect they're an infantry unit which was sent to search for survivors at Fort Mantachie. But it doesn't really matter what type unit they are. Since our invasion, we've had a tough time finding and eliminating Haven's militia. Here is a golden opportunity to wipe out a militia unit in a surprise night attack. After the attack, we'll sort out what type unit we destroyed. Are there any questions?"

CHAPTER 23

NIGHT ATTACK (MILITIA FORCES)

Helen and I arrived at camp early in the afternoon. Everyone was up and about but not much activity was occurring.

After I parked the hauler, the mechanics came over and helped me with its maintenance services while Helen contacted Colonel Maxon and sent him a detailed report on the Third Battalion's fate.

While servicing my hauler, Misty found a tracking device planted underneath the cargo bed. She had been checking the rear axle for leaks when she noticed the device.

I immediately carried the device to Helen and reported the find. "Ma'am, Private Ransom found this tracking device planted underneath the cargo bed of my hauler. I can only speculate that it must have been planted while we were checking out Third Battalion's base."

Helen looked over the device and said, "I think you're right, Private Collins. That's the only time we were away from the hauler during the reconnaissance mission. I'll contact Colonel Maxon with this news."

Turning to Frank she said, "Sergeant Delucca, place the fire team on alert. We need to position the cheetahs for maximum effectiveness. This is probably the best defensive position available because we don't know when the enemy will attack. Let's get some sensors out in order to give us advance warning of their approach." Turning to me she said, "Private Collins, have the mechanics dig foxholes between the cheetahs and see what you can do about getting our extra ammo protected."

"Ma'am, why not put the tracking device back on the hauler and let me lead the enemy away from our position?"

"Collins, when this particular tracking device was removed, it automatically switched off after broadcasting its final location. I think it's safe to assume the enemy knows our exact position. I'm not criticizing your actions; you had no way of knowing its triggering mechanism. What's done is done. Let Sergeant Delucca know when your mechanics have completed their defensive preparations."

"Yes Ma'am."

I called the mechanics together and explained our plan of action. We dug for the next three hours. Fear is a great motivator. As I was sweating over my shovel, I began to fondly think of my tracked excavator. Digging foxholes would have been child's play and done in less than five minutes.

After completing my foxhole, I checked on everyone's progress and helped Wendy and Misty finish their foxholes. We took our extra ammo off the trucks and stowed it away from the camp in a narrow ravine. When all had been completed, I reported to Sergeant Delucca then washed up and took a break.

As we ate a cold dinner, Sergeant Delucca announced watch assignments. He paired drivers with mechanics for two hour shifts.

I was fast asleep when the alarm was given, *"EVERYBODY, TAKE COVER!"* Explosions erupted in front of and behind our perimeter.

Helen and her warriors scrambled into their cheetahs. We mechanics dived for our foxholes.

I had never been under fire. The noise, concussion and smell of explosives scared the hell out of me. I kept my head down and prayed that none of the shells would land in my foxhole. I couldn't imagine anything surviving this barrage. Shells exploding nearby hurt my ears and dirt seemed to be constantly raining down on me. Air waves, created by exploding shells, pushed on my chest and made it difficult to breathe.

Suddenly, the barrage stopped as quickly as it started. My ears were still ringing when I took a quick peek into the night. About twenty yards to my front shadowy forms seemed to materialize out of the smoke and dust. A cheetah next to me began firing its anti-personnel gun at the advancing soldiers. I aimed my rifle at them and started firing, too. The next few minutes were a blur. I have never been so scared in my life. I didn't know who was winning but I was alive and knew that I must shoot them before they could shoot me.

One of our cheetahs fired its main gun. There – an explosion 100 meters in front of us lit the sky; momentarily illuminating advancing enemy soldiers. They were quickly mowed down with our combined anti-personnel gun and rifle fire. Our defensive line was holding.

Sergeant Delucca and Crystal's cheetahs began moving forward. Advancing side-by-side, they appeared to be providing one another mutual firing support. I decided to stay put in my foxhole. I could hear projectiles whizzing overhead and I didn't want to get hit. Helen's cheetah started forward. I hoped that the tide of battle was turning in favor of the good guys.

There was a large explosion to my rear. One of our haulers was burning. This was not good; our positions were being illuminated by the fire. Ralph's cheetah began moving wide to my left. Sean's cheetah was not moving nor was it firing. That seemed odd to me.

After waiting a couple of minutes and judging by the sounds of firing, the battle had moved several hundred meters to our front. I didn't hear any bullets zinging by so I slowly got out of my foxhole then ran over to the stationary cheetah. One look told me why this cheetah had not moved. Sean had been killed. His body was halfway in the driver's compartment. I heard somebody behind me say something. It was Wendy. She climbed on the hull and together we got Sean's body out of the driver's compartment and slid him to the ground; his blood smearing the hull's front slope. By this time, other mechanics had gathered around us. I said, "Let's move him further back." We carried his body to the center of our position and gently lay him down. Wendy walked over and sat down, cradling his head. I said, "Wendy is it okay if I start your cheetah?" She looked up at me and silently nodded her head.

I got into the cheetah and started the engine. I turned on the sensor array and comm unit and put on Sean's helmet. I heard Helen's voice. "Three – on your right – slow moving target – range 300 meters."

"Roger –One – target is a hauler – ON THE WAY." I heard an immediate explosion then, "Target destroyed." This was interesting; I was getting to listen to a real firefight; Helen designating targets and her teammates destroying them.

A vehicle suddenly appeared on the display in Sean's cheetah. I identified the target as an enemy cheetah slowly moving toward our campsite! Our cheetahs were chasing the remnants of the attackers and this guy had slipped by unnoticed. Nobody had picked him up as a target.

I found myself in a scary situation. As a mechanic, I had never fired the main gun. However, unless I killed this enemy cheetah, he would wipe out our entire maintenance team while Helen and her warriors were attacking a retreating enemy force.

I swung the barrel of the main gun onto the approaching cheetah. Fortunately, he didn't realize my cheetah's main gun was tracking him. I fired the gun at point blank range. The projectile hit the turret and stopped the vehicle in its tracks. My second round blew the turret off the enemy cheetah.

The fight was over in less than ten seconds. I was numb from shock and just sat in the commander's seat. Hearing Helen's voice over the comm link brought me back to reality.

"Four – multiple targets on your left – range 500 plus meters"

"Roger –One – nearest target is a hauler – ON THE WAY." After the explosion, "Target destroyed. Next target is a hauler – ON THE WAY. Target hit – am unable to assess damage. One – no lock on the other targets – they are out of range. Shall we follow?"

"Negative. All cheetahs, return to base. Good job."

When Helen and the other warriors returned, I reported Sean's death and the loss of a hauler. The warriors were amazed I had actually destroyed an enemy cheetah but that news was overshadowed by the loss of Sean.

Late that night, I awoke from a restive sleep and suddenly got the shakes. Although it was cool outside, I knew it wasn't the weather. I lay trembling in my sleeping bag for no apparent reason. My chattering teeth must have awakened Helen because I felt her hand softly stroke the back of my head and neck. The last thing I remember was hearing her say, "Shhhh, go to sleep."

* * *

Early the following morning, Helen gathered everyone and read some passages from a small religious book. After saying, 'amen' in unison, we placed dirt in the grave of Private Sean Ellis – warrior. I felt tears roll down my cheek as we filled in his grave. Sean was well-liked by everyone.

After the service, I began cleaning Sean's cheetah; removing all traces of his blood. Wendy came over and stood near me; watching as I finished my task. She said, "John, I miss Sean so much. I don't know what to do with myself. Few people knew it, but we were engaged to be married."

Wendy was right, I had no idea they were romantically involved. "Wendy, I can only imagine the pain and loss you're feeling. I know you need time to grieve. I'll ask Warrant Officer Ramses if leave can be arranged."

Between tears she said, "Thank you, John. You've been very considerate of my feelings."

Helen was sitting on the cargo bed making a report of the attack. She looked up when I approached and quietly said, "John, I'm so glad you're safe."

I climbed up, sat beside her and replied, "We're both lucky to be alive. I was scared every minute; every second during the attack. Listening to your voice over the comm link as you directed the fight was amazing. You sounded so calm. I don't know how you do it."

She smiled and replied, "John, combat training kicked in and my actions were the result of many hours spent preparing for this fight. Had I permitted myself to think about individuals and their safety, I would've failed in my job and our unit could have lost our first battle."

She continued, "I've sent a full report on your actions. When we were attacked, you returned fire and accounted for several of the enemy casualties. I also heard about you helping Wendy extract Sean from his cheetah during the fight. Most significantly, you getting into Sean's vehicle and killing the enemy cheetah which had slipped by us saved people's lives and our equipment.

"John, you did your job and more in spite of being scared. And anybody who says he's not afraid during combat is lying."

"Speaking of Wendy, is there any possibility of her getting some leave? She's really taking Sean's loss hard. I just found out they were engaged."

"I knew about their engagement. Sean told me a few days ago. I'll ask Colonel Maxon about emergency leave. However, our first priority is to get out of here before the Earth soldiers come back. Along with the after action report, I've requested another site for the fire team. Have everyone load up and prepare to move out. We can't stay here. I'm afraid of what they will bring to the next fire fight. Earth may be wrong for invading Haven, but their soldiers aren't stupid."

"Helen, about last night; I guess I got the shakes after the fire fight."

Helen replied, "That's only natural. In fact, I was shaking, too. The only difference between us was my teeth were not chattering." She grinned and continued, "I was afraid you would wake everyone."

With tongue-in-cheek I replied, "Ma'am, it's good to know you always place the unit's best interest ahead of all else." Before she could defend her comment, I left to help the mechanics load the haulers.

We loaded our haulers and made sure the batteries were fully charged. Sergeant Delucca said, "John, WO Ramses informed me how well you did in the simulations. Based on her recommendation and your action last night, I want you to drive Sean's cheetah. On the comm link, you'll be designated as India Five. If we run into a firefight I want you to hold back and protect the haulers. Your cheetah will follow the haulers and I will be directly behind you guarding the rear. Just follow my instructions."

"Okay, Sarge."

Fred's hauler was destroyed during the attack so Sergeant Delucca assigned my hauler to him.

Helen assembled the fire team and informed us of our new location. In two minutes we were moving out. Her cheetah led the fire team and Sergeant Delucca's cheetah brought up the rear. Nobody wanted to wait around for any other visitors.

This was my first time driving a cheetah for any distance. It was thrilling to drive the small but powerful vehicle. I decided I would work hard and earn the right to become a full-time warrior.

Our next encampment was a few kilometers outside the Wildlife Refuge in a small village named Sparta. Its citizens offered us fresh water and vegetables. At Sparta, a small occupying force from Earth had been disarmed and sent packing by another Fifth Battalion fire team so we were free to move in and set up. Eating freshly cooked vegetables was a real treat from having to live on a steady diet of food rations during the past few weeks.

Helen assured the mayor that we would do nothing to jeopardize the safety of the villagers. He seemed satisfied and offered us the use of several storage buildings where we could hide our vehicles.

After parking my cheetah, I contacted the village priest who offered grief counseling for Wendy after I explained our recent loss. I returned to our fire team's area and found Wendy working on her hauler. I said, "Wendy, there's a priest in Sparta who has lots of experience talking with people who have suffered the loss of a loved one. He's willing to talk with you."

"John, that's sweet of you to think of me but I'm not a religious person and don't know what meeting a priest would accomplish."

"Wendy, you've nothing to lose by talking with the man and I doubt he'll try to convert you to his religion."

"Okay, if I agree to meet with the priest, will you let me continue working on my vehicles?"

"You got it." I figured it would be therapeutic for her to stay busy and readily agreed to her request.

Since I was no longer assigned a hauler, I began scouting around and discovered an empty barn loft nearby. I stowed my personal gear among some bales of hay. It was perfect. Later, I joined Helen for lunch. Eventually she asked, "John, where are you sleeping tonight?"

"Ma'am, I discovered a barn loft nearby with plenty of hay. It has a trap door entrance accessed by a ladder and a large door at one end which is shut from the inside." I quietly added, "There's room for two."

Lowering her voice she replied, "I'll think about it."

After dark, Helen climbed up the ladder to the loft carrying her personal gear. A single lantern lit the small loft. Wordlessly, she inspected the accommodations; then closed the trap door and unrolled her sleeping bag. While she was getting ready for bed, I opened a bottle of wine I had purchased and poured two glasses.

She looked at me with a stern face and quietly said, "John Collins, you seem to be pretty confident about your sex appeal. How did you even know I would sleep here?"

Smiling, I replied, "You were invited to sleep here and this loft is a lot better than the back of a hauler. More importantly, I believe my commander deserves a glass of wine. If she believes the wine would lead to something else, I would dearly love to discuss that subject with her."

She whispered loudly, "John, you're continually making jokes while I'm taking a big chance that others may find out about us."

"Helen, with all we've been through during the past few days, do you really believe knowledge of our relationship would harm this unit?"

"Unfortunately, I do believe unit cohesion would be damaged if others found out about us."

"What if we were formally engaged?"

"I think knowledge of any personal relationship would have an adverse impact - though perhaps not as severe if we were engaged." She quickly added, "But don't construe that comment to mean I'm begging for a proposal, Lover Boy!"

I lay back and grinned. Teasing Helen was a lot of fun. Interestingly, the thought of getting married didn't scare me and that was a new feeling.

After finishing our wine, I turned out the lantern and Helen and I snuggled together. I whispered to her how wonderful it felt having her beside me. It gave me a warm feeling hearing her agree. After a couple of passionate kisses, Helen suggested we get some sleep. I'd been with enough women to know when they're not in the mood so I reluctantly agreed. With some women; it's all about patience.

CHAPTER 24

ESTABLISHING AMBUSH TEAMS (EARTH FORCES)

"Colonel Morrissey, please standby for General Dietrich."

A moment later the four task force commanders were attending their weekly staff meeting with General Dietrich over a vid network. This secure military network was established immediately after Earth invaded Haven. It enabled General Dietrich to hold face-to-face meetings with his senior field commanders without their having to travel to Tupelo. In addition to the time savings, this mode of communication reduced the chance of senior officers being ambushed by a militia unit.

"Good morning, gentlemen. According to your weekly activity reports, no militia soldiers have been killed this week. Need I remind you that we'll never completely conquer Haven until we eliminate their militia? With that goal in mind, my headquarters staff has proposed a strategy which we need to discuss.

"As you know, the militia is operating in small units and it has proven extremely difficult to locate an individual unit and stamp it out. Given that situation, my Operations Officer is suggesting each task force commander create a heavily armed ambush team and place that unit along a probable route taken by militia units. Your team may have to sit still for several days waiting for the enemy to drive by. But when he does, your ambush team should be able to obliterate the passing militia unit because you will have surprise on your side and superior firepower."

"General, this sounds like the same tactic the militia units are using on us."

"Colonel Harper, you're one hundred percent correct. My Operations Officer believes if this tactic works for the militia, it should work for us."

"Sir, are we limited to one ambush team?"

"No Colonel Morrissey. Form as many as you like. Just remember you must have enough reserves to protect your post and be able to reinforce your ambush teams should it become necessary.

"Colonel Rogers, you've been silent during this meeting. What do you think of this strategy?"

"General Dietrich, I'm trying to determine how I would implement this plan within my sector. As you know, the area of Haven north of Ripley is flat and open. That's one reason why it's ideal for growing wheat. It would be extremely difficult to ambush militia. We seldom see any trace of their presence. My own losses have resulted from militia snipers using long range hunting rifles. My men have become reluctant to leave the confines of Ripley unless they travel in platoon-sized formations. In my case, perhaps I should form sniper teams and stalk the militia snipers?"

General Dietrich thought about Colonel Rogers' idea then responded, "In your case, I believe sending out your own sniper teams may work best. You may even consider positioning your teams so that they can mutually support one another. That is, if one team is hit, the enemy militia investigating their kill would become targets themselves."

"Good point, sir. I'll let you know how it works."

"Colonel Thompson, I haven't heard from you. What about the Natchez area – could you establish ambush teams?"

"Yes sir. I believe ambush teams would work for us, too. The militia forces operating in my area are mostly infantry. I think roadside bombs using anti-personnel munitions would be highly effective."

General Dietrich added, "Don't forget any trails they may be using. You can emplace mines along trails and monitor all sites from your headquarters. And let me remind each of you; I want no civilian casualties. Make sure your target is militia before shooting.

"Gentlemen, if there are no additional comments or questions, I'll see each of you again next week. I am anxious to receive better reports from your efforts."

CHAPTER 25

RESCUE, CAPTURE AND ESCAPE (MILITIA FORCES)

With Sean's death occurring a few days earlier, nobody felt like celebrating New Year's Day. The first of January was just another day. Colonel Maxon and Sergeant Major Peters stopped by to give us an update on the war.

We assembled in the local church and Colonel Maxon began, "Ladies and gentlemen, I'm very proud of what you accomplished in December. We've had a tough time with the invaders. The Earth soldiers arrived on our planet with numerical superiority in soldiers and equipment. You met their force with initiative and courage. While every fire team has experienced some losses, your unit cohesion has held firm and you have inflicted great damage to the enemy. Through your successes, he has abandoned some of his captured locations and is withdrawing into fewer places which he can defend. Forcing the enemy into fewer places means we control more of Haven. Because of your victories, several of our production facilities are coming back on line. Additionally, Militia Headquarters has established a prisoner of war camp where captured Earth soldiers may be interned.

"That's the good news. Unfortunately, our war with Earth has only begun. I've been told we can expect a second and third wave of invaders. But no matter – I believe these Earth soldiers have been sent on a one-way mission; especially since we learned our Third Battalion was massacred. This atrocity will not go unpunished. I am pleased to announce a bounty has been placed on members of the enemy's 415th Armored Battalion. For every member of the 415th Battalion captured alive and turned over to Militia Headquarters, the person responsible for the capture will be awarded a twenty-four hour pass. Are there any questions?"

"Sir, where might we find the 415th?"

Colonel Maxon laughed then replied, "I'm told they're bivouacked in Columbus. We have to defeat the enemy located at Camp Shelby and Johnson Springs Reservation before moving on to Columbus. Don't worry; it's just a matter of time before we reach Columbus and I'm pretty sure the Earth soldiers are staying put."

"Sir, when are we going to recapture Camp Shelby?"

"I don't know. The enemy may choose to withdraw and consolidate their forces at Johnson Spring Reservation before we have enough strength to attack Camp Shelby. Militia Headquarters will decide when we're ready to launch a full-scale attack. In the meantime, our orders are to continue ambushing the enemy whenever possible and destroy him one soldier at a time."

* * *

Two days later an alert was sounded and fire team members hurriedly assembled at Helen's cheetah. She announced, "Fire Team Four has stumbled into an ambush. Colonel Maxon has ordered his fire teams to converge at Fire Team Four's coordinates and launch a rescue operation. Expect heavy fire from the enemy. We're closest so we'll be first to make contact. Let's saddle up and go. I'll give more details en route."

I climbed into my cheetah, started the vehicle and turned on the comm unit. I heard Helen's voice saying, "Five, when we engage the enemy, I want you behind me and to my left. Do you copy?"

"Roger, One. In this formation, which targets do I engage?"

"Engage targets from my six o'clock to my nine o'clock."

"Wilco. India Five out." I thought to myself, *'her instructions sound identical to those given to me on the day we first met. The only difference is I now respect the woman.'*

Helen set a fast pace for the cheetahs. Sergeant Delucca, designated as India Two, was the fifth cheetah in our hasty march. The four haulers remained behind.

Helen announced, "All Indias - here is a situation report: Only one cheetah remains operational in Fire Team Four. We'll be at their location within two minutes. Order of battle is: Sweep to the right then turn left and attack in line formation. All acknowledge."

Each cheetah warrior sent an acknowledgement.

She continued, "Five, your new position is behind me and to the right. Engage targets from my three o'clock to my six o'clock."

"India Five - WILCO"

Wham! A large explosion hit nearby and rocked my cheetah. We had arrived at the ambush site. The terrain in front was mostly open with a few low rolling hills. I could see Fire Team Four's cheetahs. They were not moving and smoke was streaming from each vehicle. I couldn't see enemy vehicles but there were some trees in the distance on my left so I concluded they must be hiding there.

Helen ordered an increase in speed and we accelerated to our maximum speed.

"One, this is Four – have been hit and cannot move forward"

"Four, shoot any target that comes your way. All other Indias – stay with me."

Even at a high rate of speed, I was almost hit by incoming rounds. The enemy was firing constantly and several rounds only narrowly missed my speeding cheetah.

"Indias – execute a hard left, *NOW!*"

Helen's cheetah slewed to the left and began moving toward the enemy fire units. I raced about thirty meters beyond Helen's cheetah before turning left. Helen had already driven about a hundred meters ahead of me but I was positioned to her right and able to spot any targets to her three to six o'clock position.

Our rapid turn momentarily threw off the enemies' aim. Everybody began firing as we continued moving forward. As we neared the enemy positions, there was no shortage of targets. I spotted an enemy cheetah to Helen's right and engaged him with my main gun. My first round hit his turret and my second blew the turret off his vehicle. That was my second kill but I didn't have time to celebrate because another enemy cheetah appeared in my sights. His shot missed me and my return shot missed him. It was now a matter of who was able to shoot first and score.

I fired a fraction of a second before my opponent and saw his vehicle hit. His final shot just missed my cheetah. Before I could locate another target, I felt my head snap back, a loud bang blasted my ears and my cockpit began filling up with smoke. I was unable to move or breathe. A surreal feeling came over me and I felt like I was floating. The lighting around me dimmed and I couldn't remember anything else.

* * *

I woke up with a splitting headache. My ears were ringing and everything looked fuzzy. Someone was talking but I couldn't understand what was being said. Mercifully, I drifted back to sleep.

Sometime later, I awoke again and found myself lying on a bed in a tent. A nurse appeared and said, "Private Collins, welcome back. How are you feeling today?"

Hesitatingly, I replied, "I feel okay, just hungry and very thirsty. Where am I and what day is it?"

She smiled and gave me a cup with a straw and said, "Today is Tuesday and you've been at our field hospital for three days."

"I remember being in my cheetah and getting hit by something but everything else is a blank."

"The doctor will want to see you. He should be making his rounds shortly. He will be able to answer all your questions. In the meantime, if you need anything, give me a shout."

After she left, I looked around the tent and noticed several soldiers were in the tent, too. Judging by their bandages, some were in pretty bad shape. I started examining myself and discovered I had a large bandage on my head. I was really sore and my head started throbbing whenever I moved.

A few minutes passed before the doctor made his visit. He was young and had a businesslike manner about him. An orderly accompanied the doctor and recorded the doctor's conversations with other patients.

The doctor stopped by each patient and briefly spoke with the person before moving on. Arriving at my bed, he smiled and said, "Welcome back to the living, Private Collins. For a while, we were afraid you might not wake up."

"Glad I woke up too, sir. Can you tell me what injuries I have?

After consulting his noteputer he said, "Collins, you received a severe concussion. The good news is you've regained consciousness. Additionally, you have a few bruises on parts of your upper torso but those are not serious and should heal nicely." He pulled up a chair and continued, "I heard that was some firefight you boys got into. What do you remember?"

"Sir, I don't remember much. I was sitting in my cheetah and I'm afraid I can't recall anything else; except I do remember being hit, and then everything seemed to go dark. I must have passed out."

He nodded then said, "That's a good start. I believe your memory will return; perhaps in bits and pieces. Tell me, do you recall to which militia unit you are assigned?"

I don't know why, but an alarm went off in my head when I heard that question. I hesitated giving the doctor an answer. Finally, I said, "Sir, I can't recall my unit designation. Is that bad?"

He replied, "No that just means that you are still recovering from a severe concussion. I have every expectation that you will fully regain your memory. In the meantime, I want you to take it easy and get lots of rest. Are you hungry?"

"Yes sir. I could eat a horse and a beer would taste wonderful."

The doctor laughed and turned to the nurse; asking her to get me some food and water. He and the orderly then left the tent.

When the nurse returned with a tray of food, I asked her, "Where are we?"

She replied, "We are just outside Johnson Springs Reservation."

"What unit is this?"

She said, "We are the 621st Mobile Surgical and Rehabilitation Unit."

"Thank you, nurse. I sure hope my memory comes back soon."

She smiled and left the tent. I lay in my cot thinking about the conversations I had heard. *It didn't make sense; why was I near Johnson Springs Reservation? That was over a hundred kilometers from the ambush site and we were told military posts had been captured by the Earth soldiers. Who does the 621st belong to; us or them?*

Things got real quiet at nightfall. Other than an occasional groan, the soldiers in the tent were asleep. I waited a couple of hours then slowly got out of my bed. As I stood up, everything began spinning around. I sat on the edge of my bed until the spinning slowed. I found my uniform and boots underneath my bed and put them on. Once dressed, I took a few wobbly steps; regaining some semblance of balance and slowly walked out of the tent into the night.

I didn't see anyone in the hospital area so I continued walking until I found the motor pool. There were a couple of floodlights at the entrance and a lone guard sitting in a chair. He had a gun on his lap and appeared to be asleep. I looked around, found a fairly large rock, and I sneaked up behind him and hit the side of his head with the rock. He slouched to one side before falling out of his chair. I picked up his rifle, checked to see that it was loaded, took his ammo belt and walked into the motor pool.

There were several haulers and ambulances parked in two rows. The unmistakable Earth military emblem was visible on the vehicle doors. I climbed into the nearest hauler and checked its battery power level. It would have been heroic to disable the other vehicles but my luck could be running pretty thin and I didn't want to chance being caught. I started the hauler and slowly drove out of the motor pool and away from the hospital unit.

It was good to be back in a hauler. The Earth vehicle was almost identical to our militia haulers. After reaching the highway, I headed south toward Sparta. As each kilometer rolled by, I began planning my next move. Continuing to drive on the highway would be stupid. Based on my previous experience, a military vehicle might be equipped with a tracking device which could pinpoint my location and eventually reveal my destination to the enemy. Also, I was a target for any militia unit waiting in ambush. Any militiaman seeing the Earth emblem on the hauler's door would probably shoot first then look inside the vehicle. The only feasible alternative was to ditch the hauler and proceed on foot.

At the first opportunity, I turned right onto an unpaved road and drove about ten kilometers before parking the hauler underneath some large trees. I took the rifle and started walking cross-country toward Sparta. It was slow going because I was still weak from the concussion. My head was hurting and each step caused a small jolt of pain. At least I was free and alive. By my estimate, I was about 350 kilometers from Sparta. It would take many days to walk that distance and I would need to find food and shelter along the way.

At dawn I arrived at a farm and cautiously walked up to the house. I left my rifle at the gate and approached the front porch. "Hello, is there anyone home?"

An elderly couple came out the front door and stood on the porch. The man was holding a shotgun which he kept pointed at the floor.

I raised my hands and said, "My name is Private John Collins and I have escaped from an Earth military hospital."

The man said, "What do you want?"

"Sir, I need some food if you can spare it."

The man asked, "Are you armed?"

"My rifle is leaning against the front gate."

Without taking his eyes off me, he said to his wife, "Sarah, get his rifle and bring it into the house." He added, "Private Collins, walk toward me and keep those hands in the air."

Holding his weapon against my back, he frisked me to make sure I had no other weapon. As he walked around to face me, he said, "My name is Larry Patterson and this is my wife, Sarah. What's your story, young man?"

I replied, "Mr. Patterson, I awoke yesterday from a concussion in a hospital run by Earth soldiers. I escaped last night and am trying to get far away from my captors and back to my militia unit."

"Lucky for you, Private Collins, we're loyal Haven residents. Come inside and we'll get you some food."

Sarah put some food on the table and gave me something for my headache. "Private Collins, you look like you are in pain. Take these tablets."

"Ma'am, I don't know how you knew it, but my head is hurting like someone hitting me with a brick. Thanks for the medicine."

I told them about my escape and Larry asked, "Where did you leave the hauler?"

"The hauler is about five kilometers to the north, just off an unpaved road underneath some trees. I figured that they might have a tracking device on the hauler and I don't want to become their prisoner again."

Sarah said, "Larry, let the boy finish his meal; you can talk later."

As I finished eating, Sarah asked me, "Private Collins, would you like to take a shower? Also, your uniform looks like it needs washing."

"Ma'am, taking a shower would be great."

"Larry, get a pair of Jimmy's socks and some underwear for Private Collins. Also, bring me his uniform and let him wear Jimmy's robe after his shower."

Larry escorted me to Jimmy's bedroom and laid out the clothing items on the bed. He said, "The shower is in the next room. When you are done, you are welcome to these items; they should fit."

"Sir, won't Jimmy mind?"

Larry looked at the floor and slowly shook his head. He said, "No, Jimmy won't mind. We buried him four weeks ago."

"What happened?"

There were tears in Larry's eyes when he answered. "He threw a rock at some Earth soldiers who were stealing meat from our smokehouse. One of the soldiers shot Jimmy in the stomach. He died in agony several hours later. We couldn't get him to the doctor because my hauler had been confiscated."

"I am so sorry for your loss. I hate Earth for invading our planet; so many people have lost loved ones during the past few weeks."

Larry looked at me and slowly nodded his head.

After a hot shower and getting dressed in a clean uniform, I felt much better and was ready to resume my hike.

Sarah packed some food and as I took my leave from them. I said, "Thank you both for helping me. Mr. Patterson, if you decide to get that hauler I abandoned, I recommend you hide it and avoid using it right away and be sure you paint the vehicle another color."

"John, where will you sleep?"

"Ma'am, probably in the woods and in barn lofts."

"Wait a minute. I have an old quilt I'll give you. As you know, it gets pretty cold at night."

"Thank you so very much for your kindness." The nights were cold at this time of the year and having that quilt probably saved my life.

They sure were nice people. I left their home determined to get some payback for their suffering.

The remainder of my walk back to Sparta was uneventful. On a few occasions, I felt that someone was following me but I never spotted anyone. I stayed off the roads and scrounged for food along the way. Sometimes I would shoot a rabbit or a squirrel and other times I would beg from a farmer. The few people I met were only too glad to help. They hated Earth soldiers and were happy to share what they had.

* * *

Helen was lacing her boots when Sergeant Delucca entered the loft. "Ma'am, there is an officer from Militia Headquarters who wants to see you."

"Thank you, Sergeant Delucca. Please tell the officer I will be with him shortly."

"The officer is a 'she'."

"Okay, thanks."

* * *

"Good morning, Ma'am. Warrant Officer Ramses reporting as ordered."

"Please be at ease Ramses. My name is Lieutenant Sarah Webber. I'm from Militia Headquarters and my job is investigating war crimes. I've read your report and watched your vid recording of Fort Mantachie. However, I need to talk with you about some specifics you witnessed regarding the Third Battalion's fate."

After a lengthy interview, Lieutenant Webber added, "Ramses, in your report you mention Private John Collins being with you at the time. Is he available for questioning?"

"No Ma'am. Private Collins was listed as missing a couple of days ago during a battle with the enemy. Because we couldn't locate his body, we believe he may have been captured."

"This Private Collins; is he about one hundred eighty centimeters tall, athletic build, with blonde hair and blue eyes?"

"Yes Ma'am. You've described his appearance perfectly. Do you know him?"

Lieutenant Webber laughed and said, "As a matter of fact, John Collins and I dated for several weeks prior to us being drafted. Can you imagine me, an attorney, dating a ditch digger? In any case, our dating served its purpose; it drove my cheating ex-husband crazy!"

Helen felt her blood pressure rising. Trying to rein in her emotions, she said, "Ma'am, Private John Collins is a brave and highly intelligent soldier. In addition to being the best mechanic I've ever known, he's an accomplished warrior who personally destroyed several enemy vehicles before his cheetah was hit."

Lieutenant Webber interrupted, "Hold on, Ramses. You don't have to defend John. I'm sure he's a good soldier." She grinned and quietly added, "I know for a fact he has lots of stamina."

Helen's eyes were blazing when she responded, "Lieutenant Webber, may I be excused? I have other duties to attend."

"Ramses, thank you for helping me with my investigation. On a personal note, I do hope John turns up. I sense he means a great deal to you."

As Helen watched Lieutenant Webber drive away, she was thinking, *'You bitch. If I ever see you again, I'll forget about rank as I beat your face to a bloody pulp and pull your dyed blonde hair out by the roots!'* This was a new feeling for Helen. She was surprised to discover how possessive she had become toward John. Helen said a quiet prayer that John would return safely. There was so much she wanted to tell him.

CHAPTER 26

THE SETUP (EARTH FORCES)

"Lieutenant Rigby, my name is Major Douglas Baird. I'm on the operations staff assigned to General Dietrich's headquarters. Colonel Morrissey informed me you were planning to release a prisoner tonight. Did you get the tracking device implanted?"

"Yes sir. We put it under his scalp near an existing cut. Both places are hidden by the same bandage. I'm sure he won't find it."

"How long will it be active?"

"Once activated, this model has a thirty-day life span."

"What preparations have you made to facilitate his escape?"

"We'll put his uniform and boots under his bed, administer sleeping pills to all other patients in the tent, remove all walking patrols, and we have a volunteer who will pretend to sleep while guarding the motor pool. We could give Private Collins a flashlight but that might tip our hand."

"Good work, Lieutenant. I hope this plan works as well as your sarcasm. You have no idea how hard it is to find the militia. We've learned militia units are no larger than squads and are scattered throughout the countryside. Being able to find one and eliminate it has been largely a matter of luck. If this tracking device works, the prisoner should lead us to his home base where we'll be able to kill or capture another nest of traitors. Incidentally, what's the prisoner's name?"

"His name is Private John Collins. We know he's a cheetah warrior but he wouldn't reveal his unit."

"Where was he captured?"

"He was captured just north of the Haven National Wildlife Refuge. His unit responded to a request for assistance. Another small militia unit had stumbled into one of our ambush teams.

"Colonel Morrissey's ambush team had wiped out a militia unit of five cheetahs when more militia units began arriving at the ambush site. Private Collins was part of the militia rescue team.

"When the militia rescuers arrived, Colonel Morrissey received a call for help from his ambush team and sent reinforcements. However, before our reinforcements could reach the ambush site, the militia had withdrawn and simply vanished. Both sides took heavy losses with nobody being able to declare victory.

"During the battle, my intelligence team was able to capture Private Collins and bring him back to our hospital unit near Johnson Springs for interrogation."

"Why did you recommend he be released?"

"Sir, Private Collins is only a cheetah warrior. We're satisfied he doesn't possess any useful knowledge. I felt it would be more productive to let him escape and track him to his unit. Had he been an officer, I would not have recommended his release."

"How were you with the ambush team in the first place?"

"It was blind luck, sir. Please forgive the pun. We had been visiting each ambush site hoping to capture a prisoner for interrogation when the militia unit came into range."

"Okay, keep me informed. I'm making a report to General Dietrich on this mission. Naturally, you can expect a reward if your plan works."

"Major Baird, what if my plan doesn't work?"

"You may find yourself assigned to an infantry unit manning an ambush site."

CHAPTER 27

TRACKING A FOX TO HIS DEN (EARTH FORCES)

Sergeant Yonas Teshome, a scout assigned to the 351st Infantry Battalion, was the best tracker in his unit. Lieutenant Gibson, his platoon leader, had personally briefed Yonas on the importance of this mission. "Sergeant Teshome, you're being assigned to track Private Collins, a militia soldier captured during an ambush. Lieutenant Rigby went to a lot of trouble to capture Collins. The payoff will be when Collins leads you to his militia unit. After you locate his home base, send me the coordinates and our battalion will crush another militia unit. This mission may take several weeks and we'll resupply you on a periodic basis. Do you have any questions?"

"Sir, how did Private Collins escape in the first place?"

"He was allowed to escape so he could lead us to his home base."

"Where is he now?"

"Collins stole a hauler from the motor pool but ditched it sometime yesterday. Here are the coordinates of the hauler. Because he drove the hauler thirty kilometers to the south of Johnson Springs, it's logical he'll continue traveling in a southerly or even westerly direction. Unfortunately, the location device implanted in Collins only has a limited range; this is why you're needed to track him on foot."

"Sir, what is Private Collins' physical condition?"

"Collins received a severe concussion during his capture. He's weak and won't be able to make fast time."

* * *

A bitterly cold wind blew across endless plowed fields awaiting spring planting. Yonas lay shivering in his sleeping bag. After spending seven days following the slow walking Private Collins, he was anxious for his quarry to get up and begin moving. Earlier that evening, Yonas had received clean clothing, food rations and fresh batteries for his tracking monitor. The 'care package' was delivered by air drop from a small drone.

Dawn began to slowly break. A feeble light enabled Yonas to quickly scan the horizon for things which shouldn't be there. Yonas thought, '*Okay Private, get up and take me to your leader.*' Yonas smiled as he used the trite expression. Tracking Private Collins had been child's play for him. A majority of the time he didn't need a tracking monitor. Collins left a clear set of boot prints any child of Africa could follow. The only thing about this mission Yonas truly hated was the cold weather. Yes, there was wind in his native Africa but the wind in this part of Haven was cold and damp.

Yonas missed his family and his village. As a soldier, he frequently spent a couple of weeks away from his village each month tracking poachers and thieves. Today, Yonas marked his fourth month away from home. Most importantly, he was not in the next village or province; he was on another planet! Yonas eagerly volunteered to serve with the American invasion army as an auxiliary soldier. He simply couldn't turn down the huge sum of money offered for his unique services as a tracker. After this job, he would be a rich man.

The monitor chirped and Yonas grinned at the thought of Private Collins commencing his journey back to his unit.

The trick was not letting your quarry know you were following him. This meant avoiding farm houses where someone might spot him and alert Collins. Yonas was amazed at the amount of fertile land available to the people of Haven. Back on Earth, his family subsisted on a meager plot of arid land. He felt extremely lucky to have been chosen to augment the American army as a tracking specialist. He thought, *'After my military obligation is fulfilled, my family and I will volunteer to settle on Haven. The Americans have been keeping this planet a closely guarded secret!'*

CHAPTER 28

HOMECOMING (MILITIA FORCES)

I finally arrived in Sparta late one evening. The streets were quiet as I made my way to the barn where I had had been sleeping. As I climbed into the loft, a single light illuminated Helen sitting on a bale of hay doing some administrative work on her noteputer. I cleared my throat and was immediately faced with a pistol pointed toward me. I froze; neither moving nor breathing.

A startled Helen said, "Who are you and what do you want?"

I slowly replied, "I'm here for a shave and a shower. We can discuss what comes next at your discretion."

Helen dropped her pistol, rushed over and gave me a big hug and several kisses.

"John, where have you been? I thought you were captured! We couldn't find your body after the attack."

Between kisses I replied, "Helen, I don't remember what happened after my cheetah was hit. I woke up in a field hospital run by Earth soldiers just outside Johnson Springs Reservation. I escaped three weeks ago and walked most of the way back here."

`'"Are you okay? Where are you hurt?"

Other than some minor bruises, I got a concussion when my cheetah took a hit. My head is still sore."

Helen suddenly let go of me and wrinkling her nose, took a step back. "John, go take a shower; you stink!"

I grinned and thought, '*Same Helen; some things never change.*'

Helen added, "There's a doctor in Sparta. After you shower and put on clean clothes, we'll go to his house and wake him up if necessary. Your bandage is filthy and I want him to check your injury."

On the way to the doctor's house, Helen continued talking about the ambush and filed me in on what happened afterward.

She said, "It's odd. You were the only militia member captured. There were losses on both sides but I didn't see anyone gathering wounded until the fighting was over. The ambushers finally retreated after Colonel Maxon committed most of the Fifth Battalion's fire teams. After the battle, we found your cheetah but you were gone."

"Helen, I have no idea how or why I was captured. When my cheetah was hit, I was knocked unconscious. At any rate, it's good to be home. You're even more beautiful than I remembered."

"Thank you for the compliment. I'm glad your eyesight is undamaged!" Helen paused then continued, "Changing the subject, did you ever date a woman named Sarah Webber?"

"Yeah, we dated some prior to my being drafted. Why?"

"She's a lieutenant assigned to Militia Headquarters. Her job is investigating war crimes. Lieutenant Webber came by a couple of weeks ago and interviewed me about our reconnaissance mission. She mentioned that you and she dated for a few months."

"Yeah, I remember Sarah. It was fun at first. However, she struck me as being high maintenance and only caring about herself. After getting our draft notices, I began to realize Sarah and I weren't compatible. Since being drafted into the militia, I guess I have become more of an operator and less of a mechanic."

Helen laughed and said, "John, you can't imagine how much I missed you. It just didn't seem the same around here without you." After pausing she added, "Speaking of mechanics, my cheetah has gone days without being properly serviced."

I looked at her and said, "Well, look who has developed a sense of humor. Ma'am, I would never have suspected you were capable of being funny."

"John, this is the happiest I've been in weeks. Try not to spoil my mood with your usual smart-ass comments. Who knows, you may get lucky when we get back to the loft. Lieutenant Webber mentioned you have lots of stamina; maybe it's time you get to prove her assertion with me."

I grinned and thought, *'Patience is indeed its own reward – whatever that means.'*

The doctor examined my head and replaced the dirty bandage. He said I was healing nicely and gave me some pain pills to take as needed.

Later that evening I concluded Helen was well worth the wait. After some intense love making, I was holding a sleeping Helen in my arms and began thinking about Helen and me getting married. *'What would it be like to spend the remainder of my life with her? Would I ever get tired of Helen and want to date other women? What if she met someone else? Would we have children? How would our marriage work if Helen stayed in the militia?'*

* * *

I got up late the next morning and joined the members of Fire Team Six for breakfast. I was really glad to see them again.

Misty said, "John, we thought you had been captured! What happened to you?"

They, like Helen, were astonished to see me alive and well. During breakfast, I told them about my experience in the enemy field hospital and escape.

Sergeant Delucca said, "John, we managed to salvage your cheetah from the battlefield. Everybody has been working on it but we can't get it back to one hundred percent readiness. Parts are scarce; even welding rods are in short supply."

"Thanks, Sarge, I'm anxious to get started. I'll talk with the mechanics and find out what we need. Maybe someone in the village will be willing to swap parts."

"I hadn't thought of that approach. That's another reason I'm glad you're back with the team."

* * *

Three hours later, the entire maintenance crew was helping me repair my cheetah when Helen walked up and said, "Private Collins, there's an officer at the church who wants to talk with you. Be completely open and tell him everything he wants to know."

"Yes Ma'am."

* * *

"Sir, Private Collins reporting as ordered."

Returning my salute, he said, "At ease, Private Collins. My name is Captain Richard Price. I'm from the Office of Militia Intelligence and I need to talk with you about your recent experience. Have a seat and tell me your recollections from the beginning of the Fire Team Four rescue operation until your return to Fire Team Six."

I told Captain Price everything I could remember and didn't omit any detail. He took notes during my recitation.

"You said the 621st Mobile Surgical and Rehabilitation Unit and they were located near Johnson Springs Reservation?"

"Yes sir. I know we were near Johnson Springs Reservation because that's where I received my militia training. I never heard of that medical unit, though."

"Neither have I, Private Collins. This could only have been an elaborate setup designed to get intelligence from you and any other captured militia soldiers. I'm proud of you for not telling them anything. Earth forces are becoming more devious and your recent experience helps confirm our suspicions. According to our latest estimates, they could lose this war unless they get reinforcements."

He continued, "However, I'm surprised you were able to escape so easily. If that medical unit doubles as an interrogation facility, their security should have been much tighter. Just out of curiosity, would you mind standing? I have an electronic detector and would like to scan your body."

As Captain Price's scanner hovered near my left ear, the device screeched an alarm. He said, "Private Collins, it's just as I suspected; a tracking device has been implanted in you. Earth forces know every place you've been since your escape. I'll notify headquarters and you go warn Warrant Officer Ramses to get out of here - and hurry!"

I ran out of the church and found Helen talking with Sergeant Delucca. I interrupted their conversation saying, "Ma'am, Captain Price found a tracking device on me. He said we've got to move!"

Helen turned to Sergeant Delucca, "You heard the man, let's saddle up!"

Looking at me she said, "John, because the device on you is still active, I want you to take your cheetah and head out in another direction. Stay away from friendlies and don't use the comm link. Take some food with you and meet me at 9:00 AM at the original Fire Team Six site two days from now. I'll bring someone who can find and remove the device."

Within five minutes, Fire Team Six had vacated Sparta and were heading to their alternate location. I climbed in my cheetah and drove into the National Wildlife Refuge.

Eventually, I reached a secluded place in the Wildlife Refuge and hid the cheetah. The sun was dipping below the tree line when I left the cheetah and went scrounging for firewood. On returning, I saw a man walking around the cheetah. He was holding his rifle at the ready position and appeared to be searching the area. I carefully laid my firewood down and hid behind a tree. My rifle was safely stowed in the cheetah which meant I was practically defenseless against a man with a weapon.

Catching a glimpse of the man in the fading light, I noted he was an Earth soldier! Not daring to breathe, I waited for him to leave.

After several anxious moments, he finally walked away from my cheetah; leaving me an opportunity to quickly sprint to my vehicle and get inside. I softly closed the cheetah's hatch and decided to wait before driving away. As I looked out my periscope, the soldier came back into view and began walking toward my cheetah. When he entered the crosshairs of my anti-personnel gun, I gently squeezed the trigger and cut him to pieces. I recovered his identification tag and collected his equipment before dragging his body into some undergrowth and covering it with leaves and fallen limbs. While examining his identification tag, I wondered why Sergeant Yonas Teshome had been tracking me. A more immediate question was why had he returned to my vehicle? Was it possible he heard me closing the hatch or had he lost my trail and was coming back to get a new start? Whatever his reason, Earth forces had been reduced by one. As I drove away, I also wondered if any more enemy soldiers were in the area.

* * *

"Sir, we've lost contact with Sergeant Teshome."

"When did he last report?"

"He sent a message yesterday at noon stating Private Collins had spent the night in Sparta and was moving toward the Haven National Refuge. Teshome failed to report in last night."

"Okay, send a reconnaissance drone to his last location and see if Collins' homing signal can be picked up. We're going to be in big trouble if we've lost track of Private Collins."

* * *

For the next two days, I drove very little; trying to simulate the kilometers I walked each day getting back to Sparta. It was cold at night and in my haste to leave Sparta, I didn't take my sleeping bag or quilt. I slept near a small fire and used the cheetah's camouflage cover as a blanket. Fortunately, I knew this ordeal would be over soon. It's amazing how much you can tolerate when you know the end is near.

I arrived at our original Fire Team Six location promptly at 9:00 AM. Helen was already there waiting with a small medical team who quickly located and removed the tracking device. It had been inserted near the wound from my concussion and was practically invisible. The doctor said, "Private Collins, keep a clean dressing on the incision. You'll be sore for a few days but it should heal nicely."

"Thanks, Doc; I'm glad to get rid of that thing. I hate having someone spy on me."

Helen said, "Private Collins, get your cheetah and follow me."

"Yes Ma'am."

Helen led me to our new location. It was on the outskirts of Okolona in a deserted factory. Inside, the fire team's vehicles were aligned and temporary partitions had been set up for our sleeping quarters. Chuck, Fred, Wendy and Misty greeted me on my arrival and took me on a tour of the facility. The bathrooms even had showers and running hot water!

After inspecting the area, I turned to the group and said, "I feel like I've died and gone to heaven."

Fred laughed and replied, "Yeah, doing without makes you appreciate the little things in life, doesn't it? Speaking of which, we have your personal items in the back of my hauler. I'll get them for you."

Following a long hot shower, shave and getting into a clean uniform, I felt human again. That afternoon, Wendy spoke with me in private. She said, "John, I want you to know that after arriving at this location, WO Ramses went back and personally retrieved your belongings from Sparta. It seems strange that she would have risked so much to get your stuff since she was always yelling at you at Camp Shelby."

I attempted to dismiss her observation by saying, "No, not strange. It's because WO Ramses has learned the value of my mechanical and warrior skills."

I could tell she wasn't buying it when she started grinning and replied, "Yeah, if you say so." I quickly changed the subject because I knew Helen wouldn't want me to talk about our new relationship.

It was good to be back working on my cheetah. Misty was a big help. She knew the vehicle inside and out because it was the same one she maintained for Sean before he died. I also inspected Helen's cheetah and made sure it was one hundred percent. After completing the maintenance, I spent most of my spare time in the cockpit running combat simulations. Afterwards, Sergeant Delucca or Helen would critique my scores.

A few days later, Colonel Maxon stopped by and inspected the unit. He brought two haulers carrying food, ammunition and some spare parts. We eagerly accepted these much-needed items. Afterwards, we assembled in a local church and listened to his announcements.

"Ladies and gentlemen, today is the first day of February. We have been fighting this war for sixty three days. After taking some initial losses, our militia units are now winning most skirmishes. While your fire team has seen action and successfully engaged the enemy, other fire teams in the Fifth Battalion have experienced similar successes. Our militia battalions have reclaimed territory and inflicted a lot of casualties throughout Haven. The enemy has retreated to our major cities and military posts. He does not often venture out with less than platoon-sized forces and his aircraft have been reduced but not totally eliminated.

"Haven's military installations and manufacturing plants were bombed during the early days of the invasion. However, we're re-establishing a production capability at New Albany where cheetahs will be produced and distributed to new armor battalions.

"Because the enemy is pretty much confined to major cities, most of our manufacturing is being shifted to rural areas where we will produce new military equipment. For example, at Morgan City we're planning to manufacture a new armored vehicle named the leopard. This vehicle requires a two-man crew, mounts a larger main gun with a longer range and has advanced targeting capability. It's fast and has excellent armor protection. Additionally, we're building a new fighter which will help our militia gain air superiority on Haven. Unfortunately, it'll take a few years for us have access to these new weapons. In the meantime, militia headquarters is relying on battalions such as ours to keep the enemy at bay until we have enough weapons and soldiers to rid our world of these invaders.

"The best news to date is our capturing an exoatmospheric transport ship. We converted the ship into a weapons platform by mounting missile launchers on its hull. On January twelfth, it destroyed an incoming interstellar transport ship loaded with military supplies. This action has severely crippled Earth's forces on Haven and saved many lives of our militia.

"I'm asking each fire team to continue making strikes against our enemy. Let's keep him penned up in the cities and make it too costly to venture out into our territory."

Cheering from the fire team erupted.

When quiet was restored, he continued, "I have one additional matter to handle. Will Private John Collins please step forward?"

Totally surprised, I got up and stood at attention before Colonel Maxon.

"Private Collins, you've distinguished yourself both in training and here in the field. It is my pleasure to promote you to the rank of corporal." I was stunned and couldn't say anything. It was normal to serve in the militia for at least three years before getting promoted to corporal.

Colonel Maxon attached the non-commissioned officer chevron onto my uniform and shook my hand. After returning to my seat, he turned to Helen and said, "Warrant Officer Ramses you're now faced with a dilemma. You have two non-commissioned officers in your unit and only one is authorized. You must decide which NCO will be assigned elsewhere. I'll bring two replacements in a couple of days to fill all vacancies in your unit." Having dropped that bombshell, Colonel Maxon left.

After his departure, I was surrounded by the fire team members who offered their congratulations. I looked over at Helen and noticed her blank expression. This was not good news for us. That evening, we didn't talk much. Helen and I went to bed early. After a tender session of lovemaking, we held one another before falling asleep. During the night, I felt her shaking with quiet sobs and knew what was about to happen.

Early the following morning Helen called the team together and made her decision public. "Ladies and gentlemen, I've been given a difficult decision to make. I have to decide which member of our fire team is transferred. Both Sergeant Delucca and Corporal Collins are outstanding soldiers and have become friends to us all. Losing one will seem like the loss of a family member. I've decided that Sergeant Delucca will remain and Corporal Collins will move to a new unit. Colonel Maxon will return in the morning for Corporal Collins." With that said, Helen quickly walked away from the group.

Later that morning, I was briefing Helen on our vehicle status when Sergeant Delucca approached. He said, "Ma'am, we've put together a picnic basket for you and Corporal Collins. We can handle things here while you take a well-deserved day off and enjoy the countryside."

Clearly shocked, Helen quietly asked, "Why just Corporal Collins and me?"

He gave her a big grin and replied, "Ma'am, when you stopped yelling at John, we became suspicious of a change. And after observing you during recent briefings, meals and any other time you were together, we knew your relationship with one another had changed."

He continued, "Ma'am, I want you to know we understand your feelings for John. He's a good man and I'm sure he makes you happy. On a personal note, I know how difficult your decision today has been. Go have a wonderful time with the team's blessing; you've earned it."

Helen looked directly at Sergeant Delucca and said, "Thank you." She turned to me and said, "John, please get a hauler, we have a picnic to attend."

Helen and I had a great time that afternoon. We drove to a secluded spot along a lake. It was a perfect place for a lunch.

After lunch Helen said, "John, I can't tell you how relieved I am that our relationship is finally out in the open. My stomach has been tied in knots over this."

"Helen, you've been under so much stress lately. Combat, hiding from the enemy, loss of Sean, fear of people finding out about us and having to transfer me elsewhere is a lot for one person to bear. There is only one thing I can say which may take some of the burden from you."

"What would that be, John?"

"Helen, will you marry me? I want to spend the remainder of my life loving you."

Tears welled in her eyes as she replied. "Yes, John. I'll marry you. I've been thinking a lot about us recently. For example, I know exactly when I became attracted to you. It was the day we met when you challenged me to get my hands dirty helping you overhaul my cheetah's engine. I was so surprised that an enlisted man would ask that of me I said yes before thinking of an alternative."

She added, "When you began playing those awful practical jokes on me, I wanted to strangle you. After the 'stuck thermostat' prank, I realized what you said about me was true - I was being a real bitch toward you. In hindsight I think I treated you badly because I was afraid of becoming romantically involved with an enlisted soldier.

"After the invasion, we stopped fighting with one another and I began to appreciate how wonderful you are. I love talking with you and learning more about you and your family.

"John, I don't know when I started loving you. Likely it was the first night while returning from the reconnaissance mission. You are so caring and considerate. I hope fate is kind to us and we survive this war. I want us to spend many years together."

Helen paused then continued, "I was also worried that you might become romantically involved with another fire team member. You're not ugly and I've overheard a couple of the women talk about wanting to sleep with you."

I grinned at her confession and responded, "You didn't have to worry about that. Getting to know the real Helen behind the façade of the perfect woman warrior won my heart and made me want to be a better man." After pausing I added, "Which women were talking about me?"

I barely managed to dodge the piece of bread thrown at me.

CHAPTER 29

REBUILDING FIRE TEAM FOUR (MILITIA FORCES)

As promised, Colonel Maxon arrived with the replacements for Fire Team Six.

"Warrant Officer Ramses, here are your replacements. Private Jim Wilson is a warrior and Private Mary Castle is a mechanic. They are recent graduates of basic training. I'm sorry we don't have any equipment replacements; they are in high demand because some fire units are experiencing critical shortages."

"Sir, Corporal Collins is available for transfer." She added, "Will you tell me where Corporal Collins is being assigned?"

Colonel Maxon said, "Helen, I'll assign Corporal Collins to Fire Team Four as their second in command. As you recall, they lost all their cheetahs and their warriors in the ambush. I need Collins to help rebuild that unit. With his mechanical knowledge, leadership ability and his transition to warrior status, he'll be invaluable to the new fire team leader."

"Thank you, Sir. I know Corporal Collins will make an exceptional non-commissioned officer."

After a quick goodbye to the fire team, I shook hands with Sergeant Delucca who promised me he would look after Helen. Fred put my duffle and sleeping bag into the colonel's personal carrier while I walked up to Helen and gave her a big hug and kiss farewell. I felt my face turning red when I heard members of the fire team cheering. Turning, I saw a bunch of smiles. Even Colonel Maxon was grinning. Without looking back, I got into his carrier and we drove away.

After getting on the road, he looked at me and asked, "What are your intentions toward that woman, son?"

"Sir, I have asked Warrant Officer Ramses to marry me and she has accepted my proposal."

"Have you set a wedding date?"

"No sir, we became engaged only yesterday."

"Well, no point delaying it indefinitely. You never know what is about to happen during these unsettling times."

"Yes sir."

We drove approximately 25 kilometers before reaching the town of Sardis. During the thirty minute ride, Colonel Maxon detailed his expectations of me.

After arriving in Sardis, I unloaded my things and shook hands with Colonel Maxon. A couple of Fire Team Four members gathered around.

Colonel Maxon asked, "Where's your fire team leader?"

One replied, "Sir, she's in town with other fire team members. We expect her back shortly."

Colonel Maxon said, "Sorry I missed her. This is Corporal John Collins; your new non-commissioned officer." Turning to me he said, "Corporal Collins, I have another appointment. Please introduce yourself and give my regards to Warrant Officer Rebekah Lloyd when she returns."

Following Colonel Maxon's departure, I looked at the two soldiers and said, "I've been transferred from Fire Team Six. My job will be to help WO Lloyd prepare you for combat. What are your names?"

"Corporal, my name is Vic Dominowski. I'm a warrior."

"Corporal Collins, I'm Mary Holloway. I have been assigned as your mechanic. I'll take you to your quarters and we can get better acquainted along the way."

"Good to meet you both. Private Holloway, lead on."

As we walked toward my quarters, Mary asked, "Corporal Collins, how long have you been in the militia?"

"I've been in the militia about five months. I started out as a mechanic then got reassigned as a warrior. What about you?"

"I've been a mechanic for a year." She unnecessarily added, "I joined before the draft." Mary paused then continued, "And you were promoted to corporal only five months after being drafted? That must be a record!"

I laughed and said, "I don't know about a record but I've been lucky so far. I've had leaders who told me what they wanted then got out of the way so I could get the job done."

"Do you intend to operate that way in our fire team?"

"That's up to WO Lloyd. I have to talk with her first to get her guidance."

"Corporal Collins, we really need your help. WO Lloyd doesn't give us the impression she knows how to run a fire team. I really miss WO Franklin. As you know, he was killed in the ambush five weeks ago."

"Mary, I'm going to need your assistance. We cannot rebuild Fire Team Four if we denigrate our leader. Instead of criticizing WO Lloyd, let's figure out how to help her succeed. And for your information, what we say in private remains between us, okay?"

Mary thought for a moment then said, "Yes sir. I now understand why you were promoted so quickly. For the first time in two weeks I believe we have a chance of becoming a good fire team."

After stowing my gear, I asked Mary to give me a tour of the site. I especially wanted to inspect the cheetahs and haulers. While reviewing the equipment logs, I heard footsteps behind me. Turning around, I saw WO Rebekah Lloyd and the other members of Fire Team Four. I put the log book down and reported.

"Ma'am, Corporal John Collins reporting for duty." As I was saluting my new boss, I was immediately struck by her beauty. She was about one hundred fifty centimeters tall with striking blue eyes and light brown hair. I thought, '*How does Colonel Maxon manage to find such beauties to command his fire teams?*'

She returned my salute and said, "Welcome aboard, John. Let me introduce you to the other members of Fire Team Four. I see you've already met Vic and Mary. Anne and Rachael are my other warriors and Pete, Brenda, Tony, and Jo Anne are my mechanics. Folks, this is Corporal John Collins. Colonel Maxon told me John is a militia wunderkind." With that comment, she gave me a big smile, flashing her dazzling white teeth.

At that moment Jo Anne Davis interrupted my fantasizing by saying, "John Collins! How the hell did you become a warrior *and* get promoted so quickly? She turned to WO Lloyd and said, "Rebekah, this guy attended mechanics school with me! He's a damn fine mechanic, too."

I spoke up and said, "Hello Private Davis. It's really good to see you." Turning to WO Lloyd, I said, "Ma'am, whenever you have some free time, I would appreciate a word between us."

WO Lloyd said, "Okay, let's meet at 9:00 AM tomorrow." She then addressed her fire team members and said, "Boys and girls, now that we have a complete fire team and have been given a secret weapon, let's celebrate. The drinks are on me!"

After they left, I resumed my inspection of the vehicles. Mary stayed with me and made notes. This was not going to be an easy assignment. Based on my initial impression, discipline was practically nonexistent and the vehicles were not being maintained according to standards.

I was nervous about the meeting with WO Lloyd. If I pushed her too much, she would turn against me and everything would go downhill. Alternatively, not impressing on her the importance of change would be disastrous for the fire team's effectiveness.

* * *

After clearing the dining room at 8:45 AM, I sat alone at a table with a cup of coffee. Mary was posted at the entrance to keep other fire team members out. At 9:05, WO Lloyd made her appearance. She wore dark glasses and reeked of alcohol.

I stood up and offered her a cup of coffee. "Thanks, John. After our celebration last night, I could use a cup of hot black coffee. Now what did you want to talk about?"

I sat down across from her and said, "Ma'am, we're both new at our jobs and I need to know your vision for your fire team and what you expect of me."

"Fair enough; those are good questions. First of all, I envision leading a highly capable unit that can complete assigned missions while remaining unscathed. Secondly, I expect you to train our warriors and mechanics so we can accomplish our mission."

"Ma'am, those are worthy goals and I'll do everything in my power to help you succeed." I paused then continued, "One key to our success will be to instill discipline within the fire team. Without discipline, soldiers may question decisions or hesitate to follow orders. In battle, this can lead to devastating results. For me to instill discipline, I'm going to need your help."

"You need my help? John, I'm putting you in charge. What more do you need from me?"

"Ma'am, you can't afford to be their friend or permit them to call you by your first name. I'll inform the fire team but implementing this change will only work if you agree this is the right thing to do."

"Corporal Collins, I intend to run this unit on a very informal basis without the usual military pomp and circumstance. I used an informal leadership style in college after being elected president of my sorority. I don't understand why that same leadership style can't be used here."

"Ma'am, from what little I know about you, I would bet anything you were very successful as a sorority president. But let's discuss some of the differences between your sorority and your fire team."

"One, every member of your sorority was a volunteer and was excited about being able to join an elite social group. Alternatively, some of your fire team members were drafted and don't want to be here.

"Two, the purpose of your sorority was to create an environment where people with common interests could bond, help one another through college, perform civic actions, and establish lifelong friendships. Contrast that with the purpose of your fire team which is to kill Earth soldiers.

"Three, if any member of your sorority became disenchanted with the organization, they could voluntarily leave or if they didn't live up to expectations, you could expel them. In Fire Team Four, what we get is what we have. If our soldiers don't meet our standards, we work with them until they do. And we don't let them quit.

"Four, and most importantly, if a sorority member fails a task, the organization could look bad and embarrass its members. Here, if a fire team member fails his or her task, someone or all of us could die.

"Ma'am, in my opinion, discipline is our key to a successful fire team. Without discipline we cannot have an effective fighting force and our casualties will only get higher."

"Wow! That was quite a speech. Corporal Collins, I take it you're not impressed with your new fire team or its leader?"

"Ma'am, my being impressed is of no importance. I'm only interested in helping you build an exceptional fire team. With better discipline and rigorous training, your fire team will be prepared to execute its assigned missions."

"And what about casualties; all the warriors assigned to Fire Team Four were killed in the ambush. I'm sure they were prepared to fight."

"Ma'am, that was a tragedy and I'm sure our mechanics have not fully recovered from losing the warriors they supported. In this war with Earth, there's no guarantee any of us will survive to the end. However, it is a fact our chances of survival and victory in each battle will improve with training.

"The commander and his four warriors in Fire Team Four were killed because they ran into an overwhelming force. In fact, I was wounded in that same battle. You should also note Fire Team Six lost a warrior and equipment in an earlier battle. Ultimately, we were able to beat the enemy. But without training and discipline, the Earth soldiers would have annihilated our unit."

"Collins, I assume from your comments that you've actually been in combat?"

"Yes, Ma'am, I've been under enemy fire on a couple of occasions."

WO Lloyd hesitated and then said, "Okay, where do we start?"

"Ma'am, leave that to me. If any fire team member approaches you about the changes, please say to them, 'talk to Corporal Collins.' I'll take it from there."

"Keep me informed."

"Yes Ma'am and with your permission, I'd like to get started."

"That's fine. I'm going back to my quarters."

* * *

Just outside the door, I found Mary talking with Brenda and Vic. "Mary, please get every fire team member into the dining room. We're having a meeting."

As the members finally arrived, I stood in front of the eight soldiers and began. "Ladies and gentlemen, my name is Corporal John Collins. You may address me as Corporal or Corporal Collins. Our fire team leader is WO Rebekah Lloyd. In the future, you will address her as WO Lloyd or Ma'am. The days of calling your leaders by their first names have ended.

"The second item on today's agenda is the condition of your vehicles. Here is a list of discrepancies I noted on your haulers and cheetahs. Private Davis, I am designating you as the senior mechanic. Your job will be to supervise all maintenance and ensure our vehicles are one hundred percent. Your first priority is the cheetahs. Keep me informed about the status of our equipment and let me know if you need parts. If you mechanics have no questions or comments, you're dismissed."

After the mechanics filed out, I turned to the warriors and said, "Ladies and gentlemen, until our cheetahs are one hundred percent, we're without training assets. For the remainder of today, I want you to construct a sand table and make ten small wooden objects to represent cheetahs from opposing sides. Also, we need a small arms firing range. Establish a safe area which will accommodate two people simultaneously firing at targets up to 100 meters away. Find something to make silhouette targets. We need one target for each fire team member. Private Pearson, you're in charge of completing these projects. Do you have any questions?"

"Corporal, what's a sand table?"

"It's a three dimensional terrain map. Use one of the dining tables. Fasten boards along each edge so dirt or sand will not spill onto the floor. Get small twigs to represent trees and use your imagination to create other terrain features. Do you have additional questions? If not, you're dismissed."

Following the meeting, I decided to talk with WO Lloyd. I knocked on her door and evidently woke her up. When she finally opened the door I said, "Hello Ma'am. I'm here to brief you on what the fire team is doing today."

"Collins, as you have undoubtedly noticed, I'm not feeling well. Why do you insist on bothering me?"

I pushed past her and walked into her room. Facing her I said, "Ma'am, I know you have a hangover. I suspect some of your fire team members also have hangovers, but I didn't let them off the hook this morning. As you should be well aware, we must lead by example."

"What does *that* mean?"

"It means we can't have a double standard. What's good for the soldier is good for the leader. If every soldier was able to get out of work because of a hangover, we'd never get anything done."

"Collins, you're a real prick. Whatever happened to, 'rank has its privileges'? Since you don't want me to be familiar with the troops, I think I'm due some extra benefits!"

I laughed and replied, "Ma'am, as leaders we endure the same hardships and become more proficient with our soldier skills than our troops. We're expected to be in better physical condition and know more about fighting cheetahs than our warriors. We're trainers and counselors. We're the first to enter combat and the last to retreat. Leaders assign tasks to subordinates; recommend some for promotion and others for court martial. We lead soldiers into combat where some or all may be killed."

I continued, "And you may be asking yourself, 'As a leader, what do I get out of this?' Well, you get more pay and recognition for a job well done. But if you're a really good leader, your soldiers will love and trust you. They will obey your orders and follow you to hell and back. In my opinion, that's the ultimate reward for a leader."

After a long pause, WO Lloyd looked at me and said, "Collins, this isn't what Uncle Morris said when he arranged for me to join the militia and receive a commission."

I asked, "Who is Uncle Morris?"

Rebekah answered, "Uncle Morris is Brigadier General Morris Barnett currently assigned to Militia Headquarters."

"What did Uncle Morris tell you about serving in the militia?"

"Well, he said he couldn't get me a direct commission until I served in a cheetah unit. After commanding a fire team, I would get my commission and a transfer to Militia Headquarters where I would work in the Propaganda Office."

"Wow! That sounds like your Uncle Morris has everything planned for you. But until you get transferred out of this fire team, how hard do you want to work?"

"What do you mean?"

"For starters, what training have you had on a cheetah?"

"I was given a one-week familiarization course by a militia captain assigned to Uncle Morris' staff. Captain Phillip Barr said I had a lot of promise."

Ma'am, that's great news. If you're willing, you may want to help me score the fire team's individual simulations. Incidentally, are you in good physical condition?"

"You mean, like running and doing exercises?"

"Yes Ma'am. All of us need to be in top physical condition if we're going to have a chance of surviving fire fights."

"I worked out at a gym before joining the militia. My trainer seemed happy with my conditioning."

"That's excellent. How long has it been since you worked out?"

"Oh I guess about a month. As you can see, there's no gym in this hick town."

"Well, we'll just have to improvise. In the back of the Soldier's Manual is a section on physical fitness. We can use that to lead the fire team in morning exercises. Maybe you and I can review the exercises late this afternoon before dinner?"

Rebekah thought a moment then replied, "Yes, meet me here at 4:00 PM."

"That's great, Ma'am. I will see you here at 4:00. Please wear your athletic gear because I know you'll want to practice the exercises with me before leading the fire team tomorrow morning."

After leaving Rebekah's quarters, I toured the motor pool and met with Jo Anne. "Private Davis, how's it going?"

Jo Anne looked up from her work and grinningly said, "It's so hard for me to get accustomed to your promotion! I'm not surprised though after reading your codex. Corporal Collins, you've survived some harrowing experiences. You're lucky to be alive!" She continued,

"Three cheetahs are one hundred percent, one is undergoing final checkout and this one needs a new fire control circuit board."

"Do we have a spare circuit board?"

"Yeah, there's one but it needs some work. I plan to do the job myself."

"Have one of the other mechanics watch you make the repair. By the way, how did you get access to my codex? Isn't that data encoded?"

Jo Anne grinned and said, "Rebekah, excuse me; WO Lloyd gave me her password. I wanted to check you out."

"Fair enough; what are the other mechanics doing?"

"They're taking a break until I get this cheetah back on line."

"Round them up and get them started on the haulers. I don't want you doing all the work around here while they're sitting around scratching their butts."

I next visited the dining facility. Anne and Rachael were working on the sand box. I asked, "Private Pearson, where is Private Dominowski?"

"He's setting up the firing range."

"Let's go see him."

We found Vic driving in the boundary stakes of the firing range. He had already built a frame downrange capable of holding two targets.

"Private Dominowski, it's looking good. Since you've done such a good job, you'll have the honor of being the first to try it out."

Vic grinned and said, "Thank you, Corporal! When do we get started?"

"Tomorrow morning after we complete our physical fitness exercises. Private Pearson, let's get back to the dining room and help Private Harris complete our sand box."

With three of us working, the sand box was quickly completed. After Vic arrived, I placed the enemy in a strategic location and put the friendly forces behind a hill. I said, "Okay, the enemy is dug in on this hill. You've been ordered to attack. I want you three to study this problem and we'll discuss your solution this evening during dinner."

Leaving them at the sand table, I got a hauler and used its odometer to mark off a one-kilometer course we could use for physical training. I marked the course with strips of cloth tied to stakes placed about one hundred meters apart. After completing this task, I took a piece of two centimeter pipe and fastened it between the back of the maintenance building and a post. It was crude but it would suffice for doing pull-ups.

At 4:00 PM I knocked on WO Lloyd's door. She answered immediately and we ran the one-kilometer course. We stopped and I said, "Tomorrow morning, we'll need to run it three times after the fire team has completed physical exercises."

"What physical exercises?"

We walked over to the back of the maintenance building and I replied, "Ma'am, we'll do sit-ups, pushups and pull-ups which work the torso and upper body muscles."

"Show me."

After completing the exercises, I watched as Rebekah took her turn doing pull-ups. She managed three before dropping to the ground.

"Good start, Ma'am. The goal is five for women and ten for men. I have some ideas for building improvised weights so you can concentrate on increasing your upper body strength."

"Corporal Collins, I don't know who thought up these exercises, but why should I have to be able to do five pull-ups? It doesn't take much strength to fire the main gun on a cheetah."

"You are absolutely right, Ma'am. Firing the cheetah's main gun is akin to pulling the trigger on a pistol. However, it takes a good deal more strength to open a stuck hatch while your cheetah is on fire and you begin to smell your hair and clothes burning."

"What a disgusting thought! How do you come up with such crude and ridiculous examples?"

"Ma'am, during the firefight following the ambush of Fire Team Four, one warrior from Fire Team Six escaped from his burning cheetah after being hit by an attacker. He reported the hatch became stuck when heat generated by the explosion warped the hull. I'm sure he had a lot of adrenalin flowing but the fact that he was in excellent physical shape and was able to force the hatch open probably saved his life."

"*Okay*! Okay, you win. I'll get in better shape. What's next on your agenda?"

"I've given the warriors a tactical problem using a sand table. Tonight at dinner, I'm planning a strategy session with them to hear their solution. I hope you'll join us."

"That's fine for dinner conversation but I thought I was the leader of the fire team. Shouldn't I be responsible for developing tactical solutions?"

"Ma'am, you're exactly right. It's your primary job. However, what happens to our three warriors if you and I become incapacitated? Shouldn't they be trained to continue the fight? I would like to know our fire team will continue fighting should we become disabled."

"What role should I play in tonight's discussion?"

"Ma'am, I recommend we simply ask questions about the warriors' solution. The main point will be to teach them how to best use their skills in various tactical situations."

On the way back to Rebekah's quarters I asked, "Have you heard when our fire team will receive its first assignment?"

"No, Colonel Maxon is relying on us to give him a date. When would you recommend?"

"Ma'am, everyone has completed their basic training. Individually, they should know their jobs. I recommend we assess the physical fitness of all fire team members and how well we handle our cheetahs as a unit. You should make your decision based on those results. The militia needs our fire team but unless we are ready, we're nothing more than targets."

Rebekah smiled at me and said, "John, your energy is amazing. You also give the impression of knowing the answers and of being in total control. Incidentally, what are your plans tonight after dinner? I have a bottle of excellent wine in my quarters." She took a step closer to me and suggestively added, "We could discuss whatever topic comes up."

I looked at her and said, "Thank you for the offer, Ma'am but I'm planning to have a good night's sleep because tomorrow will be a busy day."

"*Oh?* That's too bad, Corporal Collins. I was hoping you were interested in getting to know your commander better."

After hearing her last comment and seeing the disappointment in her face, I knew I had hurt her feelings by rejecting her invitation. I thought, *'Well John, you may have made an enemy today. Let's hope she doesn't carry grudges.'*

Later that evening as I lay in my own bed, I mentally listed my misgivings about Rebekah's fitness for command. Someone had given her a warrant officer's rank and she had never been in combat. Also, she didn't know the first thing about leading a combat team. I thought about Helen and how much I missed her. In addition to being my fiancé, Helen was a competent leader who had been tested in combat.

* * *

I woke up a grumbling fire team at 5:00 AM. Only half the fire team members could complete all sit-ups and pull-ups. We finished by running the three-kilometer course. At the conclusion, I announced, "Those of you not completing all exercises will work out with me daily at 5:30 AM until you've achieved your goal. Those of you who successfully completed all exercises will be assessed on a monthly basis. After breakfast, please assemble at the firing range."

Brenda said, "Corporal Collins, it's not fair. I'm a mechanic; not a warrior. Why should I have to complete these stupid physical fitness exercises?"

Noticing others were listening I said, "Private Childress, your warrior deserves a mechanic who is physically able to maintain his cheetah. These exercises are designed to assess your physical fitness level. According to the results of today's assessment, you need to strengthen your upper body. Once our unit is activated, there'll be times when your physical stamina will be pushed to its limit. If you're unable to do your job, the additional work will fall on your fellow mechanics. Forcing someone else to do your work is *my* definition of unfair." Following these words, I saw her defiant look fade into surrender. Turning my head to the others I said, "Does anybody else have anything to say?"

After breakfast, Vic was first to fire his rifle on the new firing range. Each person qualified but my mechanic, Mary Holloway, was the best shot. I said, "Private Holloway, where did you learn to shoot?"

Mary replied, "I grew up on a farm and my father took my two brothers and me hunting with him each year. I've been shooting since I was twelve years old."

"Private Holloway, you've earned the distinction of being designated as the Fire Team Four Sniper. I'll see to it you're issued a sniper rifle. Ladies and gentlemen, please join me in congratulating Private Holloway for her outstanding marksmanship."

I continued, "For the balance of this morning, I want all warriors to complete scenarios 5, 7, 12, and 16 on their cheetah's interactive training system. This afternoon, WO Lloyd and I will evaluate each warrior's scenario results in the dining room. Normally this is done one-on-one but I suspect our training time is short and everyone can benefit by seeing one another's successes and failures.

"Mechanics should ensure your vehicles are 100 percent. Help one another if needed. Everybody who did not pass the physical fitness test should commence exercising at every opportunity.

Improvise. For example, build gym equipment by using containers filled with water or sand as a substitute for weights. Do you have any questions? If not, you're dismissed."

A few minutes later, Rebekah received a message from Colonel Maxon. She said, "Corporal Collins, Colonel Maxon has called a staff meeting this afternoon at 1:00 PM. I won't be able to assist with evaluating the scenarios. If he should ask, what would you recommend I say regarding our unit's activation date?"

"Ma'am, I recommend you ask for two weeks and accept one week. In one week, we won't be one hundred percent but we'll be better than we are today. And if you get a chance, please say hello to WO Helen Ramses for me."

* * *

When Rebekah returned from the staff meeting, she summoned me to her quarters.

"Hello Ma'am. How was the meeting?"

"Oh the meeting was fine. We're scheduled to be activated in one week. Colonel Maxon and Sergeant Major Peters will be visiting our fire team in six days for the official assessment."

"Well that's great news. I'm sure we'll have everything and everyone ready to go."

Corporal, one other thing was announced at the staff meeting that you should know."

"Yes Ma'am?"

"I was caught completely by surprise when Colonel Maxon announced to the staff that WO Helen Ramses is engaged to Corporal John Collins! And do you know why I was surprised? After hearing you preach to me about the necessity of maintaining a separation between enlisted and officers - only to find out you don't practice what you preach. You're such a hypocrite! Do you have anything to say for yourself, *Corporal* Collins?"

I thought, *'Oh crap! How am I going to explain the difference between my relationship with Helen and Rebekah's earlier cozy relationship with her fire team members?'*

I cleared my throat and began. "Ma'am, you are absolutely correct to question the difference between these situations. From a certain perspective, there is no apparent difference. However, if you compare the environments, there are notable differences."

Rebekah sat back and sneeringly said, "Yeah, I'm waiting. This should be good."

"When I was assigned to Fire Team Six, WO Ramses made me her mechanic and rode my back constantly. There was no friendship, no pleasantness, and certainly no romance between us. It was her giving orders and me taking orders. This relationship remained unchanged until Haven was invaded. Separated from the battalion and on our own, our relationship started changing because we shared the bed of my hauler for sleeping; we ate together and went on missions together. Being close for several months enabled us to get to know one another on a personal level. It was not until the aftermath of a fire fight that I learned a mechanic and her warrior from our team were engaged to be married. Tragically, he was killed during that fire fight.

"WO Ramses and I found and reported the mass murder of the Third Battalion. Seeing carnage on that scale caused me to realize how fragile people are during war. It was during that mission my feelings for WO Ramses progressed to the point where I decided I wanted to spend the remainder of my life with her. However, it was not until I escaped from an enemy hospital and returned to my fire unit that I asked her to marry me. At no time have I ever publically addressed WO Ramses by her first name.

"Because she had already established herself as the fire team's commanding officer, the other fire team members accepted our decision to become engaged.

"Ma'am, when I reported for duty with Fire Team Four, the discipline essential during combat had not been established. The members of this fire team were lax and not prepared for war. They seemed too familiar with you which led me to question if they understood the concept of command structure and would be willing to carry out your orders during combat. Their lives are too precious for us to take that risk.

"What people say and do behind closed doors is their business. How your soldiers comport themselves in public is our business."

"Well that's a nice speech, Corporal Collins. I'll think about what you said before deciding if there is a real difference between these situations or whether I've been given a load of your bullshit. At dinner tonight, tell me about the fire team's training today and what you have planned for tomorrow. Oh and lest I forget, WO Ramses and her fire team has been assigned to serve as the enemy force for our evaluation next Saturday. And since you're obviously romantically involved with someone else, you are dismissed."

I left Rebekah's quarters concluding she was carrying a personal grudge against me for rejecting her earlier advance. My brain said, *John, it's clear Rebekah's not going to forget or forgive you for rejecting her advances; especially since she knows about you and Helen.'* My heart said, *'Too bad, Helen is the woman you love and you're not going to make a career of the militia. Stay focused on your goal - get through this war alive.'*

CHAPTER 30

ASSESSING FIRE TEAM FOUR (MILITIA FORCES)

I was proud of the progress the members of Fire Team Four made in one week of intensive training. They had converted from a mob of individuals into a unit which acted like a team. At 11:00 PM before our assessment began, everyone was on alert and placed in their defensive position. My guess was Helen would attack our position with her fire team at the stroke of midnight.

Initially, Rebekah didn't understand and was skeptical of my defensive plan. It took some time for me to convince her that WO Ramses wouldn't play by any rules of etiquette; that her goal would be to blast through our area and capture everyone by surprise. After a lengthy discussion of Helen's probable intentions, Rebekah began to grasp the strategy I was proposing.

She finally said, "Oh you clever devil; we'll let WO Ramses believe we're all asleep and totally unprepared for her assault. When she attacks, she'll be met with an enemy waiting and ready to demolish her force. I have one final question. How do you know she'll attack so early and not wait until a more reasonable hour?"

"Ma'am, WO Ramses loves to win and hates to lose. This is an opportunity for her to test our readiness and look good in front of Colonel Maxon. Knowing her aggressive nature, I wouldn't expect anything else from her. We can expect her attack as soon as the exercise clock starts."

"Corporal Collins, I seem to remember recently finding out WO Ramses is your fiancé. Won't you feel bad about beating her in simulated combat?"

Smiling I replied, "Not in the least, Ma'am. WO Ramses wins tomorrow either way. If her fire team wins, she's publically acknowledged once again as an exceptional combat leader. If we win, she feels justified in transferring me out of her fire team and knowing that I have a reasonable chance of getting through this war alive. In any case, Colonel Maxon will announce the results of this test at the next staff meeting. I think it would be great for you to be praised in front of your peers."

I added, "And from my own perspective, WO Ramses and her fire team need to be reminded they lost a valuable asset when I was transferred."

Our cheetahs were not armed with normal ammunition. Instead, we had been issued laser training devices which would sense and report hits on combat vehicles and would disable any vehicle hit in its vulnerable areas.

In preparation for the test, we used the sand table and made up a replica of our fire team's position. From this topographical map, we were able to spot the most likely approach and prepare new defensive positions.

I sold Rebekah on an unorthodox strategy. If it worked, Helen's entire force would be eliminated in one stroke. Essentially, we were going to let Helen believe Fire Team Four was asleep. She and her warriors would quietly move toward our position with their cheetahs abreast. Our plan was to let them through our forward hidden positions so we could hit them from behind. Being able to attack the enemy from his rear is an armored commander's dream. One well-placed shot from each of our cheetahs would spell curtains for Helen's entire fire team.

Someone once said, 'no operational plan survives initial contact.' In the wee hours of Saturday morning, Mary, my vehicle mechanic, was assigned to an advanced lookout post. At 1:30, she reported vehicle noises. "Lima Two, I hear tracked vehicles approaching along the projected route."

"Roger, get back to your foxhole. You've done your job."

"All Limas - tracked vehicles approaching along route alpha. Lima One will give the order to fire; wait for the command."

Vehicles slowly moved past on either side of my hidden cheetah. As expected, Helen had spread her cheetahs in a line formation in order to hit us with her entire force.

Rebekah keyed the comm link and said, "All Limas - *FIRE!*" immediately Helen's cheetahs were hit with our laser simulators. Smoke poured from engine compartments and the vehicles halted. The devices registered vehicle kills.

"All Limas - report." I received confirmation of four kills. This meant Helen or one of her warriors had survived our ambush. I thought, '*Oh crap! Either Rebekah had sprung the trap too soon or someone failed to take out his assigned target! This is a rookie mistake.*'

"All Limas - crank it up and let's get the fifth cheetah. Lima One, take Limas Three and Five with you and sweep right. Lima Four, you're with me. We're going to sweep left. Sound off when you sight that cheetah."

A few minutes later the comm link crackled into life. "Lima Two - One and Five are down and I'm taking fire."

"Roger Three. Hang on, we're on the way. Lima Four, let's get that cheetah."

The combined fire of our remaining three cheetahs finally overcame the fifth enemy cheetah.

"Limas Three and Four, help everyone out of their cheetahs. Get the mechanics to help you."

I got out of my cheetah and ran over to the disabled enemy vehicle. Smoke was billowing from the engine compartment and it was difficult to see. I scrambled up the hull, jerked open the hatch and was met with a blast of hot air and smoke.

Reaching down, I unfastened the harness of the occupant and pulled the body from the vehicle. The warrior was unconscious and really heavy. After dragging the body to the ground, I removed his goggles and recognized Sergeant Delucca. He slowly opened his eyes and grinningly said, "Hi John. I want you to remember it took three of you to disable my cheetah."

I laughed and replied, "Yeah Frank, you're stubborn as a mule and never know when to quit. That's what I admire about you. If you can get up and walk, let's round up everybody for an exercise debriefing."

Sergeant Delucca laughed and said, "You won't see the day when I can't recover from those laser-generated love taps!"

After gathering everyone in the dining room, Helen addressed the warriors and mechanics. "Good morning, ladies and gentlemen. Thanks to your being alert, our surprise attack on your position failed. You have my congratulations. Your unorthodox strategy handled our attack very nicely. And although Sergeant Delucca killed two of your cheetahs, you shouldn't feel bad. He's been a cheetah warrior for six years and is one of the best I've seen. For your information, Colonel Maxon is en route to this location and I expect his arrival any minute. He witnessed this morning's attack on a vid link."

Colonel Maxon and Sergeant Major Peters arrived two minutes later. "Ladies and gentlemen, Sergeant Major Peters and I offer our heartiest congratulations to Warrant Officer Rebekah Lloyd and her fire team. Defeating Fire Team Six is a tremendous accomplishment and indicates you're ready for combat. To that end, you'll be placed in immediate rotation with the other fire teams for future missions." Turning to Rebekah, he said, "WO Lloyd, unless you have other plans, I would like to give the members of your fire team a twenty-four hour pass starting immediately."

"WO Ramses, thank you for participating in this important unit readiness assessment. As usual, your fire team performed in a thoroughly professional manner. You and your fire team have no further assignments today or tomorrow."

Turning back to Rebekah, he added, "Rebekah, while I'm here, we should discuss your first combat mission."

As Rebekah and Colonel Maxon began discussing Fire Team Four's upcoming mission, Helen walked over to me and said, "Corporal Collins, before I return to my base, I'm interested in a tour of your fire team's area. Will you be my escort?"

I replied, "It'll be my pleasure, Ma'am."

Outside the building, I asked her, "What would you like to see first, Ma'am?"

Helen quietly replied, "I'd like to see your quarters."

After closing the door to my bedroom, Helen and I rushed into each other's arms and began kissing. Holding her close was wonderful.

"Helen, I've missed you so much during these past two weeks. I couldn't believe our good fortune when Rebekah announced your fire team had been selected to test us."

"John, you've no idea how difficult it was to convince Colonel Maxon to assign the assessment to Fire Team Six. In retrospect, I suspect he was toying with me by acting reluctant to use my fire team. We had just returned from a four day mission and were due some rest when I found out about Fire Team Four's assessment. He practically made me beg to participate." She paused and then continued, "Darling, being here with you at this moment makes everything else trivial by comparison."

"Helen, I want you so much."

She broke away from our embrace and said, "Well, let's do something about that."

As I unzipped my sleeping bag, a small wad of red cloth was revealed. Helen reached down and picked up the cloth. As she slowly unrolled the material, it became obvious she was holding a pair of women's thongs.

My heart sank and I began blushing like never before. Defensively I said, "Uh, Helen I have no idea where those came from or how they got into my sleeping bag."

Helen stared at me and didn't say anything for a while. Holding the thongs with two fingers, she finally said, "John, you've got some explaining to do. I'm engaged to be married. From the looks of things around here, I don't know what you've been engaged in."

I walked over to Helen and guided her to a chair. After she sat down, I kneeled in front of her and said, "Helen, you've got to believe me; I've been faithful to you. Darling, I love you with all my heart and would never even think about cheating on you."

In agony I looked down, thought for a few moments and continued, "Helen, since I know I didn't cheat on you, this could only be the work of a practical joker." At that moment, I looked up and saw a big grin on Helen's face. Realization dawned on me as I quickly stood up and stared open-mouthed at a woman laughing out loud.

Helen stood up and put her hands on both sides of my face. She said, "John, I remember a conversation during which I told you that someday you may want to apologize for all those awful practical jokes you pulled on me at Camp Shelby. Today, my love, you've received a dose of your own medicine. Now put those big strong arms around me and tell me again how much you love me."

As our lips met, I couldn't help thinking, *'Life will never be dull living with you, Helen.'*

CHAPTER 31

DEFENDING CALHOUN CITY (EARTH FORCES)

General Dietrich looked at each officer attending the weekly commander's vid conference. Gentlemen, our intelligence source at Militia Headquarters has given us vital information. We have been informed militia forces are preparing an assault on Calhoun City. They intend to capture and hold that city.

"Sir, what's so important about Calhoun City?"

"That's a fair question, Colonel Thompson. I'll let Colonel Morrissey give you an answer because Calhoun City is within his assigned sector."

"Thank you, General. Calhoun City is a major rail center. The switchyard at Calhoun City is the nerve center of all rail traffic on Haven. Whoever controls the switchyard controls every train on Haven. Maintaining control over the rails means we decide what gets shipped where and when."

General Dietrich asked, "Colonel Morrissey, what forces are you using to defend Calhoun City?"

"Sir, we have one company from the 351ˢᵗ Infantry Battalion reinforced by one company from the 450ᵗʰ Armored Battalion."

"I've been informed the militia will attack with one battalion of armor and one infantry battalion. I'm not sure you can defend

Calhoun City with only two companies. Do you consider that an adequate force?"

"Sir, it's all I can afford at this time. However, if I could withdraw from Camp Shelby, I would transfer those assets to Calhoun City. And may I remind the General that Camp Shelby has been bombed and is of little tactical or strategic value."

"Remind me of your force at Camp Shelby and when can you get them to Calhoun City?"

"General, I have the remainder of the 450th Armored Battalion and one company of the 351st Infantry guarding Camp Shelby. Most of these soldiers are assigned as ambush teams. It would take five days to clear Camp Shelby and move everyone to Calhoun City."

"Colonel, my intelligence source tells me the militia will attack Calhoun City in two weeks. You may withdraw from Camp Shelby and move those units to Calhoun City. However, arrange your reinforcements to arrive at Calhoun City one day before the scheduled attack. I don't want the militia to realize we've reinforced Calhoun City before they commit their forces. We can't afford to lose control over the rail network and I want to defeat as many militia soldiers as possible."

"I'll issue the appropriate transfer orders, General."

CHAPTER 32

FIRE TEAM FOUR ENTERS THE FIGHT (MILITIA FORCES)

Our newly activated fire team didn't have long to wait for our first mission. One week later, Rebekah gave us our mission briefing.

"Ladies and gentlemen, we are joining the other battalion fire teams in six hours. Our objective is to remove the enemy from Calhoun City and occupy the town. Colonel Maxon will provide command and control. Corporal Collins, what is the status of our equipment?"

"Ma'am, all laser training devices have been turned in and our cheetahs are 100%. We'll get ammunition loaded and ensure the batteries are fully charged prior to departure. How many haulers should we bring?"

"What's your recommendation?"

"Ma'am, I recommend we take everything with us. This mission sounds like the militia is launching a campaign to reclaim territory which Earth forces now occupy. I wouldn't be surprised if our base is elsewhere after the fight. If we take everything with us, it'll be a simple matter to relocate."

"That sounds logical. Let me know when the unit is ready to move out."

One hour later, Fire Team Four was en route to a rendezvous with the other battalion fire teams.

As we neared Calhoun City, we heard firing in the distance. I began monitoring both the fire team and command nets.

Listening on the command net, I heard Colonel Maxon contact Rebekah. "Lima 1, I'm sending you an updated mission and set of coordinates. Engage immediately."

Rebekah contacted her fire team and said, "All Lima haulers, here are your new coordinates. Set up a defensive perimeter and await further orders. Break. Limas 2, 3, 4, and 5 - I'm sending you the operational order. The area is hot. Advance in column formation with even numbers covering the right and odd numbers covering the left. Good luck, team. Lima 1 out."

Our first mission was clearing a street. My cheetah was positioned at the rear of the formation and my job was to spot targets others had overlooked and prevent an attack from the rear as we rolled down the street.

Clearing streets is dangerous work. I held back from the others and constantly swept the tops of buildings for ambushers. There! On the right side of the street I spotted a soldier leaning on a building parapet and pointing a shoulder held rocket launcher at one of our cheetahs. I immediately cut loose with the anti-personnel gun. I uttered a quick *'gotcha'* as I saw him spinning backward with his launcher slipping over the side of the building and clattering on the sidewalk below. There was no time to reflect on the moment because others could be preparing to fire on my team.

An explosion burst near Lima 4 which caused me to look at the top of a building on the left side of the street. I estimated at least five heads peering down as our cheetahs rolled by. I swung the main gun toward the building and fired a quick round just below the men's position. Bricks, dust and other debris exploded from the building and rained down on the street below. As I rolled past the heavily damaged building, dust was still billowing over the street and adjacent buildings. The top portion of the storefront had collapsed.

I glanced to the rear and saw a cheetah sitting in the middle of the street with his gun pointed toward our fire team. I began slewing my turret and turning my cheetah sideways to the enemy. Simultaneously, I announced, "All Lima's - enemy cheetah in our rear. I'm engaging."

No sooner than I completed the transmission, I felt a jolt that shook my cheetah. His round struck the side of my rotating turret. The accompanying sound was similar to someone beating on an empty steel barrel with a hammer. Fortunately, my turret continued to turn. I quickly got a lock on the cheetah and fired. No sooner than I had fired, the enemy again fired his main gun. His second shell hit my turret another glancing blow. A yellow light started flickering on the instrument panel indicating the turret was still operational but not one hundred percent. My next round hit the enemy cheetah between the hull and turret. His turret was blasted free of the hull. Scratch one cheetah.

I immediately began searching for another target. Rebekah came on the net and asked, "Lima 2, what is your status?"

I replied, "Hit twice but still operational."

She said, "All Lima's; proceed with original mission."

Since my turret was not one hundred percent, I said, "Lima 4 - be on the lookout for enemy on building tops. I will continue rear surveillance."

"Lima 4 - WILCO"

Having given my primary target to Anne, I kept the cheetah in reverse with my gun pointed toward the rear of our formation as we continued down the street.

Almost on cue, another armored vehicle came into view. And this was no cheetah; it was one of the new leopard combat vehicles!

I got him in my sights and fired. My round hit but didn't kill the leopard. I continued backing up and started swerving from side-to-side to make it difficult for him to get my cheetah in his sights.

"Lima 1 – I have a leopard on my tail. Need help."

"Negative 2 – do what you can to stop or slow him down; we have to complete our primary mission. Limas 3, 4, and 5 - stay with me."

I was in a dangerous situation; the leopard was not giving up and my commander was deserting me. The leopard fired and his round narrowly missed my swerving cheetah. The building on my right was hit and debris rained on my cheetah and the street. The noise was deafening. It was only a matter of time before my cheetah would be blown to scrap.

I fired again and hit the leopard on his turret. My second round didn't seem to faze the vehicle as he continued closing the gap between us. Things were getting desperate as I continued swerving while backing up. Deserting a team member during a fire fight was unheard of. If I lived through this and caught up with my cowardly commander, somebody was going to lose some beautiful white teeth.

My speaker came to life and I heard a familiar voice say, "Lima 2, this is India 1. Do you require assistance?"

Helen was on the scene! I quickly replied, "India 1, affirmative. Enemy leopard is trying to crush my cheetah. Here is my location and the leopard is about four hundred meters down the street and closing."

"Roger. Break - India 2 – go to intersection Samuel Tango and hit that leopard from behind"

"India 2 - WILCO"

The leopard fired again and this time his round hit my left track. My cheetah spun counterclockwise about forty degrees before I could disengage the drive. Now sitting dead still, I knew the leopard would kill me with his next round.

Suddenly, a cheetah flew through an intersection and crashed into the leopard. While this did not disable the leopard, it caused his next round to miss my cheetah by a meter. A few seconds later, Sergeant Delucca's cheetah fired point blank into the rear of the leopard and knocked him out of action.

"All Indias, set up a defensive perimeter around my location. Lima 2 – do you require medical assistance?"

"This is Lima 2 – negative on medical assistance. Many thanks for saving my life."

"India 2 - request haulers for two disabled cheetahs and one leopard. Break - Indias 3 and 5 - drag the crew from that leopard and hold them for questioning."

Several hours later, the hauler carrying my disabled cheetah rolled into our new camp. As I got down from the cab, Anne, Vic, Rachael and Mary rushed over to see me. Vic said, "Corporal, we were worried sick about you. We don't understand why WO Lloyd wouldn't let us go back and help you."

"I'm sure she had her reasons. Fortunately for me, Fire Team Six came to my rescue and captured the enemy's leopard. Where is WO Lloyd? I need to report."

Mary said, "She was called to a meeting with the Battalion Commander a few minutes ago."

"Okay. I'll see her when she returns. Meanwhile, I need to see Private Davis. Where is she?"

"I think you'll find her with the vehicles inside the old building to your right."

The building looked like it was used for manufacturing at one time. Today, it was filled with our military equipment illuminated by portable lamps. I saw a couple of militia working on a cheetah and walked over.

"Private Davis, what's the status of our equipment?"

She grinned and replied, "Hi Corporal Collins, we heard about your close call today. Glad you're safe. We have three fully operational cheetahs. Anne's cheetah received some minor damage and is now being repaired. Your cheetah just arrived and it looks like it has extensive damage. Mary will begin work on the turret immediately after dinner. I've already ordered a new track and a couple of road wheels from battalion. Without a more detailed assessment of its damage, I'm not sure when your vehicle will be up and running."

"Okay, thanks. Please keep me posted. If you need help, let me know."

A couple of hours later, a hauler arrived with Rebekah, Helen, Sergeant Major Peters and Colonel Maxon. Accompanying them was a general officer. They entered an empty office and began interviewing each warrior assigned to our fire team. I had no idea what was going on until Sergeant Major Peters summoned me into the office.

After I reported, Colonel Maxon introduced Brigadier General Bill Flanders from Militia Headquarters then asked me to be seated.

"Corporal Collins, this is a formal hearing investigating the events occurring earlier today. I want you to listen to a recording of the communications among your fire team members and a recording between you and members of Fire Team Six." After the recordings were played, Colonel Maxon asked me if I had anything further to add.

I replied, "No sir. The recordings accurately portray the events of today's action."

He then asked me, "Corporal Collins, do you believe your cheetah was in imminent danger of being destroyed by the leopard?"

I looked over at Rebekah and replied, "Yes sir. I hit the leopard with two rounds with no visible effect. The leopard fired three times at me. Because I was swerving my cheetah from side-to-side, his first round missed but his second blew off my track. Except for the actions taken by WO Ramses and Sergeant Delucca, I'm certain the leopard's third round would have destroyed my cheetah. They saved my life."

"Thank you, Corporal. You are dismissed and are ordered not to speak of this to anyone outside this room."

I left the office and walked back over to the maintenance area to help Jo Anne and Mary restore my cheetah to an operable status.

After about thirty minutes, I noticed the visitors and Rebekah get into a hauler and leave. Sergeant Major Peters remained behind.

He walked over to me and said, "Corporal Collins, I need to speak with you."

We walked out of earshot of others and he started talking. "John, this has been a tough day for everyone in your fire team. Morale among the warriors is low and I think you know the reason why."

"Sergeant Major, I don't understand why Rebekah refused to send help during the firefight. It's one thing to be afraid; we all are during combat. But her refusal to let the others help me defies logic."

"Well, you don't have to worry about WO Lloyd anymore. She's being transferred elsewhere. In the meantime, you're the senior soldier in this fire team and you must take over immediately. Do you have any problem assuming this added responsibility?"

I thought for a moment then said, "No. I can handle the job. How long will I be in command?"

"That's for Colonel Maxon to decide. If you've no further questions, I want you to get the fire team assembled so I can make the announcement."

"Sergeant Major, I have two questions. What are our orders and can I get our vacancy filled?"

Sergeant Major Peters said, "I'll work on getting your team to full strength. In the meantime get sentries posted and be prepared for an operations order from Colonel Maxon. Here are the primary and alternate frequencies he's using. Keep your portable comm unit with you at all times. If the frequencies are jammed, we'll send a message by courier."

A few minutes later, nine of us were standing in front of Sergeant Major Peters.

He began, "Ladies and gentlemen, WO Rebekah Lloyd has been transferred to another unit and Corporal John Collins has been given command of this fire team. I hope you will give him the loyalty and respect he has earned.

"Today, your fire team accomplished its first mission since being re-certified. I am proud of your accomplishment and believe you'll continue distinguishing yourself as we fight to rid Haven of its invaders. If you have no questions of me, I am formally turning over command of this fire team to Corporal Collins."

"Thank you, Sergeant Major. You can count on us to do our job."

Sergeant Major Peters asked, "Corporal, would you get me a ride back to battalion headquarters?"

I asked Mary to take the Sergeant Major back to his headquarters and addressed the fire team after they departed.

"Ladies and gentlemen, we've had a rough day and nobody knows what tomorrow will bring. I am making Private Anne Pearson our number two. She's in charge when I'm away.

"On a related topic, has anybody found a place where we can shower and sleep tonight?"

Private Sanders said, "Corporal, there's a hotel about three blocks away but nothing closer."

"Okay, that's too far from our vehicles. We can take showers there but we'll sleep in our haulers tonight and I'll see if I can get us something better tomorrow.

"Private Pearson, please set up a guard roster for tonight."

"Yes Corporal."

"Private Dominowski, take Private Childress with you and see if you can buy us some food from a local restaurant. Here's some money. Buy enough for nine people."

"Private Higgins, what is the status of WO Lloyd's cheetah?"

"Corporal, her cheetah is one hundred percent."

"Thanks. I'll use her cheetah until mine is repaired. We're short one warrior and I've requested a replacement."

About nine o'clock that evening, Colonel Maxon contacted me. He said, "Corporal Collins, I have a mission for your fire team tomorrow at ten o'clock. A militia infantry unit is moving into the area we captured today and will provide interior security. I want you to move your fire team to provide perimeter security. Here are the coordinates. Link up with adjacent fire teams to ensure no gaps show up in our defensive perimeter. We suspect Earth may counterattack soon and this may turn out to be the first place we get to stop a full-fledged attack. We believe they'll attempt to retake Calhoun City because of its strategic value. You'll need to dig in for a heavy fight. Use whatever materials and tools you can scrounge. Have you any questions?"

"No sir. This seems like a straightforward defensive strategy which will take a huge toll on the enemy if we're successful."

"You got it. Good luck, soldier."

I assembled the fire team at 6:00 AM and gave them the warning order. "Our next mission is to link up with other fire teams and form a defensive perimeter around Calhoun City. We can expect an attack soon so we don't have much time to prepare. Private Holloway, take my cheetah and drag it on the line if you have to. I realize it's not one hundred percent but it can still shoot. And since you're the best shot on our fire team, you are a good choice to fire its main gun. I want all mechanics to help man the perimeter. We'll take one hauler with extra ammunition, some water and food rations with us. Leave the other haulers here. Ladies and gentlemen, we've taken this city and I don't intend to let the enemy back in. Are there any questions? If not, let's roll."

Our assigned portion of the defensive perimeter was about one kilometer away. We arrived in less than five minutes and began deploying in our sector. I met with the adjacent fire team leaders and introduced myself. After exchanging frequencies and call signs, I returned and helped the team dig in. There was no lack of materials we could use since several buildings nearby had been demolished in the previous day's fighting.

Sergeant Major Peters stopped by and asked, "Corporal Collins, I've located a tracked excavator which appears to be in operating condition. Are you interested in using it?"

In answer, I immediately jumped in his hauler and said, Sergeant Major, you've made my day!"

A couple of minutes later, we arrived at a construction site and I spotted the excavator. It was an older model but it seemed okay. I got out of the hauler and ran over to make a closer examination.

After checking the battery charge and lubricant levels, I got into the cab and started the vehicle. The excavator was in good operating condition and responded to its controls.

I began moving the excavator toward our perimeter. The vehicle was not quick like my cheetah. I had forgotten how slow excavators were compared to our cheetahs. It took almost thirty minutes before finally arriving. The fire team began cheering as I quickly built firing positions for our five cheetahs. Afterwards, I drove over to the adjacent fire teams and helped them complete their firing positions. This was obviously what Sergeant Major Peters had in mind because he asked me to continue working along the entire defensive perimeter. Interestingly, I didn't see Helen's fire team and was puzzled why they weren't manning the perimeter.

I contacted Anne and told her that I would be helping the other fire teams prepare their positions and she was to assume command until my return.

As I was finishing the work and driving back to my sector, Sergeant Major Peters contacted me and asked if I needed anything. I replied, "Sergeant Major, we could use another warrior and a sniper rifle with ammo."

He paused a moment then responded, "I can get you a sniper rifle, ammo and a spotting scope but the warrior is not available at this time."

As I was parking the excavator behind a nearby building, Sergeant Major Peters arrived with the sniper equipment. I called Privates Holloway and Childress from their assigned positions. I gave Mary the sniper rifle and handed the spotting scope to Brenda. "Mary, I want you to take this sniper rifle and get up in the building behind our sector. You should avoid the top floor if possible. Brenda will serve as your spotter. Stay away from window ledges so you can shoot without being seen. Ladies, your job is to shoot enemy soldiers. I've been advised the enemy will attack with a combined force of infantry and armor. Infantry and especially warriors stupid enough to expose themselves are your primary targets. This is our opportunity to get some payback for the annihilation of the Third Battalion and the loss of our Fire Team Four warriors. Stay in touch with me via the short range comm link. Your call sign is Lima 6. If you have no questions, I wish you good luck and good hunting."

After their departure, I went to each warrior and mechanic on the perimeter and talked with them individually about the upcoming fight. I gave them my expectations and answered their questions. This was our first firefight and both warriors and mechanics were apprehensive.

I directed Private Higgins to man the gun in Rebekah's former cheetah while I climbed into my battle damaged cheetah and buttoned up. We didn't have long to wait. An alarm sounded just before shells started raining down on our positions. I was thankful for having access to the excavator. Without which, some militia would have died during this bombardment.

After the fires finally lifted, I alerted the fire team members and began scanning for attackers. The command link came into life with the warning order.

No sooner had the smoke and dust began clearing, our first targets presented themselves. I switched to our fire team link and said, "All Limas – report." After receiving confirmation that everyone survived the bombardment, I said, "Standby for enemy forces. Hold your fire until you get a target lock."

As the enemy appeared, it seemed our cheetahs fired simultaneously. Up and down the line the firing was continuous at an enemy which had moved into point blank range. Their advance was halted as we continued pouring round after round into their vehicles. Some vehicles turned around and began retreating. However, they didn't get far because retreating cheetahs are easy targets as we fired into their unprotected engine compartments.

The only enemy forces not retreating were the leopards. Those were tough armored vehicles and it took a lot of rounds to stop their advance. One or two actually breached our battalion's perimeter before being stopped. Thankfully, the enemy only fielded a handful of those weapons.

Enemy soldiers advancing behind their vehicles became easy targets for our anti-personnel weapons as the enemy vehicles disengaged and began retreating.

In the distance, I saw bright lights and felt several explosions. I was puzzled over this event until Colonel Maxon came on the command net and announced that Fire Team Six had destroyed the enemy's ammunition resupply point. He ordered all fire teams to advance and capture any Earth soldier who surrendered. He added that the militia infantry responsible for providing security within Calhoun City had established a stockade for captured enemy soldiers. He sent us the coordinates of the stockade.

Remnants of units of Earth soldiers surrendered. Facing our cheetahs, they gathered in clumps with arms raised. Cheetahs are not good for transporting captured soldiers so I ordered Jo Anne to bring our hauler. I noticed a number of wounded prisoners but we didn't have adequate medical supplies or medics available. I contacted Colonel Maxon and apprised him of this situation. He replied that medical treatment was available at the stockade. I ordered the wounded transported to the stockade first.

Other fire teams brought their haulers forward and we transported about twenty captured soldiers per hauler. As soon as a hauler unloaded its prisoners at the stockade, it returned for more.

After the last prisoner was transported, I contacted the fire team members and had them return to the perimeter and gather for a meeting.

Looking around, I saw a bunch of sweaty, dirty, and dog tired soldiers. "Ladies and gentlemen, I am very proud of each of you. We've won a great victory today. We captured over four hundred prisoners and destroyed a battalion of enemy armor. Additionally, a supply depot was destroyed by Fire Team Six. Unless the Earth soldiers are reinforced, I believe today will mark the decline of their occupation. Someday you'll be able to tell your children and grandchildren that while defending Calhoun City we defeated two battalions of Earth soldiers."

"Private Pearson, please establish a normal duty watch and give everyone else a much-deserved break. Private Holloway, come with me."

Mary and I walked away from the others. After reaching the excavator, I stopped and began talking. "Mary, I gave you the hardest job of all today. It's one thing to put sights on an enemy vehicle and fire. It's something else to put a person in a rifle scope and pull the trigger. How do you feel?"

Mary looked up at me and tears began welling in her eyes. She began talking very softly, "Corporal, I feel terrible. Brenda and I counted twelve kills. It could have been more but I was scared at first and missed several times before getting the feel of the rifle. After the first hit, I didn't miss. There are twelve people who died today by my hand and I can't get their faces out of my mind."

I put my arms around her and said, "Mary, today you killed twelve Earth soldiers who were intent on killing your fellow militia members. Tomorrow, their parents and wives will be notified that they died in combat. Your actions today means that some families of our militia members will not be notified that their sons and daughters died defending Calhoun City. By taking their lives, you saved our lives.

"Mary, war is a terrible thing and no human being should have to kill another. None of us wanted Earth to invade our home but they did and their invasion has forced us to defend our world. I wish I could erase this bad memory from your mind but I don't know how to do that. I wish I could promise you won't have to fire the sniper rifle again but I can't make that promise either. We have to use whatever means at our disposal to make the Earth soldiers leave our planet. I do know bad experiences fade from our memories over time. Hopefully, this war will soon end and we can go about making these bad experiences fade from our memories."

"Mary gave me a quick hug and said, "Thank you, John. I really appreciate you being here for us. I don't know what we would have done without you." Stepping back she added, "WO Helen Ramses is a lucky woman."

As Mary walked away I wondered, *'How did she find out about Helen and me?'*

As I was walking back to the fire team's perimeter, I received a message from Colonel Maxon to report to the stockade at 8:00 AM.

* * *

The following morning, I left Anne in charge of the fire team and reported to Colonel Maxon as ordered. Two other fire team leaders also reported. He led us to a large office in a building near the stockade where other militia members had gathered. I counted eleven people.

A colonel from Militia Headquarters arrived and announced, "Ladies and gentlemen, you have been summoned to serve on a military tribunal. If there is anyone among you who feels he or she cannot render a fair and honest judgment on another soldier, please step forward." Nobody moved so he continued, "Today, we have over four hundred prisoners of war who were captured yesterday. Each prisoner is having his or her record screened to determine if they were previously captured by a militia unit. Those who have been previously captured will be tried by this tribunal. This tribunal will remain in session until all prisoners have been given a trial. I expect it will take two weeks to complete our work. Please take a seat behind the long table and I will introduce the prosecutor and defense attorney."

A total of two hundred forty three out of four hundred fifteen prisoners had been previously captured by a militia unit. For each prisoner, a short vid was shown giving the familiar warning to the captured soldier of their fate if they were captured again by the militia. When asked for a statement, a few of the soldiers on trial claimed they didn't understand the warning but most stated they had no choice about returning to combat since they were just following orders.

Some appealed to the mercy of the court. A few stood stoically as their sentence was read while others began pleading with the court to give them one more chance to leave Haven. A couple of the captured officers argued that our tribunal was illegal and we were committing war crimes by convening this 'kangaroo court.'

At the end it didn't matter what they said. Following our guilty verdict, the presiding judge sentenced each to death by hanging. The entire session was put on a vid recording and a copy was given to the one hundred seventy two captured Earth soldiers being returned to their unit. Prior to these Earth soldiers being released, they were told to get off our planet and should they be captured again, they would be executed.

After being released from the tribunal, I was ordered to report to Colonel Maxon.

"Welcome back, John. I know serving on the tribunal was hard and disagreeable work.

"I didn't get a chance to tell you how much I appreciated you helping everyone prepare for the attack. Your expertise with the excavator saved lives and enabled us to withstand a vicious bombardment. Additionally, your fire team fought bravely and well on the perimeter. Militia Headquarters is presenting a Distinguished Unit Award to our battalion in the next few days. Each fire team member will receive this medal."

He continued, "In recognition of your personal contribution toward our victory, I have a special award in mind. What do you know about our Officer's Training School?"

"Nothing sir; I operated an excavator back home in Tupelo before being drafted into the militia. I knew nothing about Haven's militia before being drafted."

"Officer's Training School is three months in length and the next class starts in two days. I want you to attend and become an officer. Cadets undergo intensive classroom, weapons and physical training.

"John, after your recent combat experience, some of the orders given to you during the next three months will seem silly and counterproductive. My advice is to 'suck it up' and do what you are told. There is a purpose behind the process."

He continued, "John, you have little experience serving as a non-commissioned officer but that's not required in order for you to become an officer. You earned the rank of corporal based on your accomplishments. You've earned the right to attend Officer's Training School based on my assessment of your potential. It is likely some of your classmates will not have had any combat experience and that's okay, too. Officer's Training School will prepare all of you to assume the role of an officer."

"At graduation, I'll arrange to have Helen attend and will authorize a few days leave for both of you."

"Thank you, sir. Helen and I would enjoy that very much."

"Excellent! Return to your fire team and make the announcement. We are sending a Warrant Officer and a new warrior to fill your fire team's vacancies. Gather your belongings and report back."

Colonel Maxon assigned a non-commissioned officer from his staff to drive me to Officer's Training School. The school was located near Houlka, a village about 200 kilometers away.

CHAPTER 33

AFTER ACTION REPORT (EARTH FORCES)

Losing Calhoun City to the militia dealt a crushing blow to Colonel Morrissey's ego. Not only did he lose Calhoun City, he also gave up Camp Shelby. Fully one half of his area of operations had been captured by the militia. The next staff meeting was almost unbearable.

"Colonel Morrissey, please give us a final report on the battle at Calhoun City."

"Sir, it is with extreme regret that I must report the loss of Calhoun City and its rail yard. The 420th Armored and the 351th Infantry battalions have been decimated. The enemy has captured 415 Earth soldiers and I have been informed our soldiers who were captured for the second time were put on trial and executed."

"What do you mean *'put on trial and executed?'*"

"Sir, the militia has a standing order to hang any Earth soldier who is recaptured."

"Do you have proof of this practice?"

"Yes sir. Here is a vid which was turned over this morning by our soldiers who were released by the militia after the battle at Calhoun City. This is the first known instance of Earth soldiers being hanged. The vid shows a court martial, sentencing, and execution of sentence.

The vid also contains a message from General Turner, the militia commander."

After seeing the vid, General Dietrich said, "Gentlemen, hanging a captured soldier because he or she fails to heed militia warnings to leave Haven is a war crime. There is a second message in this vid. Please note General Turner alleges Earth forces, specifically members of the 415th Armored Battalion committed a war crime on December 3. Colonel Harper, what do you know about a massacre of the militia's 3rd Armor Battalion?"

"Sir, this is the first I've heard of any massacre committed by Earth forces. I would like your permission to conduct an investigation."

"No, that won't be necessary. I'll appoint a special team to conduct an independent investigation at Fort Mantachie. Ladies and gentlemen, this is embarrassing. It's difficult for me to take the moral high ground and condemn war crimes if my own forces are guilty of illegal and immoral actions. My independent investigation will take the highest priority. And I promise you this, if evidence of a massacre is found, those responsible will be punished to the fullest extent. As of this moment, Fort Mantachie is off-limits to everyone except the independent investigation team."

"Next subject - Colonel Morrissey, you've lost two companies from the 351st Infantry Battalion and the entire 450th Armored Battalion. You only have one company from the 351st and the 413th Armored Battalion remaining. Will that be enough to hold Johnson Springs Reservation?"

"Yes sir. I can hold Johnson Springs with my remaining forces."

"I hope so; otherwise I'll divide your area of operations between Colonels Thompson and Harper and allocate your remaining soldiers to them."

"Our final topic, Earth has sent me a message stating they are unable to send reinforcements or replacement equipment at this time. I have no idea when our force will be resupplied or augmented. Gentlemen, we have to be more careful with our remaining soldiers, equipment and ammunition. In one year of fighting we've lost one fifth of our soldiers and equipment and we've expended one third of our ammunition. Further, our supply ship was destroyed as it entered Haven's atmosphere. Meanwhile, militia units are getting ammunition from newly-established munitions plants. As of today, they're not getting replacement vehicles. I'm told those plants will take at least eighteen months to resume production.

"Regarding new recruits - based on Haven's population of 150 million with an estimated annual birthrate of 2 million, approximately 1 million young people will be eligible for the draft each year. However, with a majority of their young men and women currently serving in the militia, Haven can only provide that number of potential recruits for the next eighteen years. Afterwards, the number of Haven residents eligible for the draft drops to practically nothing."

"Sir, where are all these potential militia members?"

"That's an excellent question. The good news is, Haven does not have enough equipment or experienced soldiers to field more militia units. I'm told a vast majority of these young people are working on farms and in production facilities. In other words, they're not fighting us yet."

"Sir, does this mean we could be at war with Haven for the next eighteen years?"

"We're here until we win the war. Earth must have full access to Haven's agricultural capacity. Ten million of Earth's citizens are expected to die of starvation this and each subsequent year. Ladies and gentlemen, we're fighting for the people on Earth. There's no going back without total victory. As of this moment, I expect you to capture enemy equipment and ammunition for our own use. That item will be added to your weekly reports."

CHAPTER 34

OFFICER'S TRAINING SCHOOL (MILITIA FORCES)

Militia cadets entering the grounds of Officer's Training School were immediately subjected to a cadre of lieutenants yelling at us to move faster or do something better. For 90 days, we suffered many indignities at the hands of these lieutenants. We began thinking of them as the school's 'attack dogs.' Lieutenants taught us how to march, make our beds correctly, how to clean our barracks until it was spotless and led us in physical fitness training. They inspected our barracks and issued demerits for any infraction. Demerits were redeemed by performing extra duty on the weekends.

Senior officers assigned to the school were our instructors. They had combat experience and were subject matter experts. They were more restrained than the lieutenants but when they asked you a question, you had better give them the correct answer. Our time was divided between classroom and field exercises.

We learned fire team and platoon tactics. The organization of a company and battalion was presented in detail. We learned that three fire teams make up a platoon. Normally, three platoons make up a company and three companies make up a battalion. These organizational structures were designed to optimize firepower given a small number of militia members.

Because we were being trained to become platoon leaders, our tactical training concentrated on the fire team and platoon structure. Each cadet was given the role of a cheetah warrior. Fire team and platoon leader positions were rotated among us. We were evaluated on our demonstrated abilities during our rotations as leaders. We also learned that in order to be a good leader, you had to be a good follower. When a fellow cadet was serving as fire team leader, you gave one hundred percent as one of his cheetah warriors. When the roles were reversed, he or she would do the same for you.

I noted that in the 5th Battalion, our units had been organized on the fire team level because of the guerilla campaign being waged against Earth forces. Hiding a fire team was much easier than a platoon. In a conventional war, the platoon was better able to defend against or attack and overcome larger enemy forces.

Exercising command and control over a platoon of fifteen cheetahs was the most difficult thing to learn and execute. Two key concepts were drilled into us. One, having good fire team leaders who followed orders and two, the platoon leader had to 'see the battlefield.' Vids of field maneuvers being conducted by previous cadet classes were shown and critiqued in class. We also saw vids of actual engagements between militia and Earth forces. The difference between the vids was striking; during actual engagements, equipment was blown to bits and people died.

* * *

The best thing happening during my three months at Officer's Training School was a weekend pass given mid-way through our training. I didn't go home but Helen managed to get two days off and we spent the entire weekend at a hotel in Sparta getting re-acquainted. I told Helen that if married life was like this weekend, she should begin wedding preparations. The weekend ended much too soon.

*   *   *

"Cadet Collins, you have been chosen to serve as platoon leader for the final exercise of your cadet class. This is a singular honor and your platoon's performance tomorrow will be recorded and discussed in future classes. You will attend a staff briefing at 6:30 PM during which you will be given the scenario for tomorrow's exercise."

I called my classmates together and let them know that I would attend a briefing and receive the scenario for our final exercise. "Ladies and gentlemen, this is it. For the past three months we have been working and studying for this moment. I ask for your best efforts and I pledge you my best. Let's meet directly after I return from the briefing and we'll go over the scenario."

After reporting to the cadre, I was given the following information: "Cadet Collins, we have received word that a company-sized force of Earth soldiers is preparing to attack our battalion headquarters. Our other units are engaged in defending the Leopard armored vehicle manufacturing plant. Your platoon is our battalion's only defense against the attacking force. We project that they will attack at 9:00 AM from the southwest. Do you have any questions?"

This scenario was slightly different from ones we had practiced during the past three months. My platoon would be pitted against an entire company of enemy armor. My mission was clear; defend battalion headquarters against three to one odds. I needed intelligence on the enemy forces.

"Sir, can you give me any intelligence on the enemy's weapons, location and time the force was last seen and their rate of advance?"

After asking several additional questions, I left the briefing and met with my classmates and gave them the scenario. I outlined my defense plan and assigned specific tasks to each fire team leader.

Based on available data, we calculated the earliest possible time of attack and used this as a deadline to complete our defense preparations. Fire team leaders positioned their vehicles along the perimeter and I found a good location from which to see the entire area. I took a portable radio with me and checked communications with fire team leaders.

While viewing the perimeter, I spotted a flaw in our defensive preparations. If the opposing forces used their overwhelming firepower, our positions would be overrun and we would lose. Alternatively, if we set up dummy positions and moved our platoon of cheetahs into hiding, the opposing forces might bypass our hidden cheetahs permitting us to attack their formation from the rear. This was the same strategy I used against Fire Team Six during our unit readiness assessment. Fire teams posted observers to alert us of an attack while others rotated through the mess hall for a quick breakfast. Fire team leaders made a final check with their cheetah warriors and we were as ready as possible. I moved to my vantage point and ran one more communications check with the fire team leaders.

The attack was launched at 6:45 AM. Fortunately, we were ready. The aggressor forces initiated the attack with a simulated mortar barrage followed by an armored assault. Unfortunately for them, they didn't see our hidden cheetahs and bypassed our vehicles.

The fight was intense but short. We hit the opposing forces in the rear; scoring a record number of one-shot kills before they knew they were being attacked. Although the opposing forces began with a numerical superiority, our initial attack helped even the odds. With my elevated view of the battlefield, our cheetahs were able to pick apart the remaining opposing forces.

After the exercise, we were given a debriefing by the school's Commandant.

"Cadets, you successfully defended battalion headquarters from an attack by a superior force. Congratulations on a splendid defense. Fire team leaders exercised excellent command and control over your cheetahs. You systematically attacked and destroyed each vehicle as it came into range. Thank goodness you were only using training ammunition today!" That drew a round of laughter.

"Cadet Collins, your leadership during this exercise is worthy of any seasoned officer. Our school staff was greatly impressed with your attention to detail and inventiveness. We have never seen a cadet platoon defend a position by attacking the enemy. That's one for the record books."

"Let this be a lesson to all. Creativity and inventiveness can be a force multiplier during combat. This class is ready to graduate."

We stood and cheered at this news.

* * *

Graduation day started with breakfast in the mess hall. We were laughing and talking about the final exercise when Helen appeared. On noticing Helen, the entire mess hall became quiet.

When I saw her, I hurriedly walked over to her and gave her a big hug amid catcalls from my fellow cadets. "Helen, it's wonderful seeing you."

She responded, "I have missed you so much, darling. How have you been?"

"It's been lonely without you." I added, "Let me introduce you to my friends."

After the introductions, Helen sat down and one cadet said, "Ma'am, please forgive Cadet Collins' lack of manners, would you care for breakfast?"

Helen played along by saying, "I could never instill in Cadet Collins the niceties. Yes, please; breakfast would be much appreciated." A couple of cadets left and returned with Helen's breakfast. In addition to ragging on me, technically, Warrant Officer Helen Ramses outranked us. After graduation, we would be commissioned as lieutenants and we would outrank her.

While eating, Helen told us about her fire team and its recent missions. This was the first war news we had been given.

After breakfast, I gave Helen a tour of the school. Because I shared my room with another cadet, Helen waited in the auditorium for the ceremony to commence while I got ready.

The Commandant gave a short graduation speech followed by the cadets coming forward and receiving their lieutenant insignia. After graduation, we were given our assignments. I was awarded fourteen days leave after which I was to report to 5th Battalion Headquarters. Colonel Maxon came through on all promises.

After saying goodbye to my classmates, Helen and I began walking to her hauler. Helen looked at me and said, "John, it will take some time before I get accustomed to you outranking me."

I grinned at her and said, "I promise I will not make you walk one step behind and to my left."

She laughed and punched me on my arm.

"Helen, how do you propose we spend the next fourteen days?"

"I have been spending a lot of time thinking about our leave." She added, "Would you like to start by visiting the local tourist attractions in Houlka?"

"No offense intended Ma'am, but I was hoping you would suggest something else."

"As a matter of fact, I have a great idea. Let's get your things loaded in my hauler. I want you to meet my parents."

CHAPTER 35

ARMY OF OCCUPATION (EARTH FORCES)

Lieutenant Bill Anders chaffed at the lack of progress in eliminating militia units. It seemed that everybody in his chain of command was afraid of violating General Dietrich's latest edict.

"Lieutenant Anders, your proposal to serve as 'bait' in order to entice the militia to attack and expose themselves sounds too risky. General Dietrich has given orders to each task force commander to conserve ammunition and soldiers."

Bill looked around the small conference room. His fellow platoon leaders (Nancy Montgomery, James Homer and Anne Richards) seemed content to let him vocalize what everyone was thinking. "Captain Steiner, how do you propose we defeat the militia forces? We've not engaged the enemy in two weeks. Staying cooped up in Columbus allows the militia to roam freely over the countryside."

"*Lieutenant;* this level of disrespect directed at our invasion commander is unacceptable; especially coming from a West Point graduate!"

Humbled by his company commander, Bill remained quiet while thinking, '*Steiner, your days are numbered. I've finally figured out a way to get rid of you without anyone suspecting me. Just keep it up my little scar-face; your fate is sealed. You're nothing but a dead woman talking.'*

Lieutenant Montgomery finally asked, "Captain Steiner, what are our orders?"

After a brief pause, Melissa Steiner said, "Continue foot patrols throughout our sector of the city. We need to get the crime rate down in Columbus. With no Haven police available, we're seeing an increase in local criminals committing crimes against senior citizens. Remember to use minimum force when you apprehend these individuals."

She looked directly at Bill and added, "Bill, I'll talk with Colonel Harper about your proposal. He may decide your idea is worth the risk. Ladies and gentlemen, if there are no further questions, you are dismissed."

As her officers filed out, Melissa was thinking, *Bill is right; we can't do our job cooped up within the city limits. I've got to convince Miles to let us go after the militia.'*

Nancy caught up with Bill after the staff meeting. "Bill, I feel terrible each time Captain Steiner vents her frustration on you. You are so brave to stand up and say what everyone is thinking."

Bill grinned and replied, "Baby, after we send our platoons out on foot patrol, I know a way you can show your appreciation for my bravery exhibited during the staff meeting."

"Bill, speaking of which, I need to speak with you privately. I have some wonderful news for you."

* * *

Captain Steiner was immediately granted access to Colonel Harper's office. "Thanks for seeing me. Colonel, we have a problem. Lieutenant Anders has suggested he become 'bait' so we can trap militia units. His ideas for engaging the enemy are creative but General Dietrich's orders were pretty specific about conserving soldiers and equipment."

"Melissa, isn't it wonderful having young lieutenants chomping at the bit to see action against the enemy? And let's face it; Anders is both creative and aggressive."

"Miles, that little shit has been a thorn in my side since he reported for duty back at Fort Boende. To make matters worse, Bill Anders has become the unofficial spokesperson for all my lieutenants. Frankly, I don't know how much longer I can control him. But 'give the devil his due;' what he's proposing is risky but it seems like a good idea."

"Tell me all about his latest idea. I might be willing to risk him if there is a good chance of success.

"Lieutenant Anders wants to modify a luxury personal coach by converting it into a mobile night club. He proposes putting four to six attractive teenage girls in the vehicle and driving it to various Haven national parks where militia forces are likely to patrol. He will pose as the girls' pimp, bartender and driver.

"Anders believes militia soldiers, especially the young ones, would eagerly grab an opportunity to party with young, pretty girls. After paying an entrance fee, the militia would be treated to a drink laced with a powerful drug. After drinking the cocktail, they would pass out; giving Bill an opportunity to shackle the unconscious individuals. He will then give us coordinates and request a pickup. Upon notification, we arrive in strength, load the prisoners and drive them back to Columbus. Should an individual militiaman not fall for the ruse, Lieutenant Anders has demonstrated he is physically capable of subduing most men."

She continued, "Due to the small number of people involved, Anders can keep his operation secret which will enable him to use this plan repeatedly."

Colonel Harper thought about the proposal for a few moments then said, "Melissa, the good thing about Bill Anders's idea is; he'll work tirelessly to be successful. If the idea pays off, you get credit as his company commander and I get credit as his task force commander. Your responsibility is to carefully monitor his progress and stay in constant communication with him. You and I can take credit for giving our soldiers permission to try new initiatives. Once the word of 'our' initiative has leaked out, other soldiers in my task force will note the positive and creative atmosphere we've encouraged and their morale will increase. Should Lieutenant Anders fail and get killed, we rid ourselves of a troublemaker. Even if his idea fails utterly, we've only lost one soldier. Frankly, I don't see a negative on this, Melissa. Lieutenant Anders' plan is approved. Incidentally, shall I expect you in my quarters this evening? You've made me feel like celebrating!"

Melissa smiled and replied, "Miles, who could resist such an invitation? Let's say around nine thirty?"

* * *

"Lieutenant Anders, your plan is approved. Let me know if you require assistance and keep me informed throughout the operation."

"Thank you, Captain Steiner. I appreciate you convincing Colonel Harper to take a chance on this idea."

* * *

After leaving Captain Steiner's office, Nancy turned to Bill and said, "Bill, you are wonderful! I'm so happy Colonel Harper approved your plan. Is there anything I can do to help? When will you leave Columbus?"

"Nancy, while a maintenance team modifies the personal coach, I'll need your help in recruiting local teenage girls. There seem to be a lot of young girls living in Columbus. I want you to concentrate on getting sixteen to eighteen year olds."

"Why do you want girls from that age group?"

"They scare easier than older girls and will be simpler to control. Also, girls younger than sixteen are too silly and are more prone to crying. Those older than eighteen are more independent which may cause a different set of problems.

"Nancy, ask someone to help you create a sales pitch for recruiting. Equally important, we need a good cover story to keep the girls' parents or guardians in the dark. I'm certain Colonel Harper does not have time to meet with parents whose daughter has disappeared.

"I'll leave as soon as I have five or six women and the vehicle is converted. I'll buy sexy clothing for the girls when you give me their sizes. Also, each girl needs to have a complete medical checkup."

"Wow, I'm impressed, Bill. Apparently, you've been doing a lot of thinking about young girls. Is it possible that you believe I'm getting too old for you?"

"Cut the crap, Nancy. This is a job; nothing more. It's vital I use young good-looking girls in order to attract and trap militia members. My question remains; will you help me round up some girls?"

"Okay, Bill. I'll ask some women in my platoon to help me get your recruits. I suspect they'll even volunteer to help us equip your 'girlie wagon.' It'll certainly be more interesting than patrolling streets looking for muggers.

"Nancy, after the staff meeting this morning, you said you needed to talk. What is it?"

"Bill, you're going to be a father! A doctor confirmed my pregnancy yesterday. Darling, isn't that great news?"

Bill was stunned at this unexpected news. He had not bothered taking precautions but had assumed Nancy was taking some form of birth control. Bill began thinking, *'Nancy, what the hell is the matter with you? Why weren't you taking birth control pills? Do I have to do all the thinking for us? I hope you don't expect me to help you with the baby. This is totally your fault.'*

"Nancy, I had no idea you wanted a baby. Forgive me, but I don't know what to say since we never discussed having children. It's great that you're excited about having a baby but it will take me a little while to become accustomed to the thought of becoming a parent. Why didn't you tell me you wanted children?"

"Bill, this is a surprise for me, too. I guess knowing that you love me made me less cautious about getting pregnant. I assumed you would be as excited as me about the baby. However, hearing the reluctance in your voice is scaring me. Bill, you need to say something."

"Does Captain Steiner know?"

"No, you're the first one I've told."

"Okay, how do you propose we handle this?"

"I'm not sure. Perhaps both of us should tell her?"

"Nancy, before running to Captain Steiner, don't we need to think about all the options available?"

"What options, Bill? Adoption is out of the question. I couldn't ask someone on Haven to adopt our child. After all, we're at war with Haven and their citizens aren't exactly friendly toward us."

"Well what about abortion? That would be a quick solution and nobody need know anything."

"Bill, you can't be serious! I love you and want to have our baby. I would *never* consent to an abortion; that's unthinkable and I'm surprised you would even mention it as an option!"

"*All right, Nancy.* Don't wet your panties! I was only thinking out loud." After pausing for a moment, Bill continued, "When we tell Steiner the good news, she'll want to know if we're engaged to be married. I suggest we get her permission to marry before telling her that you're pregnant."

"That sounds great, Bill. When are you going to propose?"

Bill smiled at Nancy and replied, "Let's go to dinner this evening. I have something important to ask you."

Nancy gave Bill a big hug and said, "Oh my darling Bill; I can hardly wait until this evening!"

As a happy Nancy walked away, Bill was thinking, '*Nancy, it's lucky for you I need your help in recruiting these young sluts. Getting married and becoming a father is definitely not in my plans. Who knows, after I leave Columbus you may have a terrible accident. One of the soldiers in my platoon owes me a huge favor.*'

CHAPTER 36

VISITING THE PARENTS (MILITIA FORCES)

Helen's home was over 600 kilometers away in a very rural part of Haven. She had stowed a battery charger on the hauler in anticipation of this trip. We took turns driving and made the trip in less than two days.

As we pulled into the driveway, Helen said, "John, my family has not seen me for a couple of years but I've stayed in touch by writing notes. You should know I mentioned you by name in some of the notes; including those written while we were at Camp Shelby." Grinning she added, "Oh and did I mention my father is very protective of me?"

"Helen, in that case, it might be safer for me to drop you off at their doorstep and I return to battalion headquarters."

"Don't be silly. As my future husband, having you meet my parents is very important to me."

I parked the hauler and slowly got out of the vehicle. Helen was already running up the steps to the front porch. She was greeted by her mother amid squeals of joy. Her father stood nearby waiting his turn to hug Helen.

I slowly walked up the steps and stood patiently until being noticed. Helen finally broke free from embracing her parents and walked over and grabbed my arm. She faced her parents and said, "Mom, Dad, I want you to meet John Collins. John has asked me to marry him and I have accepted his proposal. We would like to get married while we're here on leave."

Mrs. Ramses walked over to me and gave me a big hug and said, "Welcome to the family, John. Please call me Martha."

I was still digesting Helen's announcement as I returned Martha's hug.

Mr. Ramses walked over and shook my hand. He looked at me sternly and asked, "How long have you and Helen known one another?"

Helen interrupted saying, "Daddy, John and I met while I was stationed at Camp Shelby."

"Is this the same John Collins you wrote about in your notes?"

"Yes Daddy, this is the man who drove me crazy with his practical jokes."

Mr. Ramses looked at me and said, "John, are you not able to answer for yourself?"

I replied, "Sir, I was not aware of any communication between you and Helen. However, I did serve as Helen's chief mechanic at Camp Shelby. Initially, Helen and I did not get along very well. It was not until Earth invaded Haven that our relationship changed."

"I see." Mr. Ramses paused then continued, "Well, you may call me Sam. Get your things and come on in. Martha, I'll put John in the guest room."

"Samuel Ramses, you'll do no such thing! Helen has already discussed their sleeping arrangements with me. John will be staying in Helen's room."

There was an embarrassing silence before Sam said, "Okay, if that's what you've decided. Come on John, I'll take you to Helen's room. Afterwards, I'll show you around the farm."

While Helen and her mom caught up on the news, I followed Sam around as he pointed out the details of farming.

Sam's farm consisted of his two-story house, windmill, workshop, large barn used to store hay and farm equipment, a chicken coop, pig sty, garden, pasture, a large pond, fenced land for crops and a hardwood forest. Sam said, "John, almost sixteen years ago, Martha and I bought this land from the government and have built this farm from scratch. We've worked hard and I had intended Helen to settle down here instead of making a career in the military. Farm work is never done and it's getting harder for Martha and me to keep things going."

He then asked me, "What did you do before being drafted?"

"I operated a tracked excavator for Ajax Construction in Tupelo."

"What are your plans once this war is over?"

"I don't know. Since being drafted into the militia, I have been living from day-to-day and haven't taken the time to think about my future."

"You asked my daughter to marry you and you're telling me you have no plans for the future?"

"Sam, you make a great point and you deserve a better answer. I love Helen and want to spend the remainder of my life with her. I'm confident I'll be able to provide for her; no matter what profession I eventually choose. Until this war is over, I can't afford to think about future employment. Winning this war is my primary focus."

"John, I can understand that. And since that's your priority, how does marriage fit in?"

"Sam, we're not in combat continuously. There is time for other things and I would like to spend that time with Helen as her husband. Also, there's a strong possibility we'll be assigned to the same unit."

We finished our tour of the farm and returned to the house. Helen and Martha were cooking dinner. As I watched Helen cook and set the table, I found myself thinking about eating home cooked meals after this horrible war had ended.

"John, you and Sam wash up. Dinner will be ready in about ten minutes."

I entered Helen's bedroom and spent about three minutes putting my toiletries in the bathroom and hanging my uniforms in her closet. Helen had found some civilian clothes for me so I changed before going downstairs.

Entering the kitchen, Martha directed me to a seat opposite Sam. She and Helen put the food on the table and sat facing one another. I hesitated before starting and it was a good thing; Sam always said a blessing before each meal. I made a mental note to ask Helen about any other things I should know about their customs.

During dinner, Sam informed Martha I wanted to marry their daughter but had no plans for the future.

Helen was quick to respond. "Daddy, how can you say that? John was drafted into our militia and recently earned a commission as a lieutenant. Until this war is over, he will continue serving as an officer. After the war, I'm sure he'll have numerous opportunities to choose a career doing something that makes him happy. I also know you were disappointed when I chose a career in the military but that doesn't mean I'm a failure."

Martha spoke up and said, "Sam, Helen and I are really tired of hearing this same conversation. You're upset because Helen chose a life in the military rather than stay home and marry a farmer. Just be honest and say it."

Sam's face got red and he snorted, "Martha, we've built a great farm and I don't understand why Helen had rather be a soldier than do something important like farming."

I could tell Helen was getting angry. She put her silverware down and began speaking softly. "Daddy, I wish I wanted to be a farmer. I know it would mean so much to you. But I love serving in the militia. I'm a respected warrior and lead a team of nine soldiers whose very lives depend on my decisions. Now John has come into my life and my future will be influenced by what we decide to do once this war is over. I love you and Momma and hope you will give your blessing for our wedding."

That evening, Helen and I were getting ready for bed when she informed me, "John, this afternoon Momma and I discussed our wedding date. If you have no objection, we can be married on Sunday afternoon which is only four days from today. Even though it will be a small wedding, there are lots of things Momma and I have to do."

"Helen, I think that's great. I wish my family could attend but they're not allowed to travel outside Tupelo."

"I know and I'm sorry I haven't had the pleasure of meeting your family. And while we're talking about wedding plans, there's one additional thing; it's my parents' custom we should not see one another on the evening before the wedding."

As Helen got into bed beside me, I put my arms around her and said, "I don't particularly care about that custom but we're in your parent's home and should try to accommodate their wishes." I paused then continued, "Speaking of which, I noticed your father praying before dinner. Are there any other customs they have I should know about?"

Helen replied, "No, I don't think so." After we kissed Helen said, "For your information, you are the first man ever to sleep with me in this bed. While growing up, I never even dreamed this would happen."

"Helen, I think we're beginning to sound like a married couple."

"Is that so bad?"

"No Darling, it's just an observation."

The following morning Sam asked me to go with him to a neighbor's farm. When we arrived, I was introduced to James Wilson who informed me he had an old excavator sitting in his barn. Sam asked, "John, can you get it operating again? James and I need additional ponds in our pastures."

"Let me take a look at it." I examined the excavator and found numerous problems. The biggest problem was the hydraulic pump. I dismantled the pump and took it apart. The hydraulic fluid looked like it had never been changed and two impeller blades were broken.

Sam and James helped me repair the excavator. It took us three days of steady work before I was able to start the vehicle. The excavator outwardly looked pretty ragged because we scrounged parts, welded and even built components to make it fully functional. We didn't spend any energy making the vehicle pretty but it worked.

James was impressed and offered to pay me but I refused to take his money. Instead, I asked that I be allowed to use the excavator to dig a pond on Sam's farm.

On Saturday, the day before the wedding, I dug a fresh water pond for Sam's cattle. After showering and eating dinner, I stayed in the barn overnight anxiously waiting for Sunday afternoon when Helen and I would be married.

On Sunday morning, Sam brought me breakfast and said, "John, I understand why Helen thinks so highly of you. In the last four days, you've proven to me that you're an exceptional man and I'm happy to have you join our family." That was quite an admission from him.

"Thank you, sir. I'm honored to become part of your family."

That afternoon, Helen and I were married by a priest in Sam and Martha's house. In addition to James Wilson and his wife, Rachael, five other neighbors attended the small wedding. Marrying Helen and hearing her say the wedding vows made me the happiest man in the world. That evening, after our first lovemaking as husband and wife, I promised Helen we would have a real honeymoon when the war was over.

On Monday, Helen and I rode over to the Wilson's house and I dug a pond in their pasture. It was fun to be back at the excavator controls and I enjoyed showing Helen my talents with an excavator. Helen rewarded me that evening with more lovemaking.

We spent the remainder of our leave visiting with Sam and Martha; helping them around the farm each day and spending wonderful evenings in Helen's bedroom.

Five days later, Helen and I donned our uniforms and began our return to battalion headquarters after bidding Sam and Martha a sad farewell.

After getting on the road I said, "Helen, after the war is over, should you decide you want to return home, I could get used to farming."

She looked at me and said, "Farming is quite a switch for a city boy. How do you know you would like it?"

"The work Sam does around the farm is manual labor which is what I did before being drafted. Based on the few days spent with your parents, I sensed they feel real enjoyment and satisfaction in their lives. Helen, I want us to be as happy."

"John, you never cease to amaze me. But I don't know if I would be happy living on a farm again."

"Helen, that may be true, but if we are going to have children, we need to ask ourselves which would be the best environment for them?"

"Speaking of children, we need to talk about something very important."

"What is it?"

"John, I have a wonderful surprise for you. I'm pregnant. We're going to have a baby."

"How do you know you're pregnant? We've only been married a week!"

"Darling, it doesn't take a wedding vow to get pregnant. Do you remember that weekend during Officer Training School?"

"How could I forget? It was the most incredible weekend I ever experienced."

"Yes it was for me, too. And what happened during that weekend accounts for a missed period followed by several positive pregnancy tests."

Realization suddenly dawned on me as I almost ran off the road while exclaiming, "I'm going to be a father!"

"John, I wanted you to be the first to know. You have no idea how hard it was not to tell Momma during our visit. Now we need to tell our parents and Colonel Maxon the good news."

"Helen, our parents will consider it good news; I'm not sure Colonel Maxon will agree."

"John, let me worry about Colonel Maxon. I'll tell him when we arrive at battalion headquarters."

"Helen, I know you've served a couple of years under his command and know him better than me. However, he will hold us both accountable. I remember hearing an old Earth expression; 'it takes two to tango' - whatever that means."

"John, tango is a dance for couples. In our case, it's an appropriate expression. I still believe I should be the one to break the news to him."

"Helen, I don't want him to think I'm being cowardly by letting you be the bearer of this news."

"Don't worry, hero. I'll set the record straight. Your reputation as a 'real man' will remain untarnished."

That comment really ticked me off but I bit my tongue and didn't say anything. After a few kilometers rolled by I asked, "Helen, why didn't you tell me you were pregnant before the wedding?"

"John, I wanted to be sure you were marrying me for love; not because you knocked me up and felt obligated to get married."

"You know Helen; your confidence in my feelings toward you leaves a lot to be desired."

"John, are we having our first fight as a married couple?"

"Probably; yes, I guess we are."

After driving in silence for several minutes I said, "Helen, look in the storage compartment. I have a small present for you."

Helen retrieved a small package and opened it. Inside was a new uniform name tape saying, 'Collins.'

She removed her name tape which said, 'Ramses' and replaced it with 'Collins.' She looked at me and said, "Thank you, Darling. I'm proud to carry your name - and your baby."

CHAPTER 37

THE PARTY WAGON MISSION (EARTH FORCES)

Nancy and her team had run a beauty and talent contest for girls living in Columbus. The top five contestants were awarded an all-expense paid trip to visit major cities on Haven. There was a lot of competition for the positions because social life had virtually stopped since the invasion. The queen and her maidens were to be chaperoned by one parent selected by Nancy while Bill assumed the role of driver and baggage handler. Parents were smiling and waving as they said goodbye to their little darlings. Some had tears in their eyes.

Nancy quietly said, "Bill, I don't understand why these parents are so excited about their daughters traveling throughout Haven. They don't seem to realize there is a war going on."

"That's right. Earth forces control the media and we have not informed the local citizens about the skirmishes occurring in the southern region. Even these idiots wouldn't permit their little darlings to travel outside Columbus if they knew about the fighting. They've been told Earth forces control Haven."

Five really cute girls eagerly crowded onto the luxury motor coach. "Okay ladies; please find a seat. Your coach is leaving on a thirty-day tour of Haven!"

Bill was perhaps more excited than the girls. He was eagerly anticipating his role and was looking forward to their training. Thirty days away from Nancy and Captain Schneider and total control over the five girls. He had one chaperone standing in his way. The chaperone was a mother of one of the girls. She was about forty years old and very attractive; especially for a person of her age.

As the coach got under way, Bill said, "Mrs. Hardy, it is so nice having you along on this trip. Please let me know if you need anything."

"That's sweet of you, Bill. Please call me Cathy. I'm looking forward to this trip and hope the girls will not be a bother."

Bill grinned as he began thinking, *'Cathy, I'm also looking forward to having some fun with you.'*

After driving a few hours, Bill pulled over at a diner and everybody piled out to eat lunch; the girls laughing and talking all the while. Bill left a leaflet with the cashier at the diner and asked her to post it on her bulletin board. Following lunch, Bill drove to a small wooded park and stopped the bus. He stood in the living room and made his first announcement.

"Ladies, there has been a slight change of plans. Access to some of the cities we were scheduled to visit has been blocked by fighting. However, we'll remain on the road for the full thirty-day period. As ambassadors of goodwill, you have an additional job which is to entertain militia members and Earth soldiers. These young men have been away from their families for a year. Surely they deserve some entertainment."

Cathy Hardy spoke up, "Bill, what's come over you? Are you crazy? People are fighting? We're not going to do this! I demand that you immediately return us to Columbus."

Bill grabbed Cathy by the front of her blouse, slapped her face and drew her up in front of him. "Cathy, your days of demanding things are over. From now on, you have two jobs; one is to keep the girls in line and the second is to take care of *my* needs." Shoving her back to her seat he continued, "Girls, Cathy's life and well-being depends on you following my instructions to the letter. Every time you mess up, Cathy will get beaten. If you run away, Cathy will die and you'll be responsible for killing her."

Bill took a collar from his pocket and fastened it around Cathy's neck. He said, "Girls, this collar contains a small but very strong explosive which can be triggered by this device on my wrist. It cannot be removed without a special key which is stored in a safe. The collar will also explode if Cathy moves beyond a certain distance from this coach."

"Girls, your job is simple; do what I tell you and you won't get hurt. When this job is done, you'll be returned safely to your families. Screw up and you won't make it back home. Are we clear?"

"Okay, let's get started. I expect some militia will be visiting us this evening. I want you girls to put on sexy outfits and entertain these young men. We've got music and drinks on board. I want our guests to have a good time. I'll serve drinks but you girls are not to drink any booze; that's only for militia. If somebody passes out, don't panic; just let me know and I'll take care of the young man.

"If you have no questions, Cathy will help me attach collars on each of you. Remember, if you run away, your collar will explode and you will die. Cathy will also die because you ran away."

Later that evening, four militia soldiers entered the coach and began partying with the girls. Bill served them drinks laced with drugs. An hour later, four unconscious men were bound and left inside a culvert awaiting pickup by Earth forces. Phase one of Bill's mission was complete.

* * *

After reporting the location of the captured militia, Bill drove to another rest area late that night. He pulled into a secluded spot, switched off the coach's engine and told the girls that they were sleeping in the living room. He pointed to a small closet where sleeping bags were stored and told the girls to use them.

"We want to use the bathroom."

"After I'm done, you have 5 minutes each to brush your teeth and get ready for bed. Nobody leaves the coach tonight."

Bill added, "Cathy, I want you to use the bathroom first. Take a shower, then I want you to wait for me in the bedroom."

"Why does my mother have to stay in the bedroom?"

Cathy spoke up and said, "Heather, don't question Bill. Just stay with the girls tonight. I'll be okay."

After Bill had taken his shower, he joined Cathy in the bedroom. He smiled and said, "You catch on pretty quick."

Cathy answered, "What's not to understand? If I don't sleep with you, you'll pick one of the girls to rape."

Bill grinned and replied, "That's right; make yourself a martyr. But I suspect the reality is, you want me just as much as I want you."

"You bastard, what do you know about a woman's desires?"

"I know your husband has not been taking care of you. I know you're a sensual woman who has unmet sexual needs. And I know I'm a man who is going to satisfy your every desire starting tonight. And when this trip is over, you'll probably thank me for giving you a great, guilt-free holiday."

CHAPTER 38

NEW EQUIPMENT
(MILITIA FORCES)

"Sir, Lieutenant John Collins and Warrant Officer Helen Collins are reporting for duty."

Colonel Maxon returned my salute and said, "John, Helen; have a seat. Congratulations on your wedding! Wish I could have attended.

"It's really good to have you back with the 5th Battalion. I have some great news for you. We have been designated as the first militia unit to receive leopard armored vehicles! And don't unpack your bags, I am sending both of you with two fire teams to the leopard manufacturing facility located at Morgan City for new equipment training.

"John, as the ranking officer, I'm appointing you platoon leader. The School Commandant informed me about your leadership during the course. He said you were a credit to your unit which reflects well on this entire battalion.

"Helen, based on your experience leading Fire Team Six, you've earned the right to command a leopard-equipped fire team." He added, "I assume you being married will not cause a problem regarding command authority?"

We both spoke up and said we had discussed that issue and it wouldn't be a problem.

Colonel Maxon continued, "Two fire teams will be reorganized into one platoon of ten leopards accompanied by five haulers. I realize a normal platoon has three fire teams but we're only getting ten leopards at this time. They are leopards captured from Earth forces and have been overhauled to 'like new' condition.

"The platoon leader and cheetah warriors will become leopard commanders. The leopard commander will also serve as the gunner. Cheetah mechanics will become leopard drivers."

"Your platoon will be assigned five mechanics who'll drive the haulers. These mechanics will report to you at the manufacturing facility where they have received training on maintaining leopards."

"Your new fire teams will accompany you to the factory where you'll receive the leopards. I didn't choose your old fire team members for this assignment. I want you to have a fresh start with new people. Here are the personnel files of your platoon members. Good luck and get back as soon as possible. I'm going to be operating at reduced strength until you return."

Before leaving, Helen looked at me and said, "Lieutenant Collins, I need to speak with Colonel Maxon. Sir, would you mind waiting outside?"

It was the first time Helen ever called me sir. I took a seat outside and waited for several minutes. During that time I could hear raised voices which were muffled by the wall's soundproofing. I suspected Colonel Maxon was not pleased about Helen's pregnancy. The door finally opened and it was obvious that Helen had been crying. She walked by me and said, "He wants to see you."

I went inside the office prepared for the worst. Colonel Maxon didn't look happy as he directed me to a chair. He finally said, "John, I was prepared to make an exception to assigning a married couple within the same chain of command. However, I can't give command of a leopard fire team to a pregnant woman. I remember encouraging you to marry Helen but I didn't say you should get her pregnant!

I simply can't afford to put a pregnant woman in command of a leopard fire team. In only a matter of months she'll be unable to get into the vehicle. The training we invest in her over the next few weeks would be wasted. Therefore, I have no choice but to assign another warrant officer to lead one of the fire teams. As luck will have it, Brigadier General Morris Barnett at Militia Headquarters has offered me a warrant officer for my first vacancy. Thanks to Helen's pregnancy, I have to take his offer."

General Barnett's name was familiar and I asked, "Colonel Maxon is it who I think it is?"

"You guessed it; none other than WO Rebekah Lloyd will be your new fire team leader. Nobody else wanted her after the battle at Calhoun City. Now you have an opportunity to instill in her a proper fighting spirit. John, I've often heard the pessimistic expression, 'no good deed goes unpunished.' In your case, that expression exactly fits this circumstance."

"Sir, what will you do with Helen?"

"I'm assigning Helen as our Battalion Liaison Officer with duty at Militia Headquarters. It'll be an easy job for her because she is thoroughly familiar with armor operations. Also, people at headquarters have better access to medical facilities. All in all, it's a good assignment for Helen at this time." He slowly shook his head and continued, "Maybe someday she'll appreciate the desk assignment."

He continued, "John, you're leaving at 8:00 AM tomorrow for the factory. I'll have WO Lloyd and your fire teams waiting for you in the battalion motor pool." He paused then added, "A word to the wise; tread carefully this evening."

"Thank you, sir. I will."

Sergeant Major Peters gave me directions to an apartment temporarily assigned to Helen and myself. After knocking on the door, a teary-eyed Helen greeted me.

"Oh John, I feel terrible. Everything was so perfect up until I informed Colonel Maxon I was pregnant. And now I'm being assigned to a desk job! I'm a warrior and I belong in combat!"

While Helen continued talking, we sat down on the sofa. I kept my mouth shut and put my arm around her shoulders and just held her as she continued talking about how unfair life was treating her.

After a few minutes she pulled away and looking at me said, "John, if we had not become romantically involved, I wouldn't be in this predicament."

"That's true. I would not have met the love of my life, we would not have spent so much time sharing our hopes and dreams with one another, and we would not be anticipating parenthood. Helen, I love you so much."

She stood up and loudly said, *"John Collins, I know exactly what you're trying to do! You're attempting to deflect my anger away from you. Well it won't work this time!"*

Not to be deterred, I also stood up and continued, "Helen, I understand why you're angry. Serving in the militia means the world to you. You've made it a career and you've become an accomplished warrior. Becoming a parent during this war is something we didn't expect. Having a baby is a wonderful event. I know you wish it could have been postponed but it happened. Darling, we are husband and wife and we've got to deal with this. Tonight, I want us to start making plans for our family. Tomorrow we'll be separated for a period of time and I regard spending this evening with you as something precious."

Helen slowly nodded. She walked into the bathroom and emerged a half hour later wearing a see-through negligee and looking drop dead gorgeous.

We decided after the baby was born, she would spend the remainder of her maternity leave at her parent's farm and let her parents care for the baby when she returned to the war. I promised I would apply for leave when she neared delivery and would take her to her parent's house afterwards. Secretly, I hoped the war would be over before having to ask Colonel Maxon for maternity leave.

* * *

During an early breakfast the following morning Helen asked, "John, do you know who is replacing me as fire team leader?"

"Yeah, I'm getting none other than WO Rebekah Lloyd as your replacement. Colonel Maxon wants me to 'instill a proper fighting spirit in her.'"

"Holy crap; I had to save your life once because of that little bitch's cowardice. You watch your back and don't trust her for one second. I can't believe Colonel Maxon would do that to you."

"Helen, he had no choice. Rebekah was the only warrant officer available. The good news is I know her pretty well and will take precautions. When I was assigned to her fire team, she was the commander. Now our roles have been reversed and she'll take orders from me. I hope she's had plenty of rest and is in good physical condition."

"John, she's a conniving bitch; don't give her a chance to stab you in the back." Helen paused then added, "And don't let her get emotional or physical with you. She's the second most attractive woman in the militia and I'd bet a month's pay she'll try to seduce you."

I reached across the table and touched Helen's hand. "Helen, you have nothing to worry about. You're my wife and the only woman I love."

After a tender farewell, I walked to the battalion motor pool to meet my platoon.

As I arrived, Rebekah called the soldiers to attention and reported.

"Ladies and gentlemen, we are the first soldiers in the militia to be issued leopards and I am honored to have been selected as your commanding officer. We're getting ten leopards which will be divided into two squads. WO Lloyd will command one squad and I the other. Our two squads will operate as a platoon. We're leaving in a few minutes for Morgan City where we'll receive and train in our leopards. Upon arrival, we'll be joined by our mechanics. They've completed their maintenance training on the leopards. Are there any questions? If not, let's move out."

After drawing food rations and loading our personal gear, Rebekah and I climbed into the cab of one of the haulers and led the convoy to Morgan City. Rebekah drove while I reviewed personnel files. I paired our militia members and divided them into two fire teams.

As we were leaving the battalion motor pool Rebekah said, "I want to congratulate you on getting your commission. I heard Officer Training School is tough but am not surprised you made it through."

"Thank you, Rebekah. It must have been a shock hearing I would be your commanding officer. I hope you won't have a problem serving in my platoon."

"No, you were an exceptional non-commissioned officer and I'm sure you'll be an outstanding platoon leader. Besides, Uncle Morris said this was my last chance at getting a commission. I realize I have a lot to learn about leading soldiers. My future with the militia is entirely in your hands."

She continued, "And for the record, I didn't feel like I was deserting you during the battle at Calhoun City. I honestly believed you would figure out a way to beat that leopard."

There; it was out in the open. I replied, "Rebekah, I appreciate your confidence in me. However, when I requested help, you should have sent one or more cheetahs to my aid. Leaving me alone against overwhelming odds made you look like a coward and it almost cost me my life."

"I'm sorry, John. I didn't realize how serious the situation was. I promise you it won't ever happen again."

"Rebekah, I accept your remorse as sincere. I suggest we put that incident behind us and move on."

Relief sounded in her voice when she responded, "Thank you, John. You won't be disappointed."

Although I was not ready to trust her, I was glad we discussed the incident at Calhoun City. It was a start. As her commander, operational necessity would demand frequent and constant communication with Rebekah. I couldn't afford to have an unresolved issue between us.

After a few minutes, Rebekah asked, "John, why didn't Helen get chosen to lead a leopard fire team? She has lots of experience with cheetahs."

"Rebekah, Helen was initially chosen but her unexpected pregnancy changed her assignment."

"Congratulations, sir! That's good news, isn't it?"

"I'm excited about Helen being pregnant."

"John, if Helen is pregnant, where is she being assigned?"

"Helen is being assigned to Militia Headquarters. You should also know that she's not happy about losing her warrior status."

Rebekah laughed and said, "That's funny. I would give anything to be assigned to Militia Headquarters and a warrior like Helen thinks it's the worst job in the militia."

We arrived at the militia post in late morning and were assigned parking space near the installation's motor pool. The post was mostly deserted, manned with only a skeleton crew which maintained security, barracks, boilers, mess hall, offices and repair facilities. After exiting the vehicles, Rebekah called the soldiers into a platoon formation and announced fire team assignments. We left one of the non-commissioned officers in charge and instructed her to arrange barracks for our platoon and get everyone settled.

Rebekah and I contacted the plant manager and showed him our identification. He was expecting us and said, "Welcome to Crane Manufacturing Company. My name is Ted Simpson. If you'll come with me, I'll show you our assembly line and vehicle staging area."

I was impressed with the layout of the factory.

Ted said, "At full production, Crane will complete three leopards each day. Currently, we have the first five new leopards at various stages of completion. The slower production is caused by the workers having to learn new assembly techniques. This phenomenon is known as a 'learning curve' and is common to all manufacturing processes."

I asked, "When will Crane achieve full production?"

Ted replied, "We hope to achieve our full production capability after we have completed the 50th leopard. Incidentally, Haven's engineers broke lots of speed records in getting this vehicle ready for production."

"Do you manufacture the parts here?"

"No. the parts are manufactured at secret locations and brought here by hauler. I'm told the parts manufacturing facilities are very small and widely dispersed. Our biggest challenge is getting enough parts to support our assembly operations."

Sitting in the staging area were 10 refurbished leopards. Ted announced, "These are your leopards. They're the first ones we've assembled. They were captured from Earth units and brought here for complete overhaul. Being able to disassemble these leopards and put them back together has been a tremendous learning benefit to our factory's workforce.

"I've arranged training classes to begin at 8:00 AM tomorrow. Please have your crews meet near the vehicles. Prior to hand-off, I'll require signatures from you for each leopard."

"Ted, I can assure you our fire teams will be ready. What about our mechanics' training?"

"The five mechanics assigned to your platoon have completed their training and I'm told are waiting for you at the post."

"Ted, is there a nearby training location at which we can maneuver and conduct live fire training with our leopards?"

"Yes, the motor pool is part of a 'mothballed' militia training post. When you get your leopards, I'll give you a map of the maneuver area and a set of keys to unlock the gates to the area. We keep it locked because we don't want local people searching for scrap metal; there are too many live rounds in the impact area and it's not safe for scroungers. Your five-day familiarization training is scheduled to start tomorrow. Eventually, another platoon will arrive to receive their leopards. One of our trainers will accompany you. In addition to leading you through exercise scenarios; he will develop a standard operating procedure for use by all leopard units."

I thanked him for the tour and his assistance and we returned to the motor pool.

At 4:30 PM, Rebekah called the platoon to attention and I began my address. "Ladies and gentlemen, our training starts at 5:00 AM tomorrow. After a morning run, you'll have time to shower and eat breakfast. We'll meet here again at 7:30 and ride over to the Vehicle Staging Area at Crane Manufacturing. Leopard commanders and drivers have been designated.

"We also have five maintenance personnel assigned to this platoon. Please welcome these men and women to our platoon. They will maintain our vehicles and drive the haulers.

"As you have undoubtedly noted, we normally have one mechanic per combat vehicle. Today, I'm announcing a workload change. Because we're only authorized half our normal maintenance staff, leopard fire team members will be responsible for washing, refueling and rearming their own vehicles.

"Ensure you get a good night's sleep and are fully prepared for class tomorrow. I'm looking forward to this five-day training course and I'm anxious, as I'm sure you are, to get back into the fight."

Rebekah and I met the new mechanics and gave them a special welcome to our platoon.

Our fire teams were assigned to Barracks 3 and 4. There was a private room in each barrack. I asked Rebekah to choose one and I would take the other. All other soldiers slept in the open bay which occupied the majority of space in each barrack.

* * *

The following morning Rebekah and I led the soldiers on a three kilometer run before breakfast. In spite of hearing some grumbling, I was happy everyone made it to the finish line within the allotted time.

At 8:00, a Crane manufacturing supervisor gave an introduction to the technical characteristics of the leopard. Following this lecture, commanders and drivers were ordered to their leopards. After signing for the ten leopards, the company trainer used his personal hauler to lead the convoy of leopards to the military installation. Leopards followed one another in a line formation. Rebekah and I were the final two in the formation.

Because my platoon members had experience operating cheetahs, our transition to leopards was relatively easy. The most difficult thing was getting accustomed to having a driver. A driver enabled the commander to 'fight the vehicle;' meaning the vehicle commander communicated with the fire team leader, located targets and fired the weapons. Maintaining effective and constant communication between the gunner and driver was a critical new task. Fully half of our field training concentrated on incorporating this task into our role as vehicle commander. As the first platoon being trained on leopards, our communications were recorded and reviewed each evening. From this, the company trainer developed and wrote a standard operating procedure. This procedure would be followed by our platoon members and given to all future platoons for their use.

My task as platoon leader was to maintain command and control over two fire teams. Rebekah and I spent additional hours developing commands to more quickly and effectively communicate different scenarios. The key to maximizing our leopards' effectiveness would be for me to 'see the battlefield' and communicate orders. This was the same issue I studied in Officer's Training School. Fortunately, our leopards used a combination of voice and digital communications. Data displays gave a picture of each vehicle with a terrain map in the background. A useful tool unique to leopards was a miniature drone used by the platoon leader. This device was about the size of my hand and its job was to fly from 90 to 150 meters above the vehicle and send back a real time view showing the command vehicle in the center of a large circular picture on a vid screen. The drone also reported the location of enemy vehicles. Enemy vehicles would be displayed on my screen and with the touch of a button; I could send this data to the squad leader.

To communicate with any leopard, I would touch a vehicle shown on the screen and communicate directly with the vehicle's commander. There was also one button used to simultaneously communicate with all leopards in the platoon.

I made it a practice to contact Rebekah whenever action was required from a vehicle in her fire team. This extra step included Rebekah in the chain of command and enabled her to maintain control over her fire team. After each simulated mission, I conducted a debriefing session with her and explained what went right and what went wrong. She readily grasped the rationale behind each scenario and seldom repeated mistakes.

During the evening of our third day of training, I entered my barracks after a debriefing session with Rebekah and heard several of the soldiers engaging in a lively debate. One side was arguing the leopard driver should be classified as a warrior while the other side was adamant that only the commander could be considered a warrior.

After noticing my presence, one of the soldiers turned to me and asked, "Lieutenant, what's the answer to our question? We acknowledge the leopard commander is a warrior but how is the driver classified?"

"You soldiers have discovered an interesting subject for debate. I don't know if anyone in Militia Headquarters has made a decision on that question. In the absence of an official determination, let's decide among ourselves. When you commanders were fighting cheetahs, you were considered warriors. Am I correct?"

Several answered, "Yes sir."

Continuing, I asked, "Your role as a cheetah warrior consisted of driving and shooting. Is that correct?"

"Yes sir. We did both as cheetah warriors."

"As a cheetah warrior, which action was more important; being able to drive or being able to shoot?"

After some hesitation, one of the commanders said, "Sir, both functions are critical to the cheetah's mission."

"That's an excellent answer, Sergeant. One final question; did you consider yourself a warrior when you were driving the cheetah or only when you were firing the weapon?"

After a few long seconds, one of the commanders sheepishly replied, "Point taken, Lieutenant; both driver and commander of the leopard should be considered warriors."

As training progressed, I observed Rebekah becoming more confident and competent as a fire team leader. Since nobody in my platoon knew her history at Calhoun City, her fire team members respected her as their leader. What I didn't know was how she would react when we engaged a real enemy.

"Rebekah, during the last scenario, you choose to hide your leopards in defilade. How could you have positioned them to better flank my squad?"

"John, I wasn't sure which direction you were taking; it seemed prudent to hide."

"In this training scenario, you knew how many leopards I have. What you didn't know was my route. Had you known my route, you could have engaged me when my formation was most vulnerable. You can't afford to miss an opportunity to attack; especially when you can pick the terrain and time of attack. Our armored vehicles were designed for attack; it's your job to find out where the enemy is located and where he is heading. If necessary, get feet on the ground and conduct reconnaissance."

CHAPTER 39

ASSIGNMENT TO MILITIA HEADQUARTERS (MILITIA FORCES)

It was a tiring trip from the Fifth Battalion to Militia Headquarters. Helen was still in the dumps over being removed from a combat role. She was thinking, *It's not fair that John gets to command a new leopard unit while I have to take a desk job! Why can't he take the desk job? After all, he's a draftee; I'm a professional soldier. Because I'm pregnant, I get stuck serving as a staff weenie while he gets to play with new toys. I should have taken precautions during that weekend. It's clear he was incapable of thinking about me getting pregnant.*

'I hope nobody at Militia Headquarters is stupid enough to laugh at my condition. I'll probably beat the crap out of them and then blame my hormones for the emotional outburst.'

Militia Headquarters was located in a large building on the outskirts of Senatobia. Camouflage netting was placed in strategic locations and vehicles were parked far away from the entrance. Helen was impressed with the size of the structure. Her driver stopped at the main entrance and Helen entered the building carrying her duffle and sleeping bags. After showing her identification, Helen dropped her bags at the building entrance and asked for directions to the Operations Center.

Room B-200; the Operations Center, was located in the basement of the headquarters building. The large windowless room contained two rows of desks occupied by civilians and militia officers; a large conference table and maps along each wall. A civilian directed Helen to a small office located in a corner of the large room. After knocking on the door, she was asked to enter. "Sir, Fifth Battalion Liaison Officer Helen Collins is reporting for duty."

After returning her salute, Brigadier General Bill Flanders smiled, got up from his desk and extended his hand. "WO Collins, I've been expecting you. Welcome aboard. It's a pleasure to have such a distinguished warrior serve on our headquarters staff. Please have a seat."

"Thank you, sir."

"If you recall, I participated in the review team a few months ago at Calhoun City."

"Yes sir. I do remember."

"Colonel Maxon is a friend of mine. He informed me about you and Lieutenant Collins and I know he will miss you very much. However, his loss is my gain. Helen, you have the practical warrior skills I need on my staff. We're planning a major offensive which will be spearheaded by armor units. I have staffers who have studied tactics and logistics, but I don't have enough officers with actual combat experience. As you might imagine, most of our officers are in the field leading troops and fighting. The few experienced officers I have on my staff are those who have been wounded in combat." He smiled and paused before continuing, "Or sent here to recover from other issues."

Helen felt her face turn red as General Flanders continued. "I'm warning you; some of us are a little rough around the edges and may give you a hard time to test your mettle. I trust you can handle yourself?"

"Yes sir, I don't anticipate any problems I can't overcome."

"Helen, you've had a long drive getting here and for the remainder of today, I want you to report to Doctor Stephanie Amos for an examination and see Mary Barnett for your quarters. Doctor Amos is in Room A-116 on the floor above. She will give you directions to Mary Barnett's office. Please report for duty here at 7:00 AM tomorrow. Have you any questions?"

"No sir. I'll see you tomorrow morning."

After knocking on the door to Room A-116, Helen heard a voice saying, "Come in." Helen entered a small office occupied by a nurse. The nurse looked at Helen and said, "Good afternoon. What may I do for you?"

Helen replied, "I am WO Helen Collins and am here for a check-up."

"Oh yes, I have your records. It says here that you've been assigned to militia headquarters and you're pregnant?"

"That's right."

"Okay, step into the next room and disrobe. There's a gown on the back of the door. Doctor Amos will be with you shortly."

* * *

"Well hello. I'm Doctor Amos and you're Helen?"

"Yes ma'am."

"Helen, I want you to lie on the examining table and put your feet in the metal stirrups. I'll put a sheet over your body since it's so cold in this room. When did you find out you were pregnant?"

Following the examination, Helen was directed to Mary Barnett's office. Mary was a cheerful and attractive woman in her early thirties.

"Hello, Helen. Welcome to Militia Headquarters! We assign two officers in each apartment. Our apartments have two bedrooms, a shared bath, living room and kitchen. Unfortunately, there's no maid service but we do furnish cleaning supplies. On the bright side, you're in luck; your roommate is a female officer and I'm sure you'll like her very much. Here is a key to Apartment 32B. It's located two blocks from the vehicle park. Please take this map, too. It contains the locations of restaurants, bars, churches, a beauty salon, laundry and shops in the area. Helen, let me know if I can be of further assistance."

"Thank you, Mary. I'm sure the apartment will be just fine; especially since I've been living in the field for the past six months."

"Oh my; I hope to hear some of your stories. I'll bet they're exciting! Not much excitement happens around here. We've been bombed twice but nothing more. Incidentally, there's a bar near your apartment named the Lucky George. People serving on the headquarters staff usually go there in the evenings and socialize. Maybe we'll see one another soon?"

"It's possible. Thanks for the information."

Helen collected her duffle and sleeping bags from the security guard stationed at the building entrance and walked to her apartment. It was several hundred yards away and she felt really tired after finally reaching the unit. As Helen opened the door, she stared at a living room cluttered with articles of clothing strewn over each piece of furniture. Helen called out, "Hello. Is anyone here?" Nobody answered. Helen walked through the clutter and found the empty bedroom. After dropping her duffle and sleeping bag on the bed, she toured the remainder of the apartment. The kitchen didn't appear to be used and there was no food in the pantry or refrigerated food storage unit. The bathroom was a total mess. Toiletries were scattered across both sinks and towels were on the floor. The trashcan was overflowing and the floor, sink, mirror, shower and commode needed scrubbing. Helen began thinking, *'What pig is living here?'* Opening the door to the other bedroom, Helen was stunned seeing the clutter on the floor and bed. Quickly closing the door, she thought, *'How could anyone live in this mess? Who is this officer? Whenever we do meet, I'm going to have a frank conversation with her and one of us is going to change.'*

Although dead tired, Helen unpacked and found the cleaning supplies. After moving her roommate's toiletries to one side, Helen cleaned the bathroom before taking a shower. She decided to skip dinner and went to bed. Later that evening Helen awoke briefly when she heard someone enter the apartment and go into the other bedroom.

* * *

At 5:30 AM Helen awoke and after a quick shower, put on her uniform and walked to the headquarters building. Her roommate was still asleep when Helen left the apartment. She ate breakfast in the cafeteria and entered her new office 25 minutes early. There was one civilian working at a desk and Helen walked over and introduced herself. "Good morning, I'm WO Helen Collins and I've been assigned to work in this office."

"Hello, Helen. My name is Jim Walsh and I'm the resident senior logistician. Welcome to the Ops Center. General Flanders announced we were getting a new officer. Your desk is across the room near the large map. The General is attending a staff meeting and I expect him back within the next 15 minutes. Let me know if I can help you."

"Thank you, Jim. I'm looking forward to working with you."

Helen walked over to her desk and noticed a name sign with 'WO Collins' had been prepared. She began studying the large map and noticed militia units were annotated on the map. She found the Fifth Battalion's position and observed its location had not changed since her departure. Helen was startled when she heard a voice behind her say, "Are you lost, Missy?"

Helen replied, "My name is WO Helen Collins and I've been assigned to this operations center." Turning around to face the person speaking she added, "And you are?"

"My name is Major Henry Kincaid and I'm your new boss." With that said, he stuck out his right arm for Helen to shake. There was no right hand; just a prosthetic hook at the end of his arm.

Helen quickly recovered from the shock and lightly took the metal hook in her hand and replied, "It's a pleasure to meet you, sir."

Henry limped over to his desk and said, "Helen, roll your chair over and let's talk."

After Helen moved her chair beside Henry's desk he asked, "What did you do before being assigned here?"

"Sir, I was the commander of Fire Team Six in the Fifth Battalion."

"How long did you serve in that position?"

"A year. I was promoted and assumed command a few weeks before the invasion."

"And what did you do before that?"

"I was a cheetah warrior for four and a half years."

"Sounds like you worked your way up the ranks and are a career soldier."

"Yes sir. I've chosen the militia as a career."

"And why are you here instead of leading your fire team?"

"Sir, I'm pregnant. Colonel Maxon reassigned me to serve as the Fifth Battalion's Liaison Officer to Militia Headquarters."

Major Kincaid laughed and said, "Well, at least your reason for being out of an operational unit is a temporary condition." Holding up his prosthetic hook and looking at it he added, "Some of us will never have an opportunity to get back to the 'fun stuff.'"

"How did that happen, sir?"

"The short version is; leaving your body exposed when a grenade explodes nearby will change your career path."

After pausing, he continued. "Enough of the maudlin stuff; let's get to work. Helen, we're planning our first major offensive of the war and you and I are going to develop maneuver plans for our armored battalions. Our job will be to integrate our plans into an overall operational plan. The Operational Plan will include armor, infantry, logistics and other units. The end result of our planning will go out as operational orders to the individual units."

"What's my job, sir?"

"You'll maintain daily contact with each armored unit. We need to know their location, manpower, equipment and supply status. The information you provide will be integrated into the overall operational plan. Based on this data, you and I will recommend missions for General Flanders' approval. Because we're planning a major offensive, all armored missions for the immediate future will be in support of this offensive."

"How do we find out about enemy forces?"

"That's a great question. Our militia has an intelligence unit which provides us information about the enemy forces. We get information such as location and movement of his units and their estimated strength. While you're collecting data on our own armored units, I'm visiting our intelligence center and getting updated information on enemy forces."

"How do I contact our armored units?"

"We have a communications center where you'll visit several times each day. A designated operator in the Comm Center will give you updated information. I'll contact the Security Office in a few minutes and request you be given authorization to enter the Comm Center. Their office is in Room B-210 and you need to speak with Doris Miller. She's our point of contact for all armored units." He added, "Helen, the work we do in this office is highly classified. Very little is written down and no paper or verbal information ever leaves this office. Do you understand?"

"Yes, sir, it's perfectly clear. I have friends serving in cheetah units and my husband is the platoon leader of our first leopard unit. There is no way I'll say or do anything to jeopardize their lives."

"That's a great attitude. If more were like you, we wouldn't have to worry about security leaks. Speaking of which, it's come to our attention that someone connected to militia headquarters is passing intelligence to the enemy. As you can well imagine, we're trying to find the traitor and plug the leak. I'm asking you to be alert to any possible security breach and report it to me. If Earth forces find out about our planned offensive, it may be doomed to failure from the start."

* * *

At 8:30 AM, Helen entered the Communications Center and asked to speak with Doris Miller. Helen was directed to an aisle of cubicles and found Doris sitting at a communications console talking with someone. On noticing Helen's presence, Doris motioned her to take a seat beside her desk.

After ending the transmission, Doris turned to her and said, "Hello, I'm Doris Miller. You must be Helen Collins. I've been notified to expect you."

"Hi Doris; it's nice to meet you."

"Helen, I notice you're an armor officer but I don't remember seeing or hearing your name mentioned."

"Doris, I recently married. My maiden name is Ramses."

Doris' mouth formed a big 'O' as she said, "*You're* Helen Ramses! Oh wow; I've been receiving reports on you and your fire team since the war started. I'm so glad to finally put a face with your name. It's an honor to meet such a distinguished warrior. Welcome to Militia Headquarters!"

"Thank you, Doris. It's a pleasure meeting you, too. I'm looking forward to working with you."

"Ah yes; Henry Kincaid notified me a few minutes ago he would be sending a new officer to collect USR's."

"What are USR's?"

"Excuse my shorthand, Helen. USR's are Unit Status Reports. If you want to wait, I'll have today's first USR completed in a few minutes."

"No problem. It'll be interesting to see how you compile the data."

As Doris resumed working on the report, a man stopped at her cubicle and said, "Doris, aren't you going to introduce me to this officer?"

Doris looked up from her desk and said, "Peter, this is Warrant Officer Helen Collins. WO Collins works in the Operations Center. Helen, this is Peter Armstrong. Peter is our resident communications technician whose job is to keep our communications network operating."

Peter looked down at Helen and said, "Welcome to Militia Headquarters, Helen. We're really fortunate to have such a cutie assigned to headquarters."

Helen stood up and faced Peter. "Mr. Armstrong, I don't appreciate being referred to as a cutie. In the future, kindly keep your juvenile observations to yourself. Are we clear?"

Shock registered on Peter's face as he mumbled something and hastily departed.

Helen sat down and asked Doris, "Did I overreact?"

Doris grinned and said, "Helen, Peter works here because he's a network engineer. As you'll notice, most of the people working in headquarters are women. With that ratio, even nerdy men have no problem finding women to date and they get away with saying almost anything. I must admit it was fun listening to you pinning his ears back. I'm sure he'll get over it and will probably spread the word that you're a lesbian or some other nonsense. Don't worry about him; he's harmless. Here's your report and please let me know if I can be of further assistance."

"Thanks, Doris. It's been great getting to know you. For future reference, when should I come by for USR updates?"

"Helen, the best times are 9:00 AM, 2:00 PM and 5:00 PM each day. It's been a pleasure meeting you and I'm looking forward to seeing you this afternoon."

When Helen returned to her desk, she noticed the First Platoon of the Fifth Battalion, Commanded by Lieutenant Collins, had been moved to Morgan City. Helen smiled and thought, *Maybe this job is not so bad; at least I'll be able to keep track of John and Rebekah at all times!"*

* * *

That evening, Helen stopped at a nearby grocery store and purchased some items for the apartment. As she entered the apartment, she almost dropped the bags when she saw her roommate. Covering her surprise, she said, "Lieutenant Webber, I didn't know you were my roommate."

Webber stood up and replied, "Helen, please call me Sarah. I was informed I would be getting a roommate but I didn't know it was you. And I see your last name is now Collins. What happened? Did you get married? Is John alive?"

Before Helen could reply, Sarah walked over, took a bag from Helen and they carried the groceries into the kitchen. Helen finally said, "Yes, John is alive. He was captured during the ambush but escaped a few days later. We were married two weeks ago."

"Congratulations. I hope you and John will be very happy. Was it difficult getting approval to marry an enlisted soldier?"

"Sarah, John is a lieutenant. He graduated from Officer's Training School three weeks ago."

"That's amazing! John is full of surprises. I know you must be very proud of him."

"I am proud of John and happy to be his wife. But what about you; what have you been doing?"

"I've been staying busy with investigations. In addition to investigating possible war crimes, I'm looking into some internal issues." She added, "Look, I know the place is a mess; I've been so busy lately that I've neglected cleaning up. I'm glad you're sharing the apartment with me. Your presence will remind me to keep things neater."

Sarah continued, "Helen, I have an idea, why don't we go out to eat dinner tonight? It's late and you look like you could use some rest. I know you've recently been in the field and it's hard to get any rest during combat."

Helen replied, "That sounds like a great idea. And you're correct, I'm pretty tired. It's been a long day."

As they walked to a restaurant, Sarah asked, "Helen, if you don't mind my asking; why have you been assigned to Militia Headquarters? From all reports, you're one of our best fire team leaders."

"Sarah, I'm pregnant so Colonel Maxon transferred me here to a desk job until the baby is born."

A surprised Sarah replied, "Well congratulations! I know you and John must be thrilled at the prospect of becoming parents. Is it a boy or girl?"

"I found out yesterday that it's a girl." Helen added, "Sarah, I love the thought of becoming a mother but the timing could have been different – if you know what I mean."

"Helen, I do understand. You're a warrior and you feel bad about being transferred from active combat. But you should know Earth intends to send two more invasion forces. It's likely you will get a chance to get back into the action." She quietly added, "And unless a miracle happens, I don't see how we can stop the next two waves. It has taken everything Haven can muster to contain this first invasion."

Helen replied, "I pray this war will be over before my child is born."

"I'll drink to that. And speaking of which, here we are. Cutter's Dining Establishment - my favorite restaurant in this town."

"It looks like a nice place."

After they were seated, Helen asked, "Sarah, since I'm new to the area, what do you know about the Lucky George?"

Sarah's expression became serious as she quietly answered, "Helen, the Lucky George is a bar about a block from our apartment. Lots of headquarters staff members go there in the evenings. If you go, be careful of what you say. I've heard that people who have different agendas frequent that bar and could be listening."

"Does this have anything to do with your internal investigation?"

"Helen, you're a smart woman and I like you already but I'm not permitted to discuss my work."

"I understand. Let's look at the menu, I'm starving."

CHAPTER 40

OPERATION SANDPIPER (MILITIA FORCES)

"Good morning Major Kinkaid, what's on our agenda for today?"

"Good morning, Helen. Our objective for today is to finalize our input to Operational Sandpiper."

"Sandpiper - what kind of name is that?"

"Helen, a sandpiper is a shore bird native to Earth. The word has no relation to our current military operation on Haven and that's the point. This operation is uniquely named but its name doesn't give any clue about its objective. Different offices within the militia can discuss Operation Sandpiper but if the enemy should only learn about the name; they can't use that to guess the intent of our operation."

"Oh I see. Who thought of that clever idea?"

"Not us. Subterfuge has been used by armies on Earth for thousands of years. We're hoping since it works for them it will work for Haven's militia."

"Does Operation Sandpiper include more than an attack on Johnson Springs?"

"Yes. There are four separate operations included in Operation Sandpiper. Earth has concentrated its forces in four sites surrounding Tupelo; Ripley to the north, Natchez to the west, Columbus to the east and Johnson Springs to the south of Tupelo. These major sites will be attacked simultaneously."

"I don't understand, sir. Do we have enough militia units to attack four major locations at the same time?"

Major Kinkaid smiled and said, "That's a great observation and you're exactly right. We're using some militia units to attack three places as a ruse while we attack the fourth with enough firepower to win. The other attacks are designed to hold the enemy forces in place and prevent them from reinforcing units at our main attack. This is one of the reasons for so much secrecy in our planning. If the enemy knew our primary objective, they would reinforce that location and our attacking force will be slaughtered. Helen, if the true intent of our operation is given to Earth forces, Haven could lose this war."

"Major, you mentioned yesterday you suspect we have a traitor within Militia Headquarters. How do you know the enemy doesn't already have this information?"

"Our intelligence sources have not detected movement of Earth forces to reinforce our primary target. If Earth units stationed at Ripley, Natchez or Columbus were being shifted to Johnson Springs, we would know our plans have been compromised."

"Assuming it takes one day to move their units and if you observed their units being relocated prior to or during our attack, what are our options?"

"Helen, that's an excellent question! We know the commander of the Earth soldiers is not stupid. He may be waiting until the last moment to commit his reinforcements. If that's the case, we must have an alternative plan. Let's call it Plan B."

"Sir, I don't understand. What is a Plan B?"

"When attacking a heavily defended position, the attacker needs a larger force in order to be successful. Let's assume the attacker requires four times the size of the defending force. That's a four to one ratio. If the defender is reinforced, the ratio of attacking to defending becomes smaller and the attack will fail. There are other factors involved but what I'm telling you is usually accurate."

Major Kinkaid continued, "Our Plan B will switch our militia units from an attacking mode to a defending mode which should change the ratio back into our favor. Plan B consists of selecting a location near Johnson Springs and preparing it for our militia units to use as a defensive position should the need arrive. If the Earth units at Johnson Springs get reinforcements, we move our attacking forces into the defensive location and decimate the Earth forces attacking from Johnson Springs. The trick is to get the Earth forces to attack our defensive location."

"How do we accomplish that?"

"We have to entice them to commit to an attack. One way is to sacrifice some of our units in order to draw them into attacking our defended position. That's akin to leaving a trail of bread crumbs toward our trap. Another option is to lure the Earth forces into our trap by pretending to lose our will to fight. A retreating militia force may tempt the enemy to lose caution and launch an all-out attack; trying to end Haven's resistance once and for all."

"Sir, which option do you propose we use?"

"Helen, I hate to think of sacrificing any of our militia. Let's start Plan B with option two. Our first decision is to find a suitable defensive position. It needs to be prepared before Operation Sandpiper is put into motion. If you had to move your fire team into a defensive position with the enemy hot on your heels, what would you want to see when you arrived at the position?"

"Major, I would want to see firing pits dug for my armored vehicles, water and ammunition stowed nearby and a medical team available for my wounded."

"Excellent! Let's see if we can find a good location near Johnson Springs which can be prepared within the next few days. A deserted farm would be perfect. We can use a couple of militia members disguised as farmers whose plan is to dig some fresh water ponds in an open field a few kilometers from Johnson Springs.

"Helen, hopefully, we won't have to use Plan B but it will be there just in case. Having Plan B might save our militia from annihilation and end up getting us the same result; this time using a defensive strategy to defeat the enemy at Johnson Springs. After I get General Flanders' verbal approval, I'll send you to supervise its construction. I know three soldiers who have the requisite skills and experience we can use. They are Sergeants Hank Powell, Edward House and Jim Watson. I'll have them get their equipment and meet you at Plan B's location.

"Helen, don't write anything down relating to Plan B and don't discuss it with anyone including people assigned to Militia Headquarters. Let's keep this on a strict need-to-know basis.

"As you are well aware, we can't afford any delay and you have the perfect motivation to get the job done on time."

"Yes sir!" At that moment, Helen wanted to hug Major Kinkaid's neck. This desk job was getting better and better.

CHAPTER 41

GOING TO WAR IN A LEOPARD (MILITIA FORCES)

After completing new equipment training, Colonel Maxon sent special haulers to transport our leopards to the Third Battalion's motor pool. That decision enabled us to return to the battalion more quickly.

I was called into Colonel Maxon's office.

"Lieutenant Collins, welcome back! Tell me about your training and give me your opinion of the new leopards. Also, what's your assessment of WO Lloyd's capability?"

"Sir, our soldiers love the leopards. They are a warrior's ideal weapon. The toughest thing we had to learn was how to talk to the driver while communicating over the net and firing the weapon. The platoon leader's remotely piloted surveillance vehicle is a tremendous tool, too. I was able to maintain a bird's eye view of the battlefield and could quickly react to any scenario in real time. The enhanced observation is a force multiplier.

"Regarding WO Lloyd; Rebekah's performance exceeded my expectations. She is enthusiastic and a quick learner. I don't know how she'll react when we go into combat but her recent performance has done a lot to overcome my earlier worries. I am ready to trust her.

Colonel, in retrospect your decision to replace Helen with Rebekah may have been the best decision. I don't know if I could have put Helen's safety completely out of my mind during combat. And please don't ever tell Helen I said this."

"John, don't worry about me telling Helen about our conversation. I'm glad everything is working out for you and I'm delighted the soldiers like the leopards because I'm giving you an important mission. Since their arrival in December, the enemy has been using Johnson Springs Reservation as a staging area from which they launch their forays into the countryside south of Tupelo. We're attacking Johnson Springs Reservation in five days and I need your leopards to lead our attack. Your platoon's call sign will be 'Sierra.'" He handed me a chip and added, "This chip contains the highly classified operations plan. Safeguard this information and only share it with your platoon members as needed."

"Sir, Johnson Springs is over 300 kilometers away. Do you have transport available for our vehicles?"

"Regretfully, I can't spare any haulers. The transport vehicles which moved your leopards from the factory will be carrying supplies and infantry. John, this operation is big. Three militia battalions are being relocated simultaneously. You'll have to drive your leopards the entire distance. Your departure time is 3:00 PM today. Take charging units with you. As you may guess, this is our first major offensive in this war. Capturing Johnson Springs is critical in preparation for the final push on Tupelo."

He added, "John, don't stop for anything and that includes targets of opportunity. It's imperative I have your leopards in support of our attack on Johnson Springs. Even if you run into an ambush along the way, disengage as best you can and continue moving toward Johnson Springs. Inform me of the ambush and its location and I'll send a force to deal with them. We've got to have your leopards at Johnson Springs."

"Yes sir, I understand." I added, "Colonel, I'm honored to be commanding the militia's first platoon of leopards."

"You earned this command, John. Good luck, Lieutenant. I look forward to seeing you at Johnson Springs. We'll have a final meeting with the other commanders before the attack. See you there."

After John left the colonel's office, Colonel Maxon called in Sergeant Major Peters and said, "Sergeant Major, when Earth invaded Haven, they selected cities to the north, east and west of Tupelo and have been using them as launch points similar to Johnson Springs. Other militia units have been given those cities as targets. Without leopards, they'll have a tougher challenge. According to information from Militia Headquarters, we haven't begun producing new leopards. I wonder why Headquarters decided to launch a major offence before all militia units were equipped with leopards."

Sergeant Major Peters responded, "I don't know, sir. It doesn't make sense unless their hand has been forced by something to which we're not privy. In any case, I'm sure glad we have a platoon of leopards supporting our attack. Getting reinforced with a platoon of leopards could be a life saver."

* * *

After leaving the colonel's office I briefed Rebekah and our soldiers. "Ladies and gentlemen, we're going on a road trip. Gather all your equipment and personal items. Make sure your vehicles have been fully charged and get chargers, spare parts and rations loaded on our haulers. If we're attacked while en route, increase speed and return fire. We can't let anything stop us and we can't afford to stop and have a showdown with an enemy ambush team."

One of the sergeants asked, "Lieutenant, with these leopards, we could defeat any ambush force. Why are we changing tactics? We've all lost friends and family; it's time for a little payback."

"Sergeant, we've been given another mission which takes priority over normal operations. We're going to bypass targets of opportunity and concentrate on our primary objective."

"Sir, what is our primary objective?"

"Due to operational security requirements, I can't say now. You'll get more information during the next few days."

Turning to Rebekah I said, "WO Lloyd, ask Sergeant Major Peters if we can get a trailer to be pulled by one of the haulers. Have everything loaded and ready to go by 2:50 PM today."

While Rebekah supervised the loading, I found a quiet place to review the operational data contained on the chip and send a quick note to Helen.

At our debarkation time, I gave Rebekah the route to our first bivouac and asked her to lead the platoon. "Rebekah, I want you to take the lead on our convoy. Spread out the vehicles with at least one hundred meters between each. We need to minimize our convoy's heat signature to reduce the possibility of a satellite spotting us. Place the five haulers between the fire teams. The vehicles can follow one another by using their sensors. Based on the distance we're traveling today, we should arrive at our bivouac by 10:00 PM. When we arrive, arrange the leopards in a defensive perimeter and post guards. No fires; we're eating cold rations tonight."

She looked at me and quietly asked, "John, where are we going?"

"Rebekah, I can't discuss our final destination at this time. Militia Headquarters has placed the highest classification on this mission. When we stop this evening, I'll be able to share more information with you. And Rebekah, in case something happens to me, you'll assume command of the platoon. Our operations order is on a chip locked in my turret storage box. The key is around my neck."

Other units of the Fifth Battalion were given separate routes and timetables. The entire battalion was on the move. I also knew other militia forces would join us for the attack at Johnson Springs.

* * *

We arrived at our first bivouac at 9:54 PM. I got two rations and said, "Rebekah, please join me for dinner." After sitting down, I told Rebekah about our mission as we ate. "Rebekah, in four days, you and I will engage the enemy by attacking Johnson Springs, a heavily defended military post. Because we're equipped with leopards, Colonel Maxon will put us in the center of the conflict. Our job will be to blast through their defenses; leaving others the responsibility of cleaning up. Breaching the defensive line will be our primary job. Once this is accomplished, we will begin destroying the enemy's remaining armor forces.

"We're going to attack Johnson Springs? Now I understand the reason for all the secrecy. John, if our attack is successful, we may force Earth to surrender."

"I'm not sure that will happen right away. But taking Johnson Springs will stop their attacks against the region south of Tupelo and that's the first step toward getting them off our planet."

"Thank you for trusting me with this information. I'm sure you've noticed during these past weeks, I've worked very hard to earn your trust."

"Rebekah, you've proven yourself to be a good fire team leader and fast learner. I've been very pleased with your performance. You've worked hard without complaining. You have only one remaining question to answer and that is, 'how will you react when we engage the enemy?' Based on what I have observed, I'm willing to bet my life you're going to perform well under fire."

Rebekah looked at me for a few moments then said, "John, I'm scared. I'm scared I'll let you and my fire team down. Not a day goes by that I don't think of that awful day at Calhoun City."

"Rebekah, you were not ready to lead a fire team at that time. Today, I believe you're ready to lead. You have the training and desire - both are essential for success. And being scared is okay, too. I'm scared every time I go into a fight. Just rely on what you've learned, trust your soldiers to do their part and you'll be okay."

"Thank you, John. I can't tell you how much it means to me to hear you say those things. I'd rather die than let you down again."

"Goodnight, Rebekah. I'll see you in the morning. We continue our road march at 7:00 AM so the platoon members need to get up at 5:30."

CHAPTER 42

PLAN B (MILITIA FORCES)

Helen arrived at the site chosen for Plan B a mere three days prior to the attack on Johnson Springs. She found the deserted farm and met the three soldiers Major Kinkaid requested for the operation. Helen and the three non-commissioned officers were dressed in civilian clothing.

"Gentlemen, I am WO Helen Collins and you are Sergeants Hank Powell, Edward House and Jim Watson?"

"Yes ma'am, we are. Major Kinkaid gave us a list of equipment to bring and he said you had a critical mission for us. What can we do for you?"

Helen outlined the plan. "Gentlemen, we have only three days to prepare a defensive position for our soldiers. This site will only be used if things go bad for us at Johnson Springs. Because the risk of successfully overtaking Johnson Springs is so high, Major Kinkaid and I have prepared a fallback plan in case we have underestimated the Earth forces' strength.

"We chose this deserted farm because it's near Johnson Springs and it's located in a sparsely populated area. However, if anyone should come by and ask who we are and what are we doing; tell them we are a family of three brothers and a sister who inherited this farm.

Because of food shortages on Haven, we've decided to put the farm back into operation."

Helen unrolled a detailed drawing and began assigning tasks. "Hank, there is a three acre grove of trees adjacent to the planned defensive position. I want you to cut a six meter wide road through those trees for access to the trench.

"Jim, while Hank is preparing the entrance, I want you and Edward to begin digging the trench for our armored vehicles. Start adjacent to the woods and extend toward the farmhouse from there. We don't have time for fancy. Dig us a trench one meter deep and five meters wide. Pile the dirt in front of the trench on the north side to serve as a berm.

"We're going to place several metal containers in the trench which will hold ammunition for our cheetahs and leopards. The metal containers will arrive in two days. When they get here, we'll set them in the trench between firing pits and cover them with dirt.

"Hank, take the logs you cut while clearing the road and place them on the berm in front of the firing pits. Our infantry can take cover behind the logs and provide small arms fire to augment our firepower.

"From the air, our digging will appear to be a narrow pond. After Hank completes the road, I'll go into the woods and emplace anti-personnel mines. This will prevent the enemy from flanking us with his infantry."

"Helen, how long should we make the trench?"

"Jim, working eighteen hours each day for three days, you should be able to build a trench 90 meters long. This will accommodate sixty five armored vehicles plus ammunition storage containers. Remember, for each thirty-five cubic meters of dirt removed, we can protect one armored vehicle. For your information, we'll attack Johnson Springs with seventy armored vehicles and infantry. Unless you have more questions, let's get to work."

Helen cooked for the men and they slept in the farmhouse. With only three days to get the site prepared, Helen and her men worked in excess of eighteen hours each day; digging, hauling dirt and cutting trees to complete the defensive position on time.

* * *

Two days after starting the defensive position, four haulers arrived one evening and unloaded twelve metal containers of ammunition for the cheetahs and leopards. By morning, Helen, Jim and Hank had placed the containers in the partially completed trench and had covered their tops with dirt.

After the third day, the defensive position was complete and Jim, Edward and Hank departed with their equipment; leaving Helen to watch over the site and wait for the militia forces to arrive.

CHAPTER 43

ATTACKING JOHNSON SPRINGS (MILITIA FORCES)

The militia leaders met in the evening prior to attacking Johnson Springs. Colonel John Maxon commanding the 5th Armored Battalion had been designated as the task force leader. Colonel Paul McGinnis commanding the 7th Armored Battalion and Colonel Lori McGraw commanding the 2nd Infantry Battalion were also present along with their officers. "Ladies and gentlemen, before we finalize our attack plans, we need to hear from Mr. Nick Durham; a local farmer who once served in the militia as a sniper. Mr. Durham has been watching enemy activity at Johnson Springs for the past two weeks. Mr. Durham, the floor is yours."

"Thank you, Colonel Maxon. Ladies and gentlemen, I was asked by Captain Richard Price from Militia Headquarters to keep an eye on Johnson Springs during these past two weeks. I was able to sneak up near the military post and found a hiding place where I could watch the entrance. I was also able to place a listening device in the guard shack one evening while the guard was temporarily distracted.

"Johnson Springs is commanded by Colonel William Morrissey who has the 413th Armored and the 351st Infantry Battalions. While the post appears to have its normal complement of soldiers, it was reinforced by a second armored battalion two nights ago. Their vehicles and men are hidden inside vacant warehouses. This means there are two full battalions of armored vehicles inside Johnson Springs. Here is a vid showing the new vehicles entering the post. Based on a conversation I overheard from someone talking in the guard shack, the new unit is the 420th Armored Battalion."

Colonel Maxon looked over at Captain Price and asked, "Captain Price, can you elaborate on this Earth unit?"

"Yes sir. The 420th Armored Battalion has been stationed in Columbus, east of Tupelo as part of the enemy's Task Force Columbus. The 420th is primarily armed with cheetahs but it has a platoon of fifteen leopards. The 420th is commanded by Colonel Veronica Williamson."

Colonel McGraw interrupted, "Which unit massacred the militia assigned to the 3rd battalion?"

"According to our sources, the 415th Armored Battalion attacked and annihilated our 3rd Armored Battalion when Earth first invaded Haven. Since that fateful day, members of the 415th have earned a reputation as being especially vicious and aggressive. They are also responsible for a majority of Haven's civilian casualties. The 415th Battalion is commanded by Colonel Miles Harper who is also the Columbus Task force Commander. However, we believe only one company within his battalion actually committed the atrocity involving our 3rd Armored Battalion."

"Thank you, Captain Price." Turning to the other officers, Colonel Maxon continued, "Ladies and Gentlemen, this changes our plan. The enemy defending Johnson Springs has been reinforced which means we don't have an adequate force to attack the fort successfully. I've been informed Militia Headquarters was aware our plans might be compromised so they have prepared an alternative plan which will be briefed by WO Helen Collins."

Helen had been standing in the back of the group and after hearing her name called, quickly made her way to the front. "Good evening ladies and gentlemen. Plan B was developed in case our primary plan was compromised. Those reinforcements arriving within the past two days are conclusive proof the enemy knows about our planned attack. In order to regain our advantage during the upcoming fight, Headquarters prepared an alternative plan designed to get the enemy to attack us while we make a strong defense."

Colonel Maxon asked, "Helen, what do we defend?"

Helen pointed to the map and said, "Sir, we've prepared a defensive position, code named 'Wiggins,' about eight kilometers from Johnson Springs which is capable of holding seventy armored vehicles. We also have ammunition stockpiled for your use.

"Your biggest challenge will be to entice the enemy to leave Johnson Springs and attack Wiggins; our defensive position."

"Colonel Maxon stated, "The enemy has never seen our militia attack in force because this is our first major offensive since their invasion. Although they're expecting us to attack tomorrow, surprise is still on our side. Ladies and gentlemen, how do you propose we get the Earth soldiers to leave the safety of Johnson Springs and come after us with all they've got?"

Nick Durham raised his hand. "Yes Mr. Durham?"

"Colonel, if we shoot the Commander of Johnson Springs, wouldn't the leader of the 420th assume command of Earth forces at Johnson Springs?"

"Yes, that's normal protocol. The senior ranking officer assumes command."

"Sir, I believe it would work to our advantage to have someone commanding the enemy forces that is not as familiar with the terrain as the commander of Johnson Springs. He or she would be more likely to fall for your trap.

"Further, having observed Johnson Springs for the past two weeks, I know where the commander lives and I know his habits. Every morning at 5:00 AM, he goes for a three kilometer run. During this run, he's frequently exposed to a potential sniper bullet."

"Mr. Durham, that's a great idea! Could you escort one of our snipers to a vantage point where the shot could be taken?"

"Yes sir."

"Sergeant Major Peters, select a sniper and have him meet up with Mr. Durham immediately. Given Mr. Durham's past experience as a sniper, he can be the spotter. Their primary target is the Johnson Springs Commander. Mr. Durham, your sniper team needs to take the shot at first light in the morning. This will be the signal for our attack. After your sniper team hits their primary target you can selectively take out anyone else who shows themself."

Turning back to the officers, Colonel Maxon continued, "Shooting the Johnson Springs commander should cause momentary confusion within the chain of command. This will give us a few minutes to use our cheetahs to fire at targets of opportunity. The objective during those few minutes is to kill armored vehicles, make noise and create as much confusion as possible. After the 420th commander takes charge, she'll assemble her remaining armored vehicles and come at us hard. That's when we begin pulling back and staying just out of range of her weapons.

"Let's show her what a bunch of cowards we are and make her believe she can win the war by annihilating our retreating force. My 5th Battalion cheetahs will run from the attack and make its way to Wiggins. Our leopards will not participate in the attack but will remain hidden until the enemy is attacking Wiggins. At the appropriate time, I will signal our leopards to hit the enemy on his flank; concentrating their firepower on the enemy leopards first.

"After defeating the enemy's combat vehicles, we'll move back to Johnson Springs and take over the post. Without armored vehicles, the post won't be able to mount a serious defense.

"Colonel McGraw, take your 2nd Infantry Battalion and position them on the north side of Johnson Springs. Wait until we destroy their armor and then you will lead the final assault on Johnson Springs."

"Roger that Colonel Maxon; we'll be standing by."

"Colonel McGinnis, I need your 7th Armored Battalion in place at Wiggins. You'll need to cover the 5th Battalion as we retreat in front of the enemy's pursuing armor. While running from the enemy and moving into Wiggins, I'm going to be short of firepower and can use your help."

"Glad to do it, Colonel. My boys will pick off several of the bastards while they're chasing you."

"Ladies and gentlemen, does anyone have any questions? If not, let's go to war."

* * *

I couldn't believe my fortune to be in the same room with Helen. Following the meeting, we greeted one another in the parking lot and took a few minutes for ourselves. Holding her close I said, "Helen, it's so wonderful seeing you. You look great, Darling and you did a super job with the briefing."

Rebekah, who had been standing nearby while Helen and I greeted one another interjected and said, "Helen, I was also impressed with your briefing."

Helen pulled back from my embrace and noticed Rebekah's presence for the first time. Helen replied, "Thank you Rebekah. John tells me you've become a good fire team leader. I wish you every success tomorrow and ask that you look after John."

"Don't worry Helen; I'll do everything in my power to keep John safe for you. You have my word on that."

"Thank you." Helen turned back to John and said, "While I was working with Major Kinkaid on Plan B, I was praying we wouldn't have to use it. John, it appears you're going to be in the thick of the fighting. Darling, please take care."

At that moment, Colonel Maxon joined us and said, "Helen, you've done a wonderful job. Your work will save many militia lives and may enable us to win the day. Thank you."

"You're welcome, sir. I only wish I could have a more active role."

"Funny you should mention that subject. It seems I am short a fire team member. A new warrior assigned to Fire Team Six broke his arm yesterday and is incapacitated. We've got an extra cheetah without a warrior. Sergeant Delucca is the fire team leader. If you're interested, go find him and give him the news. I'm sure he would love to have you join his fire team."

"Yes sir!" turning to me she said, "Bye Darling. I love you. Take care!" And she was running to find her fire team.

I laughed and said, "Colonel, you've made her the happiest woman on Haven."

Turning to me he smiled and said, "After the work she did for us, it was the least I could do for her." He noticed Rebekah standing nearby and said, "WO Lloyd, it's good to see you again. How do you like the new leopards?"

"Sir, the leopard is a wonderful machine and I really appreciate the opportunity of serving in Lieutenant Collins' platoon. He's taught me so much during the past few weeks."

"I'm delighted to hear that, Rebekah. John has spoken highly about your performance, too."

Turning to me he said, "John, according to the map there are some woods about one kilometer from Wiggins. Before the attack begins, I want you to hide your leopards in these woods, shut down and go cold. Minimize the chance of being spotted. When I give you the signal, get to Wiggins as quickly as you can and hit the enemy on his right flank. Concentrate your fire on his leopards. Make sure your identifiers are tuned to our frequency so we minimize friendly fire incidents."

"Yes sir. Your plan will hit the enemy armor from two different directions. You're the anvil and we'll become the hammer."

"That's the idea. Let's see if it works. Good luck, John."

"Thank you, sir. Luck to you, too."

When Rebekah and I returned to my platoon, she called the members together. I announced, "Ladies and gentlemen, we're going to hide in a wooded area and wait for Colonel Maxon's signal to attack. When we get into the woods, turn everything off. From the woods, it's only a three minute trip to the planned battle area. We'll attack in line formation. Only engage the enemy when you have a firing lock. Primary targets are his leopards. Shoot, hit one and quickly shift to another target. Don't wait for a kill confirmation. We'll be outnumbered so we've got to disable as many as possible before they notice us. Are there any questions?"

"Sir, after our first shots, the enemy will know we're flanking him. If they begin moving toward us, what do we do?"

I replied, "We're going to slug it out with them. This is why our first salvo must disable a maximum number of enemy vehicles. They'll have fewer vehicles with which to shoot at us. Besides, Colonel Maxon's forces at Wiggins will continue firing. This is why you need to double check your transponders." Turning to Rebekah I said, "WO Lloyd, please verify everybody's transponder frequencies. I don't want any friendly casualties."

* * *

Sergeant Major Peters contacted WO Grant, the leader of Fire Team Four, and asked for his sniper. "We've got a special mission for a sniper and I need yours right away."

WO Grant replied, "Sergeant Major, our sniper is Private Mary Holloway. I'll get her for you."

With her rifle slung over her shoulder, Mary walked up to Sergeant Major Peters and said, "Sergeant Major, WO Grant said you needed me?"

"Hello Mary. I have a very important job for you this morning. How are you fixed for ammunition?"

"I've got 200 rounds, Sergeant Major."

"That's good. Mary, I want you to meet Mr. Nick Durham. Nick is a former militia sniper who is going to spot for you. Mary, based on Lieutenant Collins' high regard for you, I've selected you for this critical mission. Do you have any questions?"

"Lieutenant Collins? Is this the same Corporal Collins who became our fire team leader during the fight at Calhoun City?"

"That's correct. John Collins completed Officer's Training School a few weeks ago. He is now the platoon leader of our new leopards."

"Sergeant Major, If Lieutenant Collins believes I can do it; then I'm your sniper."

Nick spoke up and said, "Thanks for your help, Sergeant Major. If you have nothing more, Mary and I must be off. I want to get us hidden before sunup."

"Good luck to the both of you."

As they jogged toward Johnson Springs, Nick asked, "Mary, tell me about you."

"There's not much to tell. I grew up on a farm and went hunting with my father and brothers each year. After graduating from school, I joined the militia and served as a mechanic. Corporal, uh Lieutenant Collins recognized my shooting skills and designated me as a sniper for his fire team. We fought Earth forces at Calhoun City where I killed twelve men with this rifle."

"Mary, today you have an opportunity to make history. Let me tell you about your target and why it is so important to put him down."

Nick continued, "There are two armored battalions inside Johnson Springs. Three days ago, there was only one battalion. Johnson Springs has been reinforced. If our militia attacks the fort today, we'll lose the fight. We've got to change our strategy by getting the enemy to attack our fort where we'll have the advantage."

"Mary asked, "What fort do we have?"

"WO Helen Collins had one built nearby this past week."

"I don't know that officer."

Nick replied, "I overheard someone say she's the wife of Lieutenant John Collins."

"Oh wow! Then she must be the former WO Helen Ramses. WO Ramses had the reputation of being the best cheetah warrior in the entire battalion."

Mary paused then continued, "Why is it so important that I shoot someone?"

"I'm sure you've noticed there are strong and weak leaders. A strong leader helps win battles but a weak leader makes mistakes which can lead to losing the battle. Our mission is to force the enemy to put a weak leader in charge of Johnson Springs."

And we do that by me killing the good leader?"

"You got it. That's our job."

"Nick, I don't want to kill anyone; especially a good person."

Nick touched Mary's arm and they stopped running. After catching his breath, he quietly said, "Mary, nobody said the person you were killing today is a good person. I only said he's a strong leader. He is the enemy. He invaded our world and he has killed a number of our militia soldiers during skirmishes. In fact, he is the leader of the Earth soldiers you have been fighting since the war began. Your job is to kill him so a less qualified leader will be put in command of their armored units. Your friends in your fire team are counting on you to do your job."

With tears in her eyes, Mary softly answered, "Okay, Nick. I'll do my best."

Mary and Nick arrived at Nick's chosen firing position at 3:30 AM. It was a good spot; on the forward slope of a low hill overlooking Johnson Springs. The firing position was actually a small cave with its front entrance covered with camouflage netting. Mary and Nick moved the netting and wormed their way inside. The cramped space made them lie side-by-side with their bodies touching. They didn't speak. Mary consciously quieted herself to get her heart rate down. An hour later, the sky began taking on a lighter hue. Nick pointed out prominent landmarks and described the route the commander would take on his morning run. Mary adjusted the scope on her rifle; compensating for distance, elevation, and wind. They didn't have long to wait.

Nick brought his spotting scope to bear on a man walking out of a building. "There, he's leaving his quarters. After some stretching exercises he'll begin his morning jog."

"I see him. I estimate 600 yards with no wind."

"Mary, I agree with your estimate. Wait until he starts his run, he'll keep to the ferrocrete road and will be within 400 yards in a few minutes. That's where you need to take your shot."

'*Crack*' - the sound of the bullet firing echoed in the stillness of the morning. Mary and Nick watched the target fall to the ground. They waited for signs of movement. None came.

Mary reported to her fire team leader. "Lima One, the target is down. I repeat; the target is down."

"Roger Lima Six - good job"

Two minutes later, Mary and Nick saw three soldiers jogging along the ferrocrete road. They were probably guards who had heard the shot and were investigating. When they stopped to examine the body, Mary fired again. Two more bodies went down but the third soldier escaped. Soon afterward an alarm was sounded within Johnson Springs. Lights began turning on in the buildings as enemy soldiers scrambled to get into their uniforms.

Seven minutes later, the ground began to shake as cheetahs from the Fifth Battalion appeared in a line formation on the crest of the hill behind Mary and Nick's position. The cheetahs immediately began firing into the fort. There were multiple targets for the cheetahs as exploding vehicles lit the compound. For a minute it looked like the Fifth Battalion would overwhelm the enemy singlehandedly. Mary could see Earth soldiers being hit as they attempted to reach their armored vehicles. She fired occasionally and winced each time her target fell backward.

The tide of battle turned when a large number of armored vehicles swarmed from the far side of the compound and began firing at the Fifth Battalion's cheetahs. The enemy was counterattacking with a mixture of leopards and cheetahs. Their covering fire gave other Earth soldiers an opportunity to get their armored vehicles into the fight. The additional firepower began taking a toll on Colonel Maxon's cheetahs. In quick succession, four militia cheetahs were disabled and several more were hit. As enemy vehicles began moving out of the compound toward Colonel Maxon's forces, it became apparent his Fifth Battalion could not trade blows with the enemy and survive the assault.

The battalion comm link was activated and Colonel Maxon announced, "All fire teams this is Alpha One - execute Plan Bravo." This was the signal for a general retreat. The remnants of Fifth Battalion began running for their sanctuary at Wiggins.

From their firing position, Mary said, "Nick, combat vehicles are moving out of the compound and toward our forces. The anticipated delay while sorting out who was in command of the Earth units didn't occur."

"You're right. It seems the new commander stepped in and everybody has acknowledged she's in charge. Well, nobody said this attack was going to be easy. You can take consolation from the fact you removed one of the enemy commanders."

"What happens if they find us?"

Nick replied, "Mary, if they find us, we'll be executed. I can't speak for you but I'm not going to let them take me alive. After Earth's combat vehicles move beyond us in their pursuit of Colonel Maxon's cheetahs, we can run for it or stay here and hope they don't send infantry to find us. But you should realize that soldiers assigned to Johnson Springs know their commander was killed by a sniper and I'm sure they're not happy."

"I vote we run for it when the vehicles are gone."

Nick looked at Mary and smiled as he replied, "He who runs away may live to fight another day."

Mary whispered, "Where did you hear that or did you make it up?"

"No. It's an old quotation from some Earth guy named Oliver Goldsmith. I remember reading it in my sniper's manual. It means you can stand and die heroically today or retreat and kill more tomorrow. I was hoping you would opt for leaving. And when we go, leave your rifle; it's heavy and you can run faster without it. If militia forces take Johnson Springs, you can come back and retrieve it."

* * *

Colonel Maxon came on the net. "India One this is Alpha One – pick up the pace before you're overtaken - All other fire teams have entered Wiggins"

Sergeant Frank Deluca contacted WO Helen Collins. Since Helen had rejoined Sergeant Deluca's fire team, she had been given the callsign India Four. "Four – what's your status?"

"One this is Four – I'm almost at the entrance to Wiggins. Where are you?

"Four, I've been hit - Have lost my right track - am turning to fire"

"Hang on, One - I'll come and get you"

"Negative Four – And that's an order. Take care of the others - I'll be fine"

"One, this is Three – I'm staying with you - Good luck to all - Out"

Sergeant Delucca and Ralph Taylor's heroism gave the remainder of Helen's fire team just enough time to reach the safety of Wiggins. Between them, Frank and Ralph accounted for four enemy cheetahs before being overwhelmed by superior numbers.

The remnants of Sergeant Deluca's fire team reached the safety of Wiggins as enemy armored vehicles swarmed toward the freshly dug fortification. Being overly anxious to annihilate all militia forces, they failed to realize they had fallen into a trap. The combined fire of Colonel Maxon's remaining cheetahs and the Seventh Battalion's cheetahs under the command of Colonel McGinnis began immediately taking its toll on the enemy's forces.

Militia cheetahs were protected by the fortification at Wiggins while the enemy's armored vehicles were out in the open.

Whoever was commanding the Earth forces was a capable commander. In a few seconds, the enemy vehicles had formed into a line and they began a slow and deliberate advance toward the militia's position. Although the enemy was losing cheetahs, his remaining vehicles were continuing their relentless advance.

Colonel Maxon called me saying, "Sierra One this is Alpha One – execute hammer and anvil"

"WILCO – Break – All Sierras – let's move out – maximum speed"

I deployed the remote vehicle which began giving me a birds-eye view of the battlefield and within three minutes, my platoon of leopards had moved within firing range of the enemy forces.

"All Sierras – *Fire!*"

After their first salvo, I noted nine enemy leopards were out of action. Others began turning to face their newest threat. I handed targets to Rebekah and gave individual targets to my own fire team members. As they began trading salvos with the Earth forces, I noticed two of my leopards had gone dark and one was a flickering yellow. After singling out the enemy leopard nearest my losses, I directed three leopards to fire on that one target.

It worked! The deadly enemy leopard fell silent under their combined fire. I immediately shifted view to the overall picture, spotted other prime targets and assigned these to my remaining leopards. It didn't take long before the enemy's will to fight broke under our combined fire and their remaining combat vehicles began slowly retreating toward Johnson Springs.

With victory in their grasp, Colonel Maxon ordered all militia cheetahs to leave Wiggins and continue firing on the retreating enemy forces.

He said to me, "Sierra One, take your platoon and provide support to Colonel McGraw's Second Infantry Battalion as they launch an attack on Johnson Springs. We can handle clean-up here"

"WILCO - Sierra One Out – Break - All Sierras – follow me - maximum speed"

My platoon disengaged from the ongoing battle and raced toward Johnson Springs. On the way, I contacted Colonel McGraw and asked for instructions. She sent coordinates and orders for our combined assault. I also contacted my maintenance team and gave them the coordinates of my disabled leopards. As we continued our race to Johnson Springs, I prayed Helen would remain safe.

Colonel McGraw contacted me again. "Sierra One this is November One. What is your location and equipment status?"

"This is Sierra One. I have seven leopards and am located one half kilometer from our point of attack. Will arrive in one minute - over"

"Roger, Sierra One – proceed with attack – Request you use a line formation and pave the way for my infantry"

"Wilco – Out"

"All Sierras – LINE FORMATION"

"This is Sierra Two – Wilco – Out"

With no armored vehicles to protect the base, our leopards easily moved through the installation. We dropped numerous soldiers and helped Colonel McGraw's infantry take the base. I was concerned about the retreating enemy armor and established a defensive perimeter as quickly as possible. Odds were good some of the Earth vehicles would escape Colonel Maxon's pursuing forces.

Shortly afterward, my view screen showed an enemy leopard closely followed by two cheetahs and a second leopard approaching Johnson Springs at high speed. I sent the picture to Rebekah and said, "Sierra Two – stop those armored vehicles" I thought, *'Okay, Rebekah, let's see what you've learned.'*

"Wilco – Break – Sierra Eight – you have the lead leopard –Seven and Nine –the two cheetahs – I'll take the second leopard"

I contacted the two remaining leopards in my fire team and said, "Sierras Three and Five – This is Sierra One – Provide covering fire as needed – Out"

I spotted other enemy armored vehicles appearing on my screen but they veered off to the left and stayed out of range.

Following a heavy exchange of fire, Rebekah's fire team did its job; all four enemy vehicles were disabled.

Except for a handful of fleeing enemy vehicles, Colonel Maxon's task force had destroyed or disabled two armored battalions today. That was a tremendous victory.

Colonel McGraw sent a squad to check for survivors. She had already established lookouts and had assigned other infantry collecting dead and wounded within Johnson Springs. The battle was over and we were exhausted.

The maintenance sergeant called to let me know I had lost three warriors and another three were injured and had been turned over to the medical team.

Soon afterward, Colonel Maxon and his cheetahs arrived. While vehicles were being deployed to augment the defensive perimeter, Colonel Maxon gathered the officers for a meeting.

"Ladies and gentlemen – I'm very proud of you. Today, we won a huge victory. I'm sure all of Haven will hear the great news. The effects of our victory will be felt for months to come. It was not without cost; we lost a lot of good men and women – both wounded and killed in action. Let's take a moment and bow our heads in reverence for their sacrifice."

After a moment of silence he continued, "Get the names of those killed and wounded to Sergeant Major Peters. I want their relatives to receive this vital information today."

"Colonel McGraw, please accept my thanks for your flawless work. I am extremely pleased to see Johnson Springs in your capable hands."

"You're very welcome, Colonel Maxon. I deeply appreciate the loan of your leopard platoon. They saved many militia lives today."

"Thank you, Lori. I'm very proud of Lieutenant Collins and his platoon."

He continued, "Colonel McGinnis, I also want to thank you for helping us win this important battle. We could not have succeeded without your Seventh Battalion. The Fifth Battalion's armor would have been crushed had you not been in the fight."

Colonel McGinnis laughed and said, "That's quite all right, Colonel Maxon. I always did hate to see a bully pick a fight. I also want to offer my compliments to the officer who built Wiggins. That temporary fortification enabled us to survive and break the enemy's massed attack."

Colonel Maxon spoke up. "Speaking of which, is WO Helen Collins here?"

A hand was raised from the rear of the assembly. "I'm here sir."

An immense relief came over me as I heard Helen's voice.

"Please come forward."

As Helen stood before Colonel Maxon, he said, "WO Helen Collins, as Task Force Commander, I have the authority to award field promotions to deserving soldiers. Your initiative in designing and building Wiggins and voluntarily serving in a cheetah fire team facing overwhelming odds are exceptional achievements. It is my pleasure to promote you to the rank of lieutenant with an effective date of today."

A loud round of applause and cheering drowned out Helen's thank you.

I was so proud of my wife. I began thinking, *'Helen, you're a unique person and I'm very lucky to be your husband. You're somebody who can be put in the most obscure place and still be recognized for your exceptional abilities. I love you so much.'*

After the applause died, Colonel Maxon added, "Lieutenant Collins, I've received word your talents are urgently needed at Militia Headquarters. I want to you leave first thing in the morning. To make sure you are safe, I will detail one of my officers to escort you. You may choose your escort."

That comment evoked raucous laughter from those who knew Helen and I were married.

Following the meeting, Helen and I ate a quick lunch consisting of rations. The dining facility at Johnson Springs had been destroyed and would have to be rebuilt. Afterwards, Helen visited her surviving Fire Team Six members to say farewell while I composed condolence notes to the families of my soldiers who died during the fight. Afterwards, I met with WO Lloyd.

"Rebekah, your performance during the fighting was exceptional. I'm very proud of you."

"Thank you, John. That means a lot coming from you. I was so scared; especially when you gave me responsibility for stopping those four vehicles."

"Being scared is natural. Continuing to perform your duties while you're scared is the mark of a soldier. I'm escorting Helen back to Militia Headquarters in the morning so I'm leaving the platoon in your hands. I want you to get the equipment back to one hundred percent operational readiness status, talk with the platoon members, visit the wounded and scrounge for parts and supplies. Colonel Maxon will need our help salvaging the enemy leopards. Some may require minor repairs but others will have to be shipped to Crane Manufacturing for a complete overhaul. Currently, we have the only trained leopard mechanics in the battalion. See if he is amenable to having some of his cheetah mechanics work under the supervision of our leopard mechanics. I'm going to request replacements for our personnel losses. Because the leopard training program is so new, I doubt those positions will be filled soon."

"Yes sir. How long will you be gone?"

"I'll be gone a couple of days."

"I'll take care of things while you're away. Have a good time and be safe."

"Thank you. Rebekah before I go, please assemble the platoon members. I want to address them before leaving."

"Yes sir."

As the platoon members stood before me I said, "Ladies and gentlemen, today was our first combat as a leopard platoon. We lost three brave soldiers and another three were wounded and are being treated for their injuries. We've been bloodied but we won two battles today. I want you to know that I'm very proud of each of you. It's safe to say today's victory is a turning point in our war with the invaders. This war is not over but we now have the enemy on the defensive. Today we destroyed two enemy armored battalions and captured Johnson Springs. For the next few days we'll mourn our losses, rest and repair our equipment. Thank you for your part in winning this important battle."

That evening, Helen and I slept beside one another under the stars. The excitement of her promotion to lieutenant and our victory was completely overshadowed by the death of Sergeant Frank Delucca and Private Ralph Taylor. The loss of Frank and Ralph was especially sad for both of us. It was like losing family members.

I remembered Frank promising he would look after Helen. Frank was a man of his word and I was thankful Helen was safe.

CHAPTER 44

RETURNING TO HEADQUARTERS (MILITIA FORCES)

"John, are you awake?"

"Getting there; how're you feeling?"

"I feel like I've been through a meat grinder. It's going to take several days for me to fully recover. Being pregnant is not conducive to combat. I can't believe it, but I'm actually looking forward to spending some time behind a desk."

"Well Lieutenant Collins, let's get you back to headquarters."

"John, my getting promoted is the last thing I was expecting. A year ago, I would be jumping for joy at being promoted to lieutenant. Today, it doesn't feel like a big deal; especially compared to the loss of Frank and Ralph. They were like brothers to me."

As we climbed into the hauler I added, "Yeah, the militia lost some good people yesterday. I don't know if I mentioned it to you but I lost three soldiers in my platoon. I didn't know them well, but it still hurts to lose people. Privates Mary Andrews, Ray Tisdale and Mark Powell will be missed. I met them when the leopard platoon was created and have spent the last three weeks with them. I've sent notes of condolences to their families."

"I'm sorry, Darling. I didn't know you had losses. I'm surprised, though. The leopard is supposed to provide more protection."

"Oh it's very survivable against cheetahs but our mission yesterday was to single out and fight enemy leopards. We gave a good accounting for ourselves but three of my leopards were completely disabled and three others are damaged."

"John, while I was overseeing the construction of Wiggins, I was motivated in part by wanting your platoon to be inside and protected by the fortress. I didn't know Colonel Maxon had decided to place your leopards out in the open going toe-to-toe with enemy armor. Had he put your unit in Wiggins, you wouldn't have lost any people."

"That's true but more of the enemy's armor could have disengaged and retreated back to Johnson Springs where they would have been relatively safe. The Colonel made the right decision; using my platoon to slam the enemy from the flank made sure few armored vehicles would escape."

We arrived at militia headquarters in the late afternoon. I accompanied Helen as she bought some groceries for her apartment. Helen immediately noticed a big difference in the apartment's appearance when she opened the door. Everything was neat, clean and the unit smelled fresh.

"Oh John, my roommate has been busy!"

"What do you mean?"

"You should have seen the place when I arrived; it looked like a pig sty. My roommate didn't spend any time cleaning up before my arrival."

"Well, you've got my curiosity aroused, who's your roommate?"

"Oh John, it's someone you know. I hope your curiosity is the only thing which becomes aroused when you see my roommate."

I was puzzled why she didn't mention her roommate's name. We were putting the last groceries away when I heard a key being inserted into the door. The door opened and in walked Sarah Webber! My shocked expression gave both women a laugh.

Helen said, "John, you should see the look on your face."

Sarah added, "John, you are full of surprises. I'm thrilled we could give you a surprise in return. Helen and I have talked about this for weeks."

I finally found my voice and said, "Hello Sarah. It is a small world. Helen didn't tell me you were her roommate. How have you been?"

"I've been just fine. In fact, if you no other plans, I want you and Helen to accompany me to the Lucky George this evening."

Helen said, "Sarah, didn't you suggest I stay away from that bar?"

"Yes I did but tonight will be special; I think you'll both be interested in the floor show."

Sarah wouldn't elaborate further about the floor show as we ate a quick dinner in the apartment and cleaned the dishes afterward. Conversation shifted to our plans for Helen's upcoming birth and how we would juggle family responsibilities in the middle of a war. I could tell Helen had been giving a lot of thought to the baby. With little input from me, she had developed a logical plan for minute details. In a sense, it was great that she was treating the birth of our child with such enthusiasm and thoroughness. On the other hand, I felt I was being left out of the process. It dawned on me that I was paying a price for not being with her.

Before leaving the apartment Sarah quietly said to me, "John, you may want to take a side arm. Things may get pretty rough tonight."

I didn't know what she meant but I usually wore my sidearm while in uniform and we were at war with Earth so it was no big deal.

The Lucky George was getting crowded when we arrived. Sarah finally got us a table near the bar and we ordered drinks from the waiter. People seemed to be having a good time and their conversations were loud.

Several people stopped by our table and either Sarah or Helen introduced me to them. It seemed all the patrons worked at Militia Headquarters. Eventually I said, "With so many people from Militia

Headquarters here, why don't you move the organization to the Lucky George?"

Sarah laughed and said, "I think that would be a great idea until soldiers in the field overheard loud talking and glasses clinking in the background. Pretty soon, everybody would want a transfer to headquarters and we'd have nobody willing to fight."

Sarah introduced us to Peter Armstrong and excused herself to have a conversation with him. After Sarah left our table, Helen said, "John, I've met that little creep at work and I don't see why Sarah is interested in him. She could do much better."

"I agree. I've never met Mr. Armstrong but from what I see, he's clearly not Sarah's type. It makes me wonder what's going on."

We didn't have long to wait. Sarah and Peter walked over to a booth and pointed their pistols at its occupants. A hush slowly fell over the bar as people noticed the unusual activity and stopped talking. All heads turned toward Peter as he announced, "Mary Barnett and Doris Miller, my name is Chief Inspector Peter Cavanaugh from Haven's National Police and I am placing you under arrest for espionage and treason."

A collective gasp came from bar patrons within earshot. Sarah holstered her sidearm and said, "Mary, stand up and keep your hands in sight." As Mary complied, Sarah turned her around and placed restraints on Mary's hands. The same process was done with Doris. Peter's sidearm never wavered from the two women. As if on cue, four militia soldiers entered and escorted the two women out of the bar.

For a long minute there was absolute silence in the bar as the patrons digested this shocking news. Suddenly, someone shouted, "Way to go Peter and Sarah!" Some sporadic cheering erupted and in a few minutes the place was as noisy as ever.

Sarah came over to the table and sat down. Her face was flushed and I could tell she was still on an emotional high from the drama. After catching her breath Sarah said, "Wasn't that exciting? We've had those two under surveillance for some time. Doris was giving militia secrets to Mary who was passing them to a driver working for a commercial hauling company. The driver was arrested this afternoon. They will be interrogated by Militia Intelligence and we should have the whole operation shut down in a few days."

Helen said, "I can't believe Doris was involved in espionage, she was so likable."

Sarah replied, "Yes, her personality was her best weapon against discovery. It took us a long time to uncover her role in the intelligence leaks. People who have access to frequent travel opportunities are easy suspects. Mary was identified when we established her association with the hauler driver. It wasn't until Mary relayed the operational plans to the driver that we were able to discover the source. Outside your office, only Doris had information about the planned Johnson Springs attack."

Helen said, "Where did you find Peter Cavanaugh? He really seemed to enjoy his role as a communications expert."

"Peter Cavanaugh is a highly respected member of Haven's National Police force. He loved being able to infiltrate our Militia Headquarters as Peter Armstrong and 'work the crowd.' Peter told me about meeting you. Your aggressive reaction to his clumsy advances caused him to beat a hasty retreat before he lost his 'game face' and burst out laughing. He said that anyone who messed with you was taking their life into their own hands."

Helen and I both laughed at Sarah's comment. It was true; Helen could and would take care of herself. Underneath her outward beauty lay a strong woman who was totally unafraid.

Sarah continued, "We don't know why these people turned against Haven. Hopefully, interrogation will reveal their motives. They did a lot of damage and good people lost their lives. We'll try to get them to talk before they hang."

I asked, "What information did Doris have access to?"

Helen answered, "Doris was my contact in the Communications Office. She had full knowledge of all armor units and their locations. I met with her several times each day and received her updates.

John, she knew where you and all other armor commanders were being assigned before you were told. It's easy to see why she was the key player in this espionage ring. That's why Johnson Springs was reinforced with another armored battalion and that's why Frank Delucca and Ralph Taylor lost their lives." Helen looked at Sarah and said, "If you need someone to pull the lever on Doris' gallows, just ask."

"Sarah, what about Mary? How did she fit in this group?"

"Mary was assigned to Militia Headquarters and had access to commercial haulers. She knew everybody and frequently met with people outside the organization in her job as housing officer. I won't know until we complete our interrogation but I suspect Mary was the head of this espionage ring."

I asked, "Sarah, why did you and Peter arrest Doris and Mary here tonight? Why not arrest them in a more private setting?"

"John, we wanted to make the arrest public for a specific reason. Rumors have been flying throughout Militia Headquarters about a traitor being among them. Morale was being affected and people were becoming suspicious of one another. The senior leadership felt this was the best way to get people back on track and focused on winning the war. We expose and remove our 'bad apples' and everyone remaining can get back to concentrating on their jobs. We're counting on the 'rumor mill' being more efficient than official notices. I'm confident that by mid-morning tomorrow, everyone at headquarters will know the traitors have been removed from the organization."

Helen said, "Sarah, your role in this investigation has been made public. What are you going to do?"

"Peter is being reassigned by his headquarters and I've been given an offer to join his organization. I'll be leaving in two days."

Helen said, "Crap! That means I'll probably have to train another roommate to clean up after herself."

I announced, "Ladies, I have to get back to my platoon. It's been an interesting evening but I need to get a few hours' sleep before driving back."

As we stood up to leave, Sarah said, "Good luck, John. It was really good seeing you again. This is our goodbye because I'm staying with the interrogation team tonight." Looking at Helen she smiled and continued, "Helen, you have the apartment to yourself this evening. I'm glad you two were able to see the floor show. It won't bring back your friends but it may open the door to closure."

I replied, "Thank you for inviting us to share this event. I hope it will be a lesson to other 'would-be' traitors. Sarah, best wishes on your new job and thanks again."

As we were leaving the bar I thought, '*Sarah's announcement saved us from an awkward moment. I can't wait to get Helen back to her apartment.*'

CHAPTER 45

THE BATTLE FOR COLUMBUS (EARTH AND MILITIA FORCES)

Columbus is a city of 500,000 located to the east of Tupelo. Its population was diminished because most of its draft-age residents are now serving in the militia, its children were scattered among farms dotting Haven's countryside, and some older adults were working elsewhere on Haven in critical defense industries.

Earth soldiers occupying Columbus commandeered prime housing and displaced wealthy families who could trace their lineage to the earliest settlers on Haven. These social elites were forced to move into apartments vacated by Haven's younger generation. This was but one of the irritants endured by Haven's citizens.

The most serious problem for the residents remaining in Columbus was the brutal treatment meted out by the 415th Battalion. Members of its B Company were especially vicious and most of the residents' deaths can be attributed to them. The slightest infraction of the military-imposed rules resulted in imprisonment and often fatal beatings. Members of Lieutenant Anders' First Platoon simply followed the lead of their commanding officer. Residents of Columbus stopped reporting abuses after some complainants were found dead.

Restaurants and grocery stores were restocked from a warehouse complex located on the outskirts of Columbus. Large quantities of food were delivered by train and haulers. An uneasy truce was maintained over food distribution to the general population. If Earth soldiers shut it down, the residents would starve. Fortunately, starving any segment of Haven's population was never their intention. The invasion commander had given clear instructions against such action. Ironically, Earth soldiers were fed from these same food supplies. Every city on Haven was resupplied in this manner.

Earth soldiers attempting to follow the empty haulers as they left the cities became ambush targets as they ventured into the countryside. Both invaders and defenders were happy that the invaders had holed up in a few major cities.

General Paul Dietrich, the commander of Earth's invasion forces, deeply regretted losing the 420th and 413th armored battalions. A majority of the 351st Infantry had retreated when the militia attacked using armored vehicles. He had been given intelligence that two armored militia battalions were planning to attack Johnson Springs. Having a high degree of confidence in the accuracy of this information, he quickly sent the 420th to reinforce Colonel William Morrissey, Commander of the 413th Armored Battalion. He didn't anticipate losing both armored battalions to a citizens' militia. Losing the battle at Johnson Springs cost him a big portion of his 32nd Armored Brigade and put Columbus in jeopardy of attack.

Colonel Veronica Williamson, commander of the 420th Armored Battalion, straightened in an uncomfortable wooden chair as General Dietrich looked up from the report and met her eyes. "Colonel Williamson, following the death of Colonel Morrissey, you assumed command of his 413th Battalion. I want you to tell me in your own words how you lost two armored battalions to a militia unit no bigger than your combined force."

Colonel Williamson cleared her throat as she nervously began vocalizing the contents of her report. "Sir, we arrived a day before the militia attack on Johnson Springs. Immediately upon arrival, my battalion was hidden in some warehouses where we remained until the post was attacked. Only then did we emerge from hiding and began firing at militia vehicles.

"After being notified that Colonel Morrissey had been killed by a sniper, I assumed command of the combined forces and ordered a rapid advance on a retreating enemy. We had almost caught the militia when we were fired upon by a battalion of armor hidden behind a hastily built fortification. After taking some losses, we reformed into a line and began advancing toward the enemy's position. Things were going as expected until we were hit in our right flank by enemy leopards. We didn't know the militia was equipped with leopards and I lost almost two thirds of my own leopards before we were aware of their presence. In effect, we were ambushed and only seventeen of my armored vehicles survived that murderous trap. Four were destroyed before we could escape from the enemy. Only thirteen cheetahs were able to return to Columbus.

"General, during these months as an occupying force we have been led to believe that Haven's militia is weak, cowardly and has no stomach for fighting. Whoever said that is gravely mistaken. We believed the militia were afraid to fight and were poorly led. Both assumptions were proven wrong at Johnson Springs."

"Colonel, misjudging the enemy is a cardinal sin. For example, not knowing your enemy's weapons is an error which could have been prevented. Attacking a fortification head-on without knowing how it's defended is another error. The first error can be assigned to Colonel Morrissey. He should have employed scouts in the area before the battle began. However, the second error is yours. Your unwarranted haste to achieve a quick victory cost me two battalions of armored vehicles.

"Colonel Williamson, you will report to my headquarters in Tupelo where you'll be assigned as my assistant operations officer. You will have a desk job for the duration of this invasion because I have lost confidence in your ability to lead. Your failure has cost us an important post and a full third of my offensive capability."

During General Dietrich's tirade of berating Veronica about her lack of abilities, Colonel Williamson wanted to commit suicide. Fortunately, the thought of her son back on Earth was enough to keep her pistol holstered.

* * *

Colonel Maxon moved salvaged cheetahs and leopards from the recent battle to Johnson Springs. It didn't matter if they could be driven; they could serve as stationary weapons to augment Colonel Lori McGraw's infantry battalion.

"Lori, I'm leaving fifteen cheetahs and five leopards for your use in defending Johnson Springs. They don't run but they can fire. I'm taking the remainder and using them to replace my vehicles. I've been given orders to proceed to Columbus and may need the additional firepower."

"John, thank you very much. We'll make good use of the twenty armored vehicles as we finish our defensive preparations. It'll take more than one armored battalion to take Johnson Springs away from us. Good luck on your next mission."

* * *

"Sergeant Major, please assemble the officers. I have received new orders for the Fifth and Seventh Battalions."

* * *

"Good morning ladies and gentlemen. I hope you've enjoyed your well-deserved rest because we have another mission. Militia Headquarters has decided the time is right for us to capture Columbus.

As you may know, the enemy's 420th Armored Battalion was moved from Columbus to reinforce Johnson Springs. Now that we have eliminated the 420th, we'll have less resistance when we attack

Columbus. Further, we have access to salvageable vehicles taken in battle. Specifically, we have several operational leopards available for distribution. Lieutenant Collins, as my senior operations officer what is your recommendation?"

"Sir, how many warriors and mechanics are available to man and service these additional vehicles?"

"Good question. As of this morning, we have enough warriors to man the extra vehicles. Unfortunately, we don't have any additional mechanics."

"Sir, I recommend assigning cheetah mechanics to work with our leopard mechanics. Our mechanics will supervise and cross train the cheetah mechanics. We can consolidate maintenance operations under the supervision of a sergeant or warrant officer. Leopards and cheetahs would be maintained by the same mechanics. Warriors could be given responsibility for cleaning, refueling and rearming their vehicles. This would greatly reduce the workload of our mechanics; leaving them responsible for all purely maintenance actions."

"That's a great idea. How do you propose I assign the leopards?"

"Sir, if WO Lloyd and I are the only officers trained to operate leopards, I recommend she be given my platoon and promoted to platoon leader. I will take the new vehicles and form another squad."

"Excellent. I have one additional change to your proposal. I'm promoting you to captain and giving you command of the leopard company. WO Lloyd and Lieutenant Collins, step forward if you please."

After awarding us new rank insignia, Colonel Maxon said, "Congratulations to the both of you. Ladies and gentlemen, if there are no further questions, Sergeant Major Peters has your route coordinates. Let's go to Columbus. Somebody once mentioned there is a bounty on members of the 415th Armored Battalion. Let's go round them up." His comment was followed by wild cheering.

* * *

Outwardly, Columbus did not appear occupied. Its streets were laid out in a grid pattern and they were empty of traffic when we arrived. Colonel Maxon ordered scouts to search the city and report back their findings. In the meanwhile, I arranged my leopards in a defensive configuration and powered down.

We didn't have long to wait. Sighting reports began streaming in and Colonel Maxon quickly began deploying his combat vehicles. My company was given the most direct route to the enemy concentration with the cheetah fire teams taking flanking positions on either side of my company of leopards.

"Sierra 2 – take route Alpha George – deploy your remote vehicle – recommend additional eyes on your flanks"

"Roger Sierra 1"

I had an uneasy feeling as my platoon began traveling parallel to Rebekah's platoon. I slowed my column so Rebekah's platoon would be the first to finish her assignment. Also, if she ran into trouble, my platoon would be available to provide additional firepower.

Suddenly, I heard multiple rounds being fired on the street Rebekah was clearing. "Sierra 2 – request situation report"

"Sierra 1 – multiple weapons dug in on both sides of us - request assistance"

"Roger Sierra 2 – break – Sierras 11 through 19 – advance and commence firing on your left – avoid firing directly at leopards on the next street but bring the buildings down"

"Sierra 2 – we are firing at the buildings on your right"

I decided the best way to help Rebekah's platoon was to bury the attackers on her right; giving her the ability to concentrate fire on her left.

"Roger Sierra 1 – we are firing on our left"

A huge cloud of dust and debris was created as buildings began falling. Whoever was attacking Rebekah's platoon on her right flank was being crushed by the falling debris. At that moment, Rebekah gave a similar order to her platoon and buildings on her left began crumbling and imploding.

Because we didn't stop, both columns of leopards emerged from the dust into the clear. Rebekah reported, "Sierra 1 – two units down – remainder proceeding"

"Roger – Good job"

I called for maintenance recovery as we continued our mission. A couple of blocks later, my column of leopards was hit from both sides. "Sierras 11 through 19 – commence firing – odd on left and even on right"

This opposition was not serious and we were able to easily blast through their ambush. I noticed we left a lot of smoldering buildings in our wake. I thought, *'The good news is the construction industry will have a lot of work after the war.'*

As we neared the end of the street, Colonel Maxon requested assistance at the city park. My terrain map indicated we were less than 400 meters away. I asked, "Alpha 1 - Request coordinates for our approach"

"Sierra 1 –enemy soldiers are located in the center of the park and are dug in – attack from the east – here are your coordinates"

"Wilco – Break – All sierras – maximum speed - turn right at the end of the street and prepare for a frontal assault - at my command"

During the assault, I lost an additional four leopards but we overcame the enemy's defenses and defeated fifteen cheetahs. Columbus was ours. I noticed that we were the only ones which had leopards.

Our first actions were to secure the city and get our wounded to the hospital for treatment. Securing the city included rounding up Earth soldiers and making them our prisoners. We transferred the prisoners to the local city jail. I was pretty sure some soldiers escaped as we broached the enemy's final defenses because I noticed a small convoy of haulers followed by several cheetahs leaving town. I thought, *'Oh well, we'll get you next time.'* I was given a sector to secure and asked Rebekah to post guards.

The next priority was feeding my soldiers and finding a place for them to wash-up and sleep. Salvaging and repairing our damaged leopards would be the priority tomorrow.

I sent a quick note to Helen letting her know that I was safe and would sleep in Columbus tonight. Colonel Maxon contacted me and invited Rebekah and myself to dinner at a local restaurant. We found a hotel nearby and cleaned up for dinner. The Trenton Hotel was small and could only accommodate my company by having the soldiers double up. After the hotel clerk informed me of the room shortage, I said, "Rebekah, since the hotel is full, would you mind sharing a suite with me? It has two bedrooms."

She gave me a big grin and teasingly said, "Why Captain Collins, I think that would be fantastic! I'll bet the suite has a large tub, too. Soaking in a tub sounds like heaven to me. I wonder if the room comes furnished with candles and champagne."

I thought to myself, *'Careful John, don't say anything which may get you into trouble later.'*

"Rebekah, I'm not sure you have time for a bath; Colonel Maxon has invited us to have dinner with him in an hour."

"Yeah, you're probably right. However, after dinner is another matter. Let's go see what *our* suite looks like."

During our ride up the elevator I said, "Rebekah, you did a splendid job with your platoon today. Nobody could have done better."

"Thank you, John. I have you to thank for training me and giving me another chance."

"Have you spoken with your uncle about transferring to Militia Headquarters?"

"I've thought about that and let's just say I've had a change of heart." She took a step closer to me and continued, "I love my job as a platoon leader under your command. I can't imagine I would be happier anywhere else. In fact, I sent a message to my uncle this afternoon informing him of my decision."

"Rebekah, that's very kind of you and I'm glad you enjoy being an armor officer. Uh, here's our floor." I was thinking, '*What's gotten into this girl? Is it my imagination or is she hitting on me? She knows I'm married and I've already made it clear I'm not available. I hope the room assignment this evening has not given her any ideas.*'

CHAPTER 46

RETREATING FROM COLUMBUS (EARTH FORCES)

The short but intense battle for Columbus destroyed buildings and almost wiped out the 415th Armored Battalion. With only a few cheetahs remaining, Colonel Harper reluctantly ordered a retreat.

General Dietrich was not happy about losing another armored battalion and a key post. After hearing the depressing news from Colonel Harper, he turned to Colonel Williamson and said, "Well Colonel, it appears your defeat at Johnson Springs will be heralded as the turning point of our invasion. The rebels are overrunning our vital installations one after another. Unless we get reinforcements, our future on Haven looks bleak." General Dietrich didn't mention that his well-placed spy at Militia Headquarters had gone silent. The militia's sudden attack on Columbus caught everybody by surprise. The General knew that had he been alerted, he could have sent reinforcements and saved Columbus.

Colonel Williamson didn't reply to General Dietrich's snide comment. Since being ignominiously transferred to serve on General Dietrich's headquarters staff, she was continually reminded of her failure. She knew arguing her side was pointless. Her boss was pinning his failed invasion on her one tactical mistake at Johnson Springs. Veronica's face was burning as she thought, '*It looks like I've been nominated and elected to be the scapegoat for General Dietrich's invasion defeat. I've got to figure out a way to stay on Haven when this is over. There is absolutely no future for me back on Earth. At the very least, I'll be court martialed and sent to prison or hanged. My pension will be cancelled which doesn't bode well for my son's future.*'

* * *

Bill Anders was relieved when Colonel Harper ordered the retreat. He had narrowly survived the one-sided tank battle. The leadership of B Company had been decimated. Captain Steiner and Lieutenant Horner were listed as missing - presumed dead; and Lieutenants Richards and Montgomery were wounded and probably captured by the militia. On hearing news of Nancy being wounded, Bill thought, '*My lucky day, maybe she'll lose the baby, too.*'

In addition to Colonel Harper and sixteen mechanics, Lieutenant Lance Stallings, Bill and twelve cheetah warriors were all that remained of Colonel Harper's 415th Armored Battalion. Bill placed himself as rear guard of the retreating column. Nobody questioned his motives for serving as rear guard; everybody else was only interested in getting to Tupelo alive. By staying back several hundred meters - away from the prying eyes of his fellow soldiers, Bill was able to freely shoot and kill anyone he saw. He even ran over two people scrambling to get out of the road as the column passed.

He was grinning as he thought, '*Yeah, enticing and capturing militia soldiers was pretty neat. Before being shut down, my girls and I bagged twenty-four of the bastards which was way more than any other Earth unit. And that chaperone, Cathy Hardy - I really enjoyed having her as my sex slave. She was fantastic in bed! Bet she didn't tell her husband about that part of the trip!*

But today, I'm having fun getting rid of these Haven scum. If our fearless leader had not been such a wuss, Earth could have won this war. Fear is a force multiplier and General Dietrich simply doesn't have the stomach to be ruthless. People like him belong in a classroom; not leading an invasion army.'

CHAPTER 47

PLANNING OUR NEXT MISSION (MILITIA FORCES)

After a quick shower, I went to the lobby and waited for Rebekah to come down. When she eventually arrived, we took a hauler and met Colonel Maxon at the Cattleman's Ranch, a restaurant he selected. As the 'liberators of Columbus,' we were given superb service and the meal was great.

"Sir, on behalf of Rebekah and me, thank you for the invitation to dinner. I can't remember when I had such a delicious meal."

"Yes, it was good and I'm happy you enjoyed the food. It makes my next few words a little easier to say."

I was thinking, '*Uh oh, what is he going to say?*'

After a lengthy pause, Colonel Maxon said, "John, I'm asking you and Rebekah to volunteer for a critical and highly-classified mission which is very dangerous. I'm willing to risk both of you on this mission because if you're successful, this war with Earth could be shortened considerably.

"General Flanders contacted me personally and suggested we try a bold tactic. This is not being planned by his operations center at Militia Headquarters. Only he, General Albert Turner, Colonel Lori McGraw and I are involved."

I asked, "What's the mission, sir?"

"John and Rebekah, this is top secret. You cannot breathe a word to anyone not cleared by me personally. Should you elect not to volunteer, I will ask others to undertake this job because its success is our highest priority."

I was thinking, '*Colonel, will you please get to the mission?*'

"I want you and Rebekah to volunteer to enter Tupelo and capture the Commander of the Earth forces."

I sat there stunned. As I glanced over at Rebekah, I could see the shock on her face, too. "Sir, we're going to need more than armored vehicles for this mission."

Colonel Maxon laughed and asked, "John, what do you think you'll need?"

I thought a moment and said, "Sir, as a minimum, we must have up-to-date human intelligence, infantry and haulers. We also need a timetable for this operation."

The Colonel asked, "John, why do you need a timetable?"

"We need to plan how we're going to execute and we need to rehearse. We also need to know if there is a deadline on this mission."

"There is a deadline for completing this mission. General Turner wants it done nine days from today. He wouldn't say why but I suspect he has a valid reason."

Rebekah asked, "John, why do we need infantry?"

"Rebekah, we can't capture anyone using armored vehicles. Armored vehicles are great for attacking a mobile force and defending a static position. But it's going to take soldiers to enter his quarters and drag the general from his bed and put him in a hauler. In fact, it may be easier just to capture the general and hold him in place rather than try to escape from Tupelo with him in custody. Also, the general may be too heavily protected within his headquarters. We may need to ambush his convoy and capture him en route to someplace. That's the major reason we'll need human intelligence. The sad fact is I don't know anything about Earth's commanding general."

"Okay, may I assume you both volunteer for this mission?"

"I can't speak for Rebekah but if it will shorten the war, I do volunteer."

Rebekah quickly said, "Colonel, I also volunteer."

"Excellent! I want you to keep this to yourselves as we go through the planning stages. Where are you staying?"

"Sir, Captain Collins and I are staying at the Trenton Hotel. Due to the shortage of rooms, we're sharing a two-bedroom suite."

Colonel Maxon said, "That's fine. Both of you staying in the same suite will actually work best. If you need specific intelligence information to help you with planning your mission, ask me. I prefer to be the conduit between you and others. This also means you cannot have visitors and you must keep your paperwork secure. This mission is way too important to take a chance on a security breach."

"Sir, why did you choose us for this job?"

"That's an excellent question, John. The primary reason you were chosen is because you have succeeded in every mission the militia has assigned you to perform. You've also demonstrated exceptional creativity. We're fighting a war in which none of us were adequately trained. For example, we don't have specialty teams trained for kidnapping or building fortifications. We use exceptional people such as you, Helen, and many others to accomplish a variety of missions. Another factor in your favor is both of you are from Tupelo."

"How will we stay in touch with you, sir?"

"Let's plan on having breakfast each morning in this restaurant at 8:00. John, you'll have to make something up for Helen. She's not authorized to know anything about this mission. Incidentally, if you have a safe in your suite, lock all planning materials in it whenever you are out."

"Understand, sir. Unless you have anything else, we'll see you here at 8:00 AM with a list of questions."

"I'm looking forward to it. Goodnight all."

Rebekah and I didn't talk much on the way back to the Trenton Hotel. We stopped and checked in with the noncommissioned officer in charge of the company before walking to our suite. Once inside the room I said, "I've had lots of conversations with Colonel Maxon but this one tops all others."

"John, this is so big, where do we start? I know I don't have a clue."

I started grinning and said, "Rebekah, I've never kidnapped anyone in my life. But if I had to kidnap someone, I would want to know who it was, where does he live, what are his habits, and who would want to stop me. Unless you have another idea, why don't we begin by listing these as headings and develop specific questions pertaining to each. We can give our questions to Colonel Maxon in the morning."

"John, that sounds logical to me. I'll get my noteputer."

As Rebekah wrote the questions she asked, "Wouldn't it also be helpful to know if any residents of Haven work in the same area as the commander? What are their loyalties? Could they help us?"

"Oh that's good; especially the question about who could help us. Add those questions under a new heading labeled, 'associates.' The more information we get, the better our chance of success. At this point, I don't think we should place limits on background information."

After about an hour of discussion I said, "Okay, I can't think of anything else. Unless you want to add to the list of questions, why don't we call it a night?"

"John, I've completed the list and I think the tub is calling me."

"Hope you enjoy the soak. Goodnight, Rebekah. I'll see you tomorrow."

I had fallen asleep and was dreaming about making love to Helen when I slowly became aware a naked woman was lying next to me lightly kissing my chest and neck and slowly moving her hand over my body. It took me a few moments to realize she was not Helen. After becoming fully awake, I disentangled myself from her and asked, "Rebekah, what the hell do you think you're doing?"

Rebekah softly replied, "John, I was hoping you were inviting me to share your bed. Don't you find me attractive? Your body seems to enjoy what I'm doing."

"Rebekah, my body is not in charge of me. I can't make love to you even if my body is more than willing. I'm really sorry but you have to leave. I never intentionally signaled I wanted to have sex with you. I'm a married man and made a vow to be faithful to my wife. You have to leave now. I promise you we'll discuss this tomorrow."

A dejected Rebekah slowly got up from my bed and walked to the bedroom door. As the door opened, a soft light from the living room silhouetted a naked Rebekah as she turned and said, "John, making love to you would have been so wonderful. There is nothing I would not have done for you." With that said, she closed the door.

I lay awake in bed a long time after she left and thought about what transpired. *'I'm sure having sex with Rebekah would have been great. She's gorgeous and has a beautiful body. I'm also sure Helen would not be okay with me cheating on her. What did I do to make Rebekah think I wanted sex? Damn, why do things have to be so complicated and difficult?'*

* * *

The following morning, Rebekah was dressed and waiting for me in the living room as I exited my bedroom. I pulled up a chair near her and began talking. "Rebekah, you're an outstanding officer and a wonderful person. Any leader would want you on his team and any man would be proud to call you his wife. For us, we can only have one relationship. We are teammates fighting a war to save our planet. We cannot be lovers because I'm married. My question is can you continue working with me under these conditions?"

Rebekah looked at me and said, "John, I'm embarrassed. I guess my wishing for a personal relationship with you overcame my common sense. I've wanted you from the first day we met. As you recall, I was the new commander of Fire Team Four and you were a newly-promoted corporal reporting for duty. I remember how hurt and angry I was when you rejected my advances. And when I found out that you were engaged to another warrant officer, it made me so jealous of her.

"Later, when you took me under your wing and began preparing me for command, my feelings for you changed. We've shared some dangerous moments together and I have never regretted serving with you in combat. I want so much to make you proud of me. I also want to always be there for you; to protect you.

"John, I realize you have a wife but I've fallen in love with you. That's not going to change. I can work with you on this and other projects. I also look forward to serving with you again in combat. And you should know that I will always have your back. My only regret today is not being able to make love with you last night."

After digesting her comments I replied, "That's fair enough, Rebekah. Things will become tense between us at times but I respect your honesty and I value you as a fellow warrior and friend. I suggest we get our list of questions for Colonel Maxon and get over to the Cattleman's Ranch for breakfast."

As we rode the elevator to the ground floor, I thought, '*Rebekah, you're an amazing woman. If we were in a different situation, I would have welcomed your overture last night.*'

* * *

Colonel Maxon was drinking a cup of coffee when we arrived. After our cups were filled, Rebekah gave him our list of questions. He read the list then asked, "Why do you need to know about Haven residents who may have contact with the Earth commander?"

I nodded to Rebekah and she began, "Sir, any Haven residents who work in or around the Earth Commander are valuable sources of information. We need to know where he becomes most vulnerable and when he has the least number of guards available."

"How do you know you can trust these Haven residents? They may be recent immigrants who maintain loyalties to Earth."

"We don't know the people who may be working for the Earth general. Perhaps our intelligence folks could do a background check on these people?"

I added, "Colonel, Rebekah and I grew up in Tupelo. However, we don't know of any physical changes which may have been made to our city during this past year. Locals will be able to provide that information. It could mean the difference between getting out with our prize and getting caught."

Colonel Maxon downloaded the file from Rebekah's noteputer and said, "Okay, I'll ask around. Some of this information may be impossible to obtain in the short time we have available; but I'll ask. In the meantime, keep up appearances with your company to ensure everything is okay with the unit."

"Yes sir. We'll see you again tomorrow?"

"That's the plan. Hopefully I'll have the information you've requested."

Rebekah and I visited the company. We found the warriors busy helping mechanics work on their leopards. I left some training simulations with the senior sergeant and asked her to ensure the warriors ran through each exercise.

"Captain, we can handle the training and maintenance. Is there anything I can do for you?"

"No. Colonel Maxon has assigned Lieutenant Lloyd and me a special project. We'll be working on that for the next few days. However, if you need me, don't hesitate to contact me."

Rebekah and I next drove over to the hospital and checked on our wounded. After a quick lunch, we returned to the hotel suite and began talking about the mission.

"Rebekah, we won't get any information from Colonel Maxon until tomorrow at the earliest. What information could we get locally which will help us start planning?"

"What about the Columbus library? They may have maps of Tupelo and maybe some news articles on the Earth commander."

"That's a great idea! Let's go."

As we entered the library, I noticed an elderly woman sitting at a desk. Walking up to her desk I said, "Good afternoon. I'm interested in knowing where your reference section is located."

"Good afternoon captain. Our reference section is on the first aisle as you enter the library. It starts on the left hand side."

"Thank you very much."

I looked for maps of Tupelo while Rebekah scanned news articles for information on the invasion and the Earth commander. She downloaded the data on a chip while I crammed some maps inside my uniform because a sign said visitors were not permitted to check out reference materials. Back at our hotel suite, I spread the maps on a table while Rebekah loaded her noteputer with data from the chip.

"Okay, let's start with the target. What did you find out from the news clippings?"

"Well there's not much about our boy. His name is General Paul Dietrich, Commander of the 32nd Armored Brigade. You and I know for a fact he recently lost an infantry battalion, two armored battalions and major installations at Johnson Springs and Columbus."

"Rebekah, Helen told me Earth forces are also concentrated in Ripley to the north and Natchez to the west. Including Tupelo, that's all the territory Earth controls on Haven. It appears General Dietrich is running out of manpower and places he can command. He has gone from commanding Haven to waiting for the militia to attack his remaining installations."

"John, his recent losses may make him all the more dangerous. If he's desperate and scared, he'll be suspicious of all outsiders and may be on guard for treachery from within his own organization."

"Okay, we may be able to use his fear to our advantage. What else do we know?"

"I overheard Sergeant Major Peters say Natchez, Columbus and Ripley were being attacked while we launched our attack on Johnson Springs. Are there any militia forces which could help us get into and out of Tupelo?"

"Rebekah, I'm not sure. But I recall Colonel Maxon saying Colonel Lori McGraw knew about our mission. If that's true, we may be able to get infantry from her. We need soldiers who know Tupelo. It will be too hard to prepare others for action within our city." Yawning I added, "We've done a lot of speculating today. How about we turn in early and get a fresh start tomorrow?"

"That sounds good. Goodnight, John."

The following morning, Rebekah and I met with Colonel Maxon at the usual place. He handed me a chip and said, "John, here is the information you requested."

"Thank you, sir. This will get us started on developing options. Once we have these outlined, we'd like to discuss them with you and get your input."

"Okay. That's fine. Let's meet for dinner tonight at 8 PM."

Back in our suite, Rebekah eagerly downloaded the chip onto her noteputer and projected the content on the wall. "Rebekah, let's see if all of our questions were answered."

"Okay, here is a matrix displaying the data."

Question	Answer
Who is the target?	General Paul Dietrich, Commander of the 32nd Armored Brigade and commander of Earth's invasion force
Where does he live?	107 Castle Bridge Road, Tupelo (large mansion in a gated subdivision named Sherwood Hills) Although not requested, the General's headquarters occupies the top two floors of the Tupelo City Hall

What are his habits?	5:00 – 5:45 AM jogs in neighborhood
	7:00 AM leaves for work
	12:30 PM has lunch delivered to his office
	6:00 PM returns home
	Note: occasionally gives dinners and hosts receptions at home
Who is protecting the target?	9 bodyguards assigned to protect the General – minimum of 2 on duty at all times
	Additional guards are posted at the entrance to the subdivision and around City Hall
Are there residents of Haven who work in the same area as the commander?	Haven residents authorized to work in City Hall are:
	Mayor, mayor's secretary, 6 janitors, transit manager, food distribution manager, public health director, fire chief, public works director, and police chief
	Note: Other city workers perform their assigned tasks but they do not have offices in City Hall
	There is a housekeeper, chef and two maids working at the General's home
	The General has a mistress named Stephanie Harris who resides with the General
What are their loyalties?	Unknown at this time
Could they help us?	Unknown at this time

Rebekah turned to me and said, "John, you won't believe this; but I believe I know Stephanie Harris! Of course there could be another person with that name but I'm willing to bet this is the Stephanie Harris I know."

"What? Rebekah, Tupelo is a city of eight million people. How could you know the woman who became the mistress of Earth's commanding general? And if that's not weird enough, what about the fact that you are the only female militia soldier planning the mission to kidnap her lover?"

"John, I can't explain the odds you cited. I'm sure they're astronomical. In spite of that, my mother hosted a party for my college sorority at the Tupelo Crown Plaza Hotel two years ago. Stephanie Harris was the hotel's Guest Services Manager. We met on several occasions while planning the party. She's attractive and has an outgoing personality. I'm guessing she's in her late thirties or early forties. Her position in public relations is probably how General Dietrich met her."

"Rebekah, I'm still amazed you know her. However, this could be extremely helpful. It could give you access to Stephanie when we arrive in Tupelo. She would be an ideal source of information. For example, she would know who attends the dinners and receptions at the General's home. I'm thinking about the possibility of substituting guests."

"John, we've got to figure out a way to contact Stephanie. For example, does she ever leave the residence? Where does she shop? Where does she go to get her hair done? The odds are good she has few friends because her affair with the General has branded her as a traitor. Also, any contact with Stephanie must be done carefully. For example, she would guess I'm in the militia since practically everyone in our age group was drafted. If the decision is made to contact her, I'll need a cover story which will not trigger alarm bells."

"Rebekah, since she's the General's mistress, we must assume her loyalty is to him. And if that's the case, we can interrogate her but she cannot be permitted to return to the General. Her reporting our presence would wreck our mission and endanger a lot of lives."

"John, if we can't get Stephanie to help us, we should consider substituting someone for Stephanie. Otherwise, kidnapping the General will involve force; not finesse."

"What do you mean by finesse?"

"John, if we could get someone close to the General, he could be given something to render him unconscious and taken away before anyone knew what was happening."

"Yeah, I see what you mean. If we can't use someone close to the General, we'll have to rely on force to neutralize his bodyguard. Rebekah, I don't think eliminating Stephanie would be too difficult. After all, it's likely she's not being protected. The hard part would be to get a stranger close to the General in a short timeframe.

"Speaking of which, let's turn our focus on other aspects of our plan. What about the people who live in the subdivision? Are they permitted guests? Also, are there domestic workers and gardeners? Our plan should include infiltrating the General's neighborhood. Disguising soldiers as guests and domestic workers is a good idea; especially since the General's bodyguard must be eliminated.

"Please set up a matrix on your noteputer. The first column will list our kidnapping scenarios, the second will list manpower and equipment requirements, the third will list advantages and disadvantages, and the fourth column will list missing data. We'll fill in the spaces and brief Colonel Maxon tonight."

"John, why not do it now?"

"Because we're going to check on the company and visit the wounded; it's important to the soldiers that we're visible and available."

After completing our matrix, we listed four viable options. The best one was, as Rebekah suggested, enticing the General to a tryst and rendering him incapacitated; making his capture easy and quiet. The second one was infiltrating the subdivision and capturing the General during his morning jog. The third was invading his residence and capturing him after killing his guards. The fourth was ambushing his vehicle as he was being driven to or from work. Kidnapping him at his headquarters was too risky and was only added to include all possible options in our list.

* * *

Rebekah and I were having coffee when Colonel Maxon arrived. I handed him the noteputer and Rebekah and I sat patiently as he read its contents. Afterwards, he looked up and said, "Good work. It appears you've captured all the options in your plan. I'll try to get answers to your questions for you."

"Colonel, Rebekah and I know Tupelo pretty well. However, we believe it would be a good idea to canvass other units and select soldiers who are also from Tupelo. Is this possible?"

"While you and Rebekah have been planning this mission, I have been assembling a platoon of infantry who will have about twenty five percent of its members from Tupelo. They will be available to rehearse the mission once it's finalized."

"That's great news, Colonel. After receiving answers to our final questions, Rebekah and I will present you with a final plan of action."

* * *

After a restless night, I got up early and prepared for our morning visit to meet with Colonel Maxon. Rebekah entered the living room and was surprised to see me dressed and ready to leave. She said, "Well good morning. You're up awfully early."

"Yeah, I didn't sleep well last night so I got up early."

"John, what's the matter? Is something troubling you?"

"Never mind, let's go see the Colonel."

"Okay, but you realize it's a bit early to be leaving the hotel. Are you sure you don't want to talk about what's bothering you?"

As we rode the elevator to the first floor, I was very conscious of Rebekah's nearness. I knew inside her uniform was an extremely desirable woman. *John, what the hell are you thinking? Get your mind on business. You know Helen means more to you than anyone; forget about having sex with Rebekah. Even if you gave in and made love to her, you know you're not going to leave Helen. Besides, look at the hurt Rebekah would experience when you left her and returned to Helen.*

And what if Helen found out you had been unfaithful; don't you think she would be hurt, too? You need to quit thinking these thoughts. Giving in to your desire for Rebekah would hurt everybody, including yourself.'

"Rebekah, because we've got some extra time before meeting Colonel Maxon, why don't we take a walk in the park?"

"John, that sounds like a great idea! It should be fun."

As we began walking toward the park, I said, "Rebekah, I've been thinking about your 'finesse' option. We could possibly replace Stephanie with a volunteer from the militia. I have no idea how difficult it would be to find someone willing to assume the role of a mistress. There would be a lot of personal risk serving in that role, don't you agree?"

Rebekah hesitated a moment before responding. "John, I believe we should capture and interrogate Stephanie for useful information. For example, we might find out he is attending a social event and we could arrange for someone to "accidentally" meet him at the event. As for getting a volunteer, you don't have to worry about that. I'm volunteering to be Stephanie's replacement."

"Rebekah, I think we can find someone else for that role."

"John, don't you think I'm capable of seducing the General?"

"Rebekah, you're young, beautiful, intelligent, and creative. That's not the issue. I need you to be my right hand person; not some temptress placed in a highly dangerous mission."

"John, I believe this may be the most critical job in our mission to capture the General. I need to know why you don't believe I can perform this task."

"Rebekah, it's not a question of ability. I think you're too valuable for that job."

"John, who do you think would be more capable than me for this mission?"

"Dammit Rebekah, I don't want to put you into that situation; it's too dangerous!"

"John, let's see if I have this correct. You don't hesitate to order me into battle against armored vehicles but you won't let me seduce an enemy general as part of a kidnapping operation? Wait a minute, on second thought, I see your point. I could get killed leading my leopard platoon but if I'm in bed with the general, I may have an orgasm. Captain Collins, I'm beginning to suspect you may be jealous."

"Rebekah, could we change the subject? I've given you way too much latitude in this discussion."

"Absolutely, sir; we should change the subject because I don't believe you're being honest with me. I've told you my feelings for you but I don't believe you've reciprocated."

After several long seconds, I replied, "Rebekah, you're right; I have omitted saying some things. Things I didn't mention earlier because I can't afford to act on my feelings for you. And with this admission, the subject is closed."

We walked along in silence for quite some time. I suspected she was thinking about our personal conversations over the past two days and probably replaying the entire track in her mind. I thought, *'Oh crap, I don't know how this is going to turn out but I'll bet things are going to get real tense between us before it's over.'* Thankfully, it was almost time to meet with the Colonel.

* * *

We presented our plan to Colonel Maxon at breakfast. Rebekah and I were silent as he read through our final document.

"John, I believe you and Rebekah are on the right track. Unless you have anything else, I'll see you this evening at 8:00 for dinner and hopefully give you the green light."

As we walked out of the restaurant, Rebekah excused herself saying she had some shopping to do while I visited the company and held individual discussions with our soldiers. I inspected the vehicles and noted some minor discrepancies. Afterwards, I walked to the hospital and met with the wounded soldiers. Their wounds were healing quickly and I was informed they would be released for limited duty within the week.

Late that afternoon, I entered the suite and saw Rebekah sitting at the table working on our mission. I sat down on a nearby sofa and asked, "What are you doing?"

Rebekah looked at me and said, "Colonel Maxon delivered the information we requested about an hour ago. He has given us the go-ahead and said it wasn't necessary for us to meet him for dinner this evening."

She added, "John, what can I do to rebuild your trust in me?"

"Rebekah, you've done nothing to erode my trust in you. Our disagreement is over my using you to seduce the General. We've talked about this already. I don't want you to put yourself in such a dangerous situation. We can find someone else for that role."

"Oh John, you're so transparent. You've got to get your head on straight about this."

"Rebekah, I am thinking clearly. I doubt you have any experience seducing a man in order to slip him a knockout drug."

"John, you've stated several times you plan to rehearse for this mission. Taking that as guidance, I went shopping before returning to the hotel. I'm going to dim the lights in the living room and will return in a few minutes. Please stay exactly where you are. I want to show you something."

Rebekah walked into her bedroom and closed the door. I didn't know what she was going to show me but I decided to humor her by staying put. A few minutes later, Rebekah opened her bedroom door and slowly walked toward me.

She was dressed in a flimsy nightgown which hid nothing. Her hair was down and I noticed she had put on some makeup. I thought, '*Oh hell, no man has a chance against this beauty!*' My throat began to tighten; the sight of her walking toward me was almost more than I could take.

She slowly sat on my lap and smiled while placing her hand on my left shoulder. I watched her blink her beautiful eyes as her smile grew. I felt my palms get sweaty and my heart began to beat faster. I was having trouble breathing but it wasn't from her sitting on my lap. In fact, it seemed very natural to have her sitting on my lap. Rebekah placed her other hand on my right shoulder and slowly leaned toward me. Her eyes were closed and she was still smiling as her soft lips found mine. My mouth quickly responded to hers and I felt my arms go around her body. She leaned into my chest and put her arms around my neck as we continued to softly kiss one another. My hands began exploring her body and she made small sighs whenever my hand touched the side of her breast.

After only a few minutes of heavy petting, Rebekah stood up and led me into her bedroom. I was struggling to get my uniform off while attempting to continue kissing Rebekah. I couldn't seem to get enough of her. Rebekah knelt in front of me and loosened my belt and untied my boots while I tore my shirt off.

I sat on the bed and rapidly pulled my boots off then stood up only long enough to step out of my trousers. Meanwhile, Rebekah was standing in front of me slowly removing her nightgown. As soon as her nightgown finally dropped to the floor, I grabbed Rebekah and literally held her to me as I backed toward the bed. My body had taken complete charge of me and if there was any hesitancy on my part, it was completely overcome by my lusting for Rebekah.

I lay back on the bed and Rebekah got into a sitting position on top of me. I was so ready to make love to this woman. She leaned closer to my face and my hands began exploring the small of her back down to her firm cheeks. I felt her raise her butt into the air as if signaling me to continue exploring. I felt her moving her hands from my shoulders and placing them on either side of my head. Looking up I saw her sexy smile.

Suddenly I felt a sharp prick on the side of my neck. Grimacing while grabbing my neck in pain I looked up and saw a smiling Rebekah getting off me and standing near the bed. She showed me a needle in her hand and calmly placed it on the nightstand. I sat up rubbing my neck and feeling confused. As Rebekah put on her nightgown she said, "John, thank you for allowing me to demonstrate my ability to render General Dietrich unconscious. It's really something I could not have done without your help."

I continued staring at Rebekah as she straightened her nightgown and gave me a bright smile. It suddenly dawned on me that I'd been had.

I stood up and put my uniform back on with as much dignity as I could muster. After fastening my trouser belt, I looked at Rebekah and said, "Congratulations, you've made a complete fool of me. Please excuse me while I go to my own bedroom and repair what's left of my dignity."

A few minutes later, there was a soft tap on my door and Rebekah entered. She was wearing a robe over her nightgown and sat beside me on the edge of my bed. "John, I really feel bad about deceiving you. However, I had to prove to you that I could handle the job with the General. I hope this helps ease your hurt." With that said she took my face in her hands and gave me a lingering kiss. Before returning to her room Rebekah whispered, "Goodnight my darling."

I sat on the edge of the bed for several long minutes thinking about the events which transpired that evening. I thought, *John, you've really stepped in it this time. This woman has made you feel guilty and stupid at the same time. You're feeling guilty because you were ready to cheat on Helen and stupid because you fell for Rebekah's stunt. You've only one option left; you've got to let her be the one who seduces the General. If it means she has sex with the General in order to accomplish her mission, so be it. If it happens, just chalk it up to another casualty of war.*

'Rebekah is right, being jealous is completely illogical. You have no claim on her; you're a married man. Yeah, well intellectually that may be logical but I have a strong attraction to Rebekah that's confusing the hell out of me. Is it possible to love two women at the same time?'

I lay awake for a long time before falling asleep.

The following morning as we rode the elevator down to the lobby I said, "Rebekah, your demonstration last night convinced me you can handle the mission. I don't like it but it's the best plan. I'm sure Colonel Maxon will agree."

Rebekah gave me a big smile and replied, "Thank you, John. On another subject, knowing how you feel about me has made me so happy."

During breakfast, Colonel Maxon confirmed the go ahead with our plan and informed us where we would hook-up with our platoon.

* * *

Later that morning, I contacted Helen and spoke with her briefly. "Helen, it is really great hearing your voice. How's everything?"

"John, your call caught me by surprise. I tried to contact you a few days ago but Colonel Maxon said you were on a special assignment and were not available."

"Yeah; we've finished part one and are about to embark on part two. Are you okay?"

"I'm fine and the baby is doing well. She's kicking so often I am ready to let her out so she can start walking."

"How do you know it's a girl?"

"John, doctors have equipment which permit them to see the baby as part of their examination. On another subject, when do you expect to complete your special assignment?"

"Hopefully, we'll be done in a couple of weeks. After which, I plan to ask the Colonel for maternity leave."

"John, I was hoping you had not forgotten your promise. Your timing is going to be very close to my due date. Why don't you ask Colonel Maxon for maternity leave today so he won't assign you another job immediately following your current mission?"

"That's a good idea. No wonder they have you in the planning division at headquarters."

"John, if you're hesitant to ask Colonel Maxon for leave, let me know. I'm not afraid to ask him on your behalf. This is very important to me."

I felt my temperature rising and said, "Helen, I'm not afraid to ask Colonel Maxon for maternity leave. Why would you think that of me?"

She laughed and replied, "Because you haven't asked him already. You and I know leave is supposed to be requested thirty days in advance."

"Okay, Helen; you've made your point. I'll ask Colonel Maxon this morning and will let you know what he says. Okay?"

"Thank you, John. I look forward to your call. I love you and can't wait to see you."

"I love you, too."

I disconnected the call and thought, *John, what's the matter with you? It'll be great seeing Helen again and you're going to be a father. Any man should be eager to be with his wife; especially when she's giving birth to your child! Do my feelings for Rebekah have anything to do with my hesitancy? John, sometimes you're pathetic!'*

After remonstrating with myself, I called Colonel Maxon and requested maternity leave.

Colonel Maxon said, "John, I was wondering when you'd get around to requesting leave. After this mission, you're authorized thirty days leave. According to my calculations, that will coincide with Helen's delivery."

"Thanks, sir. I know Helen will be happy to hear this news."

CHAPTER 48

KIDNAPPING A GENERAL (MILITIA FORCES)

After gaining final approval for our kidnapping plan, Rebekah and I gathered our soldiers and supplies for the mission. We drove to within 30 kilometers of Tupelo and stopped at a farm where Rebekah began training the soldiers for the mission.

I had neglected shaving for a week and after donning some coveralls, I looked like a middle-aged manual laborer. I decided to conduct a reconnaissance of Tupelo and hitched a ride on a food supply hauler and rode into the warehouse where food was sold to stores and restaurants.

As I helped unload the hauler, I began a conversation with one of the residents. "Hello. I'm John Smith and would like to know if there are any construction jobs available in Tupelo."

The man looked at me and said, "John, pleased to meet you. My name is Travis Johnson. To answer your question, I don't think there's much construction going on in the city. Do you have a pass?"

"No I don't. Why do I need a pass?"

"John, the invaders have issued all residents of Tupelo a pass. Their soldiers can spot check anyone at any time. If you don't have your pass, they'll shoot you on the spot."

"That sounds a bit harsh. What if you forgot your pass and left it at home?"

"If they're feeling generous, an officer will take you to your house and escort you inside to see your pass. If you can't find it; you get shot. If they're not feeling generous, they will simply shoot you on the spot for not having your pass."

"Travis, how do you get a pass?"

"All residents of Tupelo were issued passes a few days after the invaders arrived. I'm sorry John but I heard that no new passes are being issued. They've really clamped down on the city."

"Travis, I need a huge favor. I want you to get on the hauler and ride out of town with me. I promise to get you back to Tupelo on the next trip."

"John, you seem like a really nice person but why should I leave Tupelo?"

I had run out of options and decided to tell Travis the truth - or at least as much truth as he needed to know.

"Travis, I'm in the militia and I need to examine your pass in order to make one for myself. It's very important that I get into the city and have a close look at the enemy forces."

Travis' eyes got big as he replied, "Holy crap! You're the first militia man I've seen since the invasion! Where have you guys been? We've been waiting a whole year for something to happen but there has been nothing on the news."

"That's not surprising since the invaders are controlling all news media. They wouldn't tell you that the militia has taken Johnson Springs and Columbus from the Earth soldiers." I added, "Travis, you can't tell others what I have told you. If the Earth soldiers find out you have actual knowledge about the war, they'll lock you up and probably torture you to find out who told you."

Travis stared at me for a few moments before replying, "John, you've given me a good reason to leave Tupelo. Can I call my wife and let her know?"

"No. we don't know who may be listening to your conversation. Let's just get on the hauler and leave when we've finished unloading."

After arriving at our temporary quarters, I contacted Colonel Maxon. "Colonel, the enemy has issued passes to Tupelo residents. We're going to need passes before we go into the city."

"John, I'll contact Militia Headquarters and relay your request. You should expect someone from headquarters first thing tomorrow morning. Send me your exact coordinates. Incidentally, do you have a sample pass?"

"Yes sir. I convinced one of the civilians to ride out on the empty food hauler with me. I needed to get his pass and I couldn't let him stay in Tupelo without one. He said civilians are shot for not being able to produce their pass upon request."

"Good work. If you need anything else, let me know."

"I will and thanks, Colonel."

I next checked with Rebekah to see how the training was progressing. "Rebekah, how's everything going?"

"John, we've spent the whole day getting everyone familiar with Tupelo; especially the areas containing City Hall and the subdivision where the General lives. My biggest concern is not having up-to-date information on any changes to traffic patterns."

"I have someone who can help with that. Travis, I want to introduce you to Lieutenant Rebekah Lloyd. Rebekah, this is Travis Johnson. He's a current resident of Tupelo and may be able to shed some light on the streets and diving conditions in Tupelo."

* * *

Travis' information was a godsend. Armed with forged passes, our team was ready to infiltrate Tupelo. Because time was running out, our planning concentrated on surrounding the general's house and waiting for the best chance to rush his bodyguard. We didn't have time to implement the finesse option.

Throughout the afternoon, team members commandeered three of the city's garbage trucks at the landfill, loaded up and moved to a rendezvous point near the General's subdivision.

"Sir, the target is entering the subdivision with his escort. I count three vehicles."

"Roger. Stay alert and let me know if others show up."

"WILCO"

Our plan was simple. I stationed snipers at the front and rear of the house with orders to shoot anyone escaping. We quietly moved to our final positions with Rebekah leading the front entry team and me the rear entry.

Rebekah's team attacked first with stun grenades thrown through the windows followed by the front door being breached with a small explosive. My team entered the rear of the house exactly three seconds later using the same entry tactic. As we scattered throughout the first floor, we were met with a hail of bullets fired from automatic weapons.

Ignoring the fighting on the first floor, Rebekah let three members of her team upstairs and captured a stunned General Paul Dietrich in the midst of changing his clothing. He was quickly handcuffed and gagged. Rebekah got one soldier to gather the General's uniform and boots while two other soldiers held the General between them. They didn't move until the all-clear was given from downstairs.

My team put down the General's personal bodyguard. During the brief but furious firefight, three of my team members were killed and another three were wounded. The General's bodyguard were good soldiers but were outnumbered by our assault force. After giving the all-clear, Rebekah and her team brought General Dietrich downstairs and put him into the rear of a waiting garbage truck.

I was among the last to leave the house when one of the critically wounded bodyguards raised his machine gun and fired three rounds at my retreating back. He was instantly killed by a militiaman. My body armor defeated one round but the second hit me in the upper right arm and the third grazed my neck.

The pain was sudden and intense! I felt like someone had hit my arm with a hammer then immediately stuck a blowtorch to my neck. Thankfully, we had a medic on the rescue team who quickly stopped the bleeding and gave me a shot of something wonderful which made me unconscious.

CHAPTER 49

THE GENERAL IS MISSING (EARTH FORCES)

After a routine communication check was missed, the Officer of the Day sent a heavily armed team to the General's home to check on his status. They reported the carnage and notified the Officer of the Day that General Dietrich was missing. As the senior ranking officer assigned to headquarters, Colonel Williamson assumed command, put the Earth soldiers stationed in Tupelo on alert and contacted the remaining Earth posts at Ripley and Natchez.

Colonel Williams activated the vid link and said, "Colonels Rogers and Thompson, it is my duty to inform you that General Dietrich's home was attacked by a militia force thirty minutes ago and his personal guard has been killed. The General is missing and presumed captured. According to our dates of rank, Colonel Rogers is now the senior officer. Sir, what are your orders?"

Colonel Gene Rogers cleared his throat and said, "Colonel Williamson, go to high alert. Secure all exits from Tupelo. Begin conducting a city-wide search. Colonel Thompson, prepare your Natchez Task Force for immediate redeployment should we locate the General and his captors. I'm on my way to Tupelo. Contact me immediately if the situation changes."

Colonel Rogers called his deputy into his office and said, "Colonel Begley, you're to assume commend of Ripley Task Force. General Dietrich is missing and I've been placed in temporary command of all Earth forces. I'm on my way to Tupelo."

"Colonel, let me assign a company to escort you."

"That's not necessary; Headquarters is sending an aircraft for me."

* * *

After giving the Headquarters Operations Officer his orders, Colonel Williamson began thinking about how she could turn this situation into her advantage. With General Dietrich being captured, it was possible she could manage to get back to Earth with her reputation intact. She would need to delete some damning reports and vids but anything was possible. *'Who am I kidding,'* she thought. *'There's no way I can gain access and erase all the files and recordings General Dietrich made. Besides, the militia will likely free the General and send him home along with the remainder of our invasion force. My only way out of this mess is to desert and stay on Haven. I need to create a scenario which will convince my fellow soldiers I've been killed. If they believe I died in action, my son's future on Earth will not be jeopardized and nobody will look for me on Haven. I just need some time and luck to come up with a feasible plan.'*

* * *

Lieutenant Anders was given a squad of soldiers and assigned a sector of the city to search. He and his men loaded onto a hauler and were driven to their area. After the hauler departed, Bill got everybody's attention by saying, "General Dietrich has been captured by militia scum. We've been given this sector to search. Not only are we looking for the General, but I want to talk to anybody who might know something related to his capture. We don't have time for niceties; just kick the door in and get everybody out. I'll question them personally. Anybody not answering my questions will be dealt with. If you see somebody trying to run, shoot them in the legs and drag them here. The time for being nice is over. Start with the apartment behind me."

As his men scurried to obey his orders, Bill thought, *"At last; we have some clarity in our orders. Today should be a lot of fun.'*

CHAPTER 50

THE HOSPITAL ROOM (MILITIA FORCES)

I slowly awoke and looked around. My shoulder and neck felt like they were on fire and the light hurt my eyes. As my eyes slowly grew accustomed to the light, I noticed I was in a hospital room. Tubes were sticking out of the back of my left hand and lower arm. There was one chair in the small room which was currently occupied by a sleeping Rebekah.

I waited a few minutes before speaking, "Lieutenant, do you plan to sleep your life away?"

Rebekah slowly opened her eyes and looked at me for a few moments before jumping up and giving me numerous soft kisses on my lips. Between kisses she managed to say, "Oh John, I'm so glad you're awake! I've been so worried about you. How are you feeling?"

"Other than my shoulder and neck hurting like hell, I'm fine. What happened after I got shot?"

"Yes, I'd like to hear that, too."

At the sound of another voice, Rebekah jerked her head around and we both saw Helen standing in the doorway.

Helen continued, "I was notified this morning that my husband had been wounded in a firefight. Perhaps you both will be kind enough to let me know what's going on."

My face was aflame when I answered, "Helen, we just got back from a mission to kidnap General Paul Dietrich, Commander of Earth's invasion forces. During the kidnapping, I got in the way of some bullets."

Rebekah quickly added, "Helen, we were successful in kidnapping the General. Unfortunately, three militia soldiers were killed and four, including John, were wounded during the firefight."

Helen said, "Thank you, Rebekah, I know you must be concerned about the other three wounded and I won't delay you from visiting them. I'm sure they could also benefit from your ...uh... personal touch."

A red-faced Rebekah grabbed her cap from a table and quickly left the room without a backward glance.

Helen watched Rebekah close the door then turned to face me. "Well now I understand why I was kept in the dark about your mission. Kidnapping the highest ranking enemy must have taken a lot of planning and secrecy. Apparently, darling husband, you're good at both."

Helen walked over to my bed and leaning over to give me a kiss; then pulled back and said, "I would give you a welcome kiss, but until your face is scrubbed, I can't afford to take a chance our unborn baby may contract some social disease. There's no telling where Rebekah's lips have been prior to my unexpected arrival!"

Oh boy, this was the Helen I first met at Camp Shelby; a tough-talking, hard-as-nails, no nonsense bitch. Again, my best defense would be a strong offense so I kept quiet; waiting for an opening.

After staring at me for a long moment, Helen said, "Well, what do you have to say for yourself, lover boy?"

I replied, "Having witnessed another woman kiss her husband could make any wife angry; especially a wife who doesn't trust her husband."

An angry Helen with tears welling in her eyes retorted, "Oh I see. I'm supposed to believe what you say and not what I witnessed with my own eyes?"

"Something like that. As a point of fact, I don't know how long Rebekah was in this room. I awoke less than ten minutes ago. I saw her sleeping in the chair and woke her. She came over and kissed me as you walked into the room. But you don't need to take my word for it. As you can see; there's a vid camera near the ceiling which probably feeds a monitor at the nurse's station. Why don't you go review the vid? Maybe your 'eyes' will see a different story?"

I paused a moment before continuing in a quieter voice. "Helen, please come back when you're ready to start over."

Helen turned and quickly left the room.

* * *

A nurse stopped by a few minutes later to check on me.

"Good morning Captain Collins. How are you feeling today?"

"A bit sore, but otherwise I'm okay. Nurse, where am I?"

"You're in the recovery ward of River Walk Hospital in Columbus."

"How long have I been here?"

"Sir, you've been here two days. The doctors thought it best to have you sleep through the early stages of your recovery. You would be less inclined to move around. Your neck, arm and shoulder needed to remain stationary."

Later that afternoon, I was thinking about how difficult it was being married when Colonel Maxon entered my room followed by Sergeant Major Randle.

"John, I'm glad to find you awake! How are you feeling? Are they treating you well? I heard Helen came by to visit. Where is she?"

After answering his questions, Colonel Maxon said, "John, I have great news. General Dietrich has ordered his remaining units to stand down and return to Tupelo where they will be given safe passage back to Earth. I'm happy to say, the war is over! Congratulations, my boy; your latest success has helped us end this war with Earth.

"And John, I'm keeping you on active duty until your wound is fully healed. The Militia owes you more than we can ever repay.

"Have you given any thought to staying in the militia? I sure could use your skills in rebuilding our armored units. You'll be interested to know that Lieutenant Lloyd has decided to stay as an armor officer. To tell you the truth, I never saw that one coming."

"Sir, this is all so sudden, I haven't completely made up my mind. A lot depends on Helen. I need to discuss this with her."

"Of course; that makes perfect sense. Sergeant Major Randle, that reminds me; I need to speak with Helen. Contact Lieutenant Collins and have her meet me for dinner."

Looking back at me he said, "John, I've got to go. There are so many things to do. Stay in touch and let me know if you need anything."

"Yes sir, I will and thanks for the visit."

* * *

Two days later, I had some unexpected visitors.

"Mom and Dad how are you?"

"We're fine, John. The important question is how are you doing?"

"My wounds are healing nicely. How did you know I was here?"

"After the Earth soldiers relinquished control over Tupelo, Helen stopped by the house and introduced herself to us. She even drove us here so we could be with you. John, we're so happy for you. Helen is a wonderful woman and your mother and I are delighted that we are going to be grandparents again in the near future. I can see you've been very busy during this war."

"Yeah, it won't be long before Helen has our baby. And speaking of family, how are Jerry, Allison and Danny?"

"John, they're doing fine. Jerry was sent to work with the Ministry of Finance. He could never tell me his location but he would occasionally send notes. I couldn't talk with him because Haven's Government blocked all calls to its staff.

"Allison was assigned to teach school in the town of Clarksdale. She and her mother found a small house so they were able to keep Danny with them. Children from local farms also attended the school. From what Alison said in her notes, the classes were overcrowded and they were limited on the number of textbooks available."

Mom began laughing and continued, "In spite of the challenges Allison encountered teaching school, it was nothing compared to the adjustment forced on Rachael."

"Remind me again; who is Rachael?"

"John, Rachael is Allison's mom. At any rate, Rachael had to learn to cook, make beds, clean house and do laundry while Allison taught classes. She didn't have her maids or gardener to boss around.

"On the other hand, I believe the hardship Rachael endured has changed her for the better. I've spoken to her several times and Rachael no longer has a condescending attitude. In fact, I really enjoy talking with her. We seem to have much more in common since the invasion. I've sent her several recipes and she keeps me in stitches talking about Danny. From the pictures they sent, Danny is really growing fast and he's the spitting image of his father!"

A few minutes later, a nurse entered the room and ushered my parents out. I was really glad to see them and grateful that my family had survived the war.

* * *

Late that evening, Helen came for another visit.

Helen sat on the edge of my bed and said, "John, how are you feeling? The doctor told me, with therapy, you could expect a full recovery."

"I'm okay. The doctor said he had to replace some bone fragments in my upper arm. My shoulder and neck hurt like hell and nurses are reluctant to give me a lot of medication. They said the pain should lessen by tomorrow."

"That's good news. I met your parents. They are wonderful! Did they come by today?"

"Yes. That was very thoughtful of you to contact them and bring them here. I'm guessing you gave them quite a shock introducing yourself as Mrs. John Collins who is almost nine months pregnant!"

"That was interesting but they took the news very calmly and we had a great conversation. On another subject, I had dinner with Colonel Maxon two nights ago. We talked about our future with the militia. He wants us to stay in the militia."

"What did you tell him?"

"I told him I needed to discuss it with you before making a decision."

I laughed and replied, "I saw Colonel Maxon and gave him the same answer."

Helen paused then continued, "I also had a talk with Rebekah this afternoon. She and I discussed you at length."

This subject was making me very uncomfortable as I waited for Helen to continue.

"John, she's in love with you."

I replied, "Yeah, I know. Helen, I didn't want that to happen."

"Have you and she made love?"

"No. I have not slept with her."

"Do you love her?"

"Helen, I am very attracted to her but I don't love her. You are my wife. I love you."

"She told me about you being in the same hotel suite for several days while you planned the kidnapping. Didn't you want to sleep with her?"

"Yes. I did want to sleep with her. But I didn't."

Helen paused for a long time before continuing. "John, I'm your wife and we promised to love one another forever. If there is any doubt in your heart about your love for me, now is the time to tell me."

I looked directly at Helen and said, "Helen, I'm your husband and I love you and only you."

Helen leaned down and gave me a gentle kiss on the lips. Afterwards she said, "Now get well. Our baby is coming soon and I'll need your help." Looking at my wounded shoulder she continued, "I suspect changing diapers is a lot easier with two hands."

CHAPTER 51

BON VOYAGE (EARTH FORCES)

The sun was shining brightly as General Paul Dietrich made his way to the reviewing stand. The ceremony was being broadcast throughout Haven. Escorted by an honor guard of militia wearing dress uniforms, General Dietrich was unsmiling as he took his place beside General Albert Turner, Commander of Haven's Militia and Governor General Peter Johnson, Haven's leader. The men formally shook hands and turned toward the sound of Haven's Militia Band as they led the formation of Earth soldiers marching toward their space ship.

Officers commanding the defeated Earth soldiers were permitted to retain their side arms and the General was granted approval to keep his ceremonial sword. It was all very civilized.

The marching soldiers saluted the officers on the reviewing stand as they filed by. There were no cheering crowds; just a few hundred heavily armed militia soldiers standing in formation on both sides of the reviewing stand.

As General Dietrich dropped his salute and turned to leave the reviewing stand, General Turner gave him a folder and said, "General Dietrich this folder contains intelligence we have collected regarding the massacre of our Third Armored Battalion on the day of your invasion. While we would normally conduct a thorough investigation and put the guilty party on trial for having committed a war crime, I'm giving you this folder and am requesting that you complete the investigation and bring charges against those responsible for this atrocity. Someone within your invasion force brought shame upon your reputation as an honorable soldier. We ask that you inform us of the final dispensation of this case."

General Dietrich solemnly accepted the folder and replied, "General, you have my word that I knew nothing about this incident until a few months ago. I promise to continue my own investigation and if the accused are found guilty by a court martial, they will be punished as permitted by our law. You will be informed of the results."

He continued, "There is another matter I wish to discuss. After capturing Calhoun City, your officers conducted a court martial involving Earth soldiers. My soldiers who had been captured by the militia more than once were hanged. General Turner, actions of that nature are strictly forbidden by the rules of war!"

"General Dietrich, I gave your men a chance to save their lives. After being captured, they were informed if they were apprehended again, they would be hanged. This was no idle threat and your men could have been saved had they heeded our word."

"General Turner, you know that a commanding officer cannot permit his soldiers to be ordered about by the enemy. I vehemently disagree with your policy and will inform Earth's leadership of your inhumane treatment of your prisoners of war. It will be my recommendation that you and Governor General Johnson be officially branded as war criminals by Earth's leaders and put on trial."

Governor General Johnson interjected and tersely said, "General, your ship has been provisioned for the return voyage. Should you need anything not already on board; please contact me prior to your departure."

"I will and goodbye."

The unsmiling generals gave a final salute to one another and General Dietrich made his way to his awaiting ship.

After the Earth-bound ship roared off Haven, General Turner assembled the militia and Governor General Peter Johnson addressed the soldiers.

"Ladies and gentlemen, words alone cannot express my thanks and the gratitude of our entire world for what you have done. The price of our victory has been high. Many of your comrades in arms have fallen and some of Haven's civilians have lost their lives. But through your efforts, we've won the war.

"In the coming weeks, many of you will return to civilian life. Others may choose to remain in Haven's militia. You'll make this choice based on what you want to do with the remainder of your lives. Haven needs both a strong militia and civilians who will rebuild our world and sustain our lives in so many different ways.

"Whatever path you choose, I hope you will pursue it with the same enthusiasm and hard work as you exhibited as soldiers during these past months. You have confirmed that we are one sovereign nation living on the planet Haven."

Applause and a roar of approval erupted from hundreds of voices. All in all, it was a great day and one that we would remember for a long time.

* * *

The following day, Governor General Johnson called his cabinet together and opened the session with, "Ladies and gentlemen, we've won a great victory. While every citizen of Haven deserves to celebrate, we must remember that the war is not over. Just because we defeated the first invasion wave does not mean that Earth will leave us alone.

He added, "However, there is another aspect we have to consider. Namely, our militia units have lost people and equipment. Headquarters has run the numbers; if Earth sends two more invasion armies the size of the first, Haven loses the war because we will have depleted our militia forces and equipment. We have lots of young people on Haven but they're untrained and therefore of little use as soldiers. This is a scary scenario and not one for publication."

Looking from one surprised cabinet member to another, he continued. "I propose that we not wait for their next invasion. I believe we must take action to prevent another attack."

"Governor, we're a sparsely-populated world with a defensive-oriented militia. Even if we could build the weapons for an invasion, I don't believe we have the manpower or equipment needed to invade Earth."

"Dr. Patterson, you're one hundred percent correct. I've been giving this problem a lot of thought since December 3, 2469. And I see but three choices available to us.

Option one is to negotiate a peace treaty and hope that Earth will not send another invasion force.

Option two is to destroy Earth's capability to build interstellar transport ships.

Option three is to depopulate Earth by poisoning their atmosphere."

Without pausing, Governor Johnson looked at Ambassador Allen and said, "Ambassador Allen, what is your assessment of option one?"

"Governor, as a diplomat, I always prefer negotiation to fighting. Unfortunately, I do not believe President Williams or any other Earth leader is trustworthy. They are desperate and losing one ill-fated invasion force on Haven will not dissuade them from redoubling their efforts. I believe we can expect an even larger invasion as soon as they assemble the equipment and manpower. Judging by Earth's desperation, their next invasion commander will have little regard for our people."

"General Turner, what is your opinion of option two?"

General Turner cleared his voice and said, "Governor Johnson, if we can get the exact coordinates of Earth's production facilities, we could target them with missiles simultaneously fired from at least six transport ships stationed at critical locations around Earth. Our biggest challenges will be to collect six ships, produce an adequate stockpile of missiles and maintain absolute secrecy throughout the planning and execution of this mission. Afterwards, we would need to maintain continuous surveillance to ensure Earth did not regain its ability to build an interstellar capability."

"Dr. Patterson; as our medical specialist, what is your opinion of option three?"

"Governor Johnson, I have studied a wide range of viruses and toxins. While it is theoretically possible to eradicate Earth's entire population, committing an act of this magnitude would constitute total war; the likes of which have never been witnessed by mankind. If we failed to complete the job, I shudder to think how Earth would retaliate. Further, killing billions of our fellow human beings living on Earth could have a devastating psychological impact on those who initiated the attack. In all consciousness, I could never endorse this option."

"Thank you all for your input. Mr. Ambassador, please return to Earth and resume negotiations with President Williams. Make every attempt to get Earth to agree to our original position on trade and immigration. Add the following codicil to the agreement; 'Haven reserves the right to interview all applicants for immigration at the launch site on Earth. Applicants who are rejected must wait one year before re-applying.'

"General Turner, Please develop plans for removing Earth's capacity for interstellar travel. Dr. Winters, you are responsible for producing sufficient missiles and obtaining transport ships to implement option two.

"Ladies and gentlemen, all other assets not committed to option two will be released back to the public. I am hopeful of a quick return to civilian life. If there is no further business, this meeting is adjourned. We will reconvene in one week to assess our progress toward rebuilding Haven's infrastructure."

CHAPTER 52

THE RIDE HOME
(EARTH FORCES)

Following the ship's departure from Haven, General Dietrich gathered his staff for a meeting. Turning to Colonel Rogers, he said, "Colonel, these documents and vid recording were given to me by General Turner just prior to departure. I want you to work with Captain John Rhodes who has been investigating this incident. If evidence of a massacre is uncovered, I want a court martial convened."

"Sir, will the court martial take place on Earth?"

"If a court martial is warranted, it will take place on this ship."

"Incidentally, where is Colonel Williamson? I have not seen her since my release from the rebels."

"Sir, we received a report from one of our search teams two days ago that her body was discovered in an alley. Evidently, she had been ambushed by rebel sympathizers. Because her body was burned beyond recognition, the medical team used her identity disc as proof the body was hers."

"That's too bad. I regret the loss of Colonel Williamson. Please ensure our dispatches to Earth list her as killed by enemy action. If she has any relatives, they should remember her as a valiant warrior."

* * *

Four days later, Bill was formally notified he had been indicted for war crimes and his court martial was scheduled to commence in two days. He was given a list of officers available to represent him in court.

* * *

Colonel Rogers hammered the gavel for silence. His face was bright red as he said, "Lieutenant Anders, another outburst and I'll have you bound and gagged. I will not tolerate your loutish behavior in my court! Now sit down and shut up!"

Bill slowly sat down as the witness continued his testimony. The witness was an enlisted man from Bill's platoon. Unfortunately for Bill, the soldier had a vivid memory of Bill walking behind each prisoner and shooting him or her in the back of the head on that fateful day in December.

After the testimony and a failed attempt to discredit the witness, Bill's attorney gave Bill a look which told him everything he needed to know. Bill would be found guilty of war crimes and there was nothing he could do to get a reprieve.

* * *

General Dietrich was furious. One of his officers had been found guilty of war crimes and was about to be executed. Normally, a firing squad was used to execute soldiers found guilty of capital crimes. Two weeks away from returning to Earth, using a firing squad was impractical on a space ship. After consultation with Army Headquarters, General Dietrich was ordered to witness the Army's first execution by explosive decompression. Lieutenant Anders would be ejected from the ship and his lifeless body would drift in space. Bill's execution would be performed using sequenced steps from the ship's computer.

Five minutes before the ship ejected Bill into space, he was placed in the airlock and given last rites.

General Dietrich walked over to Bill and silently handed him a folded piece of paper containing a single pill. "Anders, against my recommendation, Army Headquarters has ordered me to use this method of execution. After the door is closed, you may want to swallow the pill contained in the paper. God bless you, soldier."

"Thank you, sir."

CHAPTER 53

DEMOBILIZATION (MILITIA FORCES)

Helen gave birth to a beautiful baby girl. Both sets of parents visited the hospital and brought practical gifts for the baby. Helen and I named the baby, Melissa Francis Collins. Francis was chosen to honor Sergeant Frank DeLuca who was killed while saving Helen's life during the battle for Johnson Springs.

Shortly after Melissa was born, Helen and I began talking about our future.

"John, I don't know what to do. I have Melissa to care for but I can't wait to get back into an armored unit. I've thought and thought and there doesn't seem to be an answer."

"Helen, maybe there is a solution to your dilemma." Helen looked at me intently as I continued, "You're the professional soldier; I'm not. I've been thinking of your father's offer to work the farm and have decided I'd rather farm than return to construction or stay in the militia. In fact, my mother and father are interested in moving away from Tupelo. There is plenty of land available. Your father mentioned to me that one of his neighbors wanted to sell his farm and move into a retirement community. If we could double the farm acreage, it would become feasible to buy larger and more efficient farm equipment. The demand for crops is going to increase greatly in the next few years. With good weather and hard work, it's possible to live comfortably as a farmer."

Helen stared at me with a shocked look on her face. "John, I don't know what to say. My mother would love to have Melissa at the farm and both parents could take turns tending Melissa while you're working. On the other hand, we would be apart for months on end."

"Yeah, well I didn't say it was an ideal plan; just one which would permit you to remain a professional soldier while I work the farm and take care of Melissa."

"John, you're making me out to be the bad person. I love you and Melissa more than life itself. You're making me seem selfish in my desire to remain a warrior."

"Helen, how am I at fault with your decision to remain a soldier?"

She thought for a minute and replied, "Well, maybe I'm the one who is being selfish."

* * *

Colonel Maxon stared at a long list of administrative actions requiring his attention. Sergeant Major, this is unacceptable. I need both Captain Collins and Lieutenant Collins. Also, if John gets out and begins farming, how long will it be before Helen quits the militia and joins him? Her desire to be with her husband and baby girl will likely become too much for Helen and we'll end up losing both warriors."

"Sir, there might be a solution. General Turner still has a mandate to rebuild the militia and we need more training capability. What if we establish a training base within twenty kilometers of Captain Collin's farm? Lieutenant Collins and others could be transferred there and ordered to train warriors and mechanics. Captain Collins may be persuaded to serve on a part-time basis. If and when we go to war, he could be immediately called back into active duty."

"Sergeant Major, you've earned your pay today. That's a brilliant idea. In fact, General Turner may be interested in establishing training facilities throughout Haven in order to retain veterans on a part time basis and keep their warrior skills honed. Further, dispersing our militia throughout Haven may one day help prevent catastrophes similar to the fate of the 3rd Armored Battalion."

CHAPTER 54

HOMECOMING
(EARTH FORCES)

There was no parade awaiting General Dietrich and the remnants of his invasion force. After the space ship settled on the pad at Cape Canaveral, General Dietrich was met by a small delegation of officers who whisked him away. Other members of his invasion force were quarantined in a little-used area of the base. Armed guards patrolled the fenced-in enclosure.

"General Dietrich, I have read your reports. I would like you, in your own words, to tell this board of inquiry what went wrong."

"General Armstrong, thank you for giving me an opportunity to address the Joint Chiefs of Staff.

"Ladies and gentlemen, our invasion began as planned. When our ships landed on Haven, my units rapidly deployed to their assigned locations and commenced operations. Within three days, Haven was effectively under my control. I maintained continuous communications with my task force commanders and provided them with support from headquarters as needed.

"Our first problem we encountered was Haven's militia. Instead of meeting us as we landed in Tupelo, they chose to use guerilla tactics. Knowledge of the terrain, support of the citizens, and access to food and other logistics were on their side during the entire occupation.

"We attempted to win the support of the citizens by treating everyone kindly and respectfully. Unfortunately, this was not appreciated nor reciprocated. In eighteen months of occupation, only a handful of Haven's citizens showed loyalty to our Earth soldiers. Haven's population is only loyal to their planet and its people.

"Haven's militia was underestimated by everybody; including Earth's senior intelligence analysts. I have never witnessed a more professional army. Although small by our standards, they were well-led, equipped and trained. Some of their officers had received training here on Earth in our own military schools. Toward the end of our occupation, Haven's militia began attacking our task forces using more conventional tactics. After losing our intelligence sources, I witnessed my invasion force being decimated piecemeal by their armored and infantry battalions. Additionally, losing our logistics support from Earth exacerbated our eventual loss.

"After I was captured, I realized we had lost the battle for Haven and surrendered the remainder of my force.

"Ladies and gentlemen, Haven can be beaten but you're going to need a much larger invasion force. Unless you have questions, this concludes my report."

"General, we thank you for your concise after action report. Please rejoin your unit and await further orders."

After General Dietrich departed, General Armstrong turned to the others and said, "Ladies and gentlemen, our scientists have created a solution for our dilemma. Delivered in aerosol containers, this new virus is absolutely harmless to plants and animals. Once applied, Haven will be repopulated with loyal American settlers. President Williams has given me verbal approval to proceed. Are there any questions?"

"General, when will the weapon be ready for use?"

"President Williams has decided to deploy the weapon in six months."

Immediately after the meeting was adjourned, Captain Bill Patch, aide to General Armstrong, called his contact at the Haven Embassy. "Stephanie, I must see you. Let's meet for dinner tonight."

CHAPTER 55

INVASION DETERRENT (HAVEN'S FORCES)

Admiral Gleason's fleet of six transport ships rapidly moved to strategic locations around Earth. Missiles were launched at precise targets within milliseconds of a tight schedule. The admiral was closely monitoring the missile impacts from his command console. A team of Haven launch specialists were also monitoring the missile warheads as they closed with their targets. Although the launch panels showed a green status, each missile seemingly malfunctioned before striking its target.

Admiral Gleason turned to the senior launch specialist and asked, "Dr. Gray, what's happening? We should be witnessing explosions on Earth's surface by now."

Dr. Gray turned to Admiral Gleason and responded, "Admiral, our missiles were not equipped with explosives. They are functioning perfectly though. Our war with Earth should be over in a couple of hours - at most."

"What the hell are you talking about?"

"Sir, we learned that Earth was planning to seed Haven with a virus which would have wiped out our entire population. My job has been to, 'Do unto them before they can do it to us.'"

"Why wasn't I informed about this change in attack strategy?"

"Sir, Governor General Johnson gave me my orders personally. My apologies Admiral, but I was ordered to avoid revealing our true mission to anyone; including you."

"And why was that?"

"Governor General Johnson was concerned other people might have developed second thoughts about killing billions of people."

"Good god man, you knew you would be responsible for killing all those people and you didn't hesitate to launch those missiles?"

"Sir, my only job was to save our fellow citizens on Haven. I have completed my task. Please inform Governor General Johnson that my mission is complete and I anticipate 98.2 percent success. Admiral, your final task before returning to Haven will consist of a detailed damage assessment. And now if you'll excuse me, I would like to retire to my cabin."

A couple of hours later, a steward opened Dr. Gray's cabin door and noticed Dr. Gray sitting in his chair facing a porthole. As the steward touched Dr. Gray's shoulder, the scientist slumped over and fell to the deck.

Calling the bridge from the cabin's intercom, the panicked steward stammered, "Admiral, Dr. Gray has died. What should I do?"

* * *

"Mr. President, we've detected incoming missiles headed toward various locations throughout Earth. Please accompany me to your bunker."

"Get my wife and children into the bunker. I'm having an important meeting; I'll be there shortly."

"Sir, your wife and children are moving toward the bunker. You must accompany me now, Mr. President. You may bring your cabinet members with you and continue your meeting down below. Please hurry, Mr. President."

* * *

Brigitte Steffen, a highly successful fashion designer, walked quickly to her personal transport in the parking garage. A group of Berlin's hoodlums had been silently stalking her. Their intent was to relieve the blonde beauty of her purse. As Brigitte reached for the door, two men grabbed her and dragged the struggling woman into a windowless storage and mechanical room in the basement of the garage. They closed the door and switched on the light. "Fräulein, you'd better stop struggling. We only want your purse. But now that I have seen you up close, I have a better idea; my men and I are going to party with you!"

As soon as Brigitte was grabbed, she activated an emergency button on her wrist. A policeman was immediately dispatched to her location. Ten minutes later, as the police vehicle neared the victim's location; the policeman suddenly became unconscious and slumped forward in his seat. His vehicle continued moving toward the storage room; stopping only when the front bumper pushed against the storage room door.

* * *

Felix Graham entered the cockpit of his tunnel boring machine. He was glad to be back at the controls; especially after the latest row with his wife. Brenda was a jealous bitch who constantly complained to Felix about him working with Francine, a young French engineer. One look at Francine and anyone would understand Brenda's jealousy; Francine was beautiful, young and smart and someone who enjoyed spending time in the tunnel analyzing rock samples. Felix turned his full attention to the cutting head and felt the slight tremors telling him that it was going to be a long day grinding the hard rock underneath the mountain.

* * *

Juan and the other children in his village had been lowered into the small opening leading to a large underground cavern. Their job was to collect bat droppings covering the cavern floor and put the smelly dung into woven baskets which were then hoisted to the surface. The droppings were used to fertilize their fields. As Juan carried his basket toward the opening, he noticed the rope had fallen and lay heaped on the floor of the cavern. Sometimes the heavy rope slipped and fell. When this occurred, someone above would send down a string to which the end of the rope would be tied and lifted back to the top. Juan called out to his father and asked for help. Getting no answer, Juan called again. Soon, other children began gathering underneath the cavern opening and adding their voices to Juan's.

* * *

The USS Mississippi (SSBN 872) cautiously sailed toward its home base in Kings Bay, Georgia. Captain Nancy Hollingsworth and her communications officer were puzzled about the lack of communication signals. They were returning from a thirty day undersea tour and couldn't understand why they were no longer receiving any radio traffic. The sonar operator was also reporting no activity from surface vessels.

* * *

Throughout Earth, similar events were taking place. In a few days, isolated groups and individuals would again walk on the surface of a planet once teeming with people. Unlike prehistoric man, these survivors would have access to many tools and modern knowledge.

Psychologically, they would be traumatized by seeing and smelling decomposing corpses too numerous to count. Practically everyone would grieve over the loss of family members. They would never fully understand why so many suddenly died but it would be written in history books as the Apocalypse of 2470.

AUTHOR'S NOTE

I deeply appreciate Mr. Jeff Hewitt's invaluable editorial assistance on this novel.

Printed in the United States
By Bookmasters